Timeless Land

Also by Rachael Treasure

River Run Deep
The Dare

RACHAEL TREASURE

Timeless Land

preface
publishing

Published by Preface 2009
First published by Penguin Books Australia in 2004 under the title *The Stockmen*

10 9 8 7 6 5 4 3 2 1

First published in Great Britain in 2009 by Preface Publishing
1 Queen Anne's Gate
London SW1H 9BT

An imprint of The Random House Group

www.rbooks.co.uk
www.prefacepublishing.co.uk

Addresses for companies within The Random House Group Limited can be found at www.randomhouse.co.uk

The Random House Group Limited Reg. No. 954009

A CIP catalogue record for this book is available from the British Library

ISBN 978 1 84809 087 3

The Random House Group Limited supports The Forest Stewardship Council (FSC), the leading international forest certification organisation. All our titles that are printed on Greenpeace-approved FSC-certified paper carry the FSC logo. Our paper procurement policy can be found at www.rbooks.co.uk/environment

Mixed Sources
Product group from well-managed forests and other controlled sources
www.fsc.org Cert no. TT-COC-2139
© 1996 Forest Stewardship Council

Typeset by Palimpsest Book Production Limited,
Grangemouth, Stirlingshire

Printed in the UK by CPI Bookmarque, Croydon CR0 4TD

For my daughter Rosie Erin
and
in memory of Jack Gleeson

Prologue

Belfast, Port Phillip, 1856

The boy could hear cows bellowing as they searched out their calves in the boggy dockside yards. He breathed in their scent and the bracing sea-breeze as if it were God's greatest perfume. Exhaling a long breath, which was more like a sigh, Jack ran towards the docks, ducking under the noses of draught horses and diving between ponies and carts that passed each other on the wide street. At the yards, Jack climbed onto a post-and-rail fence to eye the cattle that milled about nervously.

'Well, if it isn't me young stockman-in-waiting, Jack Gleeson,' called old Albert from the yard, his little terrier dancing in circles at his muddy boots. Behind him stood Mark Tully. Jack couldn't help being envious of Mark. He barely had to go to school and spent most of his days helping down at the Port.

'Hello to you both,' said Jack.

Albert coughed a raspy cough.

'Mary, Joseph and Holy Jesus, I'm workin' for me whisky today,' he wheezed. 'A penny for your thoughts on these beasts, me boy?'

Jack cast his eye over the cattle and bit his bottom lip.

'Mostly a nice lot, but I wouldn't take *her*.' Jack pointed to a small heifer on the rail. 'She has a head on her like a gargoyle and her teats are set all wrong.'

'Ah, well done. Couldn't agree with you more. And this one? What of her?' He pointed his worn cattle cane towards a short black heifer with shining, up-turned horns.

'She's all right.'

'All right nothin'.' Albert banged his stick on her rump. 'She'll have a devil of a time calving with pins as narrow as that. Look out for the likes of her, Jack. It's like eyein' over a woman – you need the gift to see beneath her clothes and even beneath her skin if she's going to be any good to you in the long run.'

Jack didn't quite understand what Albert meant but ran his eye over the heifer and nodded anyway.

'Where are they going?'

'Not goin' – they're *comin'*. They've sailed all the way over the devilish seas and they're about to be walked hundreds of miles up the road to Glenelg. If you ask me – which most folks don't – I wouldn't ship the likes of these cows halfway over the world, not a mixed lot like this. There's a real art to picking God's beasts, Jack, and some of those toffs back in the Mother Country just don't pay attention to what the Lord packaged up for us. They're too busy with papers, pedigrees and prestige to pick a good beast by eye. It's an art you'll need to learn if you and Mark are going to be the stockmen you say you are.'

Jack noticed two men riding towards them. They were big men with broad shoulders who sat lightly in the saddles of their ambling horses. Their saddlebags were full and every loop had something tied from it. A bed-roll, a pannikin, a billy full of tea and flour. Loaded up for the long drove. Jack felt his heart beat faster. Albert tapped Jack on the knee with his cane and nodded towards the men.

'Those lads have the gift – just look at them. Watch their stock-horses, look at their dogs. Watch how they take the cattle quietly along that busy street.'

The drover's dog loped forward to inspect Albert's terrier. The big black working dog circled the small wire-haired one. The black dog held his tail high while Albert's dog wagged his, low and fast.

'Hey lads,' Albert said, with a twinkle in his eye. 'Do you know why dogs wag their tails?'

'No,' said Jack, leaning forward, eager to learn more from the old man.

'Because no one will do it for them!'

Jack looked at Albert with a frown. Albert thumped him on the leg, beginning to wheeze, cough and laugh all at once . . .

Albert hobbled away to let the sliprails drop down in the mud. The drover whistled and the black dog ran around the heifers, pushing them through the gate. Jack watched them as they moved in unison, man and beast, away from the town and towards the land that Jack longed to see. Then he heard his Aunt Margaret's voice on the wind and turned to see her waving from the buggy loaded up with supplies for their trip home to Codrington. He got down from the fence and jogged over to his aunt with his hands shoved deep in his pockets and a frown on his face.

'Why dogs wag their tails, indeed,' he muttered in the broadest Irish accent he could muster.

One

Rosemary Highgrove-Jones focused on the dog through her camera's viewfinder. She chuckled, then pressed the shutter button down. Click. In the sweltering heat, amongst dozing red gums and drunken racegoers, she'd captured the image of a cocky little Jack Russell pissing on Prudence Beaton's chunky leg. Yellow urine seeped into Prue's beige pantyhose as she continued to sip, politely and obliviously, on equally yellow Chardonnay.

Satisfied, the Jack Russell snorted, pointed his stumpy tail to the sky and scuffed up dried grass and dust with rigid legs. He then turned his attention to Prue's Maltese Terrier. The two little dogs stood nose to tail, in a formation not unlike yin and yang, and began spinning slowly in a circle, oblivious to the throng of human activity above their heads. Rosemary had raised her camera again to capture the bum-sniffing on film, when she heard her mother's voice.

'Rosemary Highgrove-Jones! What in God's name are you doing?' Margaret hissed, firmly pushing the camera down. 'You're *supposed* to be working! Duncan's relying on you! You're not going to let him down again, are you?'

'Why do you think they do that, Mum?'

'Do what?' Margaret frowned, momentarily creasing her perfect foundation.

Rosemary nodded at the dogs. 'Sniff each other's bums like that.'

'Oh, Rosemary!' Margaret Highgrove-Jones took her daughter's elbow in a pincer-like grip and steered her towards the VIP tent. 'Now come on, I've got some people who are dying to get their faces in the social pages.'

Margaret, tall, slim and upright in her blocky heels, seemed to tower above her daughter. Rosemary squinted at the sun shimmering in her mother's rust-coloured organza dress and chanted to herself, 'I must not be antisocial when doing the social pages, I must not be antisocial when doing the social pages.'

'Let's huddle in close for a nice photograph for *The Chronicle*,' said Margaret as she gathered up a collection of old ladies sweating in race-day frocks.

Rosemary raised the camera, her eyes scanning the women. Her mother stood front and centre of the group, looking like a blonde version of Jackie Onassis. Click. Rosemary took up her pen and notebook and began to scribble down who was in the shot. No need to ask how to spell their names. They were her mother's regular rent-a-crowd of graziers' wives.

'Got time on your social rounds for a glass of shampoo?' Margaret asked, waving a champagne flute at her.

''Fraid I can't,' Rosemary said. 'Got to watch Sam in the next race.'

Rosemary walked through the crowd towards the racetrack. The men standing among the litter of betting slips glanced away from odds chalked up on the bookies' stands to watch the pretty girl pass. Some of them wore their dinner jackets with shorts and Blunnie boots. Others in proper suits had their shirtsleeves rolled and ties slackened about their necks. Beyond the fringe of bookies and punters, boys in jeans, blue singlets and big black hats slumped on a sagging couch on the back of a ute, drinking beer. They clutched cans in stubby holders while Lee Kernaghan's songs vibrated from the ute's stereo. When they saw Rosemary, one boy whistled.

Embarrassed, she looked away, but then stumbled as a green wheelie bin rolled past her. A tubby bloke stood tall in the wheelie bin, like Russell Crowe in a *Gladiator* chariot. He held his beer can high and roared 'Charge!' as his mate pushed him at high speed over the bumpy ground, scattering the crowd. Rosemary watched the boys until they were out of sight, then turned to see her father's serious face.

Gerald Highgrove-Jones was standing tall, like a slim grey gum, with other gentlemen of the 'tweed coat brigade'. These were the men of the district who never loosened their ties no matter how hot it was or how much alcohol they drank. Royal Show badges were pinned with pride to the thick woollen lapels of their jackets. Among them, his fine long legs clad in moleskin pants, was her brother Julian. As usual, he looked subdued and bored. Like Gerald he towered above the other men, but instead of standing upright he seemed to stoop, as if trying to hide.

Rosemary waved to him as she passed and Julian waved back, rolling his eyes to indicate boredom. At the racetrack rail she looked at the familiar faces in the crowd. Like Julian, she had tried so hard to fit in. Each year, she'd tried to get excited about the coming bush races. Weeks before, the volley of phone calls between the ladies in the district would begin. Who would do hors d'oeuvres? Salmon or shrimp in the vol-au-vents? Caramel slice or coconut ice? She tried to gush over the dresses in the latest catalogues from Maddison & Rose and be upbeat and bubbly about her mother's special trips to Laura Ashley and Country Road in Melbourne. Margaret was always striving for *Country Style* magazine perfection. But Rosemary and perfection just didn't fit.

She looked down at her now-creased white linen dress with its pattern of cornflowers and daisies. It had been ordered from Melbourne and had cost a bomb. But still, Sam had said she looked nice. She looked for him now in the area cordoned off for riders. Pretty girls in tight Wranglers, cowboy hats and singlets moved purposefully about their horses, carrying buckets, adjusting buckles, rubbing rough brushes over their mounts. They were girls her age. She'd known a couple of them at pony club, but her mother had refused to let her go on with her riding once she'd left the district for boarding school. In the years since she'd been home, the girls had barely spoken to her. Except when she was with Sam.

She saw him on the far side of the track. He was with a group of riders making their way to the starting line. Collected in on tight reins, the horses bowed their heads and swished their tails nervously. Sam's black gelding, Oakwood, loped in circles. Sam rode like a stockman, not a jockey, and he'd set his stirrups longer than the other riders as he always did at bush races. Rosemary eyed Sam's strong, tanned hands as he expertly gripped his reins. Beneath brown skin, the veins in his arms stood out. Oakwood, too, had rivers of veins running under his glossy coat. His Australian stockhorse freeze-brand gleamed against his dark coat. Rosemary felt a tingle run through her as she took in how magnificent Sam and Oakwood looked together. It was as if man and horse shared the same blood, veins pumping as one. As they came nearer she tottered closer to the rail in her high heels, waved and called out.

'Good luck, Sam!'

Sam and Oakwood spun in a circle and then leapt towards her.

'Make sure you get a winning photo of us, Pooky,' he called. His dark-brown eyes shone as he winked and smiled at her.

'I will!' She winked back. She hated it when he called her Pooky, but there he was. Gorgeous Sam. Handsome right down to his boxer shorts.

Behind him on the track rode Jillian Rogers, her long dark ponytail flying behind her. She thundered past on her leggy chestnut, yelling to Sam as she sped by, 'Are you coming to get your arse whipped or not?'

'You'll regret that, Rogers!' Sam called after her, laughing. 'See you soon, Pooks.'

Rosemary watched Oakwood's muscular hindquarters

bunch beneath him as Sam turned the gelding towards Jillian and cantered after her.

'Good luck,' she said again, but her voice was carried away on the wind.

Rosemary reached for the ring on her engagement finger and spun it around and around. As she touched the sapphire and smooth gold, she wondered again how it was that, of all the girls in the district, she was the one who was going to marry Sam Chillcott-Clark.

The voice of Rosemary's editor from *The Chronicle* crackled from the loudspeaker. Duncan Pellmet fancied himself as a race caller. He had a special nasal voice for the one day of the year that was marked for the Glenelg Bush Races.

'Well, ladies and gents, welcome back for the continuation of our Sunday bush racing program,' said Duncan. 'It's time for the feature event of the day – the Glenelg Stockman's Cup – sponsored by our very own local newspaper, *The Chronicle*. This event is open to all local stockmen and their horses. And these days, folks, "stock*men*" includes the ladies – that's right, fellas . . . look out! One little miss that'll be hard to beat this year is Jillian Rogers, riding her mare Victory. But she's up against three-time cup winner Sam Chillcott-Clark on his magnificent gelding Oakwood. Now, folks, Oakwood is no stranger to this track or the bush racing circuit. He's also a polocrosse champ, a second place-getter in the national Stockman's Challenge and gives a fair run at campdrafts all over the countryside. No surprises who the bookies' favourite is today . . .'

The public address system whined, as if complaining about Duncan's voice. But he was soon back on the airwaves talking to a crowd who had long since stopped listening.

'Er . . . now while the riders are getting ready for the start, some housekeeping . . . if anyone has seen my Jack Russell please show him to the secretary's office . . . thank you. He answers to Derek.'

The crowd hushed in anticipation as they waited for the mounted clerk of the course to drop the starter's flag. As the white flag fell, the line of horses leapt from their standing start on the far side of the track. Goosebumps rose on Rosemary's skin as Duncan Pellmet's excited commentary reverberated through her. She watched the horses bunch and gallop in the haze of summer heat, eating up dust, belting along as if they were one giant beast. As they came more clearly into view round the turn, the slower horses started falling away and from the pack emerged Oakwood and Victory, the chestnut and the black, doing battle neck and neck. Sam leant over his horse and hissed in his ear. Jillian, perched on short stirrups, called to her horse in a gutsy voice. Then with just a few lengths to go, Duncan's Jack Russell burst onto the track, yapping madly at the horses. Oakwood, a seasoned stockhorse, barely glanced at the little dog. But Jillian's thoroughbred mare, more used to showjumping than stockwork, threw her head and took a sidestep just on the line. Sam had won. The crowd erupted into cheers and the wheelie-bin boys ran onto the track to rugby-tackle the dog.

Rosemary made her way to the mounting yard where Sam, sweat trickling down his brown face, helmet under his arm, was holding onto the heaving Oakwood. He called out to Rosemary.

'Here! *Now* take your winning picture for the paper!'

She lined him up in the viewfinder. There he was, gorgeous Sam with dust sticking to the sweat on his face, a big white grin, and eyes that crinkled when he smiled. And his horse, head held high, nostrils flared and his ears thrust forward. Click.

Sam took a step towards Rosemary. 'Can you just hold him for a sec?' he asked.

Rosemary found herself juggling her handbag, camera and a set of sweat-covered reins. Oakwood swung his head around anxiously, knocking Rosemary's hat skew-whiff. He tossed his bit up and down so it clattered against his teeth. A long string of saliva trickled onto Rosemary's arm. His eyes rolled in his head and he danced on black hooves.

'Whoah, boy,' Rosemary said, stumbling as her heels sank deep into the turf. Then, as if he were telling her to shut up, Oakwood dropped his head low and rubbed his sweaty, dusty face all over her white dress. She glanced up, looking for Sam, and saw him in the corner of the mounting yard, his hand on Jillian's shoulder as she wiped away tears. She had her hat off and her dark hair had come loose, falling over her strong shoulders. Sam stooped a little to look into her eyes and smile gently at her. Then he glanced towards Rosemary, said something to Jillian and bounded back to her, the beaming smile again on his face. He grabbed the reins.

'Thanks.' He inclined his head towards Jillian. 'She's a sore loser, that one, but it wasn't entirely fair. Duncan's bloody dog. Anyway, better get this boy hosed down.' A quick kiss on her cheek and he began to lead his horse away.

'Where will we meet up?' Rosemary called out.

Sam spun around. 'Boys want to shout me a few winning beers. I won't be long. I promise. Just a couple at the pub.'

Rosemary's face fell. Sam came over and took her hands.

'Just *one* beer then,' he said.

'Let me come with you,' begged Rosemary. 'You *never* take me to the pub.'

'Your mum would tear strips off me if I took you there. You know she hates it. Besides, I heard your mum ask some of the girls back to your place for drinks. You can get on the Chards with my mum and talk weddings. Get some plans in place for when you move in.' He ran his hand over her slim waist. Rosemary wrinkled her nose.

'You're so cute when you're pooky, Pooky.' He tipped back her hat and kissed her on the brow. She looked down at her dusty Diana Ferrari slingbacks.

'All right. Piss off then,' she said sulkily.

'What?'

'I said piss off!'

'Oh! That's ladylike!' Sam said. 'I've just won the Stockman's Cup for you and you won't even let me go to the pub with my mates! Is this how it's going to be when we're married? I thought you'd *want* to go home with the girls. They're happy to do it. Isn't it good enough for you?'

'It's not that, Sam.'

'Well, what is it then?'

'I don't know.'

'You never know. That's your problem. That's why you need me!'

He pulled her to him and looked into her eyes.

'Just wait until we're married. When Mum and Dad move to the flat in South Yarra, you'll have the whole homestead to look after. You won't have time to "not know". It'll be perfect. You'll see. Okay?' Gently, he kissed her on the nose.

She nodded and smiled a little, but she still felt the frustration within her. She sighed. He could get any girl he wanted, that's what her mother said, and he had chosen her. She watched him saunter away in his tight denim jeans and his sweat-stained shirt.

Sitting in her dirty dress beside the Glenelg River, glad to be alone, Rosemary listened to the far-off sound of Duncan's droning commentary. Angrily, she swiped an unexpected tear from her cheek, then wondered why she was crying. All her mother's friends told her what a lucky girl she was, engaged to Sam. But so much seemed to be missing from her life. She wished she knew what it was like to thunder around the track on half a tonne of horse muscle, instead of just watching from the rail. She snapped a stick in half and threw it into the olive-green river. Why couldn't she be more like the other girls, the ones who'd be drinking in the pub with Sam tonight? she wondered. Why didn't he take her with him?

She turned her head towards the breeze. She wished it carried something with it, a whisper of things to come. As it lifted her straight blonde bob away from her sweating neck more tears fell from her eyes. Her mother would be looking for her. She covered her face with her hands and took some deep breaths. Suddenly she felt something warm and wet on her cheek.

Startled, she looked up. A red kelpie sat beside her, trying to lick away her tears.

'Rack off!' she said, gently pushing the dog away.

'He's just being friendly,' came a voice from behind her.

She turned and saw the silhouette of a man holding a horse. He stepped into the shadow of a red gum so she could see him clearly. It was Billy O'Rourke.

'Don't you like dogs?' he asked.

'No! Yes. I mean I do, but I . . .'

'You *should* like dogs.'

Rosie looked up at Billy's weather-beaten face. He was smiling at her kindly from beneath a broad-brimmed hat. He held his horse's reins lightly in his tanned fingers. She had seen Billy by the river often in Casterton as he schooled nervous, green-broke horses. And he sauntered into *The Chronicle*'s office each week to file his livestock sales reports.

'I do like dogs,' she said.

'That's good, because I've got a job for you. Are you in the office tomorrow?'

'Yes,' Rosemary nodded. Unfortunately, she thought to herself.

'Good. See you then.' And he began to lead his horse away.

'Hang on! What's the job?'

He turned and winked at her. 'You'll see.' Then he walked back towards the track, his legs slightly bowed and his shoulders rounded from all those years of bending over sheep in shearing sheds.

The red kelpie watched him leave but stayed sitting by Rosemary's side. He thrust his warm nose under her hand, begging for a pat. As Rosemary rubbed his velvety ears, he laid his chin on her knee, looked up at her with his chocolate-brown eyes and sighed.

'What do you want?' Rosemary asked.

Then Billy whistled and the dog was gone.

Two

The convoy of dusty four-wheel drives rattled over the grid and through the white timber gates of Highgrove station. Rosemary sat jammed next to Prudence Beaton in Margaret's new Pajero. On the forty-minute trip home, she had tried to ignore the faint smell of dog urine emanating from Prue. Now she leaned her forehead against the window and looked out at the sun setting over the high golden hills of the valley. Sheep were drifting in single file over the dry pasture towards the river for their evening drink. Their heads were slung low and the sun on their backs made their fleeces glow golden.

Only ten years ago, Highgrove station was running fifteen thousand merinos on its four thousand hectares. It was one of the oldest merino and Hereford cattle studs in Australia. The merinos bustled through the bluestone shearing shed like an endless river, leaving behind them white fleeces of bright, beautifully crimped wool piled as high as the dark rafters. But, over time, the business seemed to stall. Now stock numbers were reduced to just one third of those in Highgrove's heyday.

Rosemary sighed as she thought of the heady days when her family's merino stud reputation was at its height. Back then, her father won every broad ribbon for their stud rams and the women loved him for it. They clustered about him in their Black Watch tartan skirts and gold-buckled navy shoes, stroking the trophies, fingering the tasselled fringes of the championship ribbons and purring how clever he was. Their tweed-coated husbands thrust firm handshakes Gerald's way and offered ridiculous sums of money for his prize-winning rams. And in the thick of it, by Gerald's side, was Julian. He was the ever-present groom, holding grumpy sheep by the jowls in the line-up as the judges spent hours deliberating on their final placement. Rosemary always begged to help, but her father always refused.

'You're just too small to exhibit the rams,' Gerald had once said. 'Imagine the ruckus if one got away – it could cost us the championship.'

Instead, Margaret dressed her up in Laura Ashley prints and insisted she be involved in the home industry section. Here, her mother's flowers burst forth in showy, opulent blooms no judge could pass by. The luxurious texture of Margaret's chocolate cakes and golden scones never failed to attract blue-ribbon status, fifty-cent prize money and the accolades of other women in the district. But then the wool prices began to slump. Fewer buyers steered Gerald away to corners of the show pavilions to discuss deals. The once-bustling sheds at Highgrove fell quiet and the rams were all turned out to fend for themselves on pasture. The jackaroos moved on and were never replaced, the stud groom was given his notice, and spiders began to weave their silver webs over the felt show ribbons that hung from the rafters of the ram shed. Now only mice and rats scuttled up and over grating that, these days, only faintly held the scent of lanolin.

Oblivious to the crumbling farm, the convoy of chattering ladies drove on from the river flats towards the grand old homestead on the hill. The double-storey, red-brick house was bathed in evening light, its wide verandah casting a shadow like a frown around the building. Massive gum trees draped their limbs elegantly over the high, wrought-iron gateway that seemed to announce the prestige and privilege of the house.

It was a hollow declaration, thought Rosemary as the vehicles bumped over the front grid. She had seen her father stooped over the bank statements in his office. But her mother continued to cook up storms of gourmet food and organise party after party, as if nothing had changed.

Fat four-wheel-drive tyres crunched on the circular gravel driveway. It was fringed by a green lawn, mown to perfection. Here, the ladies tumbled out, crumpled, tipsy and tired. All were looking forward to Margaret's hospitality within the cool walls of the homestead.

Rosemary sat slouched on her mother's chintz-covered chair in the drawing room, rubbing at the stains Oakwood had left on her dress. As she watched the women flit about, drinking white wine and giggling, she wondered what Sam was up to and when he would call her tonight.

'How about you, Rosemary? More Chards?' asked Prue Beaton, bulging out of her electric-blue and hot-pink Anna Middleton silk suit. Prue perched her ample bottom on the arm of Rosemary's chair and tipped wine into her already full glass. She leant so close Rosemary could see the sweat gathering in beads on her top lip. Prue giggled before she spoke.

'When you marry Sam Chillcott-Clark, are you going to be all modern and keep your own surname?'

'Or why not just add another hyphen?' tittered one of the ladies.

'Yes!' squealed Prue. 'Perfect! Rosemary Chillcott-Clark-Highgrove-Jones! Or Rosemary Highgrove-Jones-Chillcott-Clark! Hasn't that got an air of importance to it?'

Margaret smiled as she offered around a platter of Atlantic salmon and capers on crusty, home-baked bread.

'That name is almost as long as the fencelines will be when the two properties merge,' said Prue, and the ladies fell about laughing.

Not long after that Rosemary quietly excused herself. Slowly, with a sigh, she climbed the wide stairs to her room.

Rosemary's bedroom was her sanctuary, though sometimes it felt like her prison too. On one side, French doors led to a wide verandah which looked out over the front garden and beyond, to the river valley. The view from the verandah teased her, highlighting how trapped she felt within the house, her mother's voice jerking her about like she was on a lead. Feeling the sadness creep into her again, Rosemary crossed her room to the deep bay window on the other side. The timber window seat was a perfect spot for gazing out to the cobbled courtyard below. She could see the stone archway where workmen used to come and go in battered vehicles, and the beautiful old stables made from dark, pockmarked bluestone. Tacked on in the same stone were the workmen's quarters. Sometimes, when she couldn't sleep, Rosemary had sat in the darkness trying to catch snippets of the men's conversation and the rumbles of laughter that rose up to greet her loneliness. She especially loved the sounds that came during shearing time. She could see the shed beyond the roof of the stables. She loved to hear the music belting out from the small windows of the shearing shed, competing with the whirring noise of the machines. From her regular perch at her window she would watch the sheep coming into the yards in full wool and then leave bright-white and shorn close, leaping over shadows as they galloped out the gate.

Tonight the floodlight illuminated the old hand-chipped stone of the buildings. Her mother's geraniums, in giant pots, shone in rich clumps of pink and green. Julian and her father had just driven into the courtyard. They had worked late after a full day at the races. Rosemary could tell by the way the ute doors slammed that they were both in bad moods. She heard her father swear as he tripped over an old-style barrel of daisies in the yard. He often complained that his wife had even 'country-styled' the work areas, which were no place for her roses and terracotta. In the past, the workmen and jackaroos had also shuddered when they saw Margaret coming. She'd want a hefty slab of sandstone moved, or a hedge pruned, or a load of gravel shovelled and raked on the driveway. It didn't matter that there were sheep to drench, troughs to check, vehicles to service. Rosemary had lost count of the number of workmen who had left because of her mother's demands and her father's coldness. As a result, Julian had become the main whipping boy.

Rosemary could hear her brother now, dragging shovels and other fencing tools noisily from the battered Toyota farm vehicle. Julian was just a year younger than her and lean as a greyhound. His work clothes hung on him and his plaited kangaroo-hide belt looked as if it would wrap itself around his waist several times. His hair fell in brown waves over his eyes, almost to his fine cheekbones. Despite Margaret's badgering, he always wore it longer than most of the men in the district.

The pair of them, brother and sister, didn't seem to fit anywhere in the modern world. Neither of them was into Killing Heidi, or B&S balls or text-messaging mates about trips to the MCG for a day on the grog at the cricket. The Highgrove-Jones kids were being raised by their mother to be the next generation of 'landed gentry'. Rosemary sighed. She dreamed of riding out over the wide plains and up to the rocky ridges that were part of the run country on Highgrove station. But her dreams had remained only that, dreams, and life just ticked over. The same events each year, marked on the David Austin Roses calendar. Christmas drinks, hospital fundraisers, garden open days and Church fêtes – these were her mother's domain and this was where Rosemary was expected to be.

The work events that really mattered – like shearing, crutching, drenching and lambmarking – were marked on her father's *Weekly Times* calendar. Rosemary watched them from afar. She had hoped that a world of opportunity would open up for her when she got engaged to Sam. He had the finest Australian Stockhorses in the district, and a line of sleek kelpies that were the best money could buy. Rosemary had spent hours imagining their new life together on the Chillcott-Clark property. Sam would teach her to turn a beast on the shoulder and plunge at a gallop into an ice-cold winter river; to whistle and cast a steady, prick-eared kelpie dog out wide around fresh-shorn sheep; to bustle against other horses in the flurry of a polocrosse match; to be the farm girl she'd always dreamed of being.

But, a year on, none of that had happened. Instead she found herself embraced by Mrs Chillcott-Clark, who lived in the same intense *Country-Style*-at-all-costs frenzy as her own mother. Rosemary bit her lip and curled up on her bed. As she shut her eyes she heard the shrill ring of the phone echoing in the house and out in the courtyard below. Her father was now inside the house talking in his clear voice.

'Highgrove station. Gerald speaking.'

Rosemary bounded off the bed. Her father's voice rose from the stairwell.

'Sam, my boy! You'll have to speak up. Sounds rowdy where you are. No, my lad. She is. Yes . . .'

Rosemary ran down the stairs.

'Yes, she's in bed I think. I'll tell her in the morning. Cheerio then.' And he put down the phone.

'Oh, Dad!' Rosemary wailed. 'I wasn't in bed! Where was he? Can I ring him back?'

'Sam said he'll pick you up after work tomorrow in time for the Rotary quiz night. He still had to float Oakwood home tonight so he can't drop in.'

'But, Dad!'

'Leave it at that, Rosemary,' said Gerald. He turned and walked away.

Back in her bed, Rosemary shut her eyes and thought about Sam. He was her first proper boyfriend. She remembered the taste of beer in his mouth and his hands on her shoulders the first time he had kissed her. They had gone into the kitchen to get some drinks for the guests at her mother's tennis party and he had stood close to her as she went to the fridge for a jug of homemade lemonade. He had looked at her with his melting dark-brown eyes and told her she was 'the catch of the district'. Then he had kissed her. Rosemary, knees buckling, worried that she'd drop the jug of lemonade.

'Ooops! Mum will go off if I spill this,' was all she could say, but she felt a buzz in her head and a smile leap to her lips when she looked up at Sam.

Rosemary rolled over in her bed, replaying that first day when Sam had made her knees buckle.

Meanwhile, out the back of the Glenelg Hotel, near the stack of empty beer kegs and cardboard boxes, another girl's knees were buckling.

Jillian Rogers had her head tilted back, her hands grasping Sam's muscular backside and her pelvis jammed against his. Sam's hands were under her top, moving over her small, pert breasts, and his tongue was deep inside her warm, Jim Beam-flavoured mouth. Just then, a ute revved around the back of the pub and they stood exposed, frozen in the dazzle of headlights like two copulating rabbits caught on the bitumen. Then the horn blasted out a Dukes of Hazard tune.

'Dubbo, you bastard!' called Sam. 'Thought I'd been sprung.'

Jillian tossed back her dark hair and laughed.

Dubbo leant out of the window. His rounded red face, flop of sandy hair and good-natured grin were only just visible in the darkness.

'Come on then, get in. Party's at my place. Then I can get started on the grog.' He tooted the horn again for good measure.

Sam took Jill's hand and led her to the ute.

'But the horses, Sam,' she protested.

'They'll be right in the racetrack stalls for now. Dubbo'll get me up before dawn and I'll go out and fix them then.'

He ran to the back of Dubbo's gleaming black Holden ute and began to unflip the strap of the tarp.

'What are you doing?' asked Jillian coyly.

'It's a good forty minutes out to Dubbo's. My swag's in the back. How about you and me have a little lie down on the way?' Sam gave her a cheeky grin.

Dubbo rolled his eyes. He'd stayed sober all day and now he'd be driving home on his own while his mate got lucky in the back.

'Bloody typical,' he muttered as he reached for his rollies. Sometimes he couldn't help feeling pissed off with Sam. How could one bloke have that much luck in life? The best horses, the best land, the best dogs, the best women . . . several all at once. He even had the best ute. Dubbo flicked his lighter and puffed on his smoke as he drove out of town. He and Sam had grown up together, been to boarding school together, and Dubbo would always be loyal to him. But he couldn't help feeling sorry for Sam's fiancée. She seemed like the prettiest, nicest chick. A lot on the quiet side, but she deserved better than this.

Still, as he sped on into the night, Dubbo glanced frequently in his rear-vision mirror, trying to catch glimpses of the tarp moving rhythmically up and down.

Three

Rosemary turned slowly into the wide main street of Casterton, driving her mother's old Volvo. The whole town seemed hungover from the excesses of the day before, and the street was unusually empty. Bob at the newsagency was only just putting his signs out on the pavement. He stared at Rosemary as she drove by before putting down the poster that declared 'NICOLE TO WED AGAIN' and then, in tiny print, 'Psychic reveals'.

At the takeaway, Johnno was putting up his Peters Ice-cream flags while his wife, Doreen, lethargically swept the pavement clean of dust. She leant on her broom and watched Rosemary drive past.

Rosemary parked at the back of *The Chronicle* office beside Duncan's zippy red sports car. Climbing the rickety back steps, she turned and looked behind her at the Glenelg River. There, on the flats beneath the great river red gums, Billy O'Rourke was working a young thoroughbred filly. She pranced and snorted in the morning sun as he calmly urged her on. What would it be like to have that freedom? Rosemary wondered briefly. To spend your days with animals as bright and fresh as that filly? Feeling seedy from Chardonnay and too much sun the day before, she decided to talk to him later about the job he had for her. She pushed open the door and stepped inside the dusty-smelling office of *The Chronicle*.

Duncan was there already, along with Derek, who barked excitedly and leapt up to scrabble at Rosemary's legs. Duncan was standing at his desk, shaking his chunky gold bracelet along his thick wrist. Pools of sweat were already starting to darken his salmon-pink shirt. He was talking excitedly on the phone and running his hand through his wiry blond hair, which Rosemary suspected was dyed and even hairsprayed. Pen in the other hand, Duncan was making wild scribbles of buxom women on the notepad on his desk.

'I thought your mother had sent you money for books? Yep. Ah-huh. Okay then. I'll send you a cheque. But don't spend it on dope. Or grog. No I'm not! How *is* your mother?'

Trying not to listen in on Duncan's conversation with his daughter, Rosemary slumped at her desk and turned on the clunky old computer. It too whirred over lethargically like it had a hangover. She created a new file and started to type up the captions for her race-day photos.

'Trying to hold in their after-luncheon farts at the Glenelg races on Sunday were, from left, Mrs Elizabeth Richards of Brookland Park, Susannah Moorecroft of Hillsville station and Margaret Highgrove-Jones of Highgrove station.'

When Duncan slammed down the phone and clapped his hands together, she quickly began to change the first half of her caption.

'Morning!' he said, smoothing back his hair and bouncing up and down on the spot, like a football player warming up for a game. 'All set for a big news week?'

'Not really,' said Rosemary quietly.

She was about to hand over her film to the bouncing Duncan when her mother swept through the glass front doors in a waft of musky perfume. Margaret's face was crumpled and contorted. Rosemary frowned at her, worried. It was the same anguished look her mother had worn when the sheep had got into her flowerbeds the day before the Open Garden Weekend, only worse.

'Rosemary.' Margaret faltered. 'There's been a terrible accident.'

Duncan was instantly at her side.

'Mrs Highgrove-Jones. Are you all right?'

Margaret looked at her daughter, shaking and blinking back tears.

'Mum? It's not Julian? Not Dad?' Rosemary asked as fear settled like lead in the pit of her stomach.

'Sam. It's Sam,' her mother said. 'Sam's been killed.'

On the window seat in her bedroom, clutching her knees up to her chest, Rosemary had been rocking backwards and forwards for hours. She'd been in her room now for three days. Today, though, she had to come out. Today was Sam's funeral.

She had replayed, over and over, the hours since she'd heard the news about Sam. The jolt. The sudden rush of fear. She remembered slipping off her chair at the office and crouching on the floor, her whole body beginning to shake. Then she felt Duncan's hands on her, and her mother stroking her hair. Gently, they had lifted her and helped her out on to the street. Bob came out of his newsagency to stare, and Doreen, Johnno and their daughter Janine looked at her sadly from the takeaway. She had been bundled into her mother's four-wheel drive. Her father was sitting stony-faced in the driver's seat, waiting. They took her straight home and up to her room. She wasn't sure what the doctor had given her, but she knew the curtains in her room had been drawn for days. In her mind too, she had felt heavy curtains close over like a fog. Every time the fog lifted the reality came flooding back and then she cried into her pillow until her head ached. She longed for Sam to drive up to the house in his shiny red Holden ute. She imagined him laughing, telling her it was just a bad dream. She *waited* for him to come. But he never did. He would never come again. The news had filtered through that Jillian was dead too. But somehow Rosemary couldn't deal with that thought. Not yet.

Now she must go to Sam's funeral. She could hear her mother downstairs.

'Not *that* tie, Julian! Have you got the wreath? Careful with it! Do you think people will know the flowers are from our garden? Should I make a card saying so? I'm sure it would mean more to his family if they knew I had grown the flowers. Gerald, help me fasten this clasp, will you?'

Her mother's booming, bossing voice reminded Rosemary of the time of her grandfather's death. Her family had barely let grief in.

'He had a good innings,' was all her father had said. It was as if her grandfather hadn't left the house anyway. His portraits and possessions were still in place. The paintings of Rosemary's great-great-grandfather and his wife still hung from the picture rail that ran the length of the hall, their walking sticks were still stored in the elegant hallstand and their china still stacked in the heavy sideboard. Their faces, pale and solemn, stared out from dark wooden frames.

'You can see the bloodlines carried through in their features,' Prudence said once as she toured the house. 'The pedigree of Scottish aristocracy is as plain as day.'

'Lucky the eyes-too-close-together trait didn't pass on to me,' Rosemary said. 'Or the horrible hooked-nose gene. Or the fat-in-frumpy-frock tendency.' She looked over to Prue anxiously after her last comment. Prue stood in the hallway, looking fat, in a frumpy frock.

'Oh, Rosemary!' gasped Prue. 'You just don't appreciate the past . . . *Your* past. It's your heritage. It belongs to you.'

'I don't want it. It gives me the creeps. A house full of grumpy old dead people.'

'Gosh. I'd love it if I had a big house like this and found a lovely farming lad to marry.'

As Prudence prattled on, Rosemary stared at the paintings

beside the family portraits. They were mostly still-lifes of dead pheasants, or hares lying shot and bloodied beside pewter mugs, with the weapon that caused their death carefully positioned and painted to perfection. There were also paintings of windswept Scottish moors and woolly Highland cattle with their maniac horns pointing upwards to stormy skies. Even though this was the area in Scotland where her father's family came from, it was her mother who proudly quoted historic trivia about the Highgrove-Jones ancestors. But Rosemary couldn't feel that it was anything to do with her. The river gums and the rolling hills of Highgrove were her landscape. She couldn't understand her mother's pride in the gloomy old paintings and their heritage.

A gentle knock at her bedroom door interrupted her thoughts.

'Rose, dear. It's time to go,' came her mother's softened voice. She stepped in the room and tut-tutted when she saw her crumpled daughter in the window seat. 'But you can't go like *that*!'

She stood Rosemary up. She straightened her suit, tugged a hairbrush through her hair, roughly puffed powder on her blotchy face and handed her a little cylinder of lipstick.

'Put that on.' Rosemary obeyed. 'There. All better. Come now.'

Rosemary reluctantly followed her mother down the stairs and past the portraits of the long-dead family members. Their eyes seemed to watch her as she went.

In the church, Rosemary sat looking at the blue and white agapanthus that stood tall in an urn in front of the pulpit. She swallowed down a painful lump in her throat. Her mother sobbed gently next to her. Gerald sat beside his wife, his grey hair smoothed down neatly, his eyes watery. He stared up at the stained-glass window of Christ on the cross for the entire service. Julian assumed the same position as his father. In the pew in front of them was Sam's mother, Elizabeth. She was a trim, straight-backed, precise woman, but today she was slumped in her husband's arms. Rosemary glanced at Marcus, Sam's father. He was so much like Sam that she felt an urge to leap over the pew to him and hold his strong brown hands in hers. But as he turned to look sadly at her she saw that it wasn't Sam at all. Sam was dead in the coffin that rested on a silver trolley in front of them.

When they had first come into the church, people had comforted Sam's parents with gentle hugs and whispered words of sympathy. But no one came near Rosemary. They just cast her sad glances and passed by. What did they know. Rosemary wondered? The image of Sam and Jillian in the mounting yard after the race flashed in her mind. Rosemary choked down a sob as she stared at the gleaming wood of Sam's coffin. She wanted to find love for him as she said her goodbyes, but all she could feel was the tug of fear and a suspicion that blackened her every thought.

Afterwards, standing numbly outside the church in the summer heat, she looked everywhere for Dubbo in the crowd that flowed out from the church. She couldn't see him.

'Where's Dubbo?' she asked her mother.

'Still in hospital,' her mother said curtly.

Rosemary wondered if Dubbo would have come to the funeral at all, even if he had been well enough. His best mate was dead, and he had been driving the vehicle that killed him. Would he have dared to turn up? Rosemary felt anger towards Dubbo prickle beneath her skin and she began to cry again. Her gorgeous Sam was gone.

People didn't stay long for the crustless club sandwiches and cups of tea served in Wedgwood china at the Chillcott-Clarks' homestead after the funeral. They talked in hushed tones, placed comforting hands on Marcus and Elizabeth, then quietly left the huge old house. Rosemary sat upright on the couch, running her fingers over the dimples and creases in the brown leather. Glancing down at the ornately decorated rug beneath her feet, her eyes blurred with tears. She and Sam had made love for the first time on that rug. She had felt the plush wool pressing into her lower back when Sam pushed her skirt up above her waist and pulled her shirt from her body.

'It'll be all right, Rose. Trust me.' She'd felt the rubber of the condom tug at her skin and as Sam thrust into her with increasing vigour, she had clenched her teeth and looked back over her head. Her eyes met the soulless, glassy gaze of a deer whose head was mounted above the marble fireplace.

After Sam had finished he said, 'Careful of Mum's rug, Pooky. It's imported from England, you know.' Rosemary had stifled a giggle. It wasn't exactly how she'd imagined losing her virginity, but Sam had been so nice afterwards and brought her homemade ice-cream with glacé ginger in it. They had cuddled on the couch eating ice-cream and smiling at each other.

Marcus Chillcott-Clark came to sit by her now on the couch. She had been tilting her head sideways, trying to see the deer again, upside down.

'How are you holding up?'

'I don't really know,' she said in a hoarse voice.

'Elizabeth and I would like you to come and see us whenever you want. Don't feel you have to stay away.'

'Oh,' she said, struggling to find the right words. 'Thank you. That's very kind.' Then she sat staring at the rug as a coldness settled in her heart.

Four

'Pass the gravy to your father, please,' said Margaret, sitting down at the dining table with a purple paper hat jammed over her hair and her cheeks flushed red. Rosemary picked up the gravy boat, but wouldn't look her father in the eye as she handed it to him. She kept her gaze on the plastic trinkets and the torn, shiny Christmas-cracker paper scattered over the table.

Julian began to read a terrible joke from the slip of paper inside his cracker, while Margaret served thick slices of ham and turkey and placed a plate in front of Rosemary.

'Help yourself to vegetables. Freshly shelled peas,' said her mother, proffering dishes from the sideboard.

Rosemary felt sick. How could they act like this? Carrying on as if nothing had happened. Sam had been buried just three weeks. Didn't they get it? She stabbed her fork into a steaming roast potato.

'Shall we do the tree before dessert or after?' Margaret said lightly.

'Stuff the tree,' said Rosemary suddenly.

Gerald, who had been in his usual grumpy mood over the pre-Christmas shearing, cast her an angry look. Her mother stiffened and drained her large glass of red wine. With shaking hands, she reached for the bottle. Julian bowed his head and began to shuffle the food around his plate with a fork.

The family ate in silence, the clinking of knives and forks the only sound.

At last Margaret said, 'Well, merry bloody Christmas.' She threw down her white linen napkin. 'I'll get dessert and then we can do your *stuffing* tree, Rosemary.' She stalked from the room.

Guiltily, Rosemary began to clear away the dinner plates. On the way to the kitchen, she heard the old bell clang three times outside the heavy front door. Wondering at who it might be on Christmas Day, she set the plates down on the hall table and went to open the door. Her face lit up.

'Giddy! Oh, Aunt Giddy,' she said, falling into her aunt's outstretched arms.

'My darling girl,' Giddy said as she gathered Rosemary up in a warm hug. Rosemary breathed in her aunt's delicious smell of sandalwood.

'My poor, poor darling girl.' She stroked Rosemary's hair and Rosemary felt tears prick behind her eyes. 'How are you?'

Giddy held her at arm's length, looking earnestly at her face, searching for the pain she was carrying. Rosemary tried to smile but felt her face contort as emotion welled up. Giddy hugged her again.

'Shush, my baby. I'm here.'

She took Rosemary's hand. 'Is that sister of mine still bossing you around completely?'

Rosemary nodded, looking down at the white Laura Ashley shirt her mother had insisted she wear for the day.

'Well, come on then,' Giddy said, looping her arm in Rose's and picking up her basket, 'let's see if we can't stir things up a bit.'

Rosemary smiled as she walked with her aunt down the hall.

'Lord, it's quiet,' Giddy whispered conspiratorially. 'It's Christmas for goodness' sakes! Let's get some fun happening here!'

Giddy stopped dead in her tracks when Margaret appeared in the hall.

'What are you doing here?' Margaret said coldly.

'Merry Christmas to you too,' Giddy said, her face giving away nothing. Margaret cast her an angry glance. Giddy slid her hand into Rose's.

'You didn't think I'd stay away during such an awful time for Rose? You can't always put yourself first, Margaret. It's Rosemary who needs some comfort.'

Margaret flinched, but gathered herself up tall.

'Well, don't think you're staying the night,' she said, 'because I won't have it.' And she huffed off into the kitchen.

On the couch in the drawing room, Gerald pressed a cool gin and tonic into Giddy's hands. Julian sat at her feet absorbed in the Tim Flannery book she had just given him.

'Are you enjoying the farm?' Giddy asked him.

Julian glanced up at his father and shrugged. 'It's OK,' he said quietly.

Giddy was about to ask Gerald the same question when Margaret entered the room, waving her empty glass.

'I'll have another, thank you, Gerald.'

Rosemary groaned inwardly. Her mother was drunk and she was bound to be rude to Giddy again. Rosemary looked at her aunt's dyed red hair and untidy, slightly eccentric clothes. She was always astounded by the differences between Giddy and Margaret. You couldn't get two sisters more unlike one another. No wonder they didn't get on.

Rosemary had always idolised her aunt, even though she rarely saw her. She loved her warmth and humour, and her hair that hung down in a sleek sheet of glossy colour. Rosemary was fascinated by Giddy's life in her artist's studio on the Peninsula.

She had once gone to stay with Aunt Giddy when she was about twelve and her mother was sick in hospital. Rosemary remembered her week there so clearly. The house was very different from the sprawling coldness of the Highgrove homestead. It was a tiny cottage, with low, pressed-tin ceilings, warmed with walls of books and scatterings of exotic colourful fabrics on cushions, couches and walls. More colour glowed from Giddy's paints, and from her canvases that were propped up against every piece of furniture. It was on this stay that she had heard Giddy making love to a young man who had come to learn to paint. Even though Rosemary lingered outside the window to steal a glimpse of the tangle of limbs and rampant thrusting actions of the man's white backside, it had shocked her so much she had wanted to go home.

'But, Rose,' Giddy had said gently, 'it's perfectly natural. Hasn't your mother taught you anything? When you grow older, you'll understand.'

A hot chocolate and a packet of biscuits later, Rosemary was again happily playing with Giddy's black tomcat and enjoying the strangeness of her surroundings. By the end of her visit she had come to love the tinkle of the beads that hung in the doorways and the sensual smell of sandalwood and massage oil.

A burst of laughter from Gerald broke Rosemary's thoughts. He was holding up a pair of socks Giddy had given him. Printed on them was 'Grumpy old fart'. He'd looked anything but grumpy since Giddy turned up, thought Rosemary. She had that effect on people.

'Here, Margaret,' said Giddy, holding out a beautifully wrapped box with seashells stuck to the card. Margaret shook her head and backed away.

'Terrible headache. Think I need to lie down.' She walked unsteadily from the room. 'Come and check on me soon, Gerald. I'll need more tablets. And some water.'

Later, as they bundled Giddy into her old car, Rosemary again begged her to stay the night. She shook her head.

'It's not a good idea,' she said, lifting her gaze up to Margaret's bedroom window. Rosemary looked sadly to the gravel at her feet.

'Hey,' soothed Giddy, 'there's always the phone.' She reached out through the open window of the car and touched Rosemary's hand. 'Promise me you'll get on with your life?'

'What do you mean?'

'You *must* make your own way in life, Rose. Use this tragedy to help you make your own way.'

Rosemary nodded uncertainly, feeling the anger and confusion over Sam's death and the frustration caused by her mother flood through her again.

'Promise me.' Giddy gripped her hand firmly. 'You really could fly in life if you made a dash for freedom.'

'I'll try,' Rosemary said. She stepped back from the car. Julian leant through the window to give his aunt a kiss. Then Gerald stepped forward and squeezed Giddy's hand.

'Thank you for coming,' he said, kissing her gently on the cheek. He kept holding her hand even as she started to drive slowly away.

'Merry Christmas,' he said softly as he at last let go of her hand.

With her aunt's words echoing in her mind, Rosemary resolved to stop hiding in the homestead. After Boxing Day she went back to her desk at *The Chronicle*, feeling like a soldier returned from the front line.

'You really don't have to be here, Rose,' Duncan said, peering at her from behind his cluttered desk. 'It's dead as a doornail between Christmas and New Year anyway, and you need to give yourself time to grieve.'

'No. I'm fine,' Rosemary said firmly before turning back to her computer.

Duncan shrugged. He had lived in the district long enough to know it was best to keep on the good side of women like Margaret Highgrove-Jones. He had been happy to put Margaret's daughter on staff even though she had no experience. Over the past couple of years it had actually been quite nice having Rosemary around, thought Duncan. She was very pretty, in a virginal kind of way. He wondered if she actually was a virgin? Then he mentally slapped himself. His wife had been gone eight months now and he felt like he was getting desperate. He decided to think lustful thoughts only about Rosemary's mother. Duncan found Margaret a frightening woman, but he liked to look at her. She always smelt so expensive and looked so perfect, like an ex-model. What was it about his attraction to high-cost older women? he mused this morning. His wife had been the same. Though he'd never been unfaithful to his wife, Duncan loved to flirt. He had always prided himself on looking just like Greg Evans from *Perfect Match*. But the glory days of Greg Evans had slid by. Now, his wife gone, Duncan had found comfort in food. His stomach strained against his pants and bags hung under his eyes from too many scotch-soaked nights in front of the TV.

Throughout the morning Duncan found his gaze returning to Rosemary. He wondered if she knew the details about Sam's death. Everyone else in town seemed to know.

Rosemary was shuffling through the packet of photos she had taken at the races. Her eyes came to rest on the photo of Sam and Oakwood. Sam's face, so handsome. She could still smell the sweat of him and his stockhorse. Tears welled in her eyes. Angrily, she swiped them away with the back of her hand. The vision of Sam had haunted her every day. Sam in the mounting yard after the race, his hand resting on Jillian Rogers' shoulder. She swivelled her chair around to face Duncan. Her blue eyes stared directly into his.

'I need to take a longer lunch break today, Duncan. Do you mind?'

The direct way she spoke startled him, and he got the feeling she was telling him rather than asking.

'By all means,' Duncan said. 'You know as well as me there's bugger all to do.' Before he had finished speaking, Rosemary had grabbed her handbag and was heading for the back door.

* * *

The air was sweltering. Instead of turning on the air-con in the Volvo, Rosemary wound down the window and let the hot wind blow her neat bob around wildly as she took off towards Hamilton. The radio was tuned to ABC talkback, so she turned the dial across hissing static until she found some music. An Alanis Morissette song was playing. Rosemary turned the volume up and let the bass beat through her. The angry lyrics sparked a smouldering fury of her own and she scowled and gritted her teeth as she thought of Sam and Jillian together in Dubbo's ute. She put her foot down harder on the accelerator and for the first time in her life broke the speed limit.

In the hospital car park Rosemary parked crookedly in front of the sign that read 'Disabled Only'. Slamming the door, she wondered why they didn't provide 'Dysfunctional Only' car parks for people like her. She marched purposefully into the hospital.

'Can I help you?' came the nasal voice of the mousy-haired receptionist.

'Ah, I'm not sure. I'm wanting to visit a patient. A Mr . . . Mr Dubbo?'

The receptionist frowned at her. It had been a bad morning.

When Rosemary at last found him, Dubbo was dozing in bed in a private room. His arm was in plaster. It had been attacked by his mates with a felt-tip pen and now featured a cartoon of a Bundy Bear on it. Rosemary shivered when she saw that Dubbo's legs were up in some sort of steel frame. His face still held traces of bruising and his blond hair was matted. When Rosemary's clicking footsteps woke him, he could barely meet her eyes.

'No need to ask how you are,' she said softly.

'Been better,' he said, looking towards the window, even though the blinds were shut.

'Can I do anything for you?'

'Why would you want to?' Dubbo asked bitterly. Then they fell into an awkward silence. Slowly, tears began to spill from

Dubbo's eyes. It was strange to see such a big bloke crying. His voice was still deep and strong as he sobbed, 'I'm sorry . . .' over and over. He still wouldn't look at her.

Rosemary moved to the other side of the bed so he was forced to meet her eyes.

'I have to find out what happened,' she said.

Dubbo shook his head, the tears brimming again. She leant towards him and touched his arm.

'I *need* to know.'

'I don't remember,' he said almost angrily. He lifted his plastered arm up to his forehead.

Rosemary persisted. 'Were you drunk?'

'No!'

'Were you mucking around?'

'I don't know!'

Rosemary couldn't help the anger in her voice.

'Well, why'd it happen? Why is Sam dead?'

Dubbo recoiled.

'I didn't do it! I didn't mean to! It wasn't my fault!' Dubbo's face contorted with pain.

Rosemary knelt down beside his bed. 'Tell me, please.'

Dubbo winced as his final memory of Sam flashed in his mind. Sam had been naked except for his boots. His pale body glowed in the dark night. He was leaning over the side of the ute into the driver's-side window, trying to hook Jillian's bra over Dubbo's ears while Dubbo, laughing, yelled at him to stop. Dubbo had caught the flash of Jillian's naked breasts in the mirror as she squealed and tried to drag Sam back into the ute. Then a guidepost was being ripped from the ground by the bull-bar. He could remember the sickening noise of metal ripping as the ute rolled and rolled. Then nothing. In the hospital Dubbo shut his eyes and swallowed down nausea. Rosemary spoke again.

'He wasn't in the cab with you, was he?' she asked quietly.

The muscle in Dubbo's jaw twitched.

'He was in the back with Jillian, wasn't he?'

'Just leave it! It's happened, just leave it alone!'

'They were in the back together, weren't they? In Sam's swag.' Tears began to fill Rosemary's eyes as she remembered pleading with Sam to take her to a campdraft on the Queensland border just before Christmas. He'd argued that there were no motels and she'd hate sharing his smelly swag in the horse float.

'It wasn't my fault,' Dubbo said again. 'It was Sam . . . he . . . he was dicking about. With Jillian. He . . . they . . . distracted me.'

He looked at Rosemary with pity and she could tell Sam had betrayed her like this before. She stood up to leave.

'I'm sorry,' said Dubbo. 'He could be an arsehole. A real arsehole.'

'I know,' she said. Then she picked up her handbag and left.

Five

Rosemary barely remembered the drive back from Hamilton. Images of Sam and Jillian in the swag as Dubbo's ute hurtled along the gravel road in the darkness swirled in her head. She pictured Sam's naked, pumping buttocks, and Jillian's long dark hair spread out on the grotty pillow of Sam's swag. She imagined Dubbo, distracted, and the big spotlights of the ute picking up the guideposts in front of them. The huge steel bull-bar ripping through the dirt as it hit the ditch, then snapping the wire fence like thread. The spraypainted Bundy Bear on the bonnet crumpling as the ute rolled and rolled down the embankment. Glass shattering, steel buckling, soft human flesh meeting metal. In the darkness, the B&S stickers splattered with blood. The broken, battered limbs of the lovers entwined. In the swag. In Sam's smelly swag.

Rosemary shook the thoughts from her head. She felt the anger rising again. Only this time it was for herself. For being so bloody pathetic.

'When are you going to get a life?' she screamed at her image in the rear-view mirror, before more tears blurred her vision.

She sped over the bridge and up the main street of Casterton, braking with a screech outside the cluster of shopfronts. Her Volvo beeped at her that the keys were still in the ignition.

'For God's sake! Shut up, you stupid bloody car!' She ripped the keys from the ignition, slammed the door and marched into the River Gum Country Clothing Store.

Rosemary's mother preferred to buy clothes down the street at Monica's Fashion, which stocked the latest Country Road and Anthea Crawford. Monica and Margaret often got together to put on Melbourne Cup and Show Society fashion parades. Rosemary was always bullied into modelling and as she marched rather than sashayed past the old biddies in clothes that didn't suit her, she felt the excruciating sting of their judgemental looks. If people judged books by their covers, Rosemary thought, she was going to change from the outside in, starting with her clothes.

In River Gum she stood before the shelves of Blundstone work boots and large wooden pigeonholes filled with Wrangler, King Gee, Bull Rush and RM Williams jeans. Colourful cowgirl-style shirts and T-shirts hung in racks beside sweet-smelling leather belts. A Tania Kernaghan CD played over the speakers of the shop. The coolness of the air-conditioning and the lilt of Tania's voice gave Rosemary goosebumps. This was more like it, she thought. She would show her family that she was no longer a wimp. She was going to become the person she'd always longed to be.

Behind the counter the salesgirl, Kelly, was sipping coffee and reading a glossy magazine about the psychic's prediction of Nicole marrying again. Looking up, Kelly almost choked on her coffee when she saw Rosemary Highgrove-Jones.

'Hi, um, can I help you?' Kelly said, wiping coffee from the magazine.

'Yes,' said Rosemary. 'How you going? Um, I think I need some new work clothes. You know, for out on the farm.'

'You do?' said Kelly doubtfully, looking at Rosemary's designer red linen dress.

* * *

When Duncan heard the back door open and saw the girl walk in he nearly called out, 'Sorry! Staff only! You'll have to come in the front door.' Even Derek leapt from his basket under Duncan's desk and danced to the door with his hackles up, barking and baring teeth. But to the mutual surprise of dog and owner, they saw it was Rosemary. She was wearing a blue work shirt, Wrangler jeans and Blundstone boots that were yet to experience a scuff mark. Around her waist was a leather belt with a pouch for a pocketknife stitched to it.

'Rosemary?' he said, peering at her. 'Rose?'

She walked straight up to him.

'Duncan,' she said bluntly, 'I've decided I'm not cut out for social pages and women's interest features any more.'

'Yes?' he said cautiously.

'I'm keen to do market reporting, visit the sale yards in the district. Do some farm pages. It's what I think I'd be better at.'

'But Billy O'Rourke's been supplying the stock sale figures for years! He knows his livestock. Can't take a photo to save himself, but the blokes around the yards are willing to talk to him. The farmers would have a fit if someone like you showed up in your new boots to write about complex stuff that they rely on . . . and you know I do the on-farm features. That's my job.'

'Couldn't we go week on, week off?'

'No! You need to be consistent if you want to follow market and season trends. Rosemary, please, don't make this difficult for me. You're perfect for the social pages.'

Rose felt jealousy well up in her. She longed to escape her life. To be like Billy O'Rourke, ex-shearer, stockman, horse-breaker. A man who moved about the farming crowd with ease and always had a kelpie dog at his heels.

'Just give me a go!'

Duncan shook his head. 'I can't.'

'Please!'

'Like I said, you're perfect for the social and home industry pages. I'm sorry.'

'No, you're not sorry. You only gave me this job because of who my mother is. You're terrified of her! That's when you're not dreaming about shagging her. You're pathetic!'

'That's enough, young lady!' Duncan reeled back from this uncharacteristic outburst. 'If I didn't know about the big shock you've had recently I'd sack you right here, right now! Take the rest of the afternoon off. I don't want to see you back here until you've calmed down.' The colour was rising above Duncan's shirt collar so the skin on his neck marbled red and white. Derek was dancing around barking at them both.

'Fine,' Rosemary said with gritted teeth. 'For the first time in my life, I'm going to the pub.' She grabbed her handbag, the patent leather making an odd contrast with her work clothes, and turned on her heel.

'Rosemary! Wait!'

She turned, her cheeks flame red, and almost spat the words at him. 'What now?'

'For God's sake, Rose,' said Duncan flatly, 'cut the swing tag off the back of your new boots. You look like a dork.'

Meekly she stood as Duncan stooped with the scissors to cut the label from her boots. He smiled tiredly up at her. 'Have a drink for me while you're at it.'

The pub was awash with afternoon sunlight. It seemed to highlight every worn patch and stain in the red and gold swirl carpet and every tear in the old brown wallpaper. But Rosemary didn't care, she sucked in the smell of stale beer and cigarettes and let the soothing chant of the Sky Channel races lull her tension. She'd always longed to come to the middle pub. She'd heard the people who drank there were the workers of the town. She was a little disappointed to find there wasn't a shearer in sight. In fact, there was only one other customer. She wanted to share a beer with the shearers and sit and listen to their conversations . . . like the ones that had drifted up from the workmen's quarters to her room at night.

She perched on a stool and looked down the bar. She'd imagined a grey-haired, pot-bellied barman with a strawberry for a nose, but the middle pub's barman was young, tanned and good-looking.

He was pulling a beer which he set before the crusty-mouthed regular slumped at the bar. Then he turned his lively brown eyes to her.

'What'll it be, darlin'?'

'Um . . . I don't know.'

'Beer?'

'Yes. Thanks.'

'Ten-ounce?'

'Sorry?'

He held up two sizes of glasses.

'Ten-ounce or a seven?'

'The bigger one, thanks,' Rosemary said.

'Good choice, love.' He winked in a friendly way as he handed it over.

The beer in her hand felt icy cold. She raised it to her mouth and sipped at it. It tingled on the back of her throat. Then she gulped it down in one hit. The publican leant against the fridge, folded his arms in front of his broad chest and crossed his ankles. He tilted his head as he considered the strange girl in the brand-new clothes at his bar.

'Another?'

'Yes . . . thanks.' She put her money forward.

After he'd pulled her a beer he leant across the bar and offered her his hand.

'James Dean,' he said.

'Sorry?'

'James Dean. That's me. My real name's Andrew Dean, but most people say I'm good-lookin' enough to be James Dean.' He smoothed back his imaginary fifties haircut. Then he gave her a cheeky smile, to make sure she knew he was joking.

'Nice to meet you, James Dean,' Rosemary said, shaking his hand firmly and smiling back at him.

'And you are?'

'Um.' She paused. 'Rosie. Rosie Jones.'

'Very nice to meet you, Rosie Jones.' The phone on the wall let out a shrill ring. ''Scuse me . . . that'll be my movie agent,' he said with a wink, before bounding away to answer it.

Rosie smiled at how easy it was. *Rosie Jones*, she repeated in her mind. The guy hadn't even blinked. He hadn't said, 'Ah! Highgrove-Jones, from Highgrove station? You're one of *the* Highgrove-Joneses, aren't you?' Instead James Dean had just met Rosie Jones. Plain old Rosie Jones. She downed the rest of the beer and burped a little, suddenly feeling a freedom she'd never experienced before.

James Dean hung up the phone.

'That was my love goddess – the missus. She was just ringing me to tell me there are no film offers yet.'

'Oh?'

James Dean shrugged. 'Guess I'd better keep pulling beers for you,' he said, picking up her glass. 'Or can I get you something else? How about some square bear? You look like the kind of girl who'd drink a shed full of square bear.'

'I do?'

'Well?'

'Yes,' said Rosie, not sure what she was ordering.

When James Dean set the fizzing Bundaberg rum and Coke before her, Rosie felt another rush of freedom. Being Rosie Jones was fun. Much more fun than that boring old Rosemary Highgrove-Jones ever had. She gulped down the rum and Coke like a thirsty kid drinking cordial.

It was getting dark outside the pub and Rosie had just put Tania Kernaghan's 'Boots 'N' All' on the jukebox for the ninth time in a row. Even the old drunk was starting to give Rosie sideways glances as she swivelled on her stool in time to the music.

'My friend Beccy outrides the boys, leaves 'em in a cloud of dust,' sang Rosie, almost in time with Tania. She swung her glass

in the air and pretended to strum the guitar, sloshing rum and Coke on her new jeans.

'She's the best at being a bad influence and it's rubbing off on me . . . Boots 'n' all, boots 'n' all! If you're gonna do it throw your heart into it!'

Her eyes filled with tears each time Tania sang, *'Here she comes, down the aisle, in her long white satin gown, and the shiniest pair of Blunnies ever, she's not mucking around!'*

Rosie sang the chorus that followed loudly, to control the lump in her throat. She thought of the wedding that would now never happen. When the jukebox at last fell silent, on the eleventh round of 'Boots 'N' All', Rosie grappled in her rum-splattered handbag for another five-dollar note. James Dean moved over to her. He'd guessed she must've been Sam's fiancée and his heart went out to her. Sam's death, and Jillian's, had been the talk of the town. James Dean had heard endless gossip about Sam's final fling.

As a publican, he hadn't enjoyed Sam's presence in his hotel. Sure, Sam dragged in his crowd of mates after stock-horse and sheepdog events and they put money over the bar, but they usually had a skinful and sparked trouble with the local workmen. And Sam, he was looking for either a fight or a woman, or both. James Dean was irked by Sam's private-school voice and the condescending way he ordered drinks from the bartenders like they were servants.

Now, James Dean looked at the drunken girl at the bar. He put his hand on hers and sought out her eyes.

'Rosie darlin', I tell you, I can't serve you any more bevvies. I didn't realise you'd be such a two-pot screamer. You're tanked to your eyeballs.'

'But, Buck Rogers, please . . .'

'It's time to go, mate.'

'No!' she slurred. 'Who's going to take me home?'

Rosie fell into a sulky silence. James Dean shrugged, sat a fizzing glass of lemonade in front of her and moved away to serve his one other customer. Just then Duncan appeared carrying a cardboard box full of books and papers. Billy O'Rourke followed him in.

'Good God, Rosemary!' Duncan said when he saw her perched unsteadily at the bar. Her hair fell over her face as she grappled around in her Princess Charlotte handbag for her car keys, muttering to herself.

'Stupid bloody handbag,' she slurred. Then she threw the bag to the floor. When she saw Duncan standing in front of her, a beaming smile came to her face.

'Dunks!' She ran to him and flung her arms around his neck. 'I'm sorry about what I said before, Dunks. Sorry. Sorry.'

Duncan put his box down, took her arms from around his neck, and sat her back down on the stool.

'Rosemary, I think I should drive you home,' he said.

'Rosie,' she said.

'What?'

'My name's *Rosie*. Next article I write my by-line's going to be Rosie Jones! No more of this hyphen bull!'

Billy O'Rourke smiled.

'That's just what Duncan and I came in to talk to you about, Rosem – Rosie.' Billy picked up the box and sat it on the bar, while he searched out her eyes.

'We can't let you do the market reports,' he said, 'it's out of the question . . . but we have another cunning plan.'

'So you're giving me the sack! Ha! Mum will love that!'

'No. Not the sack!' Duncan shook his head.

Billy put a hand on Rosie's shoulder. Suddenly she felt like one of his young horses, calmed beneath his touch.

'Remember I had a job for you?' he asked. Rosie nodded. 'I've been meaning to see you. But with the accident and everything . . .' His voice trailed off for a moment. 'I'm very sorry about what you're going through.'

Rosie nodded again.

'But I need you now. Duncan and I want you to research something for us. We need you to set up a weekly series for the paper and help with a marketing campaign. You can do it from home . . . you need to take some time of your own, Rosie, to get over your grief.'

'Grief,' Rosie echoed, the image of Sam flashing into her alcohol-addled brain.

'Yes,' said Duncan. 'You'll love it. It'll be a boost to the town. It involves going out to interview stockmen,' he said enticingly. Rosie looked at him, a glimmer of interest on her face.

'It's Billy's idea. We need you to research an Irish stockman by the name of Jack Gleeson who used to work around Casterton. Tell her about it, Bill.'

Rosie looked up into the kind eyes of the stockman who stood before her. His legs were slightly bandy from a lifetime spent in the saddle. His hands were as brown as the leather reins he held daily. It was hard to tell his age, maybe late forties, but his summer-sky eyes held a youthful energy.

'Well, they reckon this Gleeson fella got himself a pup that he named Kelpie, and she's the foundation bitch for the whole kelpie breed. It's a bit of history that only a few people know about, but it's worth celebrating and it could really kick-start something for this town.'

He waited for Rosie to respond, but she just blinked her blue eyes slowly. Billy soldiered on.

'The story goes he swapped his stockhorse for the pup on the river bank somewhere near here. We need you to research it and write it up.'

'Bollocks!' Rosie said suddenly.

'Pardon?' said Duncan.

'Bollocks, bollocks, bollocks! You just want me out of the office!'

'It needs doing, Rosem – Rosie, and I don't have the time. Billy here's been barking at me for ages to get on to it. It's a perfect job for you.'

'It's a great idea!' said James Dean. He sauntered up to them and leant both elbows on the bar.

'Bill has the following in the dog world to get the nation's largest kelpie auction up and running here in the town, based on this yarn. It'd have to give this whole place a boost and that sounds great to me. It might even mean a few more boozers coming in the door of this old dungheap,' he said, looking around.

'No offence, Neville!' he called to the old man who was dozing at the bar. 'Come on, Rosie. Get off your arse and do something for your town. If we all get behind Bill on this one, who knows where it could take us? National fame and fortune . . . even the big screen . . . you never know your luck.'

'Well, what do you say, Rosie?' asked Duncan.

Rosie looked at the three men standing before her. Did she really want to take on something like this? She tried to process their request in her muddled brain. She didn't know what she wanted to do in life now Sam was gone. But could she handle working from home? What did she know about kelpies? She was about to argue that she might not be the person for the job when suddenly the pub door opened. Billy's red kelpie nosed his way in and trotted over to the bar.

'Outside, Trevor!' Billy said, but the dog wagged his tail and put his paws up on Rosie's knees, begging for a pat.

'What is this?' she asked. 'A scene out of *Lassie* or something?' She picked up the dog's front paws.

'Come on, Trev. Let's boogaloo till we puke!' She began to dance.

'Boot 'n' all, boots 'n' all, if you're gonna do it, throw your heart into it. Everything you do, throw your heart into . . . Red dirt gum tree country, red dirt gum tree country. Boots 'n' all.'

Leaving Trevor to bark and bound around her feet, Rosie picked up the box of books and danced to the door. The men watched her from the bar as she and the dog danced out into the street.

'I think you can take that as a yes,' James Dean said with a wink to Duncan and Billy.

That's if she remembers in the morning,' Billy said, shaking his head.

Six

It was the first morning since the accident that Rosie Jones had woken without stinging thoughts of Sam's death. Instead, she woke feeling excited, despite her hangover. History books and pamphlets were scattered over the bed. She reached out and picked up one of the books.

'A Green and Pleasant Land,' she read out loud. She picked up another. *'Still Stands the Schoolhouse by the Road.'* She tried to remember what Duncan had told her about researching the Irish stockman and the sheepdog. Where should she start, she wondered?

CODRINGTON, VICTORIA, 1861

The tiny stockman's hut stank of stale urine and of smoke from a now cold fireplace. Old Albert lay withered and shrunken between grimy sheets, his mouth hanging open and his eyes sunk deep into their sockets.

'Good Lord Jesus. Is he gone already?' said Jack to the Reverend Shinnick.

'No, Jack,' said the Reverend. 'Go to him. But mind you wake him gently.'

Jack moved slowly to the bed and tugged hesitantly on Albert's sleeve. The old man gurgled phlegm in his throat and began to lick his dry lips as he awoke. He peered at the tall young man who stood at his bedside.

'Ah, Jack . . . me boy.'

'Albert. Can I do anything?'

'Only bring me our sweet Mother Mary so I can go meet her Son in Heaven,' said Albert. 'I've had enough of this world.'

Albert weakly patted the empty space on the bed beside him.

'Even me little dog gave up on me.' He began to cough.

Jack stood waiting, not sure what to do or say. Then the old man spoke again.

'Go out the back now, Jack. Go to the stable and pick yourself out what gear you need. Then ride the mare home. Her colt will follow.'

'Your horses, Albert?' said Jack, wide-eyed. He knew Albert's prize stockhorse mare had thoroughbred bloodlines. A box crammed with coins and rumpled pound notes had been emptied to buy her. Then, after a good win at cards, old Albert had sent his mare to the best imported stallion in the district. And now he was offering Jack that very same mare, and the handsome colt that she suckled.

'Take 'em, boy.'

'But, Albert –'

'Don't be arguin' with a dyin' man, Jack.' Albert wheezed. 'You've got a gift. I've seen you with animals. It's a rare thing. Don't waste it by being a potato grower for your uncle James. That store he wants to open in Koroit – it's not *your* dream, Jack. If you don't go now, before you know it you'll be servin' fussy little ladies and sellin' wine to old drunks like me. You'll pine away inside.'

Albert paused for breath.

'So just take the mare on the road. Break her colt in as you go. Take to the road, Jack, it's what you're destined to do. Make a difference to this earth with your gifts – don't waste 'em.'

Jack felt the words of his old friend touch him deep inside. It was here that Jack held his frustration, a frustration he struggled with each day of his life on the farm with his kindly uncle and aunt, who had loved him and raised him as their own. Though he loved his family, Jack longed for the freedom to ride into the vast interior of this new country. Turning beasts on the run in the scrub, then calming the cattle to a steady walk along a track; a working dog leaning on his leg at night as he gazed into a campfire. This had always been his dream.

He felt the old man's hand reach out to touch his.

'It's time for me to sleep now, boy. Take good care of them horses for me. It's your turn to be the stockman. Be the best you can.'

'Goodbye, Albert,' Jack said, tears spilling from his eyes. Then he turned and walked away.

Outside in the sunshine, birds skittered about in the pear tree. Beneath the tree were two mounds of dirt. The grave for Albert was already dug and a cross made from palings was lying in the grass. The second mound was smaller, a miniature grave that bore no cross. Jack knew that underneath it lay the old man's little terrier.

He shook the chill of death from his shoulders and walked on into the stable, comforted by the smell of horses and leather. He ran his hands over the cool snaking twist of a stockwhip and well-oiled straps of a bridle. Under a sweat-crusted saddle blanket sat a magnificently crafted stock saddle. It was old and worn, rubbed smooth with work, lanolin and love. Jack had always dreamed of having a saddle like it. He opened the stable's creaking back door and stepped into the stockyard. There the mare stood dozing, one hind hoof lifted slightly, her foal nuzzling at her teats. The mare, Bailey, was a deep chestnut with a flaxen mane. She was strong and stocky for a horse of her breeding and she had soft brown eyes that looked at Jack calmly. The bright-eyed colt, about three months old now, was a sleek, long-legged bay. The colt turned his head to Jack and watched him cautiously. Jack stood looking at the shining coats of the heavenly creatures, barely daring to believe they were his.

Then Bailey whickered and took a step towards him, reaching out her neck to sniff at his shirtsleeve. She moved closer and leant her face to Jack's chest. When Jack stroked her strong neck he felt the excitement of possibility charge through him.

'Oh, lass. Will we have some adventures together!'

Rosie snapped out of her daydream and began to jot down some notes. As she did, she heard the clatter of hooves on cobbles and whinnying from outside her window. Climbing from her bed, she pulled back the curtains to see Julian and Sam's father unloading Sam's chestnut mare from the float. Even Rosie could see that she was heavily in foal. Gerald was holding Oakwood, who was looking anxiously around at his new surroundings. Chained to the back of the Chillcott-Clarks' ute were three sleek, sharp kelpies, which Rosie recognised as Sam's dogs. Two were black and tans, the other was an unusual blue and tan, the colour of campfire smoke. The sight of Sam's animals sent a chill through Rosie. Surely Sam himself would soon step out from the stables or emerge from the horse float? Rosie spun the ring around on her finger, frowning as she watched Julian lug dog food and bags of chaff into the stables.

'What is going on out there?' she asked herself before she scrabbled in her cupboard for some clothes.

Splashing cool water on her face seemed to ease her hang-over a little as she searched for the strength to face Sam's father. From the bathroom she heard her own father calling to her from downstairs. The impatience in his voice grated on her nerves.

'Rosemary? Rosemary! You have a visitor.'

'Coming!' she yelled.

Margaret Highgrove-Jones always insisted guests be ushered into either the northern sunroom, overlooking her herb garden, or the drawing room. No talking at the kitchen table for her. Unless, of course, the visitors were workmen or stock agents – *they* took their tea on the glassed-in back verandah.

Rosie found Marcus Chillcott-Clark in the sunroom, perched on a white wicker chair. His face was grey and great shadows darkened his eyes. For Marcus, every day since his son's death had been a walking, waking hell – but the nights were worse. In the darkness, lying next to his sobbing wife, he relived the call over and over again, the one asking him matter-of-factly to make his way to the Hamilton hospital.

By the time he and Elizabeth arrived, it was too late. Sam was dead. Their strong, beautiful boy lay bloody and still on a steel trolley in the hospital morgue, and Marcus could not get that vision out of his head. Each day, when he went to feed Sam's dogs and horses, he found himself ripped open with grief. The animals triggered so much trauma that soon Marcus couldn't bear to go near them. For several days, the dogs and horses went unfed and unwatered. He knew it was wrong, but he couldn't help it. Gripping a post at the corner of the kennels, he bent double, vomiting up the pain and grief. Early one morning he found himself standing before the dogs with a rifle in his hands, until Elizabeth came screaming from the house in her night-dress to drag him inside.

The dogs, as if they knew they were doomed, fell to howling in an eerie chorus. Elizabeth huddled like a frightened rabbit in the corner of their bedroom as Marcus bellowed out the window, 'Sit down! Sit *down*, you bloody dogs!'

When the dogs continued to howl and Sam's horses belted wildly up and down the fenceline, calling to each other, Elizabeth watched as her husband gave in to grief.

'That's it,' he said, grabbing for his boots. 'They have to go. All of them.'

The dogs yelped as he violently dragged them by their collars and flung them on to his ute. Then he hitched the float and marched away to catch Oakwood and the mare.

Back inside the house, his wife lurking near like a shadow, he talked to Gerald Highgrove-Jones on the phone in soft tones. Elizabeth sobbed when she heard Marcus asking if Gerald would take the animals on.

Now, sipping his coffee in the Highgrove sunroom, Marcus wondered if he'd made the right decision. Gerald was saying something about the responsibility for Sam's animals being his daughter's domain. Marcus glanced doubtfully at Rosie. She looked smaller and younger than usual in her baggy track-suit pants and an oversize teddy bear T-shirt. Her face was pale, her eyes red-rimmed. She looked like a little kid at home from school with the flu.

'I don't know the first thing about looking after them,' she said, 'let alone working them.'

Marcus sat forward on the couch and leant towards her.

'You can call me any time for advice,' he said. 'Please, Rose. It upsets Elizabeth too much to see them every day. We could never sell them. But we don't want to give them to just *anybody*. You know how much they meant to Sam, that's why you should have them. You'll be fine. I'm sure your family will help you,' he said, already doubting his own words.

'Okay then.' Rosie nodded uncertainly. 'I'll give it a go. I'll take them on.'

She could almost feel Marcus' relief. He came over to her and hugged her. It wasn't a warm hug. He simply encircled her in his arms for a moment. Then he took a step back and muttered. 'We would've loved you as a daughter-in-law. You were perfect for Sam's future.' Swallowing down tears, he walked quickly out of the sunroom.

Rosie sat in silence, watching her father putting the cups and untouched biscuits back on the tray.

'Now what do I do?' she asked eventually. Rosie had been so preoccupied with Sam's death that she hadn't paid attention to her father in weeks. He looked . . . different. There was such a faraway, vacant expression on his face that she felt like she was looking at a stranger.

He blinked at her, then said coldly, 'I can't help you. I've got enough to think about.'

'But, Dad!' Rosie said incredulously.

'Get Julian to help you.'

'I want *your* help! Why won't you ever help me?'

Gerald turned his back to her.

'You're just a stingy, grumpy old bastard!' Rosie yelled. Gerald spun around. His face was white and drawn.

'That's *enough*, Rosemary. I've sacrificed a lot for you. You have *no idea*!'

'What? Shelling out for school fees and designer clothes? What about *time*? That's all I want, Dad, some of your time. Why can't you teach me about farming, and looking after Sam's animals? I bet if Sam had left me some Wedgwood china you'd be fine with that! Much more suitable for a bloody grazier's wife! And stop calling me Rosemary – I'm Rosie from now on! Plain old Rosie Jones. I'm not taking this Highgrove-Jones crap any more!'

Frustration and anger brimming over, Rosie flung her arm across the silver coffee tray, knocking cups and biscuits to the floor. Black coffee grains splattered over the couch. The coffee jug smashed on the polished timber floor.

'How dare you!' Gerald yelled. 'After all I've done for you! I should've known it would come out in you in the end.'

Rosie stood shaking her head.

'What? What do you mean? Dad?'

'Ask your mother,' he spat at her, before storming from the room.

With her father's words echoing in her head, Rosie pulled on her boots and ran across to the stables. In the stalls, Oakwood and the mare tugged hungrily on hay nets. The sound of the two horses chewing rhythmically comforted Rosie. She breathed in the sweet smell of horses and fresh hay. In the third stall she heard the rustle of straw, and water being lapped up thirstily. Standing on tiptoe, she peered over the stable door to see Sam's dogs sniffing around their new surroundings. Dixie, the smoky-grey bitch, was lapping at the water. Rosie noticed, with a panicky feeling inside her, that the bitch was heavily in pup. Suddenly the two black and tan males noticed Rosie peering at them from over the door. Anxious, hackles raised, they began to bark loudly at her. Rosie took a step back and the panic rose higher. What was her father on about? What had he meant? A terrible feeling gripped her. She had to get away from this place.

Leaping into her father's work ute, she turned the key, not bothering to wait for the diesel glow light to go out. Then she revved her way out of the courtyard, away from Sam's animals and Highgrove homestead.

James Dean tried not to laugh when he saw the girl in the tracky-dacks and teddy bear T-shirt standing at his bar.

'Hair of the dog, eh?' he said, smiling at her.

'No. No more dogs please. And sorry about my hair.'

Rosie came and sat on a bar stool in the empty pub. James Dean waited for her order, but no order came.

'What's up?'

When he stooped down to look in her eyes, she burst into tears.

'Oh, now come on! There's a surcharge for bawling at my bar.' He came around the counter to her. 'You're messing up my clean bar mats. We've only just washed them! Come on, darlin',' he said, putting his arm across her shaking shoulders. 'Come out the back. My missus, the lovely Princess Amanda, is here today. She'll make you a cuppa and you can tell her all about it.'

He steered Rosie through the bar.

'Mands!' he called out. 'Got a basket case for ya!' Then in a quieter voice he said, 'Just joking, love. We'll sort you out.' And he patted her on the back.

Seven

When Rosie sobbed her way into the pub's kitchen, Andrew 'James' Dean introduced her to his wife. Amanda had the longest, brownest legs Rosie had seen. She had cropped blonde hair, wore runners and shorts, and would've looked more at home pole-vaulting than standing amidst the stainless steel of the pub's industrial kitchen. She looked at Rosie with warm, almond-shaped eyes, eyes as kind and pretty as a jersey cow's, Rosie thought. Amanda made her hot chocolate with marshmallows melting lavishly in the steaming mug, then pushed a packet of chocolate teddy bear biscuits towards her.

'They match my T-shirt,' Rosie said, laughing between sobs and wondering why she was here seeking solace at the kitchen table of a complete stranger. James Dean lingered in the kitchen, telling Amanda the story of how Rosie had written herself off the day before.

'Rosie was Sam Chillcott-Clark's fiancée,' he said to Amanda. 'You know. The bloke who was killed in Dubbo's ute accident.' He didn't try to sanitise the accident with sterile words like her mother's friends did, or talk softly or gently around it. He was straight to the point, and his frankness was comforting to Rosie.

For the next two hours she found herself pouring her heart

out to Amanda about Sam and Jillian, about how she didn't fit into her family, and then the fight with her father. How she'd come to town not knowing where to go or what to do.

'Then, to top it all,' she said to Amanda, 'Sam's father has dumped Sam's beautiful horses and dogs in the stables for me to look after. How am I supposed to deal with them? I've seen Julian and the workmen with the dogs, but I've never been allowed one of my own . . . and as for horses . . . I learned to ride on Trixie . . . but that was years ago. Sam *never* took me riding. He always said I couldn't handle his style of horse. That I might ruin them with my inexperience. And now . . . there they are in the stables! What is Sam's dad thinking?'

Amanda listened intently as she peeled and chopped vegetables for the counter meals that evening. When Rosie paused for breath, Amanda said, 'Name three things you love most in life. Off the top of your head.'

'What?' asked Rosie, wondering how this was relevant.

'Come on. Three things,' Amanda said, nonchalantly waving a kitchen knife at her.

Rosie sat back and frowned. A few things sprang to mind . . . like gardening? Entertaining friends? Redecorating? But of course it was her mother who had told her to be interested in those things. Rosie grimaced as she realised how lost she was. How her mother dominated her every thought.

'I don't know,' she said, wrinkling her nose.

'You do. Try harder,' said Amanda as she cranked a can opener around a massive tin of sliced beetroot. Rosie thought.

'Shearing time!' she said suddenly. 'For some reason I look forward to it every year, even though Dad chases me out of the shed because I have to help with the cooking instead . . . but I love the sounds and smells of shearing. I try to take the smoko in every time and I stay there for as long as I can, until Mum chucks a spazz when I don't get the cups and basket back to her in time to wash them up.' Rosie sighed and thought some more.

'Then there's watching the dogs work. I love that. We've

had a few stockmen over the years who had brilliant dogs. There's those stockmen that were hopeless . . . their dogs would crap in the back of the work ute every time and bark like mad and the men would belt the bejesus out of them. But the men with good dogs . . . oh, I love to watch them in the yards. And then there's the sheep. I love to watch them walking on to water in the evening, or eating excitedly when they've been moved onto a fresh paddock, and especially I love to watch them when they think.'

'Think?' said Amanda doubtfully. 'You're trying to tell me sheep think?'

'Yes. Of course they do. If you watch them when they don't know you're there. You know . . . the look they get on their faces when they could be thinking. I'm convinced sheep do actually think. At least I *think* they think . . . I think?'

Rosie shook her head. 'Anyway, they're things I love . . . oh, and . . . and I love the hills on Highgrove station. I love the way the sun makes them glow and the way the trees cluster in green patches in the gullies and along the ridges.'

'Great,' said Amanda, smiling at her. 'It sounds like you are born and bred to be on the land that you love . . . a stockman and a drover.'

'A stockman?'

'Yep.'

'But Dad's never allowed women stockmen on the place. It's men-only in the quarters.'

'That's like saying it's women-only in the kitchen,' said Amanda.

'Unless the man calls himself a chef.'

'And then he leaves the washing-up for the women.'

'Sucks, doesn't it?' said Rosie.

'Only if you let it. It doesn't have to be that way. You don't have to live by those rules. Andrew and I share everything. It's my shift today in the kitchen, then his tomorrow, then his mum, Christine, comes in the third day. She's raised him to take on all the domestics.'

'Not like our family! I've never been encouraged to do anything the men do. Never. Mum always needs a hand with the house, or the garden or the "community events".'

Rosie rolled her eyes.

'Dad's just as bad. Farm work is work for Julian, not me. I don't belong out there and he lets me know it. And I guess in a way, Sam was the same . . . it's funny but I hadn't noticed how adamant he was about it. He barely even gave me a tour of his place. It was like he assumed I wasn't interested.'

'But the land and the animals could be your true passion,' Amanda said. 'And a life without passion isn't really much of a life. Why should you let other people dictate where you can and can't be?'

Rosie looked down at her lap.

'But I don't know where to start.'

'Start where your heart is. And by telling your mum and dad to stick their old-fashioned ideas up their arses.'

'Mmm. Just like a suppository!'

'Yeah! Just like a suppository, I suppose. Go, girl!' said Amanda, punching the air with her beetroot-stained hands.

The girls fell silent with smiles on their faces. Rosie slowly peeled a spud as she thought about all the possibilities awaiting her out on the crackling golden hills of Highgrove.

'Ah, got her to work at last,' said James Dean as he bounded into the kitchen with a box full of lettuces. 'Save me doing that job!'

'You'll never guess what Rosie's inherited from Sam,' Amanda said.

'The clap?' he said. Rosie shot him a glance. 'Sorry, just slipped out. Not funny really.'

'No. It's fine. It *is* funny really,' said Rosie, 'when you think about it . . .'

'So what's in your inheritance from Mr C-C?' he asked. Amanda answered for Rosie.

'Three well-bred stud kelpies and two registered Australian stockhorses! Prize-winning ones at that. And she's going to learn how to use them on her place. Imagine the adventures she's going to have with them!'

Rosie had never considered Highgrove as 'her place'. It belonged to her father and to the pale faces of the dead ancestors hanging in gilded frames in the hallway. Rosie had always known Highgrove would one day be Julian's place. It was *his* right to drive around the paddocks and hillsides . . . never hers. But, Rosie realised, that could change. There was nothing to stop her joining Julian on the farm. Nothing to stop her except herself.

'I suppose I *could* have adventures with Sam's animals. We've got run country in the bush up the back of the place. There's a hut there, high above the river. Julian and the stockmen camp there when they muster the runs, but I've never been. *I've never been there*. Can you believe that? You can only get there on horseback. I could work for Dad, outside, and ride out there this year for the muster . . . I could ride out on Sam's horse and take a dog with me!'

'Of course you could!' Amanda said.

'Sure you can, darlin',' chipped in James Dean.

'I guess I've got what I've always longed for, but I didn't know it.'

'Exactly. So get out there and have a go!' James Dean said, pointing a lettuce firmly at her.

'But I can't imagine it.'

'Well, start.'

'Mmm. I don't know.'

'She needs something other than Blundstone boots to convince her,' James Dean said. He paused. 'I know! She needs a ute. Her life will be transformed if she gets a ute.'

'A ute?' Rosie asked.

'Yes. A ute. You can't have dogs and horses and drive them about in a Volvo. This girl bloody well needs a ute.'

'Are you sure?'

'Yep . . . in the famous words of the Uteman himself, a ute without a dog is like a shag without a sheila – it's kinda lonesome. And likewise for the dogs who don't have a ute!'

Then he clicked his fingers and pointed at Rosie.

'Aha! Have I got a deal for you!'

'What are you up to now?' Amanda said with narrowed eyes.

'Neville!' he said to her. Amanda paused and thought about it. She started to grin.

'Yes! Neville,' she said, and they both ran out to the bar.

'Neville?' Rosie asked as she followed them, completely confused.

Neville was sitting slumped at the bar watching Sky Channel and prodding his smouldering rollie in the ashtray with fat yellow fingers.

'Doing any good with the dish-lickers?' James Dean asked, nodding towards the greyhounds on the screen.

'Nah,' rasped Neville.

'Never mind. Next race.' James Dean patted him on the back. 'Now, old sunshine, you remember Rosie from yesterday?'

'Bloody jukebox queen,' Neville said, squinting at her through cloudy eyes.

'Yep, the boots 'n' all girl. Well, now she's got some boots and she's got herself some dogs, so the next step is she'll be needing a ute.'

'I will?' Rosie asked.

'Yes,' Amanda said. 'It's your dream to have a ute.'

'It is?'

The next thing Rosie knew she was listening to Neville and how his gout was giving him hell in his leg.

'Can't change the gears. Clutch leg, you see!' He tapped at his left leg and moved it slowly back and forwards, dangling it from the bar stool. 'Bugger of a time with me gout.'

'An automatic would mean old Nev here could get about some more, see?' said James Dean, smiling.

'And a ute would mean Rosie Jones and her dogs could get about more too,' said Amanda.

'So you want me to swap Mum's old Volvo for Neville's

old ute?' Rosie looked at them all, terrified at what her mother would say.

In the next moment, she found herself sitting next to Neville at the bar. They were rehearsing the art of the column shift. They waved their arms about, hands clutching the imaginary gearstick.

'It's three on the tree. Up for first,' Neville wheezed.

'Up for first,' repeated Rosie.

'Down for second. Back and up for third.'

She followed his moves, concentrating hard.

'And reverse?' Neville asked.

Rosie showed him the action for reverse and he clapped her on the back, smiling and laughing.

'You got it, girl. And what about your car? How do I get about with that?'

'D for drive. And when you don't put your seatbelt on, ignore it when it bloody beeps at you. Simple as that,' she said and then she started laughing. Rosie Jones now had a Ford ute to put her dogs on!

'Simple as that!' she said again. After she had bought Neville a beer and a lemonade for herself, she turned to him and asked, 'Hey, you don't know anything about the good old days and what it was like to be a stockman way back when . . . we're talking mid-1800s?'

'I might be an old bastard,' slurred Neville, 'but I'm not *that* old!'

'I didn't mean that. It's just I'm trying to find out about this Irish stockman. A guy called Jack Gleeson.'

Neville set his beer down and smiled.

When Rosie left the pub she was feeling a whole lot better. James and Amanda had worked wonders. Not by serving her alcohol this time, but by providing a good old cup of tea and a chat. Rosie squinted into the sun and smiled. She was going to follow her dreams . . . now that James Dean and Amanda had helped her discover what they were.

Instead of getting into her father's ute, which she had parked in the main street, Rosie walked around the side of the pub to the gravel car park. Her mother's old Volvo was still sitting where she had parked it yesterday. The car stuck out at an odd angle next to the stack of empty beer kegs and looked as if it was sulking from being abandoned the night before. She patted its square boot. 'Sorry for leaving you behind last night, but I have to say – so long, good riddance and goodbye.'

In the palm of her hand she tossed a set of keys. The bronze name-tag attached to them was engraved with the name 'Neville'. She made her way towards a clunky looking old XF Ford Falcon ute. She ran her fingers along its dinted side and then unlocked the door. She slid onto the crimson vinyl bench seat and proudly sat behind the wheel, breathing in the smell. With the vinyl heating in the sun, she was sure the ute still smelt of the seventies, the heady era in which it was made. Slipping the keys into the loose ignition switch, she turned the key to the charge position. She smiled when she found the vehicle, unlike her Volvo, didn't smugly beep at her because she hadn't clicked her seatbelt on. She pushed the sloppy clutch in, tugged a bit on the column-shift gearstick and turned the key over. The Ford ute grumbled to life with a throaty growl.

'Awesome,' Rosie said, and she drove off down the main street, out towards Highgrove station.

Eight

The sun was glowing red in the sky when Rosie drove over the garden grid to the front of the house in her 'new' ute. The Falcon rolled to a halt outside the grand homestead and then let fly with a bang and a blue puff of smoke as Rosie switched off the engine. Her elation seemed to die with it. She breathed in deeply before she got out. As she entered the house, a feeling of dread settled in her.

Outside the kitchen door, Rosie hesitated. She could hear her parents' voices hissing within. They were barely able to restrain the angry words flying from their lips.

'How could you?' Margaret said through gritted teeth. Her father mumbled something back. Rosie stepped closer and put an ear to the door.

'You *promised* never to say anything to her.'

'*You* started this!'

'That's not how I remember it,' Margaret said icily.

'Forget who's to blame. She has to know the truth sooner or later.'

'She's already had one big shock with Sam!'

Rosie could stand it no longer. She pushed the door open and saw her parents standing at the sink, her mother looking ridiculous in a floral apron and her father with his glasses sliding down the bridge of his nose. Their faces were ablaze with anger.

'The truth about what?' Rosie said.

They started, and turned to her with worried looks. Margaret untied the apron and slipped it over her head. Gerald pushed his glasses back along his nose.

'I've tried to accept it,' he said, shaking his head and walking to the door. 'But it's gone on too long. I'm sorry, Rose.' He cast Rosie a glance she couldn't read. 'This is between you and your mother now. I can't be part of it any more.'

'Don't you walk out again!' Margaret yelled. 'Come back here and face this!'

'Face what, Margaret?' said Gerald from the doorway. 'It's not my place to tell her. It's *your* mess. You created it. You sort it out!'

Margaret was shaking. 'Please, please! You have to help me tell her! This is about all of us, not just you!'

Tears rolled down her cheeks and she clutched a teatowel so tightly that her knuckles were white.

'I've put my life on hold long enough for you. No more, Margaret. You hear me? No more!'

Rosie, completely bewildered, watched her father walk away. She turned back to her mother.

'Mum? What the hell's going on?' Margaret just shook her head and cried even harder.

'Mum?' Rosie urged with fear in her voice. Just then Julian walked into the kitchen.

'Nice outfit,' he said, taking in Rosie's teddy bear T-shirt and tracksuit pants, teamed with the Blundstones. But the friendly mockery in his voice dropped away when he saw his mother.

'Are you okay, Mum?'

All Margaret could do was shake her head.

'Mum's got something to say to me, Julian,' Rosie said, 'and she's going to say it *now*!' A quiver had crept into Rosie's voice as she took a step forward, grabbed her mother by the shoulders and looked her straight in the eye.

'I'm sorry,' Margaret sobbed, 'I'm sorry. It was a mistake. It was all a mistake. I didn't mean to.'

'For God's sake, Mum, just tell me!'

'Gerald isn't your real father,' Margaret blurted out.

Rosie blinked. An image of the dusty stud record books that lined the shelves in the office flashed before her eyes. They contained the Highgrove station bloodlines. Her grandfather had laid them out before her and let her trace her small finger along the bloodlines of the bulls and rams. Then he had done the same with an old family album. She had traced the lineage of her family all the way from her forebears in Scotland to the spot where her finger had come to rest on her own name. Rosemary Margaret Highgrove-Jones . . . daughter of Gerald and Margaret.

Suddenly she felt adrift on a huge sea. The line that had connected her to a sturdy proud ship was cut, and she was drifting. Lost. She swallowed away her nausea. Grappling to control her rush of thoughts, Rosie felt one question surfacing in her confusion. Who, then? Who is my father? She was frozen. She couldn't move and was unaware of Julian's hand on her shoulder. She was only aware of her mother's red-rimmed eyes that were spilling over with tears. Rosie stared at her, and swallowed hard.

'So, who is my father?'

'I don't know,' Margaret sobbed.

'You don't know?' Rosie asked incredulously.

Margaret shook her head and scrunched her eyes tight shut. 'It meant nothing. Nothing! It was an accident. I can't talk about this, Rosemary. I can't deal with it now.'

'But, Mum!'

'I'm sorry. I can't deal with this now! I have to find Gerald!'

Margaret fled from the room. Stunned, Rosie looked at Julian. There was pity and panic on his face. He reached out to hug her, but she pushed him away.

'No!' she said. 'Leave me alone!' She had to get out of the house.

Her head still pounding, Rosie shut the heavy oak door of the stables behind her and caught her breath. Under the stable lights the animals' coats gleamed. The dogs sniffed at her legs as she squatted down amongst them.

'Hello,' she said, tears brimming as she ran her fingers along their lean backs. 'I'll clean out your stable, then I'll find you something to eat. We can go for a run in the morning.'

The dogs pricked their ears and looked up to the door, wagging their tails.

'Not now,' she said to them sadly. 'You'll have to wait.' Their tails stopped wagging at the word 'wait'.

Emotion welled up in her. Sam had trained his dogs to perfection. She wished he were here now to tell her what to do. She felt another stab of anguish as she realised Sam wouldn't have taken her mother's news lightly. She swallowed back tears and fought the fear inside her. She had to be strong.

To distract herself, she turned her attention to Sam's animals. They needed her. She felt her heart beating fast. She'd have to get in with the horses to feed them now and it terrified her. They weren't like the shaggy ponies she'd played around with at pony club. She looked at the large horses in the stalls. If only someone was here to help her, but her father had sacked the last workman this month. It was after her mother had declared that he couldn't bring 'strange women from town' back to the property.

Huh, thought Rosie now, her mother was a fine one to talk. Rosie recalled how the workman had looked at Margaret, standing tall, elegant and proud before him. She looked every bit the grazier's wife and was doing her best to make him feel every bit the worker. But this bloke had met women like her before and took pleasure in telling her that what he did with strange women in his own time was his business. Then he'd added, with a sly smile, 'I reckon you're just jealous, Mrs H-J. Not getting enough from the old man, are ya?'

After that Gerald had little room to move, and so another workman had packed his things and driven off Highgrove for the last time.

Rosie walked to the cluster of feed bins at the end of the stable. She lifted the heavy lids and peered in, wondering which grain was what and which chaff was which.

'Just get on with it, Rosie,' she told herself angrily, then screeched and dropped the lid as a mouse scuttled over her hand. Rosie took a deep breath to calm herself and stooped into the bins. At the sound of grain being scooped into feed buckets, the horses whickered eagerly.

'Coming! I'm coming.'

She lugged the buckets to the stalls and entered Oakwood's first. He craned his neck to sniff at the black plastic tub and threw his head up and down as if to say, 'Hurry up!'. Rosie gave him his food and reached out to stroke his long, smooth neck. She could feel her own heartbeat settle as she watched him chew contentedly on his chaff. There was nothing to be frightened of with Oakwood, she realised. He was a gentle creature who just got revved up on race days, as any horse would.

In the next stable, Rosie stroked the golden chestnut mare as she ate. She ran her hands slowly over the mare's swollen belly, hoping to feel the movement of the foal inside her. The mare ignored her, chewing stolidly, until Rosie touched a place on the top of her tail. Then the mare leant into the pressure of her hand, so Rosie began to scratch her harder. She remembered how Julian's pony Trixie had liked to have her face rubbed. Rosie scratched the mare's rump for a while, trying to remember her name. Sam had talked about her at tennis, his new brood mare from the Hunter Valley. Her name? Rosie tried to summon up the image of Sam's sexy mouth speaking the name. Sally? No. Sassy? Yes, that was it. She was certain.

'Sassy,' she said aloud, then she began to cry. She stood for a long while, her arms looped about the mare's neck as images of Gerald flew through her head. The times when he had yelled at her. Ignored her. Looked at her in disdain. It was all falling into place.

Rosie went outside and looked across the yard to the

homestead. She could see the light on at one end of the house. Gerald would be in the sitting room, reading the newspaper and dozing in front of the TV. Trying to pretend nothing had happened. Her mother would be holding in the tears and taking her wrath out on a vase or stainless-steel pot, cleaning furiously. Julian would be in his bedroom with his earphones on, listening to Radio National or reading. Rosie looked up to the second storey of the house. Her bedroom light was on. But there was no girl at the window, looking down on the courtyard. The window seat was empty and the girl had gone.

In the workmen's quarters, Rosie lay exhausted on an old striped mattress. The night was warm, but still she curled her legs up to her chest and hugged herself. She looked around the room. It was a good place to be, despite being dusty and empty of anyone's things. It smelt musky, like the smell of men. Real men, who worked hard in dirt and dust. Men who would sweat and eat mutton chops and wipe their mouths with their sleeves, who'd swig on enamel mugs, swilling sugar and tea leaves around in the bottom.

Rosie had always watched the stockmen with intense fascination, longing for their freedom. She wanted to work hard all day long outside. To be grubby and grimy and dog-tired. To satisfy herself with a big hearty meal, washed down with beer. To come in sun-tired after a day of fencing, or droving or rouseabouting, to shower sore muscles and be satisfied that the day was done. She wanted a life like that. She wanted to be one of them.

Outside the door of the quarters she heard one of the horses snort and shuffle about. Then there was a knock on the door.

'Rose?' Julian put his head around the door.

She curled up in a ball.

'Go away.'

'Are you all right?'

Rosie didn't answer. Julian came in and sat on the edge of

the bed. 'Dad asked me to come and find you. To make sure you're okay.'

Fury bubbled up in her. He wasn't *her* dad. Why hadn't her mother come? As if reading her mind, Julian continued.

'Mum's taken some tablets. To help her sleep. You know how worked up she gets.'

Rosie buried her face under the pillow.

'Come on, Rose,' pleaded Julian, 'come inside now. Please?' He pulled her arm, but she tugged it away from him.

'No! There's no way I'm going back in there.'

'Look, if it makes you feel any better, it's shocked the hell out of me too. I don't want to be in the house with those two either.'

'But you're Dad's golden boy. Even more so now,' Rosie said, sitting up.

'Rosie, if only you knew,' Julian said tiredly. 'The number of times I've felt like punching his head in, or telling Mum to stick it. I don't know why I've stayed and put up with their crap for so long. And now with this bit of news, that Mum was unfaithful to Dad and you . . . well, everything feels so weird.' He fell silent, then added quietly, 'I'm sorry they've hurt you so much.'

Rosie began to cry again and Julian pulled her to him. He held her as her mother's news sank in with full force.

Some time later, Rosie wiped her eyes and looked up at Julian.

'Will you help me run away?' she asked.

'Course I will. Where to? Anywhere. You name it.'

'To the farm. To here. I want to live here now.'

'Come on then,' Julian said, dragging her up from the bed. They crept inside, stepping carefully over the creaking floorboards. She and Julian threw her belongings into a backpack, gathered up towels and bedding, and crept back down the stairs with the box of books from Duncan in their arms.

The old kettle rumbled in the corner of the quarters while

Julian rinsed out chipped enamel mugs. Rosie plumped the pillows on the bed and sat her clock on the bedside table.

'There you go,' said Julian, handing her a steaming cup of sugary tea. 'There's a dash of something stronger in there too. Pinched it from Mum's grog cabinet. She won't miss it.'

'Thanks,' Rosie said, taking the cup and sitting down at the kitchen table.

'You all right now?' Julian asked.

'Sure, I'll be fine. What about you?'

'I'm fine. The more I think about it, the more it explains . . . you know . . . how uptight they always are. I thought it was just marriage. But something's been wrong for a long time between them.'

'Are you going back in?' Rosie asked. 'Or do you want to bunk down here on a swag or something?'

Julian shook his head.

'I'm OK. I have plans of my own. You'll see one day.'

Rosie smiled. 'Well then, I'll see you for work tomorrow.'

'You bet,' Julian said. 'You could head out on Oakwood and check the stock for me. That'd be a real help.' Then he smiled at her kindly before going out into the night.

The thought of riding Oakwood filled Rosie with fear. She tucked it down inside herself, along with the shock of finding out Gerald wasn't her real father. Instead she reached for Duncan's box of history books.

At the old kitchen table in the men's quarters, carved with the names of workmen from days gone by, Rosie settled down to read. She was trying hard to lose herself in the history contained in those pages. Better by far to explore other people's lives, than to face her own right now.

Albert's Stables, Codrington, 1861

The brush glided over Bailey's coat while Jack Gleeson spoke softly to her in the dawn light. He let her sniff at the saddle and blanket before he placed them on her back. When he lifted the flap of the saddle and let the stirrups down he felt a sadness for Albert. There was a well-worn groove where the buckle had rested, the leathers kept in one spot for years. Jack flicked the reins over the mare's head and stepped up easily into the saddle. It felt strange, like he was putting on another man's worn old shoes, but Jack knew that, with time, Albert's saddle would come to fit him like a glove.

Bailey stood patiently as he got off to tie his pannikin to the saddle. Then he added the bags of sugar, tea and flour. His strong fingers fiddled with the smaller buckles of the saddlebags stuffed with his belongings. He strapped his coat on the front of the saddle and firmly tied Albert's old swag at the back. The colt stood by his mother, his ears flickering with curiosity. He stretched out his black nose and sniffed at the saddle and then began to nibble and tug on the flour bag.

'Get out of that, you cheeky mite,' Jack said, slowly reaching out a hand. The colt snorted but stood still as Jack ran his hands down his glossy bay neck and scratched him on his wither. 'You eat my tucker and you'll be in strife.'

Jack gently slipped the halter over the foal's head and told him. 'It won't be long till you'll be carryin' your fair share.' The colt dropped his head and shook the halter, but he would soon take to being led from the mare.

Jack thought of the long hours ahead of him on the road. There'd be plenty of time to dream up a name for the colt.

He led Bailey out of the stalls, the colt following them. He turned away from the sea-breeze that was rushing in off the grey water, and walked along the road that headed north. He didn't look back.

Nine

The sound of the horses moving about their stalls woke Rosie at dawn. She stretched and stood, thinking only of the animals, ready to go, not bothering to wash or change. Not wanting to face her mother or the truth. There was no sign of Julian. He must have slept in, Rosie concluded.

In the stable Oakwood stood as still as a queen's guard horse as she reached up and struggled to put the bridle over his ears. He waited patiently while she heaved the stock saddle on to his back. So far so good, thought Rosie, as she tugged the girth up a notch. But out in the courtyard he was a different creature. He danced on his hooves, and each time Rosie put pressure on his bit, he tossed his head.

'Stand still!' she cried in frustration as Oakwood turned in circles. She had a fine sweat on her brow from nerves. She stood for a moment, taking deep, slow breaths, trying to calm down. Then she took a firm grip on the reins.

'Stand up,' she said in a commanding voice. This time Oakwood stood. She clambered up into the saddle and was relieved to feel the horse relax. His slim neck seemed to stretch out forever in front of her and his ears flickered back and forwards as he looked about the courtyard. She felt a long way off the ground. Sassy, now in a yard behind the stable, trotted anxiously up and down the fence and whinnied to him. Rosie felt Oakwood shudder beneath her as he let out a loud reply.

'Oh, come on!' she said. 'It's not *that* bad!'

She had let the dogs out before saddling Oakwood and they were now sniffing about the courtyard. The largest black and tan, Diesel, was leisurely lifting his leg on Margaret's pot-plants and the smoky-coloured bitch, Dixie, was pooping in the middle of the yard.

Rosie watched them, feeling almost smug. Anger towards her mother began to bubble up again. All those years of being bossed and berated by Margaret, who pretended to be Mrs Perfect – but it was all a lie. Her mother had lied to her! Well, she was going to live out her dreams from now on, no matter what her mother thought. Rosie used her feelings to steel her nerves as she urged Oakwood forward, through the archway, past the shearing shed and then on beyond the yards.

'Dogs! Come behind!' she called out like a true stockman. Then she set off on the lower track, which she knew would eventually lead her to where the river rolled out from the hills.

She had been on the horse for just half an hour when the dogs caught scent of the sheep. Rosie saw them sniff at the wind and then crouch down and move in a slink, rather than a trot. In the distance she spotted the sheep drinking at the dam in the morning light. The dogs crouched, their ears pricked. They stalked forward.

'No,' said Rosie. 'Come, dogs.'

But they ignored her. The youngest dog, Gibbo, was quivering with excitement. As they neared, a sheep lifted its head from the water and sprang back, startling the rest of the mob. They began to move nervously away from the dogs. Gibbo took off like a whippet, running full pelt at the sheep. Diesel cast out and around, while Dixie, slower and full of pups, cantered to the other side of the mob.

'No! Dogs! Come here! Diesel! Gibbo! Gibbo! Dixie! Come! Bugger you!'

The dogs took no notice. With youthful exuberance, Gibbo cut a few sheep out of the mob and ran them hard, snapping at their faces, while Diesel and Dixie did their best to work the whole lot into a mob. They ran them round in circles towards Rosie, pushing them closer and closer to the dam.

'Leave them!' Rosie yelled.

But the dogs would not. Soon sheep were up-ended in the dam, their legs and hooves flailing in the air like beetles on their backs. Rosie instinctively kicked Oakwood to a trot, but he was no kid's pony, so the feeling of her boots in his sides jolted him straight into a canter. Rosie careened awkwardly in the saddle as they headed towards the dam, screaming at the dogs as she went.

'Come behind!' she screeched. She hardly recognised the voice as hers. Her heart raced as Oakwood cantered up and over the dam bank. Like the brilliant campdraft horse he was, he skidded to a perfect halt at the water's edge. Rosie felt air rushing around her as she flew over his neck. Still clutching the reins, she fell down and down as if in slow motion. At last, cold water splashed around her as her backside hit the muddy bottom of the dam with a jarring thud that shocked the air from her lungs. Sheep thrashed all about her as the dogs worked hard to bring the mob to Rosie. Gasping, she dropped the reins. She grappled for a stick floating on the muddy surface and waved it angrily at the dogs.

'Sit! Sit! *Sit!*' Hearing the fury in her voice, each dog sat. The sheep on the edge of the dam seemed to calm. Rosie stood puffing, her breasts rising and falling beneath her wet teddy bear T-shirt. Her tracky-dacks, brown with mud and smeared with sheep manure, sagged below her bum. Oakwood had waded into the dam up to his knees and was pawing at the water. Rosie grunted with effort as she hauled heavy wet sheep to their feet so they could totter to dry ground. The movement of the waterlogged sheep again sparked Gibbo to rush in at the mob, but this time Rosie ran at him waving the stick.

'Sit, you little bugger! *Sit!*'

Gibbo backed off a few paces, glancing nervously at her, and slowly put his backside on the ground, though he continued to stare intensely at the sheep.

By the time she had collected Oakwood from the dam and convinced the dogs to come away from the sheep, Rosie was exhausted. A sharp pain was rising in her right bum-cheek, probably from landing on a rock. She sat on the dam's bank and looked at her mud-caked hands. With a jolt she realised Sam's engagement ring was gone. She waded back into the dam, scrabbling through the silt and mud, looking for the gleam of sapphire and gold. Sobs rose in her throat.

'Oh, no! Oh, Sam!'

When Rosie at last gave up searching for the ring, she stood up in the middle of the dam. Arms outstretched, she let out a long frustrated wail that made the dogs flatten their ears and look away. Then she flung herself backwards into the water, as if she was being baptised.

As she sunk beneath the vile-smelling dam water, Rosie wished she would drown. She held her breath and shut her eyes and listened to the thud of her heart. But when her lungs felt as if they would burst, she surfaced again, to see the three dogs sitting on the dam bank anxiously watching for her. From the dam's edge they whined and barked at her, as if begging her to come out.

'Okay, okay,' she said sadly. 'I get the message.'

She waded out, crouched down and hugged the dogs to her.

Ten

Back at the homestead yards, still wet and muddy from the dam, Rosie took up a shovel at the dog kennels and flung open all the gates. The wooden slats were heaped up with piles of dog droppings that had dried white in the sun. In one of the pens, Julian's shaggy collie dog leapt up and down and barked loudly at Sam's dogs who trotted around nearby. Rosie scraped the blade of the shovel along the grating, trying not to breathe in the smell. Then she unwound a hose and sprayed the grating clean. The dogs hovered about, sniffing, squatting and lifting legs in the sheepyards until Rosie called them over. She asked each dog to 'hop up' the way she'd seen Sam do when he put his dogs away. Diesel and Dixie obliged, but Gibbo hung back. Rosie crouched and held out her hand.

'Gibbo, come.' He hung his head and ambled up to her. 'Don't hurry or anything,' she said, scratching behind his ears. She lifted him into the kennel, shut the gate and turned back towards the stables. It was then she felt the dread settle over her. She'd have to go into the house at some point. Sooner or later she'd have to face her parents . . . or at least, face her mother and the man who was no longer her father. God, she thought, what did she call him from now on? She shut her eyes and again held back tears.

In the kitchen, Margaret was crashing about with pots and

pans. Normally she'd prepare her weekly Meals on Wheels for the elderly in the district with an air of precision. But today she had tossed the too-pink slices of roast lamb and undercooked vegetables on to the plates and roughly covered them in aluminium foil. Rosie noticed how unsteadily her mother stacked the meals in a wicker basket. When Margaret looked up and saw her daughter, caked in mud and manure, wearing the same clothes she'd had on yesterday, she burst into tears. Her hands were shaking as she groped in her handbag and pulled out her car keys.

'I'm going to town,' she said defiantly.

Rosie shook her head and sighed. Her anger towards her mother now mingled with pity. Suddenly *she* felt like the parent.

'Not like that you're not.'

Margaret turned her back to Rosie and leant on the bench.

'I have to get the meals in on time,' she said in a shaky voice.

'Will you stop pretending like nothing's happened?' Rosie yelled. 'We have to *talk* about this!'

But just as she let her anger fly, Rosie noticed the little jar of pills by the kitchen sink, and the bottle of whisky beside them. Oh God, she thought, she wasn't going to get any sense out of her mother now. She sighed and heard herself saying, 'I'll drive you, Mum. Just give me a chance to have a shower.'

But there was an edge to her voice, a bitterness that Margaret had never heard before.

Margaret stared vacantly ahead as they drove towards Casterton in the Pajero. Rosie willed herself to speak gently.

'So, how did it happen?'

Her mother kept her eyes on the road.

'It was a long time ago,' she said.

'Yes, Mum. Twenty-three years ago, actually,' Rosie said sarcastically.

'Don't be angry with me, Rose. Your father's so angry with me. I couldn't bear it if you were too.'

'*My* father. Mum, Gerald is *not* my father – not any more, according to you!'

Margaret winced and shifted in her seat, trapped in the moving vehicle.

'Please. Please don't be angry.'

'Surely I have a right to know who my own father is?' cried Rosie, thumping the steering wheel.

'I know this is a big shock,' Margaret said. 'But now's not the time. At the moment, it's important to keep our family together. It's important to keep your father happy. I know you need to know.' She put her hand on Rosie's knee, her first offer of comfort. 'We *will* talk about this, I promise. But not now. I can't deal with it right now. Please understand.'

Rosie glanced at the mud that was drying beneath her fingernails and longed to be back in the stables with the dogs and horses. She pushed in a cassette of The Corrs and turned it up loud, signifying to her mother that the subject was now closed – for the moment. She stared at the countryside that was rushing past them. The leaves of messmates hung limply, dulled by dust from the road. Roadside grasses waved as the vehicle sped by. She didn't want to think any more about her own life. She wanted to escape to Jack Gleeson's world. Would he have travelled this road, Rosie wondered? Would Jack Gleeson have ridden past that very same old tree, the one with the gnarled dead branch that speared through its own living leafy growth? She tried to imagine Jack riding along the road into Casterton.

Cobb & Co coach track to Glenelg, mid-1860s

Early one Friday afternoon in late February, on the rutted track next to the Wannon River, Jack caught up to a coach that was making slow progress. He rode alongside the vehicle and saw gloved hands waving to him from inside. A young woman's voice called out, 'Declare you are *not* a bushranger, sir, for I fear we might all faint!' Then there was a peal of giggles, followed by the stern, scolding voice of their chaperone.

'And how can I be sure it's not *you* who might rob me blind, young lady?' Jack called out to the passengers hidden behind the heavy curtains that swayed in the coach windows. He rode past the carriage so he was level with the driver. The colt tugged a little on the lead rope as he shied from the creaking, rattling coach. Jack admired the muscular backs of the bay four-horse team that pulled the coach over the difficult ground.

'Good day to you, sir,' said the driver, sitting straight as a gun barrel in his seat. He held the reins with precision and Jack noted that his neatly groomed beard was trimmed exactly to meet the edges of his starched collar and tie. The man was not much older than Jack, but his long English nose and neat suit made him seem more mature. Beside him sat a boy of about sixteen who eyed Jack cautiously. The boy was in no mood to joke about bushrangers. For him, bushrangers were a reality that caused him daily anguish in his job. His hand was resting beside him under a coarse woollen travel rug and Jack was certain his fingers were wrapped about a pistol.

'G'day to you, sirs. I'm Jack Gleeson,' he said, tipping his stockman's hat. 'I'm headed for the Crossing Place in search of station work.'

'Ah! Another man with dreams of adventure journeying to the wild west! You're bound to find your work, Mr Gleeson . . . and your adventures.' The driver smiled at him, sizing up the fine-looking man on the fine-looking mare.

'I'm Thomas Cawker. I'd shake your hand, but I daren't let go of the reins, for I have precious cargo on board.' He winked.

'So I saw when I rode by,' said Jack with a smile.

'A party of ladies bound for the three-day meet at the Casterton Races. They are the daughters and nieces of a fine gent from Geelong, who'll ride out and meet us there.'

'It sounds like I've timed my arrival right,' said Jack.

'Are you a racing man, Mr Gleeson?'

'Well, I'd like to be. The old stockman who owned this mare said she has won her share and her colt is sired by a very fine thoroughbred.'

'Yes, I can see his blood is rich with quality – which is more than I can say for your dog!'

Jack looked at the old dog that followed him, his head and tongue hanging low, his eyelids sagging down to reveal the pink flesh that surrounded his cloudy eyeballs.

'Ah yes, the dog. Idle's his name. He was a gift from an old widow I did some work for along the way.'

'She mustn't have been too happy with your work,' laughed Cawker.

Jack looked sceptically at the black dog with the greying muzzle and arthritic legs. He'd accepted the dog out of politeness, but also knew he'd need at least one working dog if he were to get a job on the big run stations further west.

'I've had to carry him most of the way! It looks as if he's not keen to take on the life of a drover's dog.' Jack chuckled to himself and shook his head. 'I must be getting in the habit of taking on dead men's animals! One day I'm going to choose the best dog myself . . . not an old scoundrel like him! And with a name like Idle, I suspect I'll be lucky to get any work out of him.'

'And what have you named your colt? Surely Quality suits him well.'

The colt was now used to the road and led beside the mare easily. His feathery foal's tail was growing nicely and his hindquarters were filling out with sleek sinewy muscles.

'I've named him Cooley, after a story my aunt used to tell me. The Cattle Raid of Cooley. But an English gent such as yourself may not know the legend.'

'Can't say that I do,' said Cawker.

Jack had found on his travels that his Irish heritage was looked down upon by many that he met. This Englishman seemed accepting enough though. His days as a coachman must've taught him to read a fellow traveller's intention with a glance. Jack himself was careful with the company he chose on the road. He tended to keep to himself, or to his own kind. Some of his fellow Irishmen had told him he was mad to leave the civilised area of Koroit for the uncertainty of the interior. They warned him away from the wild towns where men fought bare-knuckled in the streets and drank until they fell into the mire. It was a place few decent single women would choose to be, the travellers would say, eyeing the handsome young man. Then the stories would unfold – men who copulated with pigs and Godfearing churchmen who shared their beds with boys; attacks from natives and gruesome butcherings beside campfires; bodies of blackfellas strung in trees; the stench emanated by corpses in the hot scrub, and the swarms of flies as thick as mud, with buzzing wings loud as the north wind. But Jack had ignored the stories. Nothing would turn him back. He was headed west to find the great sheep and cattle runs that he had dreamed of.

Some nights, with his heart in his mouth, he gestured to passing Aborigines to join him by his campfire and together they shared food. Surely better to share with them than be speared, he thought. With time, Jack came to love the smell of kangaroo fur singeing in licking yellow flames as the skin bubbled and spat. The native men tore at fresh-cooked flesh with teeth as bright and white as stars. But in the mornings the men's smiles would disappear, replaced by a wariness in their solemn eyes. They were men at war. They would pick up their belongings and walk quietly along the track with Jack for a time, as if protecting him. Then they would slip into the scrub and out of his sight.

Jack turned back to Cawker.

'How far until you deliver your precious cargo, Mr Cawker?'

'For us, with the road the way it is, another three hours – we'll arrive before dark, so there'll be no need for young Ted here to light the lanterns. But you, sir, on your pretty mount, you'll arrive long before us.'

'Could you suggest some lodgings for me and my horses when I get there?'

'There's the Glenelg Inn, of course, but it can be a rowdy place – especially during race meets. If you'd like to offer your services, you could put your animals and yourself at my new place of business. The Livery and Letting Stables. I offer first-class accommodation and attentive grooms. I'd be delighted to accommodate such a fine mare and colt.'

'And I'd be delighted to offer my services as an attentive groom,' said Jack with a smile. 'At least until I find work on a station.'

'Well then, Mr Gleeson, we have an agreement. We shall meet you there this evening.'

Jack tipped his hat again and rode on, with Idle trotting at Bailey's heels. The mare had a spring in her step, as if she knew she was headed for Mr Cawker's stall of fresh sawdust and a nose-bag full of oaten chaff.

Eleven

Rosie and Margaret pulled up outside Mr Seymour's rickety house in Casterton's main street. Rosie carried a plate of food to the front door and followed her mother inside. She felt a darkness swamp her, and musty air fold over her skin and clothes. In the living room, the smell of cat's urine was overwhelming.

The low-ceilinged room had drab wallpaper covering damp walls. Rosie's eyes scanned the collection of framed black-and-white photographs from another era. They were mostly of elegant, long-legged racehorses, their jockeys holding up trophies by the track. In the corner, looking as worn, untidy and dirty as the room, was an old man slumped in a grotty armchair. The chair sprouted tufts of horsehair, as if it were growing whiskers like the man who sat in it.

'Mr Seymour? This is my daughter, Rosemary,' Margaret shouted at the shrivelled old man. Resting his gnarled, knuckly hand on his walking stick, he leant forward and peered at Rosie.

'Pretty,' was all he said.

'Here's your roast lamb,' yelled Margaret as she took the plate from Rosie, removed the foil and placed the meal on a tray. She set a knife and fork on either side of the plate and sat it on Mr Seymour's lap.

'Fine filly,' he said, looking at Rosie. 'Want to go to the races?' He slapped his thigh so hard that the tray nearly tipped off his lap.

'Oh eat up, you silly old goat,' muttered Margaret as she steadied the tray and began to cut the meat into small pieces. He continued chattering and staring at Rosie.

'Good days, race days. Fine fillies on race days . . . good set of legs. Bloody good set of legs.'

'Ex-jockey and stockman,' Margaret whispered to Rosie. 'His father was a jockey too. Dreadful family. Dreadful. This one's deaf as a post and silly as a wheel.'

She rolled her eyes and stooped to yell at the old man, 'See you next week, Mr Seymour. Mrs Chillcott-Clark will drop in tomorrow with your lunch. She can deal with the cat's litter. It's wash day tomorrow too, so have your clothes handy for her.' Then she rose to her full height and looked down her nose at him with distaste.

'No need to treat him like an imbecile. He's just old,' Rosie whispered. Margaret cast her a hurt glance and walked back along the hall.

Cautiously, Rosie walked over to Mr Seymour.

'Mr Seymour? Er . . . excuse me, but you obviously know a thing or two about horses. How do you know when a mare is going to have her foal?'

'Filly. Fine one,' he slurred as a dollop of gravy slid from his chin. Rosie touched the old man on his arm and asked the question again. He turned his head and looked at her. The directness of his gaze startled her.

'Your mare in foal?'

'Yes, she's in foal.'

'Ah!' he said, as if the penny had dropped. 'She's off her tucker first. Then her bag goes spotty. White spots. And she'll kick. At her belly, she'll kick. And her twat. Gets a nice loose spring in it. Nice loose twat along with her bum-cheeks. Loose bum-cheeks, not tight like yours. Then her teat wax goes clear. Yellow then clear. And she'll eat fast and back up. She'll back up. You hear, girl? She'll have a fine colt, that mare. Or a fine filly. With good legs and a tight backside.'

'Thanks. I'll know what to look for now,' said Rosie.

'She's been on a bender that mum of yours,' he went on. 'Been on a bender. Can smell it. But you'll be right.' The old man laughed, and Rosie could see the half-chewed food in his mouth.

She backed away, saying, 'Thank you again, Mr Seymour. See you. Bye.'

As she hurried along the crooked hallway she wondered if Mr Seymour knew anything about Jack Gleeson. Perhaps she should go back and ask him? She was halfway along the hall when she jumped in fright and screamed. She had just bumped into what she'd thought was a shadow, cast by the coats hanging on the hallstand. But it was a man, not a shadow, silhouetted against the bright light of the open doorway. Rosie pressed her back to the wall and looked down at the floor as she let him pass.

'Sorry. You gave me a fright. Sorry. 'Scuse me,' she said. Goosebumps rose on her skin as he passed her. She looked up and caught the glance of a gorgeous guy with the bluest eyes. She sucked in a timid breath and then bolted from the house.

Her mother was waiting impatiently in the passenger seat of the Pajero.

'What were you doing in there with that dreadful old man?' She saw her daughter's pale face. 'What is it? You look as if you've seen a ghost.'

Rosie shook her head and started the engine. 'Where to next?'

'Just two more to drop off. Then we're due at Susannah Moorecroft's for a late luncheon.'

Rosie turned to her mother incredulously.

'You're joking?'

'Now, Rose,' her mother cautioned, 'it's been on the calendar for –'

'No! No way, Mum! You can stick your friends. I've had *enough*. I'll drop you there and you can find your own way home!'

Later, after depositing her stunned mother on the Moorecrofts' driveway, Rosie drove back into town to hunt around the old Casterton museum on the railway siding. She stood for a long time looking at the old bottles and bits and pieces that sat silent and still in the glass cases.

Then she drove to the big hill overlooking Casterton. She got out and sat in the long yellow grass, letting the warm wind touch her face as she looked out across the river and up the main street. She stared at the photocopy of an old photograph of the town that she held in her hands. Is that how it had looked to Jack Gleeson when he'd come riding into town?

Casterton Town, The Crossing Place

Bailey's ears shot forward when Jack pulled her to a halt on top of the big hill overlooking the town of Casterton. He looked down at the bridge spanning the slow-moving water of the Glenelg River. It was flanked by impressive red gums that cast an olive-green reflection over the river. Near the bridge he could see the stone front of the Glenelg Inn. It stood on the corner of a wide, dusty street that ran up a hill away from the river and was lined by a scattering of buildings. Despite the February heat, smoke drifted from chimneys as women inside warmed water for washing or cooked the evening meal.

Jack descended the winding track and Cooley danced and snorted on the bridge at his own hollow-sounding hoofbeats. On a shaded river bank, a woman standing outside a tent placed a pot on the smouldering campfire and then stood up stretching her back. She watched Jack pass. He tipped his hat.

Jack rode up the main street, whistling Idle in close to the horses as he went. He rode past a blacksmith's shop, a post office, several huts and wattle-and-daub houses. At the top of town Jack turned around outside the doctor's house, noting the red lantern, unlit, hanging from the window. Then he rode back down the street and dismounted outside the Livery, glad to be out of the saddle. He led Bailey into the dim entrance of the stable that bustled with grooms and horses. The town was humming like a hornet's nest in anticipation of the race meet. Jack felt his life as a stockman would begin in earnest in this very town.

At the Casterton races the next morning, in the shade of the river red gums, Jack sipped on a cup of tea. Ladies stood beneath a large canvas shadecloth in their best white dresses, high lace collars and large straw hats decked with silk ribbons and bows. Children in their Sunday best ran about calling to each other with shrill voices. A scattering of gentlemen stood among the ladies. Silver fob chains hung from their waistcoats and their knee-high riding boots were polished to gleaming.

'Jack.' Thomas Cawker stood a little way off and was motioning him over.

'Come, I'd like you to meet a gent.' Thomas inclined his head towards a short man with pasty skin and hooded dark eyes. He carried himself importantly and stood beside his even shorter wife, who was dressed in dull navy blue.

'George Robertson,' whispered Thomas. 'He and his wife are childless, so they have dedicated their lives to their magnificent station, Warrock. It's reputed he looks after his staff well and encourages them all to worship our Lord regularly on the station, although I think not in your faith, Jack. Shall we seek his attention and ask him if there's work for you?' Jack nodded and they moved over to the short gentleman wearing a top hat.

'I'd like you to meet George Robertson, of Warrock station,' Cawker said. Jack offered his hand but sensed Robertson was loath to shake it.

'Jack's in search of work as a stockman,' Cawker explained. 'He's a fine horseman, and honest too.'

'It's good of you to present him to me, Mr Cawker, but I'll not be needing any more men this year,' Robertson said a trifle gruffly. 'I'm afraid you'll need to inquire elsewhere.' He began to walk away. Then, as if regretting his snub, he called back to Jack, 'I'd advise you to try Muntham station.'

'Come, Jack,' said Thomas as he handed his empty cup to a lady in a pinafore. 'We're bound to find you work. But for now, let's get some fun under our belts.'

Jack had never seen such a fine collection of horses. All were lean and fit and their coats reflected sunlight. Many were tethered to carts or trees, waiting to be saddled for the races to come. Jack's eyes came to rest on a tall, muscular, bay thoroughbred. The man who saddled him was striking too. His black hair was parted neatly in the middle and his moustache and sideburns framed a lean, determined face and stern dark eyes. His face softened to a grin when Thomas approached him.

'Why, Mr Cawker, a pleasure to see you again.'

'Mr Cuthbert Featherstonhaugh!' Thomas said as he vigorously shook the man's hand. 'What red-blooded courage and recklessness will you exhibit to the crowd today?'

'Ah, Mr Cawker, I'll grant you my blood will be up when I ride against that rascal Billy Trainor!'

Jack detected the Irish lilt in the man's voice, much like his own.

'I'd like you to meet a newcomer to the Crossing Place – Mr Jack Gleeson.'

Jack offered his hand and Cuthbert shook it with enthusiasm.

'Don't let the flowery nature of his name fool you, Jack,' said Thomas.

'Aye. My mother wasn't right in the head the day she named me,' said Cuthbert with a wink.

'It might sound like a name for a gentleman as soft as butter,' Thomas went on, 'but Cuthbert will ride a horse over anything and his horse here, Robinson Crusoe, will gallop eight miles and jump seventy fences before raising a sweat.'

'Aye, he's as mad as the man who rides him,' laughed Cuthbert. 'Will you be riding around the track too, Mr Gleeson? The novice events are open to anyone sober enough to scramble on to his horse.'

'Yes, I'll be riding today,' said Jack. 'My mare's fit from the road, though she may throw her head about a bit when she leaves her colt.'

'When she lines up with the rest to race, she'll soon forget him! Good luck to you then,' Cuthbert said.

'Jack here is looking for station work,' continued Thomas. 'Would it be worth his inquiring on Muntham?'

Cuthbert shook his head.

'Not likely this time of year. We've already got twenty men for the New Year. But work is about. I'd try for Mr Murray's Dunrobin station. He's always in need of good men. Now if you'll excuse me, gents, I'll take my leave and see if I can't kill myself this time round the jumps.'

Jack felt his heart sink a little as he watched Cuthbert lead his horse away. Last night at the stables he'd heard tales of Muntham Station and of Cuthbert Featherstonhaugh's legendary horsemanship. He had met a rowdy group of workers from the place. They had told him Muntham was some seventy-seven thousand acres and Jack had already ridden over some of it on his journey into town. On its bush runs it carried fifty-five thousand sheep, eight thousand fat Shorthorn and Durham cattle, and five hundred horses. Some of the tough, nuggety horses from Muntham were at the races today. Jack longed to work and ride alongside Cuthbert but it sounded like it wasn't to be. He frowned a little. Thomas sensed his disappointment and patted him on the back.

'Come now, Jack. We've got three days of racing ahead of us. Let's enjoy the company of ladies . . . a rarity in these parts, you'll find. Though don't expect to begin courting any in earnest. These girls are mostly in search of a grazier whether he's a gent or not. They barely cast a glance over a mere coachman or stockman.'

Jack scanned the pretty girls who stood about in the shade.

'If only that weren't so,' he said.

At the end of the meet, Jack found himself standing on the filthy sawdust floor of the makeshift bar at the racetrack. Cuthbert had one arm slung over his shoulders and was holding a mug of ale aloft.

'To the district's finest new rider, Jack Gleeson,' he declared, before sculling his drink.

Jack had yarded the colt and saddled up Bailey for as many novice races as he could. She had triumphed in the Hurdle and the Steeplechase. He could feel the heart and soul of the mare as she leapt the jumps, her ears flattened back and her neck stretched out. Like Jack, she gave the races her all. By the last day of the meet many of the racegoers were talking about the new Irish lad from the south.

Jack looked around the bar. Some of the crowd were singing songs and dancing jigs as a young lad whipped his bow in double time across a fiddle. Others slumped on rough-cut benches, leaning against the tent posts with pipes smouldering in their hands as they recounted stories of the race meet. Many relived the vision of Cuthbert pelting down the track over the last jump, his horse dark with sweat and bleeding from the spur. The roar of the crowd as Cuthbert overtook Billy Trainor at the post to win the Hurdle Race lingered on in their ears. He'd also won the Sweepstakes of three miles, and his horse was saddled up again to win the Open Handicap of two and a half miles. Robinson Crusoe now stood tethered in the racetrack shelter with his head down, sound asleep. Not even the sounds of fistfights and the shouts of drunken men could wake him. In the next stall Bailey dozed too, Cooley nuzzling at her flank, relieved to be back by her side.

Yet another mug was thrust into Jack's hands. He took it with glee. There was much to celebrate. Not only had he shone in the novice field but he had also secured a job. Tomorrow he was to ride to Dunrobin station, and present himself to Mr Murray for work.

Twelve

Rosie parked her mother's car beside the cluster of buildings at the Casterton racetrack. Her eyes scanned the empty track, heat shimmering above treetops in the distance. The grandstand stretched open like a wide mouth in the midst of a yawn. The expanse of dried lawn, no longer buzzing with people, took on an eerie emptiness.

'Hello?' she called out as she ducked her head inside the secretary's office. No answer. Just the click of heat in the iron roof. Then she heard hoofbeats behind her. Swinging round she sucked in a breath as a man astride a fidgety horse loomed above her. With the sun behind him it might have been Sam on Oakwood. But as the horse danced into the shade she realised it was Billy O'Rourke, riding another of his client's youngsters.

'Hello, Rosie. Are you searching for your Irish man?' Billy said.

'I am,' Rosie answered, admiring how confidently he sat on the nervous young horse.

'Go on in. There's a cupboard full of old stuff in there. You're welcome to rifle through it. I'll track down the key and be back in a sec.'

Standing in the secretary's office, Rosie looked at the photos on the wall while a fly bashed itself against the windowpane.

In one photo ladies in white dresses stood chatting beneath the shade of giant red gums. Rosie's eyes scanned the photo for the men in the crowd. There were very few amidst the ladies. Perhaps, she thought, they were all off looking at the horses. She spun round as Billy came through the door, a smile on his face.

'This'll be interesting,' he said.

When Rosie drove over the grid at Highgrove station Julian was driving towards her, his collie dog leaning eagerly over the side of the ute. She stopped and wound down her window. Julian pulled up and got out.

'Where's Mum?' he asked.

Rosie shrugged. 'I dumped her.'

'You serious?'

'No. I wish. She's getting a lift home, I think.'

'Oh. Well, can't say I would've blamed you.'

'Where are you off to anyway?' Rosie asked, noticing the bags in the back of the ute.

'I'm leaving.'

'Got something on in Melbourne?'

'No. I mean I'm *leaving* leaving. You know.'

'You're what?' Rosie leapt out of the Pajero and stood in front of her brother. 'You can't!'

'Yes I can.'

'But what about Mum and Dad?' Rosie shook her head. 'I mean your dad.'

'This isn't about them. It's about me,' Julian said.

'But . . . the farm? You –'

'It's not *my* farm. I've never wanted it – not with Dad breathing down my neck.'

'But I *need* you. What about Sam's horses and dogs? I need you to give me a hand.'

'That's just the thing, isn't it?' Julian said, his jaw clenching in anger. 'Anyone need a hand? Call on Julian! He'll fix it, he'll lug it, he'll feed it, he'll drench it, he'll weed it, prune it, cut it, cart it. No, Rose. I've had enough of this place. I'm leaving.'

'But –'

'Don't you get it? The pressure's been on me all my life. Now that the truth's come out about you, that pressure's been upped tenfold. I don't *want* to be the one and only golden boy. Stuff them! Dad will have to rely on you now, whether he likes it or not. You're the only family he'll have left for this place. I sure as hell don't want it. I never have.'

'But, Jules . . .' Rosie put a hand on his sleeve and took a step towards him. He looked beautiful and vulnerable.

'Don't, Rose . . . don't make it harder.'

'Where will you go?'

'Like I said before, I've got plans. And I've got friends. Blokes I was at school with.'

'But you can't leave me!' Rosie could feel hysteria rising in her voice. 'Not now.'

'You don't need me. You'll do great things on your own here. It's time for me to start doing what *I* dream of. Bugger what Dad says. Or what the community says. I'm not going to be scared any more, Rose . . . and neither should you. Life's too short. Sam's death has convinced me of that.'

Julian hugged her and Rosie felt the warmth of his muscular, angular body against hers. She breathed in his smell. It was so foreign to her, to hold him close like this. Their family rarely hugged.

'I know you'll cope, Rosie. And I'll keep in touch, I promise. You'll be fine. Trust me.'

She nodded sadly, and pulled him to her for another hug.

And then he was gone. Rosie watched the tail-lights of his ute until they disappeared.

Parking the Pajero in the garage, Rosie noticed the buzz of a shearing machine coming from the shed. She saw a handful of crutched lambs in the yard. Who had Gerald found at such short notice to crutch the lambs, she wondered? Frowning, she walked towards the shearing shed. Inside, at the far end of the long row of stands, Gerald was bent over a merino wether lamb. Sweat dripped from his brow into the wool and his face was pink. A fan positioned behind him was blowing locks into a pile against the catching-pen walls, like flotsam left by a tide. The whole board where Gerald stood beneath the shearing machine was scattered with dags and crutchings and pizzle-stained wool.

'Dad?' Rosie grimaced. Should she still call him that? She shut her eyes for a moment at the impossibility of it all.

Gerald glanced up but didn't stop the machine. He continued to finish the last blow. Then he let the lamb scrabble to its hooves and it scuttled out the chute to join the rest of the crutched and wigged mob. Gerald stretched his lower back and mopped sweat from his face with a towel. Rosie suddenly realised he was also wiping tears away. She wondered how Julian had broken the news that he was leaving. Did they have a roaring fight? Or had Julian just quietly said goodbye? Suddenly she felt sorry for Gerald. Julian had been his security, his future for the farm. And now he was gone.

'Can I help?' Gerald didn't answer her. Instead he pushed through the catching-pen doors and tipped over another lamb, dragging it to the board. Rosie picked up a broom and began to sweep. A twinge of annoyance crossed Gerald's face.

'Don't just sweep it all up into a pile, woman,' he said impatiently. He put the lamb back in the catching pen and grabbed the broom from her.

'Look. Anything stained goes into one pile. Heavy dags in another. Wigs and clean crutchings into the butt. Pizzles can go into this butt of stain here.' Gerald picked up each type of wool as he spoke. Rosie nodded earnestly and concentrated hard on sorting and sweeping. They worked on in silence. Thoughts tumbled in Rosie's head about Julian leaving and how her mother would react. How Gerald must be struggling under the weight of despair. But she kept on working, gaining speed with her sorting so that soon the board was tidy and she had fallen into an easy rhythm of sorting the wool. She noticed how Gerald groaned and strained with each sheep. She had hardly ever seen him do manual labour and it was clearly wearing him down. When he had at last emptied the catching pen and stretched his back and mopped his brow, he stood up tall and went out to the back pens to gather more sheep to crutch. As she sorted the last of the dags, she could hear him trying in vain to fill the catching pen with the flighty young sheep. Rosie glanced over the pen nervously as her father swore.

'Damned creatures!' he said when the wethers again baulked at the gate. 'Dashed things won't run,' he said, flinging a young, confused wether in the direction of the gateway. 'For God's sake, Rosemary, get out of the way! They won't run with *you* there!'

'They won't run whether I'm here or not. So don't blame me!'

Gerald looked up at her.

'Well, why don't you grab one of those expensive dogs?' he said tiredly. 'Seeing as your brother took his half-useless dog with him, you'd better find a job for Sam's.'

When Rosie picked up the broom again she felt elation creep into her soul. Diesel had trotted obediently into the shed behind her heels and when she said 'Go back' he had leapt the fence and brought all the sheep to her. When they crammed into the catching pen's gateway and wouldn't run, she had clapped and whistled. Diesel had leapt up on to the backs of the sheep and barked. Within minutes the catching pen was full. Calling him onto the board she said 'Sit, stay' and he settled down with his paws together on the cool wooden floor, his serious brown eyes watching the lambs as they were dragged across the board. She had hoped her father would say 'Well done' but the sight of the full catching pen seemed to make him angry again.

He roughly dragged out another sheep and was about to put the machine into gear when Rosie said, 'Can you teach me?'

Before he could say no she had moved into position, almost bumping him out of the way. She gripped the front legs of the lamb as it sat upright on the board. She saw a look of disgust cross Gerald's face. But he was too tired to argue, and too relieved that he was standing upright. He walked away to the experting room, flicked the switch that turned on the fluorescent lights above the board and began to instruct Rosie on how to crutch. Rosie felt the warm handpiece come alive, vibrating in her hands. She was shocked at the heat of it and the life of its own that it seemed to possess. But as she began to push the comb and cutter through the wool, she glanced up at her father.

'Look, I'm a natural!'

Gerald looked at her sourly before sweeping the dags away.

Thirteen

For the next few days, Rosie tried to settle into the strange new shape of her family. The three of them tiptoed around each other and skirted away from the problems they carried with them like sacks of stones. The stiff veneer that hid her parents' pain was now firmly back in place. They barely mentioned the fact that Julian had only called once from the city. And even then, Margaret had asked him about the weather. Her mother and father were still not speaking to one another, their marriage as fractured as the cracked dry soil in the dusty paddocks. They used Rosie as their go-between, or left short sharp notes for each other on the kitchen table. Gerald retreated to his office at night and spent hours on the phone. Margaret stole sips of the cooking brandy, and at night tipped pills down her throat to make her sleep.

Rosie set herself up in the quarters. Her mother's fine linen doona cover looked strange in the rough old quarters, but with the shelves full of books and cupboards full of work clothes borrowed from Julian, the place began to feel like home to Rosie. She stocked the tiny kitchen with packet noodles and tins of spaghetti for those times she felt she couldn't face her parents. Her body was still adjusting to the hard physical work of the farm, and her mind was still struggling with all the shocks of the past couple of months. During the day Rosie spent her time with Sam's dogs and horses, and at night she delved into the history books Duncan had given her, trying to blot out her pain. She read of fistfights, and of handsome stockmen who dared each other to jump their horses off the bridge into the Glenelg River for a bet. She read of shepherds murdered by natives, and of natives murdered by shepherds. She read of a settler's wife who buried all five of her sickly children, digging the last one up to cut a lock of the baby's hair before she moved on to another district.

Each night Rosie sifted through long-winded historic accounts, looking for shreds of information about Jack Gleeson. She made notes for her newspaper series before her eyes grew heavy and she at last sleepily reached for the bedside lamp. Listening to the horses snorting and chewing in the stables next door, Rosie would stare into the darkness and imagine how it felt to live in an isolated shepherd's hut.

Dunrobin station

Jack wrapped the woollen blanket about his shoulders and peered at the pages of the book. Its small print was illuminated by candle-light that flickered in the draught which crept through the gaps in the stringy-bark walls of his hut.

In the text Charles Dickens had written:

> *I know a shaggy black and white dog who keeps a drover. He is a dog of easy disposition, and too frequently allows this drover to get drunk. On these occasions it is the dog's custom to sit outside the public-house, keeping an eye on a few sheep and thinking.*

Jack sighed. He had been on Dunrobin a month now and was longing for a good dog. Idle was the laughing stock of all the men who worked on Dunrobin. Instead of keeping vigil on the mob at night, he would scratch at Jack's door and whine to come in and doze by the fire. He slept through the night, so that Jack's sheep found gaps in the flimsy night-yards and would scatter some distance throughout the unfenced river-flat country. Some would even cross the shining midnight river and would be grazing the banks of Warrock station on the other side at dawn. On such mornings, Jack would swing into the hard cold saddle at sun-up and ride Bailey in a vast circle, picking up the strays and crossing the sheep back over the river. Idle, having slept soundly all night, danced at the excitement of it all and occasionally helped Jack gather a stray from a tricky section in the bush. Jack longed for a well-bred dog. A dog he could trust.

Jack shut his book, blew out the candle and bent to throw a log onto the crackling fire. He stared into the flames, remembering the day he had ridden up the drive to Dunrobin homestead for his interview with Mr Murray. When he had knocked on the back door, Mr Murray himself came to answer, and in the shade of the back verandah he and Jack shook hands. The agreement was made: Jack was now a stockman.

At first he tailed an older man about his duties, getting the lie of the land and an eye for the earmarks and brands of the stock. Dunrobin was licensed by the government to run thirty thousand sheep, but so far only nineteen thousand sheep grazed the unfenced pastures. Jack was put in charge of a mob of his own and instructed to head north along the Casterton-Apsley track, grazing the flock by the Glenelg River which bordered Warrock station. He was given a packhorse laden with food and equipment. Bobby was a flea-bitten grey with feathery hocks and a large ugly head. But he was a good horse, and took care not to scrape the packs when the journey brought them through thick stands of stringy-bark. Jack set out from the homestead for the day's journey to the shepherd's hut.

The hut was set amidst some river red gums. Jack savoured the spot. Magpies chortled above him in the treetops, and not far away the river slid silently by. He spent that first afternoon swinging the axe, felling saplings and larger trees. He used them to patch up the rough yards where he would pen the sheep overnight to protect them from wild dog attacks.

Days at the hut slid into weeks. Stockmen would come by and share his camp site. The men talked often of Warrock as a place where good dogs could be found. Jack was determined to go there soon to see for himself. Some Warrock sheep had strayed across the river in his flock, so he would ride out there and put them in George Robertson's yards. Then he would inquire about the purchase of a good, handy and true dog.

Jack climbed into his swag by the fire and was just dozing off when Idle again scratched and whined at the door.

'Goodnight to you, Idle,' Jack said angrily, but he couldn't help letting some humour creep into his voice. 'But don't worry. If what they say about Warrock dogs is true, it won't be long before you can retire.'

Rosie stirred sleepily beneath the sheet, then kicked it off. She lay dozing, in a white cotton singlet and knickers, her brown limbs sprawled out in the heat. She knew she'd overslept, but her body, tired from drenching sheep and dehorning wethers, refused to wake.

'Does the sleeping beauty come with the quarters?' she heard a man's voice say. The voice was thick with an Irish lilt.

Rosie's eyes flew open. In the doorway stood the tall silhouette of a young man.

'Jack?' she said, rubbing her eyes and thinking she was going mad.

'Rosemary!' her mother's voice came from outside. 'For goodness' sake! I thought you were up and gone!'

When Rosie realised that the apparition was no apparition at all, but a real-life man, she hastily pulled up the sheet and, wide-eyed, asked, 'Mum?'

Margaret stepped past the man into the room.

'This is my daughter Rosemary.'

'Rosie,' retorted Rosie firmly.

'This is our new stockman. Jim Mahony.'

'No need for introductions now, Mrs Highgrove-Jones. Shall we let her get dressed first?' Jim said with a smile in his eyes.

Rosie realised they were the same blue eyes she'd seen in

Mr Seymour's hallway. Jim Mahony was no ghost. He was a modern-day Irishman, wearing jeans and a blue work shirt. The colour of his shirt and his tanned face seemed to make his eyes even bluer. His face moved easily into a smile each time he spoke and his broad shoulders nearly filled the doorway. Rosie couldn't help noticing his lean hips and stomach, set off by a plaited leather belt, and his R M Williams boots, polished to shining.

Suddenly anger flashed inside her as she realised that a new stockman meant no room for her in the quarters. Her mother had been meddling again.

'Come on, Mr Mahony. We've got time for a cup of tea now. We'll leave Rose to get dressed and gather her things so that you can move in.'

'Well, if it's no trouble, I don't want to move anyone out of where they belong.'

'Oh, not at all! Rose doesn't belong here. She just sleeps in here when the weather gets too hot, don't you, dear?'

Margaret ushered Jim out the door and began to make small talk with him across the courtyard. She settled him down on an old squatter's chair on the glassed-in verandah. She went into the kitchen to make tea for him – in mugs, not cups – and put out a plate of biscuits – packet, not homemade.

Rosie quickly dragged on her Wrangler jeans. Still in her singlet, she hobbled barefoot over the courtyard cobbles and slammed the screen door into the verandah.

''Scuse me,' she said, red-cheeked, as she ran past Jim into the house. He watched her pass, then crossed his ankle over his knee and began to flick through last week's *Weekly Times*, wondering what on earth was going on in this family.

In the kitchen Rosie hissed at her mother, 'Just what do you think you're doing?'

'It's not my fault you weren't dressed.'

'No! Not that!'

Margaret poured boiling water into the teapot – the old china one, not the silver. 'Well, how else would I get my daughter back under the roof where she belongs? And it's a much-needed surprise for Gerald. Now Julian's gone, it's even more important to keep him happy.'

'Geez, Mum!' said Rosie, exasperated. 'We're doing fine on our own – and besides, *nothing* would make Gerald happy. He was born grumpy.'

'Look,' Margaret said, 'your father's on the brink of walking out, I just know it.'

'Stop being so paranoid,' spat Rosie. 'And he's *not* my father. Remember?'

Margaret shook her head sadly. Rosie narrowed her eyes.

'Where'd you find this bloke anyway? Under a shamrock?'

'Don't be silly, Rose. I met him when I delivered this week's meal to Mr Seymour. Their families are somehow connected back in Ireland and Mr Mahony was visiting the Western District with the hope of finding station work.'

'Right. What's he good at – growing spuds?'

'He's had more stockwork experience than you, young lady, so I'm not hearing another word about it.'

Margaret turned her back on Rosie and left her in the kitchen. She carried the tray out to the verandah, rearranging her face into a gracious smile as she went. For the sake of her marriage, she was determined to make sure this workman stayed.

Fourteen

Soft sunlight crept through French doors of the upstairs verandah and began to spread light across the room. Rosie sat up, her hair tangled in a bird's nest, angry from a sleepless night in her own bed. She felt trapped back in the house. The wooden floorboards were cool on her bare feet as she padded over to the window and peered down to the courtyard. The light in the workmen's quarters was on, but she couldn't see Jim. During the night she had tried to imagine him sleeping in what had briefly been her room. She clenched her teeth, furious at the way her mother had pushed her into coming back into the homestead.

Rosie crossed her room and flung open the French doors, stepping onto the verandah in her singlet and knickers. Across the valley, she watched the sun beginning to illuminate the short-grazed pasture. A fine white mist had settled over the bush in the gullies. She breathed in the fresh air and began to plan her day. She would be working with Gerald, helping with the foot-paring. She stretched her arms in the air. Although tired, her body had never felt so good. Small, newly formed muscles bunched up in her arms. She flexed them proudly. She did a few muscle-man poses just for fun. All she needed was some baby oil, she thought. As she did a clean and jerk with her imaginary barbell, a movement caught her eye a few hundred metres from the house. She squinted down from the verandah, beyond the garden. The new stockman was trotting towards her on a chestnut colt, looking up at the house. The colt's nostrils were wide from exertion and each breath came from its nose in a white mist. As Jim rode up the steep hill towards the iron gates of the house, he waved.

'Oh my God! Oh my God!' whispered Rosie as she ran into the bedroom, her hand to her mouth. Jim Mahony had just seen her doing the clean and jerk in her undies. How embarrassing! She fell face first onto the bed and groaned.

In the shearing shed, out the back on the grating, Jim had set up the panels and foot-paring machine and dragged the compressor over to the work area. A red pup, just a few months old, trailed him about the shed on padding paws that seemed too big for its body. Gerald was in the experting room, sharpening the blades of the parers. He shouted to Jim from where he stood.

'I really should've got a contractor in to do them.'

'Not to worry,' called Jim. 'We'll get them done. If your daughter keeps the sheep up to me, we'll have them trimmed up in no time.'

'Are you certain you don't want me to hang about for the day?' Gerald asked. 'Rose isn't all that experienced. And the dogs . . . they aren't exactly hers, so they can get in the way.'

'She'll be fine,' Jim called back.

Gerald shook his head and sighed. He just wanted out. Since Sam's death, Margaret's pill popping and preaching had hit overdrive. Yet still she insisted on carrying on as if nothing was wrong. She was already planning her Christmas list for this year. Gerald felt panic creeping into his soul. Earlier that morning, he had stared at the piles of manual cashbooks in the office that dated back to the early 1900s, fearing his would be the generation that spent the lot. Lost the lot. He'd seen it happening around him as the wool prices crashed, the rain failed to fall and the grand old gum trees on the property began to die. He imagined his own end . . . from heart attack, a farm accident or even by his own desperate hand. He longed to pass things over to Julian. But Julian was gone. And now he was stuck here. Stuck in a life he never wanted. Should he phone Giddy again? he wondered. She would know what to do. Gerald carried the parers over to the machine and attached them to the compressor. Jim's voice broke his train of thought.

'Have you got a portable handpiece?' he asked. 'I could give any daggy ones a crutch on their way through if you like.'

'Yes, good idea. The porta-shears are up at the workshop. I'll grab them.'

Normally Gerald would've sent the workman to get them but he needed this one to stay. At first Gerald had been furious at Margaret for making a decision behind his back. 'You know we can't afford him!' he had yelled at her.

But Jim had agreed to a lesser wage if he could have the weekends for dog trialling. And so here he was . . . another stockman. Gerald removed his glasses and rubbed his tired eyes, before walking from the shed.

A moment later, Rosie, still chewing on a piece of Vegemite toast, ran into the shearing shed with Diesel and Gibbo at her heels.

'Sorry I'm late,' she said to Jim, not looking at him.

'Thought you were up early this morning, doing your exercises,' he teased.

Rosie glanced up to see his eyes glinting. 'At least you've managed to put some clothes on this time,' he went on.

Rosie's shyness began to turn to irritation.

'Shall we get to work?' she asked coolly.

'By all means, but first, could you stop your dog trying to mount my dog?'

Rosie turned, red-faced, to see Diesel humping away at Jim's young male pup.

'Diesel! Come here!' she said, but Diesel ignored her.

Outside the shearing shed, Jim had two dogs tied up to a fence on short chains. They were handsome-looking kelpies, a bitch and a dog. From under the shade of the work ute an old black dog with grey paws ambled out, his tail wagging low and slow.

'Ah, here he is,' said Jim fondly to the old dog. The red pup gambolled up and licked at the dog's greying muzzle. The pair of young dogs sat tall, staring beseechingly at Jim to let them off for work. Rosie trailed behind him, embarrassed at having to work with someone so obviously competent.

'We won't be needing this many dogs,' Jim said to her. 'I'll leave mine tied up and you can work yours, if you like. Bones . . . the old dog, Lazy Bones, he won't be offering his services today anyway, will you, mate?' He stooped to scratch the dog's ears.

'He was retired before he even started, but an old bloke gave him to me when I first came to Australia and I wouldn't be without him as a mate. And his main purpose in life is to remind me not to baulk at paying good money for good genes. If you want a top dog, you need to study a pup's bloodlines. Now Bones, he's got any manner of non-working lines in him. Not like this little fella.'

Jim scooped up the pup and held it like a baby, scratching at its belly.

'This little one is by that bitch and dog. Daisy and Thommo, and their bloodlines go back to the best. Even at this young age, I can see he's got it. He's working already, although he's too small for the likes of those big wethers. He's likely to get skittled.' Rosie watched the way Jim's strong tanned fingers travelled up and down the pink belly of the little red pup. His Irish accent made everything he said seem wonderful. Rosie swallowed. Jim, seeing Rosie's glazed eyes, bent and clipped the pup to another short chain and stroked him firmly down the back.

'I'm sorry. I'm rattling on about dogs again. A bad habit of mine. Sorry to bore you.'

'No! No, really. I'm really interested,' Rosie said. 'Why don't you use your dogs? I'll tie mine up.'

'No, no. I insist. I've got a dog trial on this weekend. It'd be good not to let them do too much rough forcing work beforehand. Thommo can go a bit psycho and Daisy, she sometimes bites a bit hard when she's revved up.'

Before Rosie could protest, Jim began to walk away. She called Diesel and Gibbo to her and followed Jim around the side of the shed to where the sheep were yarded. Her heart beat fast. She was so scared about working the dogs in front of Jim that she felt her back trickle with sweat.

'Gibbo's only young,' she said as she climbed the fence. 'He's a bit deaf.'

'Dogs have at least forty times better hearing than us so I don't believe for a second he's deaf,' Jim said with a wink.

'The dogs aren't really mine. They don't really work for me.'

'Come on. They'll be just fine,' said Jim.

But the dogs weren't just fine. Gibbo singled sheep out and chased them to the fence. Diesel kept running to the front of the mob and blocked the entranceway to the shed. Heat prickled under Rosie's collar and frustration showed on her reddened face. Her voice began to rise.

'Diesel! Diesel! DIEEEEE . . . SEL!' she yelled.

Jim stood back with his arms folded and watched the chaos. Gibbo was the worst. He ran backwards and forwards, barking and forcing the mob onto the rail, cutting one out and racing it to a fence with a crash.

'Gibbo! Gibbo! *Sit!*' Rosie shouted. But in the high excitement of sheep bustling, leaping and running, Gibbo ignored her.

'They don't always work well,' she said to Jim, feeling humiliated.

'Do you mind?' he asked, stepping forward. 'Your father will blame me if we don't get the job done. And it'll come out of my wage if we have sheep with their necks broken.'

Rosie backed away and leant on the rail of the yards. One minute Jim was standing still. The next he was dancing about in the dust, clapping his hands and putting his hands high in the air in front of Gibbo. He set his body square on to the young dog and matched his every move, so that Gibbo had no choice but to look away from the sheep and up to the tall man who had so much presence.

The moment Gibbo glanced at Jim, Jim praised him. Soon Gibbo was coming to Jim and sitting when he asked. Much to Rosie's annoyance, Jim's voice never even got above normal speaking level. It remained calm and firm.

Diesel, too, was now aware of Jim's presence in the yard.

'Diesel, come behind,' Jim said, followed by a shrill whistle. Diesel obeyed and soon the sheep were flowing into the shed and the dogs were trotting at Jim's heels.

'I can get them working like that when other people aren't around,' said Rosie furiously as she slid the old gates shut in the shed.

'I've no doubt you can,' said Jim gently, but with a smile on his face.

For hours Rosie worked by Jim's side, burning with humiliation. The rhythmic hiss of the pneumatic foot parers and the shutting on and off of the air compressor left little room for conversation. In the smaller, more confined race, Diesel and Gibbo worked the sheep well from outside the rails, barking each time the next sheep was due up into the cradle. Though Rosie was still sulking over the morning's disastrous dog display, she couldn't help notice the flex of Jim's muscles as he tipped the cradle over and began to trim the hooves of yet another sheep. He worked with intensity, allowing Rosie to study his profile. His hair was fair and clipped short. His skin was honey-brown and his square, clean-shaven jaw gave him a strong, masculine look. Although there was a toughness about Jim, his eyes conveyed a gentle kindness that came from within. Rosie tried not to let her eyes travel to him too often, but it was hard. She attempted to focus her attention instead on the stubborn sheep that propped and wouldn't run up the race.

At morning smoko, Jim switched off the compressor and the noise died down to silence but for the sound of hooves on grating and the panting of the dogs.

'Thanks for your help, Rosemary,' he said, looking directly into her eyes.

'Rosie.'

'Sorry. *Rosie.*'

He walked away from her towards the washstand in the corner of the shed. Rosie wished they could talk. She wanted to know where he was from. Obviously he was Irish, but what was he doing out here? How had he learned his Australian stockman skills? She wanted to ask him personal questions, too, like . . . did he have a girlfriend? Instead she followed him across the shed and asked, 'How did you get the dogs to work for you like that?'

Jim's face warmed with a smile.

'It's all about how *you* are as a person, Rosie – it's nothing to do with the dogs. In life, if you let people or animals give you crap, that's just what they'll do. Or if you demand things of people or animals, they'll eventually switch off. But if you get a bit of grunt about you and ask for respect . . . people and animals will do anything for you, willingly and with joy. So get a bit of grunt about you, girl! And I don't mean by yelling. I mean *grunt* . . . from in here.'

He tapped at her stomach, before turning to wash his hands.

'Grunt?' Rosie frowned and her hand moved to her stomach. She didn't understand.

'It's all about communication,' Jim said. Suddenly he turned to her and stood, eyes wide, yelling, 'Rosie! ROSIE! ROS-IEEEE!'

She jumped at the harshness of his voice and took a step back, confused.

'See?' he said. 'You're confused and confronted. That's what you were doing to Diesel out there in the yard before. You were yelling his name but not asking him to do anything. How's he supposed to know what you want? You need to be clear with your communication, be direct but not demanding. And use your body language to show him what you want. What if I was to say, "Rosie. Come here to me"?' He opened his arms up to her and inclined his head enticingly.

When he said the words again they sounded like melted butter. 'Rosie. Come here to me.' Soft, inviting and delicious. Rosie's wide blue eyes looked willingly into his.

'Rosie. Come here.' He urged her again with his eyes and with the lightness of his voice. Instinctively she took a step towards him and instantly his words danced with warmth and praise as he said, 'Rosie! *Good girl*!'

Rosie couldn't help but smile. She felt a warmth for Jim rush over her.

'See? It's just the same for dogs. Clear communication. Say the dog's name without the anger, then state the command with a tone that asks, not demands. Then praise. Not just with your voice, but with your energy. Got it? It's all about being a good boss.'

Demonstration over, Jim turned his back on her and began to scrub his arms in the sink. The warmth Rosie felt for him suddenly dissolved into resentment. He wouldn't suck *her* in with his gorgeous body, good looks and, above all, his accent. He had just called her over to him like he'd call a dog. Rosie bet he had seduced a million women with his blue eyes and Irish lilt. He was just like Sam, good-looking and able to get anything he wanted. She'd had enough of Jim Mahony. She was about to excuse herself and let another batch of sheep out of the footbath when her mother walked into the shed. She was carrying a giant wicker basket in the crook of her arm.

'Smoko!' Margaret sang out. She put the basket on the woolshed table and proceeded to lay out a cloth. On it she placed a thermos, cups, milk and sugar. Then she uncovered a plate of steaming sausage rolls. Scones, biscuits and cake followed.

'Mum? You *never* bring smoko to the shed.'

Margaret glanced in Jim's direction.

'Don't be silly, darling. Of course I do.'

Jim ambled towards her with a towel slung over his shoulder.

'Mmm. This looks wonderful, Mrs Highgrove-Jones!'

'Do start then,' Margaret said, offering him a sausage roll.

'Shall I throw up now or later?' Rosie muttered as she walked away.

Fifteen

Rosie stared at the dark wood of the dining table as her parents ate their dinner in silence.

After the meal. Gerald stood up and stalked out of the room. Her mother watched him go and threw down her napkin angrily.

'Thanks for the meal,' she said through gritted teeth as she began to clear the plates. 'Now that Jim's got everything under control, you're free to come with me to town, Rosemary. And you can help me get ready for my end-of-season tennis party. I've ordered the meats from the butcher in Hamilton and then it's just a matter of calling into the bakery . . . then doing the flowers . . . I've rung Ida and she'll come in to clean tomorrow while we're out.'

Rosie felt the fury rise up in her. How could her mother keep pretending everything was normal, after all that had happened?

'Perhaps I could ring Sage,' Margaret went on. 'She could give you a trim, Rose, and I'm due for my eyelash tint.'

Rosie was about to tell her mother what she could do with her eyelash tint when the bell rang outside the back verandah.

'I'll go,' Rosie said, desperate to escape the stuffy dining room and her mother's pretence.

Jim, dressed neatly and scrubbed for town, was standing

with his back to the door. He turned when he heard Rosie open it.

'Ah! It's you! I thought it'd be the maid. Or do you double as the stockman and the maid here?'

'What do you want?' asked Rosie icily.

He sensed her mood and smiled at her gently.

'I was just wanting to see your father – I'm off to town. Old Mr Seymour wanted some things doing at his house, so I'm ducking in there to help out. If you could let him know.'

'You don't have to report your *every* move to my parents,' Rosie said, folding her arms and narrowing her eyes at him. 'They won't, for example, need to know every time you fart.'

'Won't they now? Well, that's good to know. Thank you. I've had some of your baked beans in the quarters for tea so I expect I'd be reporting in fairly regularly after that. I'll make sure I replace your supply though. Seems you'll be needing them. You sound a bit bound up to me.' He turned away, but before he got to his ute he stopped and looked at her.

'Ah. The other thing I meant to tell you before I went . . . I think your bitch is about to whelp.'

Rosie's mouth hung open as she watched Jim drive off. Bitch? Whelping?

'Dixie!' she cried out. Her mind flew into a panic. She pulled on some boots at the back doorstep and ran over to the dog kennels, cursing Jim as she went. He could've offered to stay and help.

In the dusky light she could see the other dogs chewing the mutton that Jim had just butchered for them. Dixie was scratching and whining in the end kennel. Hanging on the gate was a plastic shopping bag. Rosie untied it and looked inside. There was a book, *Every Dog*, and a torn piece of newspaper marked the section on whelping bitches. Rosie undid the kennel and dragged Dixie out by the collar. Her pupils were wide and frightened and her pink tongue hung out further than Rosie had ever seen before.

'Come on, girl. We'll get you settled.'

In the stable, installed on some old hessian bags and a thick layer of straw, Dixie scratched at her bedding. She circled around and around and then lay down to whine and pant. She licked at her flank and then moved around some more. Panting. Always panting. Rosie sat cross-legged under the glow of the naked bulb that hung from the old beams of the stable. She read the book intently, occasionally putting it down to inspect Dixie's rear end.

When she saw the first pup arrive, Rosie gasped in amazement. The bitch strained and licked quickly at the tiny head that was emerging. Rosie placed her fingers on the warm slippery bulge and gave a gentle pull. Out slithered a sac, filled to capacity with a kelpie pup. Rosie tore at the tough membrane, as Jim's book had instructed, and the little black pup began to squirm, gasping in air. It looked more like a rat than a kelpie. Rosie smiled with delight as Dixie licked the pup, rolling it over and over and chewing gently at the umbilical cord. Within minutes the pup was blindly but instinctively searching for Dixie's warmth and a teat to drink from. Rosie checked her watch. It was now a matter of waiting for the next pup to arrive, according to the book.

'Good girl, Dixie. Good girl.' Rosie stroked Dixie's silver back and the dog seemed to find comfort in her touch. The excitement of seeing a tiny kelpie pup born made Rosie think of what she'd read recently about the dogs on Warrock station. Did people get as excited back then about the birth of a litter?

Warrock station, circa 1870

Splashing over the river on Bailey, the mob of Warrock strays picking their way up the river bank, Jack was excited at the prospect of seeing Warrock station. He had heard George Robertson was a Scottish cabinet-maker from Port Glasgow who had wasted no time over the past twenty years in putting his sawpit and his staff to good use. Now Jack would see it for himself.

When he saw Warrock's homestead and outbuildings, Jack was

certain he'd ridden into a small fairytale village. There were at least thirty buildings, all styled with finials that pointed proudly and prettily from the gables of the roofs. Each building was beautifully proportioned and decorated with gleaming paint, decorative shutters and timber latticework. As Jack ushered his small mob of Warrock sheep towards the shearing shed, he rode past a skin house, a branding fluid shed, a shambles filled with fat sheep carcasses for the station's rations, all decorated with pretty finishes. Even the shearers' lavatories had impressive timber designs.

A man wearing dungarees, his shirtsleeves rolled up, emerged from the gloom inside the shearing shed.

'Not more of the woolly beggars!' he said with the remnants of a Scotsman's accent. 'I thought our day was nearly done!'

'They were out grazing on Dunrobin, where I work, so I thought I'd bring them by.'

'Well, Mr Robertson will be mighty pleased with your deed.' The young man jumped over a fence, his boots hitting the dusty ground with a thud. He undid a gate to the yard. Then, instead of walking around the sheep, he whistled.

'Come!' he called. Two black, prick-eared dogs scuttled out from somewhere inside the shed, their eyes wide, their tongues lolling. They cast around wide of the mob and steadily hunted the sheep through the gate where the man stood.

Jack looked back at Idle, who lay panting in the shade of a gum.

'Could you learn from that in any way, Idle?' Jack said as he jumped off his horse. He turned to the man. 'Where'd you get your dogs?'

'Oh, if only they were mine. They're the boss's dogs. From Scotland. The best you can buy. He's very strict with 'em though. Only lets his senior men use 'em,' he said proudly. 'Archie McTavish,' he said, holding out his hand.

'Jack Gleeson.' They shook hands firmly as Archie eyed the tall, fair-haired man before him.

'Come, Jack, you can deliver the news to the men that there's more sheep to be washed and shorn! But it won't take long. We've twelve men on twelve stands in action. It's a sight to behold when the blades fly. And because it's close to knock-off the men are in good spirits. I'm sure they'll only be mildly angry at you.'

Before the bell rang for the final sheep of the day, Archie ushered Jack out of the shed.

'What say I give you a tour of the place before the sun is down?'

Leading Bailey about the station, with Idle and the collies at their heels, Archie proudly pointed out the shearers' quarters further up the hill. Then he showed Jack the large dining room from which wafted the smell of roasting lamb.

'You'll find a place for your bed-roll in the hut by the kitchen fire after the men have had their meal. I'm sure Mr Robertson would be pleased for you to join them for their supper after the favour you've done.'

'That'd be grand,' said Jack, his face lighting up at the prospect of an evening with company.

'There's also a blacksmith's shop over yonder, towards the homestead. You can stable your horse there. Mr Robertson is good to men who are honest and hardworking and I'm sure he'll make no exception of you. He himself works tirelessly at his lathe. A man who loves wood. I'll show you his workshop and saw pit, if you like, before I take you to his office.'

Jack was more anxious to see some of Robertson's dogs. He'd noticed that the black bitch who tailed Archie had milk in her teats, so there must be pups about. Just then Archie led him past the finest kennels he had ever seen. They were made from red brick and from within the slits of the walls the muzzles of hounds sniffed and bayed. White wrought-iron posts spiked skyward to prevent the dogs leaping out.

'Well, that would be more luxurious than my shepherd's hut, to be sure!' said Jack.

'Aye,' agreed Archie. 'The kennelman is mighty proud of this abode. Here, take a look at Mr Robertson's kangaroo hounds. The finest from England.'

Jack peered in through the slats of the solidly built gate. Four hounds with drooping eyes and ears bayed at him from their stone-floored kennel.

'And in the next kennel we have the Scotch collie dog litter from this wee sheepdog here. The dog and the slut were knotted on the boat sailing over, and this is the result. The best pups in the land.'

Archie stooped to stroke the ear of the black collie bitch who was patiently waiting to get in to her pups. Jack could hear excited and startled yaps from the pups as they woke up inside the shelter of the kennel. When Archie opened the door, five little black and tan and red and tan pups rushed to their mother and began grappling at her teats.

'She won't take much more of that rough treatment. They're eight weeks old and about weaned.'

The pups squatted on their haunches and began to suck strongly, their sharp little claws kneading their mother's teats. Their mouths worked like clamps. Each one sucked with all its might, bunting and nuzzling its mother as she stood with her legs apart and a pained expression on her face. As their bellies began to swell, the bitch turned to growl and bite at the strongest of the pups. Her teeth gnashed near the ears of a black and tan bitch. She walked away then, leaving the pups sprawling on the ground and looking about frantically to seek her out. She leapt up onto a box in her kennel, out of reach of her pups, and began to lick at her sore nipples. The pups danced about the box looking up and barking at her. All except one. The little black and tan bitch pup sat with a full belly and solemn eyes at the feet of the men. She looked up at Jack and gave one sharp clear bark before pouncing on his bootlaces.

'May I?' said Jack to Archie.

'Go right ahead. The kennelman says the more handlin' of them the better.'

Jack scooped the little pup into his hands and held her up to his eye level. She didn't struggle or whine. She just relaxed in his hands and looked into his eyes with her deep brown ones. She sniffed slightly at him.

'Oh, you're a find, you are,' he said to her gently, and the pup wagged her tail.

'What would it take for me to buy this little pup?' asked Jack.

'Well,' said Archie, 'it would take quite a bit.'

Rosie clasped the tiny newborn pup in the palm of her hand and held it up to her face. As she gently set it back down next to Dixie, she heard the stable door opening. It was Jim.

'How many did she have in the finish?' he asked, squatting down beside Dixie and the squiggling mass of pups.

'Um. Five. The last was born at ten.'

'It's almost twelve now. She'd be finished for sure.'

Rosie looked down at the collection of tiny blue, red and black pups that nuzzled at the nipples of their exhausted mother.

'Ah. They're a fine lot,' Jim went on. 'Don't you think some tucker would be nice for her during the night? I've got some in my quarters. I'll bring it out for her.'

'You don't have to . . . I can . . .'

'I know I don't have to. But I'm offering.'

Rosie frowned at him and tugged a piece of straw from her hair.

'Why are you being helpful now? Why didn't you stay before?' she asked suddenly.

'You didn't need my help. The book tells you what to do. Besides, how will you learn if you just sit back and let the men do it all?'

'What do you mean by that?'

'I've been talking to your friends at the pub. James Dean and his lady. They told me about your troubles. I heard about your fiancé. I'm sorry.'

Rosie turned away from the kindness in Jim's eyes, afraid she might cry. She decided to give up being angry with him. She turned back to him and smiled sadly.

'Thanks for your sympathy – but I'm sure James Dean told you the real truth about Sam and our . . . relationship.'

'You're a fine girl, Rosie Jones, I'm sure,' Jim said, patting her firmly on the back.

'Thanks.' She looked back to the pups and began to stroke Dixie's flank.

'Well,' said Jim, 'I'll be seein' you in the morning then.'

'It already is the morning, you big Irish git,' Rosie said with a smile.

Jim pulled a face at her and laughed a little before he went out to his quarters and shut the door firmly behind him. Rosie sank back down in the straw to watch the pups sleeping, their tiny sides moving up and down, their coats already glistening. She couldn't bring herself to go back into the house and up to her own bed. She felt so alone up there. She had wanted Jim to stay . . . she wanted to know more about his life. Did he have brothers and sisters? What did his parents do? What did he really think of Rosie Jones without-the-hyphen and her mother and father with-the-hyphen? Rosie shrugged. For now she'd have to wait. Instead she turned to stroke the pups with her index finger.

'What tiny miracles you are,' she said softly.

Sixteen

'Venus Williams or what?' called out one of the Moorecroft brothers as Rosie slugged a tennis ball over the net towards him. It bounced once and flew past him like a missile. Little did he know she was really aiming for his head, so in her mind it was a poor shot. Behind each slam of her racket, Rosie surged with anger.

For the past few weeks she had busied herself outside on the farm, despite Gerald's silence and sighs. She had tailed Jim, watching, learning. Having a go at whatever it was he was assigned to do. She was like his shadow, even though she knew she got in the way sometimes. If time allowed, Jim tried hard to teach her as he worked. But Rosie couldn't help feeling he only put up with her because she was the boss's daughter. She bombarded him with endless questions and frustrated him with her cack-handed approach to handling wire or tools or driving vehicles. But still he encouraged her. Was it because he liked her? Or was it obligation? Rosie longed to tell him the truth . . . that she wasn't Gerald's daughter at all. But somehow she couldn't say the words out loud. For now, she wanted to forget.

There were times, at the end of the day, when she hooked her arms over the yard rails and watched Jim handling his colt, that she felt like Sigrid Thornton in *The Man From Snowy*

River. It seemed so impossibly romantic when she caught his eye and the corners of his delectable mouth turned up slightly in a smile. Then she'd shake the attraction from herself with a cold shiver. It was too soon after Sam – wasn't it? Only four months since the accident. Though the guests at her mother's end-of-season tennis party obviously thought she should move on. Margaret and her friends had been parading eligible men in front of her all day. Even Dubbo had been invited.

Men be damned, she thought, as she slugged again at the tennis ball. Sam had betrayed her. Her real father had obviously cleared off. Gerald ignored her, and Jim was somewhere on the runs being free in the saddle, riding his young colt out to check the ewes.

Rosie herself felt anything but 'free'. Here she was in a crisp white tennis outfit, playing co-host at her mother's annual Indian Summer barbecue and tennis match. She felt trapped, and miserable, and furious with her mother.

When Rosie first saw Dubbo, looking gaunt and pale and leaning on a walking stick, she felt a pang of sorrow for him. He had leant over and given her a kiss on the cheek, his fair hair flopping over one eye as he did. Still, Rosie felt stung. Dubbo's presence reinforced the reality of Sam's death. He had actually been there, there in the darkness when Sam and Jillian were killed.

'Yikes!' said Rosie's opponent as a tennis ball slammed onto his tubby thigh, leaving a reddened welt.

How could her mother do this to her? Rosie glanced over at Gerald, who was hovering on the fringes of the party. He dutifully continued to pour Pimms and lemonade for his guests but he was so detached and remote from the general festivities, people gave him a wide berth. Rosie could tell Gerald had closed down. She had seen him withdraw before, and she could see it in his eyes now. Though he'd never been this bad. Rosie served the ball with a crack and the Moorecroft boy ducked.

Beside the court, lounging on Margaret's new jarrah furniture, arrogant young men drank beer and stared at Rosie's fine legs. Thirty-something Prudence sat among them, giggling loudly at their jokes and playing with her black curly hair. Despite her expensive tennis dress and glowing white sandshoes with matching wristband, Prue looked anything but sporty. Her chunky legs bubbled with cellulite when she crossed them and her upper arms flapped about when she clapped Rosie's winning shots. Lapping up the new male guests at the Highgrove-Joneses', she put on 'the voice' to impress them. Her over-enunciated words were delivered between lips smeared with hot-pink lipstick.

'Good show, Rosemary! That's one for the gals!' she bellowed.

Rosie stomped off the court with some satisfaction, after whipping the Moorecroft boy's fat little arse. But her mood soon plummeted when she heard Prue talking loudly.

'Yars!' Prue said to the boys. 'I'll be thar Fraa-day and you can buy me a Chaaardonnay.' She looked out from beneath her dark lashes at the men who clearly squirmed at her request. Rosie slumped into a chair, threw her tennis racquet down and sighed loudly. Her mother sashayed up wearing her flattering navy tennis outfit, a silver antique fob chain draped about her neck.

'Rose darling, why don't you pop into the kitchen to get some fresh lemonade and glasses? It's a heavy jug. I'm sure David will go with you to help you carry it.'

Margaret placed a firm hand on Dubbo's shoulder and he quickly put down his beer.

'Yep. Sure. Yep,' he said, jumping to attention. Eagerly he limped after Rosie across the lawn and into the cool of the house.

In the kitchen, all the lunchtime salads had been covered with a tight film of clingwrap and were neatly stacked in the fridge like transparent drums. The bench was wiped clean and afternoon tea was already waiting, draped with clean white gauze embroidered with golden bumblebees. Pristine glasses were stacked on trays.

'Lemonade's in the fridge,' said Rosie gruffly as she fished a tray of icecubes from the freezer. Dubbo's brown eyes leapt her way nervously for a moment, wary of the angry energy Rosie was putting out.

Rosie glanced at him. What could her mother be thinking? Of course, in Margaret's eyes, Dubbo had the bloodlines. His family had one of the largest grazing properties around, and important connections in the city! Never mind that this was the man who was at the wheel when Sam was killed! Emotions clustered and banged about inside Rosie as she thought back to kissing Sam here in the kitchen. She cringed at the thought of history repeating itself . . . with Dubbo. Although he had been Sam's best friend, she barely knew him. Seeing him here in the kitchen seemed to open up the fresh scars of Sam's death and his unfaithfulness to her. When she failed to budge the icecubes from the tray, she pelted the plastic mould at the sink and swore.

Dubbo looked up from where he was peering into the huge fridge, clearly startled at her outburst.

'Let me,' he said. He walked over and with his strong farmer's hands twisted the ice out with ease.

'I'm sorry,' Rosie said, feeling guilty and awkward.

'Understandable,' said Dubbo. 'I'm not sure what to say to you either . . .'

She summoned up a smile for him. The poor bloke, she thought, bearing her wrath.

'I'm not angry at you,' she said. 'It's my mother. She drives me nuts.'

'Yeah. I know what it's like. Since the accident my mum's been treating me like I'm twelve again, at home from school with a bug. It's been crap. Stuck at home with her fussing over me every day!'

'So you haven't got back to work on the farm yet?'

'I'm getting there. I'm riding the four-wheeler about. Helping Dad with this and that.'

'Oh?'

'Well, to be honest, we're just working on controlling footrot in our sheep. They're predicting a wet winter after this terrible dry so we thought we'd get stuck into them now. But don't spread it about, will you? The fact we've got footrot.'

Rosie's face lit up. 'Oh! Me too.'

'Sorry?'

'We've been doing the same – footrot control. Did you use zinc sulphate or formalin?'

'Zinc sulphate this time, but we'll use formalin next time round.'

'Jim, our stockman,' Rosie said eagerly, 'reckons it's best to let them stand about in the yards a bit after you've footbathed them – gives the stuff more time to work into the hooves rather than let them straight off into the paddock. We drained them off on the grating in the shed this year, which is different to how Dad and Julian did it last year.'

Dubbo stood holding the jug of Margaret's homemade lemonade with his mouth open. He had never seen Rosemary Highgrove-Jones at a sheep sale, like some of the other girls her age in the district, yet here she was chatting knowledgeably to him about footrot and zinc sulphate. She was a bag of surprises, he thought.

'Don't you hate it when you've got the sheep upside down and you're working on the back hooves and the sheep lets a warm smelly one rip?' Rosie went on with a smile.

Dubbo raised his eyebrows and then nodded.

'Yeah! Pure methane!' he agreed.

'I reckon you breathe in so much of it during the day, at night your own farts smell like sheep farts.'

'Can't say I've actually noticed.'

'Next time, think about it. I'm sure it's true. Give yourself a mutton dutch oven.'

Dubbo looked at her for a moment, then threw his head back and laughed. Rosie chatted on as she put the icecubes into a dish and arranged the lemon slices the way her mother liked.

By the time they strolled back across the lawn towards the other tennis players, Dubbo and Rosie were talking comfortably. They had even agreed on a time for him to come and look at Dixie's pups working. He'd insisted Sam's kelpie bloodlines were too good to just give away, but Rosie said, 'Don't worry about it. I don't want money for them!'

Margaret smiled warmly at the sight of them. Plans bubbled in her head as she tried to recall the size of Dubbo's family landholding. She knew it was large. Enough to get Gerald out of trouble, she thought. When Rosie delivered the tray to the table, she noticed her mother smirking at her.

'Thanks,' Rosie said abruptly to Dubbo. She immediately moved away from him and slumped down in a chair as far away from Margaret as she could get. Dubbo, bewildered, cast a hurt look in Rosie's direction.

Just then Jim trotted around the corner of the homestead on his gangly colt. The colt shied a little at the clutter of people and furniture on the normally bare lawn, but Jim kept him calm enough to ride right over to Rosie. The guests looked up, startled by the sudden presence of a dancing young horse and tall stockman in their midst. A warm feeling rushed through Rosie. She was so glad to see Jim, especially here. He had clearly come to seek her out.

'It's your mare, Rosie,' he said, his thick Irish accent cutting through the polite burble of guests. 'I think she's about to foal. And it looks as if she'll have a hard time of it.'

Rosie's eyes grew wide with excitement and urgency.

'Let's go,' she said as she leapt from the chair and raced towards the stables. Jim wheeled the colt around and followed her.

'Rosemary,' called her mother, 'you have to play another game in the roster!'

But Rosie was gone.

Later under the glow of the stable light, Jim and Rosie looked down at the foal.

'Oh, he's a beauty,' said Jim, beaming like a proud father. He was cradling the colt to steady him as he stood for the first time. Then he let go, and the chestnut foal tottered on his pointy little hooves. He craned his neck, stretched out his pretty head with the white blaze and sought out a drink. Sassy snorted contentedly as she ate, while the foal wrapped his muzzle over her teat and suckled.

'Have you thought of a name for him?' Jim asked.

'I think I'd like to call him Morrison,' Rosie said softly. 'You know, after Van.'

'Ah, one of Ireland's greatest musos. But have you thought long enough on it . . . are you sure you don't want to call him Sinead?' Jim looked at her cheekily.

'Nah . . . he's got too much hair. Morrison will do.'

'Bono?' Jim suggested.

'No! Not U2!'

'What do you mean not me too?'

'No! Not U2. Oh just give up, Jim. It's Morrison,' Rosie said, frowning at him. Was he flirting with her?

'You could go Scandinavian and call him Bjork.'

'It's *Morrison*!' Rosie crossed her arms in a pretence of frustration.

'Just trying to help,' Jim said sheepishly. Rosie fell silent.

'And what about the other little 'uns?' Jim said, inclining his head to indicate the stable next door where Dixie lay in a straw nest suckling her tiny, squirming offspring.

'I just can't think at the moment.'

'Are you going to get them registered with the Kelpie Council?'

Rosie shrugged.

'You'd be able to get papers for all these animals. You could set up a stud, for both the stockhorses and the kelpies. Get some return for them. That's what I'd be doing if they were mine.'

'Who'd want to buy working dogs and horses from me? I don't know anything about it.'

'You'll never find out if you don't have a go . . . and besides, the genes in these beauties will give you all you ever need to know. You just have to learn how to read them. Good animals teach their handlers. What do you reckon?'

Rosie looked at Jim. There under the warm glow of the stable light, surrounded by the sweet smell of hay and horses, she just wanted to kiss him. She *had* to kiss him. She stood up on her toes, shut her eyes tight and put her lips to his. She felt him kiss her back, at first tentatively, then with rising passion. He pulled her closer to him and she felt his whole body responding to her. But just as suddenly, he pulled away.

'I'm sorry, Rosie,' he said. 'You're a gorgeous girl, but . . . I don't know.'

Rosie felt embarrassment flush her cheeks red.

'Oh God. I'm sorry. I thought you . . .'

'No! I mean yes. I do find you attractive.' He ran his hand through his hair and looked shyly away. 'You're gorgeous. It's just, I want to stick around on this place, so I'm near Ronnie Seymour and can lend him a hand now and then. And if your father found out I was carrying on with his daughter . . . well . . . I don't want to lose my job.'

Rosie smiled and stepped forward, ready to tell him that Gerald wasn't really her dad, but Jim kept talking.

'I mean, let's face it. You're too posh for me. Common is what the Poms call people like me back home. So I know what you're up to. You're not serious, are you? You're just looking to have a bit of fun with the hired help.'

His words stung Rosie. Anger rose up in her.

'You think I'm a bored little rich girl, don't you? But you don't know the first thing about me! You've got it wrong, Jim Mahony. You've got it so wrong!'

'Hey,' soothed Jim, 'I didn't mean to –'

'Never mind. Forget it,' Rosie said, backing away from him. 'Just *forget it*.' She flew out of the stables and back across the courtyard into the house.

Seventeen

Warrock homestead

A sprawling garden swept around the Warrock homestead, isolating it from the work buildings. At the wrought-iron gateway into the garden, Jack hesitated. It was as if the green land of England had been transplanted and, against all odds, carefully maintained beneath the harsh Australian sun.

'Should've worn my Sunday best,' he said, smoothing down his dusty jacket and tugging on his sleeves. He thought of his uncle and aunt and how they would chastise him for meeting Mr Robertson in such a state. His boots were scuffed and dirt lay etched in the lines of his hands. The gravel of the driveway crunched underfoot as Jack and Archie rounded the hedge that lined the tennis court. From behind its leafy wall, Jack could hear the giggle of women on the court and the shouts of young men. Strolling ladies in white dresses shone against the greenness of the garden like sulphur-crested cockatoos, accompanied by young men proud as wood pigeons in their woven waistcoats, straw boaters and ties. Not far from the court, a handful of guests lounged in the shade of a Moreton Bay Fig tree, like lions after a big feed.

When George Robertson saw Archie he excused himself from his guests and strode over. Jack immediately recognised him from the races. He was a short man with white skin as iridescent as a trout's belly. His long lean nose ended with a crooked tweak and the bridge of it was flanked by small, narrow black eyes.

'How is it with the shearing, Archie?' he asked.

'All is fine, Mr Robertson,' Archie said. 'We have more to shear thanks to the honesty and vigilance of Mr Gleeson here. He mustered a sizeable mob on Dunrobin's run and brought them back across the river for us.'

'Ah, Mr Gleeson,' said George Robertson. Lines creased his high forehead when he lifted his brows and surveyed Jack's face. 'We have met before, I believe, at the Crossing Place race days. I saw you ride to victory on more than one occasion. A shame we didn't have a place for you here on Warrock. A fine horseman you seemed to be.'

'When I see your magnificent station and your remarkable collie dogs, I can't help but think it was a shame I could not find employ here, sir.'

Mr Robertson turned to Archie.

'Make sure Mr Gleeson is well fed and comfortable for the night before he returns to his pastures on Dunrobin.'

'Aye. That I will.'

A young lady's voice rang out from where the guests sat in the shade.

'Well, if it isn't the bushranger!' She ran towards Jack, her skirts swishing and the locket around her neck thudding gently on her breast. Her dark hair was looped up in ribbons and her cheeks shone from her exertions on the court. 'We saw you on the road a few months back . . . on our way to the races.'

George Robertson was frowning at the young lady and looking at Jack as if he might bring trouble.

'Oh, Uncle George,' giggled the girl when she saw his stern face, 'he's not *really* a bushranger – I was just teasing. Won't you bring him over so we can hear what adventures he's had? We're all frightfully bored with tennis . . . some stories will jolly us along.'

With an elegant toss of her skirts, she turned away, assuming the men would follow her command.

'That, Mr Gleeson,' said Mr Robertson wearily, 'is my nephew's fiancée. I'm afraid we must do as she pleases.'

'Er, excuse me,' said Archie uncomfortably, 'I've been away from the shed too long. I'll meet you at the dinner hut on sundown, Jack. Take your horse to the blacksmith before you come.'

'Thank you, I will. See you there.' Jack felt torn. He would rather be surrounded by shearers in their lanolin-soaked dungarees than in the thick of the well-dressed ladies and gents beside the tennis court. But he pulled himself up tall and strode over, mustering as much Irish pride as he could.

Beside the smooth trunk of the Moreton Bay Fig, Jack glanced about the party of men and women before settling his eyes on George Robertson, who sat amongst them as if commanding the whole occasion. Jack cleared his throat before he spoke.

'Mr Robertson, may I know how you came across such fine working dogs as the two collies in your kennels?'

George Robertson sipped at his tea, then set his cup down on an ornate cane table before he spoke.

'Well, Mr Gleeson, where shall I begin?'

He had the long fine fingers of a craftsman. And like the wood he turned, his hands seemed polished and smooth. He picked up a tiny fork and sliced through a fat wedge of sponge cake.

'They are from none other than Mr Richard Rutherford's kennels of Sutherlandshire, Scotland. A man with an exceptional eye for dogs. Ah, Scotland! How I miss the bite of the fresh sea air and the salty tang on my tongue! In the early mornings we would run his dogs along the sand and they'd dance by the seashore in the gleaming wet kelp. Barking, bounding and growling at each other like a wolf pack . . . but when their master whistled they would abruptly give up their play and come to heel like well-behaved children. Mr Rutherford had a way with the dogs.'

'Sutherlandshire?' inquired one of the young men who lay on the grass. 'Is that where they burn kelp for iodine?'

'Indeed it is, William. I can still smell it.' George Robertson sucked in a breath through his long nose as if to prove that he could. 'Bonnie Scotland!'

'Aye!' said William, raising a bottle of ale to the air.

'You, Mr Gleeson,' said Mr Robertson, 'you are of Irish blood, are you not?'

'Yes, I am.'

One of the young men muttered and a few of the girls stifled giggles. Jack felt his Irish blood rush to his cheeks as he felt the judgement of the group fall upon him.

'Well, you make the best of what you are given,' said Mr Robertson, a smile playing at the corner of his crooked mouth. Before Jack could think of anything else to say, a buggy drawn by a team of dapple-greys drove into the sprawling greenness of the garden.

'Oh, it's George,' exclaimed the young girl as she ran towards the buggy.

'My nephew, George Robertson-Patterson Junior,' Mr Robertson explained to Jack.

Jack looked over to see a finely dressed young man stepping down from the buggy. He greeted the girl with a smile and a kiss on the hand. She danced about him like a puppy, her hand tucked into the crook of his arm. The other men rose and walked over to greet him.

'Well,' said Jack, 'it's time I headed back to the men's quarters.'

'Indeed,' said Mr Robertson. 'I thank you again for returning my stock.'

'A pleasure, sir.'

There was a silence between them for a moment before Jack blurted out his request.

'May I be so bold as to ask if I could buy the black and tan female pup that is housed in the kennels, Mr Robertson?'

Robertson's eyebrows drew down over his eyes in a stern frown. He placed a heavy hand on Jack's shoulder and began to speak in a lowered voice.

'Jack, my good man. You must realise that as a gentleman establishing my own empire within this land, I've invested much time and money in bringing those bloodlines from the far shores of northern Scotland. No bitch pup of mine is for sale, nor will be for sale. I may consider parting with a few males, but of the creatures born, all are promised to gentlemen friends of mine.' George Robertson held out his hand. 'Good evening, Jack.'

Jack took his hand and shook it, but he had taken Mr Robertson's snub, too, and there was tension in his grip.

In the morning, bleary-eyed from a late night beside the fire with Archie and the shearers, Jack began to saddle Bailey. Dark clouds had rumbled in from the west at midnight and so by morning the rain came in steady sheets and a wind blew the red gums about wildly. Archie had warned Jack off asking Mr Robertson again about buying the pup.

'The answer will still be no, Jack,' he said with conviction. 'I know him, and he won't budge on any decision he's already made. You can see from this place how determined the man is. But if I come by a good dog, I'll bring it to you. I know which shepherd's hut you're at now, so I'll be sure to stop by.'

Jack thanked him, but his heart was low as he swung up into the saddle in the pouring rain. He could still see the face of the little black and tan pup with the floppy ears. The one that had looked him in the eye and pounced so playfully on his boots. She was the only dog he wanted.

'Come on, Idle, you useless codger, we best get back to our own sheep.'

The dog yawned before gingerly stepping out into the pouring rain.

'Mind crossing that river on the way home,' said Archie from beneath the shelter of the shearers' quarters' verandah. 'Keep your wits about you and beware of the kelpie spirit.'

'The what?' said Jack.

'The kelpie spirit. We have them back home in Scotland. On dark stormy nights they come out . . . looming in the mist, in the shape of a giant horse. After you see one, someone is sure to drown. They are a warning, Jack, so be mindful of where your horse places her feet in that river.'

'The *kelpie* spirit?' Jack said.

'Oh she's a warning, Jack. Look out for her.'

'You Scots and your superstitions!' Jack said, with laughter in his voice.

'You Irishmen and your scepticism,' said Archie in the same tone, and they both laughed before Jack rode away with his collar up and his face turned away from the rain.

Eighteen

Confused and embarrassed by Jim's rejection after their kiss, Rosie ran along the dark hallway.

'Bugger!' she said as she tripped over the croquet mallets left by her mother's guests. She could see a square of light on the carpet from the kitchen's open door. The smell of something burning drifted upwards to the ceiling.

In the kitchen Margaret was wearing her robe and pouring herself a drink from a bottle of gin. A frittata was bubbling and charring black under the grill.

'What are you doing, Mum?' Rosie said as she grabbed the frying pan and switched off the grill.

'It's your father's supper,' Margaret said absently. Rosie tossed the hot pan into the sink where it hissed beneath the tap. She tore the bottle from Margaret's grip.

Margaret slipped her hand into her pocket and took out a plastic container. She pulled off the lid and tipped tablets out onto the table, pushing them into piles with her index finger.

'Mum? What are you doing?' Rosie repeated.

'What does it matter? My life is over.'

Margaret was shaking.

'What are you talking about?'

'Your father is leaving me.'

'*Leaving* you? Why?'

Margaret turned to her, her eyes strange. 'Why don't you ask your precious aunt?'

'What?' Rosie asked, shocked.

'She's always wanted him for herself.'

Rosie tried to take in what her mother was saying. Giddy and *Gerald*? At first it seemed absurd. So absurd that Rosie wanted to laugh. But then memories of Giddy and Gerald together flashed into her head. Like last Christmas, when Gerald had kissed Giddy so warmly and laughed so loudly. He'd wanted her to stay. He'd held her hand. That very same day he'd changed from being silent and surly to whistling and happy. And then there was Margaret's frostiness towards her sister. It was always there . . . that feeling of bitterness between them.

'Are you sure?' Rosie said, still struggling to grasp this latest development.

Margaret knocked her forehead on the table gently and began to laugh hysterically.

'Am I sure? Do you think I'd have slept with a shearer if I hadn't found Giddy and Gerald together? What do you take me for?'

Do you think I'd have slept with a shearer? The words echoed in Rosie's head. She backed away as the pieces started falling into place. Margaret finding the lovers together, all those years ago, then taking her revenge. A fling with a shearer. A *shearer*. Her father. Rosie couldn't breathe. She began to stumble down the dark hall. She could still hear her mother yelling in the kitchen, her voice echoing about the house.

'There's never been a divorce in the Highgrove-Jones family,' Margaret ranted. 'Never! Ha! Now look! After all these years, Gerald's running off with my sister!'

Rosie ran on to the front verandah in time to see Gerald pulling away in her grandfather's old Mercedes. In the glow of the verandah light she could see he was staring straight ahead, his face set like stone. He didn't see her. He just drove off, the tail-lights, like narrow red eyes, getting further and further away.

'Dad?' Rosie yelled after him, then winced at the impossibility of it all. He hadn't even said anything. He'd left without speaking to her. Panic at feeling so alone and so unwanted swamped Rosie. She couldn't bring herself to go inside to face her ranting mother, nor could she face Jim.

'Oh, God,' she muttered. 'What am I supposed to do now?'

Out in the yards, Rosie roughly bridled Oakwood, threw a saddle on him and opened the gate. Jumping on him, she booted him to a gallop and rode off into the mist.

Bleary-eyed from sleep, Jim came to stand shivering on the cobblestones in his bare feet. He peered out into the darkness of the cold night.

Oakwood stumbled a little in the mist and slowed to a trot, holding his nose close to the ground, smelling his way, snorting and peering into the darkness. Low limbs of messmates scratched Rosie's face and left red welts on her cheeks but she barely felt them. Thoughts rushed through her head so fast that her temples pounded and a pain stretched across her forehead. She rode on into the night. The track suddenly took a dive down a hill and Rosie leant back in the saddle as Oakwood's haunches bunched under him. He half-skidded, half-loped down the embankment, Rosie's body jarring at each step. She wasn't sure where they were going, but she didn't care. She didn't care if she got lost for days out here in the tangled scrub that flanked the river. Anything to get her away from her crazy family and the huge old homestead filled with gloomy portraits of people who were no longer her relatives.

At the base of the bank, Oakwood picked his way through a tunnel of thick ti-tree that was barely more than a wallaby track. Rosie's feet were often yanked from the stirrups as they hooked on slim trunks. The ti-tree scratched her arms and left the sensation that she had spiderwebs draped over her skin and spiders crawling down the back of her neck.

At last, drawing clear of the scrub, she felt as if she'd just travelled through the magic wardrobe and emerged in Narnia.

The mist peeled back to reveal a sheltered clearing. A hazy moon shone chilly light down onto a serene grassy river bank. Large white gum trees reflected the moon's light and the low silvery river slid silently by. A frightened bird took flight, bashing its way blindly through branches and startling Rosie, but not her horse. She slid down from him and looped his reins over a fallen log. Then she sat in the wet grass and began to cry. Her tears were silvery and silent, like the river. She hugged her knees to her chest and shivered in her damp jeans and T-shirt. Her teeth began to chatter. She wiped hot tears across her cold, bloody cheeks and began to rock back and forth.

After a time, the shaking became uncontrollable. Rosie knew it was from shock as well as cold. She put her arms around Oakwood's solid neck and warmed her face under his long mane. She put her hands under the heat of his saddle blanket and cried more tears onto his neck. She felt like she could die here. She wished the river would rise up and wash her away forever.

Then she heard a rustling in the ti-tree and her heart leapt in fear. A black shape emerged. At first Rosie thought it was a wild dog. But the black shape's tail was wagging and soon Diesel was whining and licking her hands in delight.

'You followed me!' she said to Diesel. 'But how did you get out of your kennel?'

Diesel barked at her excitedly and then ran back into the bush. A few moments later, Jim emerged from the ti-tree on his bay mare. He could see Rosie's white T-shirt in the moon-light and make out the gleam of the stirrups and the bit on her horse.

'How did you find me?' she asked angrily.

Jim rode right up to her. Oakwood whickered gently as he stretched out his nose to greet Jim's mare.

'I didn't find you. The animals led me to you. They're far smarter than me.'

'Go away,' she said, turning from him, ashamed. He slid from his horse and put his hands on her bare arms.

'Oh, but you're freezing! Here, let me.'

He opened up his big oilskin coat and folded it around her, pulling her close to him. He looked down at her face and gently smudged the grime and blood from her cheeks.

'You've cut yourself.'

'I know. It stings.' Rosie dabbed at her cuts with her fingertips. She felt awkward standing like a pathetic girl in Jim Mahony's arms. She didn't want to be weak and pathetic. He tipped her face up towards his. 'What's upset you like this?'

She shook her head, not knowing where to start.

'Dad's just left Mum.'

'Oh.' Jim pulled her to him.

'Only it gets worse. I'm not really a Highgrove-Jones at all. I just found out Mum had a shag with some shearer. And *he's* my real father,' she said, bursting into tears again.

'Shush,' Jim soothed, cupping her head in his hands as she rested her cheek on his broad warm chest. 'I've got you now.'

Rosie looked up at him and then suddenly he was kissing her. She felt the passion run through her. His lips were so warm. She tilted her head and began to kiss him back. Wanting him more than anything. Desire tightened in her chest as she kissed and kissed Jim Mahony, the Irishman, there by the river. She could taste him and taste her own blood from a cut lip. The pleasure and pain was excruciating. She wanted to lie down now with him in the long grass and pull him into her. She invited his hands to slide across her back and up under her damp T-shirt. His huge hands, rough and warm, slid over her smooth cold skin. She felt his body pressed against hers. Then Jim pulled away. He looked at her face and stroked her hair behind her ears. Desire glimmered in his blue eyes.

'Ah, Rosie,' he sighed in the most gentle Irish lilt, 'you're so beautiful, like a siren. A water spirit. Like you've come up from the river to tempt me. Where are you leading me, girl?'

His voice was husky with emotion. Rosie wasn't used to

gentleness, she had only known Sam's rough, non-communicative ways. But here, with Jim, the very sound of his voice and the emotion in it made her melt.

Jim took Rosie by the hand and made her sit down on a log, then sat close to her. All the while he looked into her eyes and stroked her hair from her face. She ran her fingers through his soft fair hair and over his square jaw that, by morning, would be smudged with a rusty-brown stubble. She took in his full lips and smiling eyes.

They sat by the shimmering river, looking into each other's eyes, until the mist rolled in again and a huge black cloud slid over the moon. It was like the curtain had just fallen on the most romantic scene in Rosie's life. She giggled when Jim's face blacked out to nothing.

'Holy shite, it's dark,' she said, mimicking his accent. The fine mist became heavier and soon it drifted down in soaking sheets of icy rain.

'Come on!' Jim laughed, taking her hand. 'Let's get out of here! We're going to get soaked.'

Riding towards home in the darkness, Rosie breathed in the beauty of the night around her, despite the freezing cold and the rain that trickled down the back of her neck.

'Jim?' she said as she ducked beneath another branch.

'Mmm?'

'Do you reckon it was a night like this when Jack Gleeson got his kelpie pup?'

'If it was, I hope he was wearing more appropriate clothing than you,' Jim said. 'At least you've got your headlights on so we can see the way.'

'My what?'

Jim grinned, and Rosie realised that in the dim light he was eyeing her nipples, clearly visible beneath her clinging wet T-shirt. Rosie pulled Jim's coat tighter across her body and reined Oakwood in beside him to punch him lightly on the arm.

Nineteen

GLENELG RIVER, CIRCA 1870

Jack Gleeson pulled on his coat and put another log on the fire in his hut. The evening had gone so slowly. He didn't know how many times he'd flipped open the leather case of his pocket watch. But now it was time to leave. He carried the lamp outside. The light created an eerie sheen in the mist but failed to penetrate the thick white veil. Jack saddled Bailey, gathered up Cooley's lead rope and swung on to the mare's back.

'Stay,' he said to Idle, but the dog clearly had no intention of moving from his warm dry spot on the horse blankets beneath the lean-to.

Jack took the stiff cold reins and the lead rope in one hand, and with the other pulled his collar about his neck against the chill. He urged the mare on past the sheep that were contentedly chewing their cud in the yards. He could hear Bobby, hobbled nearby, tearing up clumps of grass. Jack ducked his head to avoid branches that emerged from nowhere. Bailey was careful not to scrape her rider's knees on the gnarled trunks of river gums as she picked her way along the track. Her ears darted about, alert to the sounds of wild dogs in the scrub and possums rustling in the trees. As he rode, Jack thought back to his encounter in the Glenelg Hotel and the events which had led to this midnight ride.

* * *

After months in the shepherd's hut, Jack was given three days off to do with as he pleased. He'd spent a morning with the blacksmith in Casterton, getting Cooley fitted with some shoes. Cooley was now broken to saddle and Jack was pleased by the way the colt moved beneath him. Good bloodlines coursed through the colt's veins and people would stop Jack in the street to ask about Cooley's breeding.

In the blacksmith's, Jack had run his hand along Cooley's neck to calm him as the farrier went from anvil to hoof, fitting the shoe, shaping it with rhythmic tings of his hammer.

'I've got myself a good horse, but it's a dog I'm after now. A good slut to breed from,' Jack told the farrier.

'Ah, there are plenty of dogs about,' he replied as he ran the rasp over Cooley's hoof and sent white slivers much like coconut on to the dirt floor.

'But there's this one. Just the one that I want. She has the brightest brown eyes and is marked with black and tan. But George Robertson refuses to sell her to me.'

The farrier set down Cooley's hoof and began to laugh so that his belly shook.

'Anyone would think you were a man struck down with an obsession for a woman.' He placed some gleaming nails between his bearded lips and took up a shoe. As he tacked the shoe onto Cooley's neat little hoof, he spoke through thin lips that still clamped the nails between them. 'Pups are like women, there are plenty out there!'

'That may be, but I know this is the best pup for me. She is the one!'

'How do you know she's such a good dog?' the farrier asked as he clinched down the nails. 'Plenty of men have been wrong about women in the past, and I'm certain the same applies for collie sluts. Sounds like you need to find yourself a few lady friends while you're about in town. That would set your mind straight!'

Jack had replied only with a smile.

'Suit yourself. If it's dogs you prefer!' laughed the farrier.

He was running his rasp over the last hoof when George

Robertson's nephew drove up in his buggy, his team of greys prancing like circus horses in their harness. Entering the gloom of the workshop, young George stopped in his tracks.

'By God! What a colt!' he exclaimed. He stepped forward, seeming to ignore Jack and the farrier. He ran his hands over Cooley's shoulder. 'A mighty specimen! Surprised he doesn't have wings . . . he looks as if he'd fly like the wind.'

'Aye. That he does,' said the farrier, setting down the last tidy hoof, now glinting with horseshoe and nails. 'He has hooves as sound as granite rock. This here's his owner. Jack Gleeson. He's brung the colt along and taught him well.'

George Robertson-Patterson turned to survey its owner. Jack knew the man's thoughts. He was wondering how such a horse could belong to a shabby-looking stockman.

'Tell me he's for sale,' George Robertson-Patterson said. 'Ask your price!'

'That he is not,' said Jack curtly, annoyed by the haughtiness of the stiff-backed man before him. 'Now, if you'll excuse me, I've business to attend to in town.'

He promptly thanked the blacksmith, paid him his earnings and led Cooley away. The sound of the newly shod hooves sliced into the gravel. Mounting Bailey, Jack took up Cooley's lead rope and rode away in search of Tom Cawker and his grooms for company for the rest of the day.

By seven that night, Jack and the grooms were well-oiled in the hotel, singing and slinging back ale. A hush fell over the bar when George Robertson-Patterson strode in, in his coat-tails. He walked straight to the bar and ordered two whiskies, handing one to Jack.

'Word has it you've got your eye on a particular pup bred by my uncle at Warrock,' he said.

The blacksmith was clearly a man who liked to talk, Jack thought. He took in the shine on George Robertson-Patterson's slick black hair and the thin-lipped smile that spread across his pale face.

'That's right. Two weeks back your uncle refused my offer to buy a pup. The little black and tan slut.'

'Well, I'm certain my uncle told you he wants to keep all the breeding bitches in our family, so as to regain some of the expenses in sailing them out here. And he's hanging on tightly to the bloodlines.'

'Understandable,' said Jack, disappointed.

'Yes. However,' said George, pausing to sip on his whisky, 'he did give me the little bitch as a gift. On the condition I *never* sell her.'

Jealousy, fuelled with the rush of rough whisky, flared within Jack. How could this man, who would rarely work a dog, be given such a prize? Ignoring the flash of anger on Jack's face, George went on in his clipped educated voice.

'I promised my uncle I would not *sell* her. And on that score, I intend to honour my word. But what would you say, Mr Gleeson, to a *swap*? A swap is certainly not a sale, is it?'

'A swap?'

'Yes, Mr Gleeson. Your colt for my pup.'

Jack looked into George's eyes. Was the man drunk? How could he suggest exchanging a fine colt like Cooley for a pup . . . no matter how good her breeding? Jack flung back the whisky.

'Not on,' he said immediately, imagining old Albert shifting in his grave beneath the pear tree. A dog for a colt! An unlikely deal.

George was unrattled by the flat refusal.

'Just think, man! Think of the training I could provide for that colt. You'll never get him race-fit out on the runs, doing the work you do. He's likely to get staked on a sapling and his days will end before they've begun.'

'But what if he doesn't? What if I do bring him on for racing and he runs home enough to be a champion? Should I give up all the service fees you are sure to gain?'

'Come now, Mr Gleeson. How could you stand a fine horse like that at stud when you are on the road? He'll only be used over rank, poorly bred mares if he lives his life with you. Whereas *I* can give him the best start in racing, and in later life as a sire.'

Jack knew George was right. Cooley was too good a horse to have his hocks knocked and damaged on fallen logs, and hooves bruised on flinty ground in the pursuit of wild cattle. He belonged in a fine stable, with his own groom and a belly full of chaff, not struggling, rib-thin, on native pastures.

'Besides,' continued George, 'you'll make a better go of it taking on a Sutherland bitch to breed from. You can sell the pups for good money to station hands and graziers alike. There are some good trials starting up in the north and they now pay handsomely for trial bloodlines. You can't get a better pedigree.'

Jack sat, considering. His heart hankered for the bitch. He wasn't sure why, he just had to have her.

'Buy me another drink, Mr Robertson-Patterson, and you may have yourself a deal,' he said at last.

'My uncle will string me up by my tackle if he finds out,' said Robertson-Patterson. 'We must complete this deal in secret . . . at night.'

'Fine,' said Jack, his eyes glimmering with excitement.

'Do you know the shallow crossing place on the Glenelg River between Dunrobin and Warrock?'

'I do,' said Jack.

'I'll meet you there at midnight in five nights' time . . . on Thursday . . . I'm certain my uncle is departing for Melbourne that day.'

Now, close to midnight, as he led Cooley towards the river, Jack felt the sadness of saying goodbye to the colt. Should he turn and head back to the hut with both horses? Forget the deal?

He could just make out the shadow where the ground dropped away to the Glenelg River's dusty bank. Bailey shook her head and her bit jangled in the night. She slid down the river bank and cautiously snorted at the water before placing her front hooves at its lapping edges. She stretched out her neck once to pull some length in the reins, then again, to put her head down to drink. Cooley came to drink beside his mother. He was nervous and wouldn't put his hooves in the water, as if something sinister was sure to clench his fine legs in its jaws and drag him thrashing to his watery death.

'Oh, go on with you!' said Jack, stroking Cooley's wither from where he sat. 'You big sook!'

He sat listening to the long slurps and rhythmic swallows of the horses and the tinkling of the water that fell from their soft muzzles onto the river stones. Though it was dead still on the ground, when Jack looked up through the branches he could see the mist in the higher reaches of the sky, blowing past the glowing whiteness of the moon. The landscape was grey, silvery-grey, with shadows as black as hell. High above him, the mist cleared enough for a sliver of moonlight to drop onto the surface on the river. It illuminated the water that trickled over the rocks on the crossing, and in the shadows of the deeper pools it danced on ripples.

Bailey and Cooley heard the horse approaching before Jack saw it. Cooley shied and pulled back on the rope, while Bailey jumped back in fright. A gloomy, shadowy shape of horse and man emerged from the river mist, as if walking on the water's surface. Jack's horses snorted nervously as he held tight to the reins and the lead rope.

The sight unnerved him. Perhaps it wasn't George Robertson's nephew at all, but an angry George Robertson himself, come to blast Jack with a shotgun for conspiring to steal a pup from him. The figure didn't speak as it slowly approached, splashing silver drops of water from its hooves. Jack thought maybe he was dreaming and he was about to wake up in his hut. But then a voice came from the shadowy figure.

'Gleeson?'

'Indeed,' said Jack lightly, hiding the fact he was as nervous as a fox in a lair with the hounds bolting by.

'I would've said *six* nights' time, if I'd known it would be a night such as this,' said Robertson-Patterson as he rode up. He was wearing a fine woollen coat and warm gloves.

'I see you haven't changed your mind,' he went on, his eyes roving over Cooley who was now sniffing gingerly at Robertson's horse.

'And you?' asked Jack, seeing no sign of the pup.

Robertson-Patterson undid the top button of his coat and out popped the little black and tan head of the pup. Even in the darkness, Jack immediately recognised her beady brown intelligent eyes and floppy ears. Robertson dropped his reins, reached in and pulled the pup out.

'I'll be a tad less warm on my journey home without her,' he laughed.

Jack took the pup in his cold hands and felt the puppy warmth of her. He scooped her inside his own coat and she nestled down against his chest. Then, with a wave of sadness washing over him, he handed Cooley's lead rope to Robertson-Patterson. Sensing Jack's regret, Robertson-Patterson offered a little comfort.

'I'll be sure he has a fine life. It's a fair swap.'

'That we shall see,' said Jack, still not fully trusting his decision.

Robertson-Patterson cleared his throat.

'And now, Mr Gleeson, might I ask that you move on quickly from this place? The sooner you are gone from the district, the safer your future with that pup.'

'It's time for me to take to the road anyway. I never plan on staying too long in one place.'

'Good luck to you,' Robertson-Patterson said, turning his horse and Cooley away.

'And to you,' said Jack.

Jack watched the man and two horses become shadows as they splashed away across the river. He thought of Albert as he took a last look at Cooley's rounded bay rump and black feathery tail disappearing from view. Then he pulled the tubby little pup from his coat. She was heavy and solid.

'Hello, Miss,' he said to her, and she wagged her tail and flicked her tongue out to lick at the misty air. 'What's a name for you then?'

Jack thought of George Robertson at the tennis party, and the images he had conjured of Sutherlandshire and the dog breeder with his dogs, dancing in the kelp on the beaches of Scotland. Then he thought of Archie, the Warrock overseer, who had warned him of the kelpie water spirit, a horse-like shape that looms from the mist to warn men of drownings. So here, down by the river, just after midnight, Jack Gleeson slid from his horse. He squatted with the pup in his hands. He cupped his hand into the cold water and sprinkled some drops of the Glenelg River over the broad brow of the little pup.

'I christen you Kelpie,' he said with a smile.

Then, with the pup tucked safely in his coat, Jack Gleeson mounted his horse and rode away into the mist, back towards the warmth of his hut.

Twenty

Jim and Rosie arrived back at the stables, drenched and shivering. Their icy, stinging fingers fumbled with wet, stiff girth straps as they hurried to unsaddle the horses.

At last the horses were bedded down in the stalls for the night. Jim stood close to Rosie outside the stable door, holding her hands and looking down at her.

'Are you sure you're okay?'

'I'm fine,' she said, smiling at him, but shaking from the cold.

The rain hung in the courtyard floodlights like a sheer sheet of gauze. It fell not in thick heavy drops, but in a heavy mist that landed on the tin roof of the stable in a comforting shush. It had been dry for so long that Rosie felt excitement course through her as water clattered in the downpipes and beat gently on the windows of the stables. It washed a calmness through her. She turned her face up to Jim. He looked so irresistible with the curling tips of his wet hair oozing raindrops on to his tanned cheeks. His shirt clung to his body and his dark eyelashes framed his eyes, eyes that held within them the sky of sunny days. She put her arms around his neck and kissed him hard, her tongue sliding into the warmth of his mouth. Soon all there was for Rosie was the sound of the rain and the warmth of Jim's kiss.

She took Jim's large hands in her own.

'Come on,' she said as she led him towards the men's quarters and into the tiny bathroom. She turned the shower on full blast. 'I need your body heat, so you'll have to take all your clothes off to warm me up,' she said cheekily.

'Oh, will I now?'

In the haze of warm steam, kissing him, she began to peel off his wet clothes, revealing smooth golden skin that rarely saw the sun. She ran her cold fingertips over his broad shoulders and kneaded the muscles in his strong arms. She kissed him down his neck and over his chest. Jim undid the buckle of his belt and peeled off his jeans. Soon they stood naked, each of them gasping as they stepped into the shower. The hot water blasted their freezing skin. Their limbs slithered together in a wet, warming embrace as they kissed over and over. Jim rubbed soap over Rosie's body so that she glistened in a soft white lather of bubbles.

'You're so beautiful,' he said.

'The bed, let's go to the bed,' she said, pulling her mouth away from his. They dried each other with scratchy clean towels, their skin reddened by the hot water. She lay on the bed, her eyes locked with Jim's.

'I wanted to do this the first time I saw you here, in this very bed,' said Jim.

Rosie pulled him down with her and they started kissing again, long and deep, and trailing fingertips over each other's skin. Jim explored her body leisurely. Rosie felt she would burst with desire. The rain outside beat down and she was swept along with the comforting sound. Their lingering kisses began to build in momentum, and soon their passion was coursing through them like water through the dry creekbeds that tonight had come to life.

So intense was their need for each other, they didn't have time for first-night nerves or shyness. Rosie arched her back and writhed beneath Jim, longing to feel him inside her. The roar of the storm was like a freight train rattling over the stables and the homestead. Deafening thunder rumbled and shook the tin on the roof and vibrated through their bodies. For a split second, lightning illuminated the room. The bright flashes revealed the lovers riding each other wildly, both possessed by a kind of madness. The air was charged with an energy from the storm and it took Jim and Rosie to another place. They were no longer in this world, or of this time. Exhilarated beyond belief, they forgot all else. All they knew at this moment was each other and the passion and power of nature around them. Nothing else mattered.

In the morning, the sun sulked behind a thick grey wall of cloud that shrouded everything in a dull light. Gum leaves drooped luxuriously as rain slithered down to their tips and fell in thick drops to the ground below. Fat kookaburras dropped down from fence posts and pulled worms from the dampened soil. With their feathers ruffled to keep out the rain, the birds looked like plump ladies in fur coats, dining out in their finest. On the short pasture, where the grass seemed to have begun to green overnight, parrots strutted about picking up insects. They drank fresh rainwater from clear puddles in the paddocks and tiptoed in the rain as if dancing. Their iridescent green and red feathers were now washed clean with fresh rainwater and they brought dabs of glorious colour to the dark grey day.

Inside the quarters, Jim and Rosie were missing nature's show. No sunlight had crept through the window to wake them. The darkness of the day had left them peacefully slumbering in each other's arms well past dawn and their seven o'clock deadline to rise.

A little later, Rosie stirred to the sound of the phone as it rang and rang. The outside bell echoed round the empty courtyard. Rosie kissed Jim's shoulder. He smiled sleepily.

'Can't you just leave it for your mam?'

'I need to check on her anyway.'

Rosie slipped out of bed and pulled on her clothes. As the

phone rang on and on, she began to worry. Where was her mother?

As Rosie ran into the house, the phone stopped.

'Typical,' she said, thinking of Jim and the warmth of his bed.

The kitchen was empty. Dirty dishes were piled up on the sink, and the table was scattered with half-empty coffee cups. The lavender her mother had picked last week was drooping downwards in the vase.

'Mum?' called Rosie. There was no answer. In the hallway she called out again, this time more loudly. 'Mum!' But the huge house lay silent. Walking up the stairs and along the hallway, right to the end, she knocked gingerly on her parents' bedroom door. Clothes were falling out of the large blackwood cupboard as if it had suddenly sneezed. The gold clock on the mantelpiece above the fireplace chimed importantly to itself. Rosie saw her mother, lying beneath a rumpled doona on the bed.

'Mum?' she said, stepping forward. Beside the bed were a scattering of her mother's prescription tablets. Rosie's heart leapt in fear. Gingerly, she lifted up the doona and peered beneath it.

Margaret looked out at her, puffy-eyed and pale.

'I know what you're thinking,' she said in a husky voice. 'But I'm okay. I haven't done anything silly. Just drunk a little too much.' Then the phone began to ring again. 'Would you get that for me, darling?'

'Sure.' Rosie patted her mother's shoulder before she turned away.

'Rosie. I'm sorry,' Margaret said quietly, but Rosie had already thudded back along the hallway. She was just about to run downstairs when she noticed a note under her bedroom door. She picked it up, the phone still ringing insistently. Rosie quickly scanned Gerald's tidy writing.

'Dear Rosie, You and Jim will have to manage on your own for a few days. I'll call you soon. I'm sorry.'

He'd signed the note with a G, and an X to mark a kiss. Not allowing herself to feel the stab of pain at Gerald's leaving, Rosie stuffed his note in her pocket and ran downstairs to answer the phone.

'Hello?'

'Is that you, Margaret?' came a man's voice on the other end.

'No. It's Rosie.'

'Ah, Rosie. It's Marcus Chillcott-Clark here.'

'Hi. How are you?'

'Look, I just wanted to make sure you've got the fax from the bureau.'

'The fax?'

'There's a flood warning. A big one. I'm just on my way out now to move the stock. Your father needs to do the same. We'll catch up another time? Bye then,' and he hung up.

Rosie stood in the quarters, dripping from the heavy rain. Jim's face lit up when he saw her.

'Hello again,' he said.

'This fax has just come through,' she said, holding it out to him. 'They've had one hundred and fifty millimetres upstream overnight. They're warning that a flash flood's on the way. There's stock all along the river paddocks. What should we do?'

'How much time do we have after that amount of rain?' Jim asked, taking the fax from her. Rosie shook her head.

'I don't know. I've never –'

'Would your mam know?'

Rosie shook her head, feeling angry with herself and Margaret for being so ignorant.

'Have you got a number for Gerald? He'll be able to tell us.'

Rosie shrugged. 'He just left me a note saying he'd call. But I'll try Giddy's and meet you back here.'

She turned and ran.

'Shite,' said Jim as he got up and began to pull on his

clothes. He didn't need this kind of drama in his life. But Jim had been in big floods in the Kimberley river country. He had seen bloated cattle left hanging from fences in piles of flood debris, terror frozen on their faces. He wasn't about to let it happen to the cattle that now grazed the Highgrove river flats. Not if he could help it. He gathered up his coat and hat and went into the stables. Soon Rosie was back by his side.

'Couldn't reach him,' she said.

'And your mam? Have you told her what's happening?'

'She was asleep. But I wrote her a note,' she said, buckling the throat lash of Oakwood's bridle.

'We'll have to hurry, just in case,' Jim said. 'You take the vehicle and move the weaner ewes off the front river paddocks. Put them up round the sheds here for the time being. Stick to the tracks, mind. I'll shift the wethers from the back run country onto the big hill.'

'And the cows and calves?' Rosie asked. 'They're all on the other side of the river on Cattleyard Swamp, aren't they?'

Jim frowned, thinking.

'We'll have to get across to open the gate to let them into the bush run. Otherwise they'll go under for sure. It'll be too boggy for the ute. I'll lead Oakwood out there and meet you at Murphy's gate.'

'Right,' said Rosie, trying to picture Murphy's gate in her mind and wishing she'd paid more attention to the paddock names.

Jim tugged the surcingle tightly round the belly of his mare. He strapped two leather saddlebags onto the brassy rings of his saddle. He was in the habit of taking the saddlebags everywhere, even on the smallest of jobs. They were neatly packed with emergency rations, matches, paper, tea, sugar, sweets and a small first-aid kit. The Western District seemed so tame to him after his years in the red, rugged country of north-western Australia, but he still felt compelled to take his saddlebags with him.

Unlatching the stable door, he led the horses out into the rain, his mare and Oakwood following him with their ears flattened back as they felt the first cold drops land on their warm dry rumps.

Twenty-one

As Rosie roared away in the ute towards the front paddocks, the dogs cantering behind, she vowed she would do a good job for Jim and for the sake of the stock.

Diesel and Gibbo cast out perfectly around the mob on the river flats. Jim had taught her to work her dogs using their natural instinct to pull the mob towards her. She drove slowly towards the gate, knowing she could rely on the dogs to guide the sheep to her.

After shutting the gates around the house paddocks, Rosie drove quickly along the track, the fat tyres of the ute splashing mud up over the doors. The windscreen wipers smeared brown droplets over the glass and Rosie leant forward trying to see where she was going as the ute bounced, bumped and fish-tailed along the track. At last she saw Jim waiting at the gate with the two horses. She got out and ran to him.

When they pulled the horses up at the river bank, Rosie sucked in a breath. The river looked sinister. White froth tinged with brown gathered beside the swirling eddies and clung to the tangled heaps of bark, sticks and branches at the river's edge. In the centre of the river, water surged forward as if it was boiling over. Further downstream, rapids roared over rocks in the shallows and threw up white spray. Rosie sat back in her saddle in fear when she saw it. Steam rose from their hot horses as Jim and Rosie surveyed the scene.

'Where do you think we should cross?' Rosie yelled through the rain.

She had been out to the ford before, on picnics, when the river had gleamed and was still; she had launched her body into its comfort and coolness in summer heat. But the prospect of crossing the river in flood terrified her. On the other side, the cows were stranded on low rises in the marshes, bellowing at their calves. The calves gambolled in the shallows of the rising water, lifting their little tails and kicking out their hind legs. They seemed unaware of the danger they were in. The cows trotted after them, lowing urgently.

'It's not so bad here at the ford,' said Jim, his mare dancing on the slippery rocks and mud at the river's edge. 'The horses will be fine. I've crossed worse than this in the Kimberley.' He stretched out a cold reddened hand and touched Rosie's face. 'Trust your horse. He'll carry you through.'

'And the dogs?' she asked.

'Current's too strong. We'll have to give them a lift.'

He whistled the dogs to him. 'Hop up,' he said, and Thommo and Daisy leapt up to sit at the front and rear of his saddle. His mare flattened her ears back as she felt the dogs land on her, but she stood still.

'See if your dogs will do the same,' he said.

Rosie patted her leg and said, 'Hop up.' Diesel and Gibbo ignored her.

'Say it like you *mean* it, girl!' said Jim. 'We don't have time to waste.'

'Hop up,' she commanded in a voice that didn't seem like her own. Diesel instantly leapt up and settled himself at the front of the saddle. Sam had clearly trained him to do that. Gibbo whined and hesitated. He put his paws gingerly on Rosie's foot in the stirrup and tucked his tail between his legs. She reached down, spilling rain from the brim of her hat onto the ground, hauled up the lanky dog and draped him over

Oakwood's rump. Oakwood gave a small buck at the sensation, then settled.

'Right?' said Jim.

Rosie nodded, swallowing the fear down into the pit of her stomach. Following Jim on his mare, Oakwood ambled into the river as if he was on a pony club trail ride. Then his ears shot forward in excitement and he snorted as he felt the current racing past his legs. Branches skidded by over the rocks and Jim's mare shied a little, but he talked to her and gently urged her forward, giving her time to find her footing. As they moved deeper into the river, the current swept past with terrifying strength. The horses grunted with effort, trying to keep their footing on the round river rocks that lay unseen beneath the frothing rapids. The water rose to Oakwood's chest and Rosie could see the tail of Jim's mare being swept sideways downstream by the current. Sticks and leaves were catching in it. Icy cold water soaked into her boots and rose up her jeans, but just when she thought they must be swept away, the water level began to drop and the horses seemed to walk more freely.

Shaking more from fear than cold, and sighing with relief, Rosie began to relax. But suddenly Oakwood stumbled, his front legs tumbling deep into a hole. His shoulder fell away from beneath Rosie and his nose dipped below the muddy waters. His hooves flailed. Then his body surged sideways, and he fell. Rosie went with him. The dogs were washed from Oakwood's back, and from the corner of her eye Rosie saw their tiny heads being swept away. Then she felt the water grasp her chest. It constricted her breath as coldness and fear choked her. She felt her legs float and lift away from the saddle as she was submerged in the angry water. It tugged her feet from the stirrups and began to pull her body downstream.

'Jim!' she screamed. She and Oakwood had been washed from the crossing and were now in the deep swirling water, moving rapidly downstream. She saw him turn and the look of terror on his suddenly pale face was the image she took with her as she was dragged under by the current. Her fingers grappled to find Oakwood's mane or saddle. Anything. Whatever she could reach. She slung her arms about his neck. Oakwood's every muscle was taut with fear and exertion as he battled to swim against the current to the bank.

When Rosie surfaced, clinging to Oakwood and his reins, she saw the terrified roll of his eyes. His nostrils were flared up, red, like a dragon's, then they would flatten and close as he breathed heavily and snorted, his big hooves thrashing in the current. Rosie felt the river's fury. It sucked her boots from her. Her coat was drawn from her body like a rabbit's skin. Time and again, she and Oakwood were pulled under, spinning about. Logs battered them. Sheep, long since drowned, ghoulishly bunted them as their bloated bodies floated past, their tongues swollen and pale, their eyes glassy.

Beneath her, from the bottom of the muddy river, it was as if the fingers of the dead were grappling Rosie's ankles, dragging her down. One moment she was in the dark raging underworld, then she was back looking up at the grey sky and watching the river bank pass by. She could feel Oakwood beginning to give up the fight. He was getting tired. Her muscles screamed with exhaustion too. The panic in her head, that fierce instinct to survive, was subsiding. Rosie began to relax. She realised in a calm, strangely detached way that she and Oakwood and the dogs were going to drown.

Sometimes they were carried in the centre of the river, at other times they were thrown to the edges. Tree branches scratched at Rosie's face and her skin was grazed by submerged rocks. As they swept round a sharp bend, the river took them under a cluster of willows. Their branches hung down like tendrils and bent with the current. Rosie reached up and grabbed a handful of slender willow branches. She felt the leaves pull away beneath her grip as the river tugged at her body. Desperately she grasped more willow branches as she passed and managed to hold fast, dangling there, the current pressing against her. With her other hand she clung to Oakwood's reins. He thrashed his legs hopelessly, trying to stay with her, but it was no good. Rosie knew she had to let him go. She watched him wash away from her downstream, his eyes rolling in his head, his breath coming quick and fast. She was numb with sadness. She had ridden a beautiful horse to his death. She had drowned the dogs too. Her shoulders ached as she clung to the tree in the freezing water. She tried to swing like a monkey to a sturdier branch but the current held her. She was stuck. Resigned to her fate, she turned for a last glimpse of Oakwood.

To her surprise, instead of being swept out of sight, he was still swimming just a few hundred metres downstream. The river had taken him to the edge of an eddy. His ears were now flickering forward as he began to swim in the heart of its calmness. He was making progress. He was out of the current and swimming towards the bank. Rosie watched as he heaved himself up and out of the river. His hooves slipped on mud, but soon he was standing on the bank, looking out towards her. He dropped his head low to the ground and shook the water from his coat, his sides heaving. His saddle hung beneath his belly. The blanket had been tugged from him and taken by the river. His bridle was pulled over one ear, the reins broken and dangling beneath his jaw.

Hanging there in the willows, Rosie knew she had to let go. She had to chance being washed into the stillness of the same eddy. Let fate decide. Before she unclasped her frozen fingers from the willows, she closed her eyes and pictured Jim. If she were to die, she wanted his face as her final image. His gentle, kind eyes and his full kissable lips. The way one of his smiles could light her up or soothe and calm her. She felt so blessed to have met him, this stockman, Jim Mahony. The first man who had touched her soul. Then the river took her. She stretched her arms out in front of her and let the logs and sticks bump past her. Rolling on to her back, she watched the grey clouds looming low in the sky. Then she felt a stillness about her as she was gathered up and spat out with the other flotsam the river had captured. And with her last bit of energy she began to swim.

Twenty-two

Standing shivering on the river bank, Rosie slung her arms about Oakwood's neck and panted. Then she tugged at the buckle of his girth. The sodden saddle dropped to the ground like a giant dead stingray. It was too heavy to pick up, so she left it there and led Oakwood away from the river. They waded through wet marsh country until they found the fenceline. Rosie knew to travel upstream, but she didn't know how far. She had to find Jim and the cattle again. Standing on a fallen log, she swung up onto Oakwood's back. She felt the warmth of his body through her wet jeans, but still she shivered uncontrollably. Time slipped away as she followed the fence, balancing carefully on Oakwood's bare back as he weaved through the scratchy fingers of ti-tree. Every now and then she called out to Jim, but the wind and the rain swept her words away.

When Rosie at last came to a clearing she saw the Cattleyard Swamp sprawling out before her. The rusty red dots of cows and calves were still standing on the ever-shrinking islands that rose up from the shallows. There was no sign of Jim. She looked about and screamed out his name. Tears came to her eyes. Had he followed her and drowned? She scanned the silver sheen of water that now covered the river flats, trying to turn every tree and every dark shape on an island into Jim.

But the rain continued to fall and it washed away her hope. Rosie slid from her horse and sank onto her backside there in the mud, beginning to sob. Having just experienced the savageness of the river, she was certain Jim was gone. She began to think of the kelpie spirit . . . the horse-like ghost looming up from the river. And she began to pray to it. She prayed for the dogs, the mare, and for her stockman. As she began to chant 'Please let them live' she felt a warm sensation on her scalp. She looked up to find Diesel sniffing at her and licking at her ears. Gibbo stood nearby, his tail wagging, sticks and leaves still caught under his collar.

'Oh, my dogs! My dogs!' Rosie clutched them to her. Frantically, she looked about for Jim and called out again and again, but only the furious wind in the treetops answered her. She felt panic flutter in her stomach but she resolved to ignore it . . . she couldn't let the cows on the river flats experience the terror of a drowning death. She had to finish the job that she and Jim had started.

Rosie summoned up all her strength and clambered back onto Oakwood. She had to be brave. She had to trust her dogs and her horse. Just like Jack Gleeson would have.

WESTERN WIMMERA

Jack ducked forward in the saddle, his heart beating fast, as Bailey plunged into the fast-moving river. He held Kelpie tight to his chest beneath his coat and dragged Idle along in the water by the scruff of the neck as he felt the mare's legs striking out as she began to swim. He gasped as the water crept up through his clothes. But Bailey was strong, and the river was clean of debris, so she was soon wading through the shallows again, safely on the other side. Bailey shook the water from her and moved on in a sprightly walk along the track beneath low-slung gums. Then Jack let the young dog leap down from the horse, while Idle grumpily trundled on behind them.

'You're my good-luck charm when it comes to river crossings,'

Jack said to Kelpie as she shook the water from her coat. He wondered when the drizzly rain would stop. He'd had a torrid few days crossing the waterlogged plains. He looked up hopefully to the ridges which were washed grey in the distance. He'd have to ride fast if he were to find a dry camp site for the night. Jack was aiming to reach Ballarook station before shearing. He had his heart set on the Wimmera, where the men said sheep grazed in their thousands. Wool was cut by the ton and bullock teams as long as a mile towed wool bales as heavy as bullions of gold. But so far the Wimmera hadn't been a golden landscape for Jack. Instead it was drab and grey. Mud and dangerous river crossings had marred his journey and he had been cold and wet most of the time.

When Jack at last rode up onto the ridge above a flooding billabong, he was relieved to see a clearing ahead where smoke trailed up to the sky like a thin skein of spun wool. The fire was struggling against the damp weather, but the camp site looked inviting.

'Hello?' Jack called out as he approached, but no one answered. The campfire smouldered lazily, its coals barely glowing. A billy, half full, sat on the edge of the fire, ashes clinging to its rusty sides. A neat black gelding with a white snip on his nose pricked up his ears from where he was tethered under a tree. He stretched out his neck and whickered a greeting to Bailey. In the treetops, pink and grey galahs screeched and danced like jesters.

'Hello!' Jack called louder. Then there was a yipping and barking of dogs as they scrambled excitedly up and over a creek bank. There were three of them, all wet and dancing with excitement. With frantically wagging tails held up in the air like flags signalling peace and goodwill, the dogs sniffed at Idle and Kelpie. Jack noted they were healthy, happy types of collies with good breeding. He was amazed to stumble across such impressive-looking dogs. He felt as if it were an omen. Was it not by water that he had first gained Kelpie? Then he heard a high-pitched whistle from below and within a split second the dogs had scuttled past him, over the bank to their master. Jack could see a man washing the carcass of a kangaroo on the lake's edge while his dogs danced about him.

Jack's jaw dropped in amazement.

‘Be buggered! Tully? Mark Tully? Would that be you?’

‘Holy Mary, mother of God!’ Mark said, standing with the roo’s tail grasped in his large hands. He scrambled up the bank. Jack slid from his horse and the two young men shook hands, embraced, then shook hands again, laughing into each other’s faces at their chance meeting. Memories of their boyhood down at the portside yards came flooding back and Jack felt his skin bristle with goose-bumps. A good omen it was.

With the fire stoked back to life and the billy boiling merrily. Jack and Mark huddled beneath an old canvas cloth that was strung beneath a thick canopy of trees and tripped over their words in their haste to recount their adventures since leaving their homes.

‘So here I am heading back to Ballarook with not a single cow in my herd. The boss is going to be as dark as this night.’ Mark jabbed the fire with a gnarled old stick and let out a breath through his nostrils. ‘But I know you can sweet-talk him, Jack. You’re good at that. It’s not my fault his other stockmen let them wander and the silly beggars picked the wrong bit of dirt to stand on when the floods came. He’s always getting me to clean up the other men’s muck-ups. But just you wait till shearing. It’ll be grand.’

‘I can’t wait to break this young lass in here with the work. She’s ready to start,’ said Jack, nodding towards Kelpie.

‘What’s her story? She’s a nice type.’

Mark listened to the story of the secret swap in disbelief.

‘Bloody hell! Albert would take his cane to you for sure. Swapping his colt for a pup! Are you mad?’

‘I know it sounds that way but I have no regrets,’ Jack said. ‘She’s a smart one, and once I find a good sire dog for her she’s bound to throw good pups.’

He pulled his damp coat about him and looked at Kelpie. She was watching him with her head tipped to one side and her lop-ears pricked up, as if she knew he was talking about her. Within a matter of weeks, she was leaving the pudgy pot-bellied pup stage behind and growing into a lean, fine type of northern collie. She rested her chin on her paws, her eyes glued to Jack for as long as she could keep them open. Then she let out a snuffling sigh and drifted off to sleep. All Jack's hopes rested in the little dog that lay before him. It was his dream to supply her pups to others so that Kelpie's bloodlines would flow on like a river throughout the countryside. He began to tell Mark about his vision.

'I want people to be able to trace her pedigree through the landscape like tracks on a map,' he said earnestly. In his travels he wanted to scatter Kelpie's well-bred pups along the way, as if scattering the seeds of a precious new plant that would change people's lives.

'And I vow I'll give the pups to any man, rich or poor, grazier or shepherd, so long as he can guarantee them good training, good tucker and a life full of work.' He reached down to ruffle Kelpie's long black coat and scratched her tenderly on a small white patch that marked her chest.

'A vision splendid, indeed,' said Mark, grinning.

'Ah, you can mock me,' Jack said, nudging his friend. 'But I see you pride yourself on keeping the best dogs.' He nodded at Mark's three, curled up nose to tail beneath the sheltered side of a tree trunk. 'How did you come across such a fine line?'

'They're Rutherford's stock. You know him?'

'Indeed, I've heard of Mr Rutherford. The one from Yarrawonga way, with family in Scotland?'

'One and the same,' said Mark. 'I did some labouring for a fella who had naught to pay me . . . so I asked for his Rutherford pair and his old dog. I don't think he knew their true value as he gave them up gladly. So there I was, with Rutherford dogs, imported from his family's stud in northern Scotland! The best about.'

'Of that I'm sure. My girl here has similar lines. I'm looking for a good sire for Kelpie when she's old enough. A good strong dog that will throw classy types. Not just any old mongrel hound. Would you be interested in selling me a pup one day when they have a litter?'

'*Sell* you a pup?' said Mark with a scowl. '*Me?* Sell *you* a pup? Oh, don't be daft. There's no way.'

Jack looked at Mark's face. His mouth was set in a serious line. Jack tried to disguise his hurt and disappointment. He was about to beg when Mark's mouth stretched upward in a smile.

'I wouldn't *sell* you a pup, Jack, you big eejit. I'd be happy to *give* you a pup though . . . you can take one when the bitch whelps. And I'd be honoured to have one of my dogs sire pups with your slut. I'll show you their work at Ballarook this very shearing – but take my word for it, they're both strong, hard-working dogs. There's none better about.'

A few hours later, after a fine supper of potato and kangaroo stew, followed by damper and treacle, Jack and Mark Tully joked by the fire as if they were fourteen years old all over again, remembering Albert's tall tales and laughing until their bellies hurt and their faces ached. Then, when they had fallen silent for a time, Jack slapped his old friend on the back.

'You know, Mark, some days they just pass as days, but others, oh my Lord, other days . . . you just know the universe is working to make things happen. Great things will come from this meeting, of that I'm sure.'

The firelight illuminated Jack's handsome face as he spoke. 'This is just the start of something much bigger than you and me and this night and these dogs. When we're no longer here on this earth, and these dogs have gone to dust, there'll still be blood flowing in the veins of living dogs far off from now . . . the blood of our dogs here.'

'Oh, Jack. Don't talk like that now when it's so late in the evening and my belly's too full for my brain to think. All I'd like to know is that in the future my blood will be getting about in the veins of my grandkids . . . that way I know I've lain with a woman!'

'That's all you ever think about,' laughed Jack.

'Well, it's better than all you ever think about – dogs, horses and stinking bloody sheep and cows!'

'And what's wrong with that? At least you don't get God looking down on you seeing all your sins.'

'Oh, Jack, you'll be wanting confession once you see the girls on Bunyip station.'

'Bunyip station?'

'Aye. It's next door to Ballarook and in the house there are the prettiest sisters I know. Good strong girls too, out of a brood of eleven. Some are prettier than others, but when you've been bent double over a sheep all day, even the plainest daughter sets your head in a spin.'

'Are you courting one that's taken your eye?'

'Bah! Don't be daft, Jack. They are the daughters of Launcelot Ryan. He's put together the three properties of Bunyip, Eldorado and Mount Elgin, so the station he owns is some seventy thousand acres all-up. He wants better than us stockmen for his lasses.'

'I don't reckon a grazier's daughter would have eyes for the likes of us anyway,' said Jack, staring into the fire.

'Well, for tonight let's forget the women – and we ain't got no wine. So we'll have to settle for some songs . . . shall we sing a few from the old days?'

And they began to sing the folk songs they had learned in their childhood, their Irish voices carrying over the river into the night. They held their heads up to the sky and sang to the darkness, and soon all the dogs began to howl along, causing Jack and Mark to fall about laughing.

Twenty-three

Rosie urged Oakwood on through the shallow floodwaters and rode out towards the cows and calves. Gibbo and Diesel hovered on the dry bank watching her go, their tails jammed between their legs, whining anxiously. But their loyalty drew them out into the shallows, following their master.

Rosie had only ever worked her dogs on sheep in dry paddocks. The sheep just drifted along in mobs if the dogs worked them right. She was surprised at how hard the cows and calves were to shape into a smooth, flowing group on the waterlogged river flats. They baulked at the deeper drains of water and wouldn't cross. They refused to stick together as a herd, preferring to run after their calves. And some cows turned and charged the dogs.

Rosie soon realised she would have to ride harder and closer to the cattle if she was to move the herd to safer ground. She urged Oakwood on, her thighs gripping his bare back. When a cow turned back towards them, Oakwood's instincts switched on. Rosie sat back on his spine and grabbed a fistful of mane as his stockhorse genes came to the fore. He worked the shoulder of a beast, matching the cow's every move. His legs darted beneath him as he weaved in front of the cow and shouldered her back towards her mates. Rosie let Oakwood take her. Trusting him. Encouraging him. Every now and then she'd lose her balance and slip from him, landing solidly on the ground that lay beneath the shallow water, but he would stand and wait until she clambered back on.

The dogs, too, were proving their worth and seemed to understand the urgency of the situation. Diesel and Gibbo were working hard to push the lead cows and calves through the water spilling rapidly across the river flats. The furious cows, protecting their calves, bellowed at the dogs, slinging their heads low to the ground and storming forward at a charge. The kelpies teamed up, snapping and barking at the cows' open, moaning mouths. With a nip of the hocks, darting from the kick, the dogs soon had any rogue cows back in the herd.

They worked like this for a full hour, moving slowly towards the high ground, the terrifying roar of the rising river behind them spurring them on. The cows plunged through drains and emerged on the other side, edging closer to the bush that rose up beyond the fenceline. Pin rushes were replaced by low ti-tree and dog bush and, beyond the fence, gum trees rose up overhead.

Rosie looked back. It seemed silver sheets of water were taking over all that had once been land. Oakwood heaved, steam rising from his body, while the cattle mooed restlessly, trying to mother-up with their calves. The dogs stood panting in the rain. Though Rosie had succeeded in moving the cattle, she was now stuck on the wrong side of the river – and Jim was missing. She felt anger rise up in her against Gerald as she heard his voice in her head: 'Don't you know those bloodlines trace back to the original Crondstadt Hereford bull imported from Herefordshire?' So what if they did? Rosie thought. They had nearly cost her her life, and now they had surely cost Jim his.

Rosie shivered. She knew she had to find shelter for herself and for the cattle.

'Which way to the gate?' Rosie said to Oakwood. The cattle were already drifting south along the fenceline.

She heard Jim's voice in her mind saying 'Let the animals teach you', so she called the dogs in behind and began to follow the herd. The lead cows ambled along at a decent pace, their red ears flickering back and forth. Rosie's feet stung and a numbness was rising up her legs. She wriggled her toes in the wet fabric of her socks and felt them burning hot with pins and needles.

As the last of the cattle trailed through the bush gate, she turned Oakwood's head to face the river. She wanted to go back to look for Jim, but the pain in her feet had now shot up to her knees and she was shivering uncontrollably with no boots, no coat and no hat. Also, it was getting dark. Heading back down to search for Jim along the river would only put her dogs and horse in danger again. She turned her back to the floodwaters and headed up the hill, looking for the track that, she hoped, would lead her to the hut.

On top of the ridge the wind blew madly and the rain pelted horizontally at Rosie. She couldn't feel her toes or fingers at all. She wasn't sure how far she was from the hut, or even if she was on the right track. She knew hunters and trail riders sometimes used it, but she had never been allowed on those trips.

'Oh, Rosemary's not at all horsey,' her mother would say when the trail leader offered to take the slim quiet girl up with the group. 'She's terrified of horses, actually,' her mother would add, laying an arm across Rosie's shoulders.

From when she was very young, Rosie had believed the stories her mother made up about her. She started to fear everything and avoided adventure, despite longing to go with the riders. Now, out here in the blustery wind and the flood, she had never felt more fearful, yet at the same time she had never felt more brave. She looked ahead on the track and imagined that Jim was riding in front of her. She pictured him, the rain running from his oilskin and trickling down the rump of his horse as he sat tall in the saddle, proud and strong, defying the elements. But when she blinked the image was gone, and she was all alone under the sodden gum trees tossing wildly in the wind. Rosie thought of Jack Gleeson, riding onwards with his pup and his stock-horse, and she felt a shiver run through her. Suddenly the bush around her seemed to shut out time itself. There was only place. This wet, cold world that was so beautiful, yet so savage, like a dream. There was only her and the animals, moving through a landscape that was terrifying in its fury and chill, yet so full of life. Rosie ducked beneath a branch and there, on the edge of a clearing, was the hut.

A lean-to at the side provided shelter for Oakwood. She hitched the slimy leather of his broken reins to the solid upright verandah posts and covered his hindquarters with an old hessian sack she found on the verandah. It would at least keep his kidneys warm, Rosie thought. Then she threw open the door and ducked her head as she stepped inside, inviting the dogs in with her. Stooping, she lit the tiny potbelly stove that stood in the centre of the hut. Someone had set it previously, as was the unwritten rule, so it crackled to life immediately, startling the spiders that had made the stove their home. Rosie lit two candles that were stuck in old whisky bottles and set them down on a shelf so she could see better inside the dim light of the hut. A sagging single camp bed, its bursting mattress covered in possum and rat dung, was in one corner. She swept the mattress clean with the sleeve of her shirt, then dragged it from the bed on to the wooden floor next to the stove. Then she curled up in a ball beside the fire, her arms slung about the dogs, and began to cry. They licked her tears with their warm wet tongues until she settled.

Thank God for my dogs, she thought. Without them she was sure she'd go mad. Still shaking, she began to long for the arms of her stockman around her. And then it hit her – she was in love with Jim. The emotions that welled up in her were so much more powerful than anything she'd ever felt for Sam. And in that very same moment, the thought that Jim could have drowned tore into her soul, so that again she found herself crying uncontrollably.

BALLAROOK STATION, CIRCA 1870

Work in the shed had ground to a halt because of wet sheep, so Jack sat about the quarters listening to the raucous carry-on of the men. He didn't join in. He was too busy thinking of Mary Ryan. He couldn't shake her from his mind.

He had first seen Mary in the orchard, picking lemons with the station children. She had honey-coloured hair, tied in a navy bow, and she was holding a cluster of lemons in her pinafore. A short distance away, her black pony tore at the sweet green grass of the orchard, while the children filled the pony's saddlebags with lemons. Jack had smiled at her and she had smiled back.

Since that day they'd fallen into an easy friendship, peppered with flirtatious comments. Mary would laugh at Jack, and taunt him, then with her shining blue eyes entice him into talking more about his plans for Kelpie. And she'd listen, seemingly spellbound, as she watched his full lips move. Jack had been breaking Kelpie in during shearing, but the dog was making the most of her day off today by dozing at Jack's side, resting her tender paws and stiff muscles.

He looked up from his book when the sun broke through the clouds and shone through the window. A cheer rose from the men as they tumbled outside, made restless by too much idleness.

Jack stretched and looked back to his book, waiting for the afternoon to end so he could escort Mary home to Bunyip station. A moment later, he heard Mark calling to him. Walking outside, with Kelpie at his heels, he saw that the men now stood around in a raggle-taggle circle.

'We have a wager for you, Gleeson,' Mark said. 'A game which only one man and dog on this station could win.'

The men threw coins into the battered hat Mark waved under their noses. Even the cook had come out of the mess and rounded up the homestead staff to see the display of 'tinning the chicken'. Mary ushered the children from the schoolroom and they clustered around her, a little way off from the men. Jack glanced over at Mary and gave her a wink. She bit her lip, stifling a smile.

As a girl growing up on a station in the west, Mary was used to young workmen coming and going, flirting with her and her sisters. But Jack was different from the rest. There was a seriousness and gentleness to him, and she loved the way he spoke to his animals, from his lazy old dog to the bright young Kelpie. Jack was rugged-looking, his skin tanned from outside work and his hands rough and dirty, but his face was so handsome with his blue eyes and high cheekbones, his hair cropped short and neat. And unlike the rest of the men, he was always clean-shaven by Sunday, his skin smooth from the blade. He even spoke like a gent. Mary felt goosebumps rise on her skin as he emerged from the cluster of men and stood in the circle with Kelpie at his heels.

'Bets are now closed,' Mark called out as he set the hat on a post. Then he put down an old tin in the centre of the ring. It lay on its side in the dirt, its shiny surface gleaming. He then took up a sack and on the edge of the ring shook out a flustered chicken. It was part-way between a grown fowl and a fluffy yellow chick. Its beady little eyes and snip of a beak were still chick-like, yet it had the long gangly legs of a grown chook. It flapped its tiny wings and shook its whole body to reorganise its feathers, then cheeped nervously as its eyes adjusted to the sunlight. The crowd looked at the pullet and the tin.

'Not likely!' called one of the spotty roustabouts. 'There's no way he can do it!'

Kelpie glanced up at Jack, quivering with anticipation. She was just six months old. Jack had worked her hard during the first weeks of shearing at Ballarook but nothing quenched her desire to herd. She was an ordinary collie to look at, but her eyes showed such intelligence and her lop-ears pricked up keenly when she worked. And work she did. She would work anything from chickens to ducks, rams to bulls, from lambs to the snotty-nosed kids that lived on the station. Kelpie's herding instinct was so strong she would even try to work swallows as they darted about their nests under the eaves of the station's outbuildings. But guiding all Kelpie's instincts was a connection to Jack that was unbreakable. His voice steered her spirit, led her in all that she did. It was as if she lived for him.

In a quiet voice Jack called, 'Kelpie, get over.' She cast out clockwise, deftly trotting over the boots of the men, trying to place as much distance as she could between herself and the chicken. It began to run away in flustered jerky steps. But quick as a whip-crack Kelpie was around and blocking the path. She dropped to her belly and let the chicken settle for a moment. Then, by raising first one paw, then the other, Kelpie stealthily moved forward, crouched, belly low to the ground, as steady as a cat. The chook moved away from her, but was blocked in her path when Kelpie appeared as if by magic on the other side of the ring. Gradually Kelpie worked the chook towards Jack, into the centre of the circle.

Jack moved to the opposite side of the tin. Kelpie glanced up. As if connected to him by a secret language she moved too, mirroring Jack's position, crouching on the other side of the tin, the chicken between them. As Jack whistled a low steady whistle, Kelpie crept forward. The chook clucked gently and strutted closer to the tin. The men watched in silence, hands folded across their broad chests or thrust deep in the pockets of their dungarees. The little yellow chicken, tilting its head to the side, eyed the tin suspiciously.

'Kelpie,' Jack said quietly, 'walk up.'

Kelpie closed in on the chook with precise movements, stopping if she felt the chicken would run. As the seconds ticked by, the chook relaxed, and seemed somehow mesmerised by the unblinking eyes of the collie dog. Kelpie crept forward until she was just inches from the chook. Then, bowing its head as if submitting, the chook gingerly looked into the dark round space within the tin. Its thin eyelids blinked slowly over its beady brown eyes. A hushed sigh of amazement ran round the group of men. The spotty boy's mouth fell open and Mark licked his lips in glee at the money he would win. The chicken placed its claw-like foot in the tin, ducked its head and then shuffled its whole body inside. It lay inside the tin, peering out as a loud cheer went up from the shearers. They slapped Jack on the back with their big, lanolin-coated hands and shook their heads and tugged their beards. The children danced up and down and clapped their hands.

'Well, I'll be blowed!' said the biggest and burliest of the shearers. 'I've never seen the likes of it, ever!'

'Fleeced by a dog!' cried another, pulling the innards of his pockets out and laughing.

'I told you Jack and his dog could work the devil back down to Hell if he wanted,' said Mark. Then he scooped the chicken back into the bag.

Jack looked beyond the crowd to where Mary stood with the excited children bouncing about her. He winked at her and she gave him a smile.

The men, in good spirits from the show, walked into the dimness of the cookhouse to take up a card game. Mary whispered something to her sister Clare, who set about getting the children back to the schoolroom. Mary remained, a flush of colour on her cheeks. As the men drifted back into the quarters, Mary walked up to Jack.

'Would you show me again what she's like on the sheep in the shed? They say she'll pad over their backs from one end of the shed to the other,' Mary said invitingly.

Jack's eyes widened. 'Are you sure? If word gets back to your da that you've been spendin' time alone with me, he'll string me up.'

Mary said nothing, but took his hand and led him into the shed.

Inside, Jack felt the heat of desire as Mary stood near and slid her small, warm hand up his arm.

'You don't really want to see my dog work, do you?' he said, turning and looking down at her.

'Of course I do.' She smiled up at him. 'But maybe a little later.'

Jack breathed in the humid air, thick with the smell of sheep. Outside, black clouds rolled over the sun again and a clap of thunder shook the shed.

Mary jumped and let out a little gasp.

'I'm terrified of storms,' she said, not looking terrified at all. She leant against his chest.

Jack put his arms around her.

'There's nothing to be scared of, Miss Ryan. I've got you,' he said.

'Indeed you have got me, Mr Gleeson.' She reached up on her tiptoes. They kissed while the storm unleashed a torrent of rain and a wind that whipped in through the let-out chutes and sent the locks flying over the board.

The tin roof banged in the wind and the door of the hut slammed shut. Rosie woke with a start. She squinted at the doorway from where she lay, curled up by the pot-belly stove. Diesel and Gibbo sprang to their feet, each letting out a sharp startled bark. There in the doorway stood a tall figure. Rosie breathed in sharply, not sure if she were dreaming.

'Jim?' she whispered, hardly daring to believe that he was real. She stood and moved towards him. He was soaking wet and shaking with cold. Rosie stood on the tips of her toes and flung her arms about him, putting her warm lips to his ice-cold mouth.

'My God! I thought you were drowned,' she said. 'Here, let's get you warm.' She began to undress him, kissing his neck and shoulders as his work shirt slipped away.

'Oh, Rosie. Rosie! Thank God you're safe,' Jim said as he began to pull her clothes from her. He cupped her breasts in his large hands and stooped to kiss them. Rosie ripped at the buttons of his jeans with trembling hands and began to peel away the stiff denim from his cold white legs. Soon they were naked beside the stove, shivering, wrapped in each other's arms. As they lay together on the old mattress, Jim searched out Rosie's eyes.

'I thought I'd lost you,' he said.

Rosie held Jim tight as warmth for him flooded through her. Her fingertips roved over his skin, his pulse fluttering beneath her touch like a butterfly caught. He was alive and so was she. They moved together as if in a slow dance of celebration, drawn hungrily towards each other's life and warmth. As Jim slid inside her, Rosie let out a groan and tilted her head up towards the shingled roof above. Jim began to thrust into her. As she clung to his strong body, Rosie felt the bitter-sweet pain of having so much passion for a person run through her. And then they were both shuddering and crying out above the noise of the wind and the rain.

Afterwards, Jim held her so tenderly and whispered to her so lovingly, Rosie thought her heart would break.

'Oh, Rosie, beautiful girl. Thank God I found you,' he murmured into her hair.

Twenty-four

The next day, the rain had eased to drizzle yet still no sunshine could break through the brooding grey clouds. Jim and Rosie dressed in their dry clothes, then Jim knelt and wrapped pieces of hessian around Rosie's feet and tied them with orange bale twine.

'Not exactly the latest fashion, but better than going barefoot.'

'Wonder where my boots and coat ended up? Probably six foot up a gum tree by now.'

'Or six foot under the silt in the riverbed!'

Jim tried to insist that Rosie take his saddle, but she persuaded him she was happy to ride Oakwood bareback. She liked the feel of the horse beneath her. The warmth of him and the flex of his muscles seemed to ease her stiff, sore body.

As they rode along the ridge, Jim told Rosie how he'd searched for her the day before, up and down the river bank for hours, until it was too dark to see. His face clouded as he re-lived his sickening panic at seeing Rosie taken by the river.

'I thought you were dead,' he said, so softly Rosie could hardly hear him. 'But then my dogs seemed to get on a scent and I knew. I knew you were up at the hut.'

'Thank God for the dogs and horses. I'd still be out there, lost or drowned, if it wasn't for them.'

Rosie shivered as a vision of the swirling floodwaters flashed through her mind. Jim pulled his horse up and looked at her.

'I can still hardly believe you're real. But it's okay now,' he said. 'We're both here. Together.'

'It's the same for me,' said Rosie. 'I thought you were drowned too. It's made me realise . . . well, it's made me realise life's too short.'

Jim leant over on his horse, shut his eyes and kissed her.

At the top of the ridge they pulled their horses to a halt, checking the river levels in the valley below. The swamp area, where cattle once grazed, was now completely underwater. The floodwaters reflected the greyness of the sky. In the distance they could see the swollen river. It had escaped the sturdy red gums that normally flanked it like sentinels and was running riot.

'Not a hope in hell of crossing that,' said Jim, casting his eye over the awesome sight of the flood. 'We might as well turn back to the hut. We've got enough tucker for a few days. We'll just have to sit it out.'

'It's funny, but I really had hoped the flood was this bad. I don't want to go back, Jim. I want to stay out here forever.'

'We might have to. It doesn't look like your mum's done anything. Do you think she's okay?'

Rosie shrugged, not wanting to think about her family.

'I hope so,' she said. Then she remembered Dixie, shut in the stable with her pups, and Jim's old dog who needed special soft food because he now had only worn-down stubs for teeth. She imagined poor Dixie, her thin frame getting thinner as the pups sucked her dry, and old Bones trying hopelessly to bite through the old sheep hocks that lay about the yard. At least Sassy and Morrison would be okay out in the horse paddock with plenty of feed and shelter.

'If you're fretting about the dogs, don't. They'll be fine,' Jim said, reading her mind. 'Dogs are tougher than you think. And ingenious. They'll figure it out.'

Jim tethered Oakwood and his mare in a clearing near the hut so they could graze on the native grasses. Rosie went to boil the billy. She filled the blackened kettle from an old 44-gallon drum that was set to catch run-off from the roof. Beside the campfire, she sat back on her heels and looked up at the low grey sky. She shut her eyes and breathed out slowly.

'What is it?' Jim asked.

'Wouldn't it be nice to live up here? Just you and me.'

'And the dogs and horses,' Jim added.

'Of course and the dogs and horses,' she said, throwing the driest gum leaves she could find onto the fire.

'Could you really handle it?' asked Jim, dragging a log of wood over for them to sit on.

'With you, I could handle anything.'

He stooped down next to her and kissed her lingeringly. I really could stay up here forever, Rosie thought dreamily. Live the simple life, like Jack Gleeson. A life full of hard work, horses, dogs and stock. A life lived out in the bush with the simple things to bring joy, like rain and sunsets and birds and the antics of animals.

When Jim broke away from their kiss he shook his head ruefully.

'I'm not sure your family would be too pleased about it, though.'

By the next afternoon the flood had subsided and the roar of the river had calmed. At the crossing the rocks were covered in sticks and grasses where the water had sunk away. Oakwood snorted at the edge, and Rosie felt his body tense beneath her, but at her urging he stepped into the water and carried her across to the other side. They rode on in silence along the track, splashing through pools of water that lay trapped in the dips and sinking into mud in the gateways. The dogs trotted behind, hollow and hungry from their days away.

Jim, Rosie and the dogs had gone nearly three days without

a proper meal. They'd found a few tins of peas and carrots and baked beans in the hut and combined them with Jim's Cup-a-Soups. By this time all of their stomachs had started to rumble, and they had laughed at the strange chorus they created in the hut.

'Symphony of hunger,' Jim had called it as he poured hot water on the last packet of Cup-a-Soup to share between them.

Jim and Rosie had cast their eyes out across the river regularly, looking for CFA members who might be searching for them. They had turned their faces to the skies to look for helicopters and stood still, listening for four-wheel-drive engines. But none had come. Rosie had begun to worry about her mother. Had she taken too many of those tablets that lay beside her bed? As they rode on towards home, Rosie began to fear the worst.

She squinted ahead in the distance.

'What's that?'

Jim followed her gaze.

'Looks like your dad's ute.'

As they got closer to it, Margaret jumped out and began to run towards them. The dogs bolted over to her, barking and wagging their tails.

'Oh, thank God! Thank God!' she said. 'I thought something terrible had happened! I didn't know what to do!'

Rosie got down from Oakwood and Margaret hugged her tightly. Then she turned to Jim.

'Oh, thank you! Thank you so much for bringing her home safe to me. I was so worried.'

'Mum,' Rosie said, trying to calm her, 'what are you doing out here anyway?'

Margaret turned red. 'I got your note very late. I slept, you see, right through until dark. I thought I'd wait for you, that you'd be home by morning. But when you hadn't got back by lunch, I thought I'd better come looking for you.'

'Why didn't you call someone to help you look?'

Margaret shook her head. She said quietly, 'I didn't want anyone to know Gerald had left me.'

Rosie cast her a dark look. 'For God's sake, Mum, we almost drowned!'

'I know! I know how stupid I've been! I put you at risk because of my bloody pride! Rosie, I'm so, so sorry!' She hugged her again. 'I've realised.'

'Hang on a minute,' Rosie said, prising her off. 'What are you still doing out here?'

'Come with me,' Margaret said, turning and walking back towards the ute.

As they neared the ute, Jim let out a laugh. 'You did a proper job of that, Mrs Highgrove-Jones!'

It was as if the back end of the ute was being swallowed up by the earth.

'Bogged, to kingdom come,' Margaret said. 'And when I got so cold last night I started it up to put the heater on, but then I ran out of petrol.'

'I doubt it,' said Rosie tiredly.

'What?'

'It's a diesel.'

'Oh. But it was awful in the cold, and it was dark too, so I put the lights on.'

'So now the battery's flat too?' Rosie asked. Margaret nodded. 'Then why didn't you just walk home?'

Margaret shut her eyes for a moment, then looked down at her muddy tennis shoes.

'I was lost.'

'You were lost on your own property!' laughed Rosie. 'That's bloody hilarious!'

A small smile crept onto Margaret's face. 'I did find some peppermints in the glovebox.'

'That would make all of us very hungry then,' said Jim, swinging out of the saddle. 'Let's give you a bunk up on to Rosie's horse and let's get home.'

Rosie climbed back onto Oakwood and waited while Jim

helped hoist Margaret up behind her. Rosie felt her mother's arms clasp around her waist. A few days ago she would have been angered by her touch. Now, after nearly drowning in the river, she felt differently. As Jim swung onto his mare's back, Margaret turned to him.

'Thank you so, so much, Jim. You've gone above and beyond the call of duty, you really have. I'll make sure you're paid a generous bonus, or you can take some time off in lieu for your trouble.'

Rosie saw a cloud pass over Jim's face as he kicked his mare on towards home without saying another word.

Jim rode into the yards looking surly, barely smiling as old Lazy Bones waddled out barking a greeting. He swung off his horse and landed solidly on the flagstones, then helped Margaret to scramble down from Oakwood.

'Let's get showered and warm, then I'll fix us something hot to eat,' Margaret said to Rosie. 'Jim, you're very welcome to join us if you like.'

He nodded to her as she walked away.

Rosie hitched Oakwood to a rail and followed Jim inside and into Dixie's stall. The pups scrabbled at Jim's feet, yapping and wagging their little tails. Their eyes were now fully open and were a pretty marbled blue. Dixie was overwhelmed to see Jim and Rosie. She put her paws up on Rosie's hip and licked at her hands, whining and bouncing on her hind legs in the stale-smelling straw. At least she'd had water, but Rosie was worried about the lack of calcium for the lactating bitch.

'We ought to get her a special meal of milk and eggs,' she said to Jim, trying to search out his eyes.

'Fine,' he said and walked past her. 'I'd better get the horses fed.'

Rosie followed him, watching his broad hands stir the rich-smelling horse feed in a bucket. His face was stern and the muscles in his jaws were clenched.

'Jim, what's the matter?' Rosie asked.

'I'm fine.'

'No! You're not. Tell me what's wrong.'

Jim flashed an angry look at her.

'Didn't you see how she treated me?'

'Who? Mum? Oh, don't be silly.' Rosie waved her hand. 'That's just her. She's like that with everyone. Don't worry about it.' She put her hand on Jim's arm. 'We'll tell her what's happened between us. She doesn't even know yet. Then she'll be fine.'

Jim shook his head. 'Maybe I should find work on another place?'

Rosie frowned. 'Don't be daft. How can you say that? Besides, I need you! How am I supposed to run this place with both Gerald and Julian away? I *need* you, Jim. In more ways than one.' She pulled him to her and reached up to kiss him. 'Don't the last few days count for something?'

Jim looked down at her. 'Sure they do,' and he held her tightly. 'I'm sorry, Rosie. I'll get over it. You go feed your dogs and I'll meet you inside for some of your mam's famous cooking.'

'You're a legend, Jim Mahony,' Rosie said, with another quick kiss. She had almost said 'I love you', but something stopped her. Maybe it was too soon for him? But Rosie knew that's just what she felt for Jim – total, undying love.

Ballarook station, 1871

Mary no longer came to teach the station children. Word was out that her father had banned all his daughters from Ballarook, after he'd learned of Jack and Mary's courting. Even Jack's friend Mark Tully had rolled his swag and gone, taking his good dogs with him. The week after he left, Kelpie at last came on with her second heat. Instead of being joined to Mark's dog, as they'd planned, she was now shut up in the bitches' box, and miserable.

The station owner had put Jack in charge of the livestock and men at Ballarook. Jack spent long days debating whether he should confront Launcelot Ryan again on the matter of his daughter. But each night

Jack came home exhausted, dusty and sunburnt, and in no frame of mind to go anywhere near Ryan. His animals were in the same sorry state from the work and the heat. The leathery pads on the dogs' paws were split from walking on mile upon mile of rocky ground. And they limped, lame from the sharp pricks of burrs. Some days, old Idle just lay on the verandah and refused to come to work. Even Kelpie was looking ribby and gaunt, despite the scraps Jack saved for her from his own plate.

The late afternoon was still sizzling hot as the sun set below the horizon. At the bore, Jack pulled off his dusty shirt and hauled up a bucket of water. It was laden with minerals and had an unpleasant smell about it, but Jack sloshed it over himself and savoured the coolness of the water. He rubbed a rough cake of soap over his body.

'Don't forget behind your ears,' called toothless Cookie as he ambled from the meat shed with a leg of mutton slung over his shoulder.

Jack was just rinsing off when he heard hoofbeats approaching. He swung about to see Mary cantering her black pony towards him, but his smile faded when he saw anguish on her face. The pony propped at the well and Mary slid down from the saddle. She ran to him and put her arms about his neck, her cheek on his wet chest.

'Hey, hey. What's all this about?' comforted Jack as he held her at arm's length and bent to see her face properly. He saw that her eyes were red from crying.

'Oh, Jack. It's all gone through. The bullock dray's packed and Ma's sweeping out the house.'

'What are you on about?'

'My da. He's sold up . . . all three places.'

'Sold?'

'He's got it in his head he wants a grander run. And now we're going. Leaving first thing. I had to come see you. Despite what he says.'

Jack frowned. 'Leaving? For where?'

'We're headed up the Bygoo way – he's bought a place there. A property called Wallandool.'

'Doesn't he know that his stock will be dyin' of thirst in country such as that? I've heard tell the Mirool will not always flow and it has conned many a grazier.' Jack pulled her to him and held her close. 'But whatever your old man's choice, I won't be kept from you, Mary Ryan. I'll follow you.'

'But my da –'

'I'll be following you as soon as I can, Mary. I promise.'

Mary reached up and touched his freshly scrubbed cheek. Then, standing on tiptoes, she kissed him and ran her fingers through his wet hair.

'I love you, Jack Gleeson,' she said.

Twenty-five

Rosie scooped up another lamb and hooked its spindly legs into the metal bars of the cradle. Gently, she clamped it down and spun the cradle round. With practised hands she clipped a small 'v' from the lamb's ear, apologising as she did it, then scratched the scabby-mouth vaccination fluid over its skin. Next, she took up the vaccinating needle and pierced it through short wool and into tough skin. She moved on to the next lamb. Across from her Jim worked in silence, docking the lambs' tails with the hissing gas knives, then picking up his knife from the disinfectant to slice the small sacs of the ram lambs.

Rosie and Jim had their hats jammed on and collars upturned against the biting wind. Too focused to speak, they worked quickly in the hope of finishing the lamb marking early. The lambs clustered in the pen bleated endlessly for their mothers, and when Rosie lay down to sleep at night, she could still hear them. It was the third mob they'd marked this week. She felt her shoulder muscle spasm as she picked up yet another fat lamb. But she was slowly getting used to the hard physical work, the sudden, fine sprays of blood that shot from tails and ears, and the cries of pain from the lambs.

'I know it looks gory, but it's good for them in the long

run,' Jim had said when he first showed her how to mark a lamb, and Rosie had turned pale and winced. 'The alternative to this is much, much worse,' he'd continued. 'In a day or two, they'll be back, galloping about like silly buggers. You'll see.'

Rosie had seen lamb marking before, but had never done it. At first the feeling of metal slicing through skin and cartilage was sickening, but now, after marking over two thousand lambs, it felt routine. And she knew it was essential.

Fencing had become routine too. She and Jim spent days beside the river, re-fencing after the flood. Rosie's hands cramped as she slammed the post rammer's metal sleeve over steel fencing droppers and pulled the wire tight in a twitch. Sweat crept down her spine as she lugged logs off fencelines and chainsawed tree trunks.

Then at night, in Gerald's office, she'd tackle the books. Her eyes were so tired she found herself not following the cash-book lines. She'd write down a drenches and dips expense in the repairs and maintenance column. Then she'd add the GST instead of subtract. At these times her anger at Gerald would rise again, but she knew the farm's sorry state wasn't all his doing. She had to count her blessings, she reminded herself. This was what she'd wished for, after all. She thought back to the day she'd last seen Gerald.

Rosie and Julian had driven down to the Peninsula for a family meeting at Giddy's cottage, not long after the flood. Gerald sat in a chair by the small fire that ate up grey driftwood with crackling orange flames, while Giddy placed a tray of herbal teas on the Balinese table. When Rosie looked at Gerald, he seemed like a different person. He was no longer stiff and neat. Instead he wore ordinary jeans and a poloneck jumper the colour of sand. His feet were bare, and on his lap Giddy's black cat purred steadily.

'Thanks for coming to see us,' he said a little awkwardly. Rosie glanced at Julian, his cheeks flushed pink from the warmth of the room. He looked different too. His hair almost reached his shoulders and he looked more filled-out and somehow happier. Giddy came to perch on the arm of Gerald's chair and crossed her slim legs.

'I know this must be a shock for you both,' Gerald said, 'seeing me here with Giddy.' He put a hand on hers. 'But we've loved each other for years. I'm sorry we hid it from you for so long.'

Rosie shifted uncomfortably in her seat while Julian reached for his mug of tea.

'We never wanted to hurt your mother,' Giddy added.

Rosie wished Jim was with her now, but he'd stayed behind on the farm, insisting that it wasn't his business to come . . . and besides, there were the animals to care for.

And of course, there was Margaret. Since the scare of losing Rosie in the flood, she was no longer sloshing down alcohol or slinging back tablets, but she was as fragile as a china doll. Jim opted to stay.

'Mum?' Rosie had said cautiously to her. 'I'm going to see Gerald.' She paused, wondering how her mother would take the news. Then she added the sting. 'At Giddy's.' Instead of collapsing into hysteria, as Rosie had expected, Margaret just nodded and remained silent.

When it was time to leave, Rosie stood beside the Pajero as her mother walked towards her with a crumpled look on her face. Rosie felt her mother's pain. She knew Margaret was terrified of what the meeting would bring. That she might lose the house in which she had spent most of her adult life. And the pain of knowing Rosie was going to the place where Giddy and Gerald now lived, *together. Happily*.

'Drive safely,' was all Margaret managed to say.

Now in Giddy's cottage, Rosie swallowed nervously. She was waiting for Gerald to tell them he was going to sell the farm. He leant forward in his chair.

'Now, I'm going to be as clear as I can. I'm sorry if I sound cruel. But I have no intention of going back to Highgrove . . .

or your mother. Ever. I know that will come as a shock, but I've lived a lie for too long.' He cleared his throat.

'Therefore, I think . . . sorry,' he looked up at Giddy and squeezed her hand, '*we* think it's best if I transfer ownership of Highgrove over to you two.'

Rosie and Julian blinked, barely believing what they'd just heard.

'You're *giving* us the farm?' Rosie asked at last.

Gerald nodded. 'As long as you look after your mother. The farm needs to support her too. And, if the finances will stretch that far, I'd like to take a modest annual allowance from it.'

Julian and Rosie were speechless. Everything they had ever believed about Gerald as a father, a farmer, and their mother's husband, no longer applied. They both stared at him as he sat there holding hands with their aunt. Julian let out a breath.

'Well? What do you think?' prompted Giddy.

'But, but . . .' stammered Rosie. 'Shouldn't Julian get it all? I mean, you know . . . since I'm not your . . . your real daughter.'

'Oh, Rosie,' Gerald said. 'I'm not proud of how I've behaved in the past. But you must know I was never angry at *you*. I was angry at *everything*. My life was one big lie, but I was always too gutless to change it.'

'But you've never –' Rosie protested, but Gerald held up his hand.

'I don't know how I can convince you to believe me, but I promise you, from this moment I'm going to be someone you *can* rely on. I know I can rely on you. Julian told me how we nearly lost you in the flood. I'm so very sorry I left you and Jim in that mess.'

'I saved all your breeding cows for you,' Rosie said, trying not to let bitterness into her voice.

'I know you did. Julian said how brave you've been and how you're running the farm like clockwork. I'm so proud of you, and so grateful.' Gerald paused, tears gathering in his eyes. 'And so ashamed. I kept you from the farm because of my own stupid anger. Giddy's shown me that. I'm so sorry, Rosie. I love you as my own. I do. Nearly losing you has made me see that.'

Rosie sat back, tears pricking behind her eyes. Giddy smiled gently.

'And what about you, Julian? How do you feel about your father's decision to split Highgrove between you and Rosie? Do you think you ought to inherit it all?'

'No! God, no!' Julian said, suddenly jumping to attention. 'It's just, it's such a shock. All of it. You know, a change of mindset. I'm happy for Rosie to be included, really I am. But to be honest . . .' Julian winced. 'I don't think I'm ready to come home yet.'

'That's fine,' said Gerald. 'Take all the time you need to make a decision. I know I've put too much pressure on you in the past. Take your time. That's if it's okay with Rosie? You and Jim have got things in hand, haven't you? If you're happy to run the place it will buy us all some time to settle into the idea. What do you think? Want to take it on, Rosie?'

Rosie nodded, smiling, as the prospect of running Highgrove raised goosebumps of fear and excitement on her skin.

When Rosie got back to Highgrove, Jim was standing in the courtyard in his faded work clothes. He put his arms around her and held her to his chest. She breathed in the smell of him and felt his solid muscles under her hands.

'I missed you,' Rosie said.

'You were only gone one night,' he said with a smile.

'Still . . .' She'd put off telling him the news over the phone, though she was dying to share it with him.

'So, how did it all go? When do we have to move out?' Rosie looked down at the ground and paused for dramatic effect.

'*Never*!' she said gleefully. 'He's not going to sell it! He's handing it on to Jules and me!'

She jumped up and down in front of him, holding his hands. Jim hugged and kissed her, but soon held her still and looked at her with a serious expression.

'Are you sure you want to take it on? It's a big, big job. Farming can break some people. And it's not as if he's handing it to you with healthy books, healthy soils and foot-high pastures.'

Rosie looked into Jim's eyes.

'Of course I'm sure. With you here, of course I'm sure.'

'So what work have you got for me today?' Jim asked.

'Can't we just go to bed for a little while? I've had a long, tiring drive,' Rosie said innocently, running her hand under his shirt and stroking his flat, smooth stomach.

'Not on your life!' he said, pulling her hand away. 'There's too much to be done.'

'Okay,' she agreed a little sulkily. 'But promise me you'll take me to the pub tonight?'

'Sorry, no deal there either,' Jim said. 'We have to get this place on track. And don't forget your promise to Duncan. He'll be wanting those articles for the newspaper soon. You'll have research to do at nights. And the farm during the day. So we won't have time for pubs. Just work and research.'

'Can't I just research you?' Her hand slid around into the warm curve of his lower back and her fingertips began to stray beneath his jeans. Again he held her at arm's length.

'Work,' he said firmly.

'Oh, you're such a tough boss,' she said.

Jim flashed her another serious look.

'No, Rosie. You're the boss now. You need to learn to be responsible. Work hard now. Play later.'

Rosie knew he was right. She probably *had* been spoilt by her upbringing. Now there was real work to do. Backbreaking, soul-destroying work as crops failed, or red-legged earthmites decimated pastures, or wool prices fell to half of what they had been the year before. She wasn't just playing at farming any more.

'Yes. Yes, I know. Thank you,' she said. 'But first, I need to go and tell Mum about the meeting. Then I'll meet you in the machinery shed.'

Rosie knocked gently on her mother's door, and pushed it open. Her mother had all her 'after five' clothes out of the cupboard. Silk skirts and satin dresses clustered colourfully together on her bed.

'You're back,' Margaret said, looking up as she folded a fur coat and put it into a garbage bag.

'What are you doing?'

'I'm taking them all to Melbourne to sell next week. I figured if we have to move, I won't have room for them. And besides, we need the money.'

'You don't need to overreact.'

'No,' Margaret said, 'I'm not. It's time I started to live sensibly. So, how was he?'

'Great.'

'Really?' said Margaret, hurt.

'Well, what am I supposed to say, Mum? That he looks shocking? He looks just fine.'

'I see. And when is he putting this place on the market?'

Rosie moved over to her mother and took a dress out of her hands so that she'd calm down and listen.

'He's not.'

'What? Oh, so I have to move so he and Giddy can come and live here?' Her cheeks were red and tears rose to her eyes.

'No, Mum! Stop being a drama queen. He's handing the whole lot over to Julian and me . . . on the condition that we support you.' Margaret's mouth dropped open.

'But you have to knuckle down,' Rosie said, pointing a finger at her. 'I'm not going to keep you in the manner you've been accustomed to. From now on, Julian and I are calling the shots.'

'Does that mean I can stay here?' Margaret asked breathlessly.

'Yes . . . but I'd still advise you to sell your clothes, and mine along with them. I've seen the books and we're up the creek. We could lose the lot if we don't make some changes.'

'Of course,' Margaret said, almost collapsing with relief at Gerald's decision.

'Listen, you have to promise me you're going to be really responsible with money from now on.'

'Yes. Yes, of course I will. I'll be sober and sensible from now on.' Then a smile played on her lips. 'But I can't promise you that I still won't get the urge to cut his balls off.'

'That's fine, Mum,' Rosie said, starting to laugh. 'You can deal with that urge any time you like. Just don't involve me.'

Now, months later, here Rosie was splattered in lamb's blood, tired but happy after marking the last lamb. She and Jim were towing the portable yards back towards the homestead, looking forward to a hot drink and some food. Rosie knew how lucky she was to be living her dream. She looked over to Jim as she drove and smiled at him. He'd been so wonderful. He never stepped in and took over. But he was always there, sharing the load, helping, advising and cajoling her, making her laugh, flirting with her, kissing away her frowns.

She loved the nights with him. He'd take her hands and bend over them, pulling out thistles and putting bandaids on her blisters. In the quarters they'd cook up toasted sandwiches, swig on beer, and talk into the night. But perhaps their best times of all were when they trained the pups. They were five months old now and Rosie had decided to keep the whole litter and sell them later as started dogs. She thought back to the very first lesson Jim had given her in training the tiny tearaway puppies.

'But they're so little,' she'd said as she fastened a red collar around the neck of one puppy.

'Pups are never too young for training, Rosie. You need to give them a good foundation of obedience first before you even let them see a sheep,' Jim had said, squatting down and putting a collar on another.

'But I don't even know where to start!'

'Well, names would be good. You can't teach a pack of dogs to respond to commands individually if they don't have their own names.'

'Mmmm. Names? All right, let's think of some. But none of this Bono or Bjork stuff, okay?'

'Don't be getting pernickety with me about my naming skills.'

'Pernickety? What sort of a word is that? You Irish with your funny words and names! If only you could spell your names how they sound . . . I mean, it's ridiculous! Look how you spell names like Siobhan and Grainne. How's a normal person supposed to work out how to say them?'

They fell silent for a time, thinking.

'I know!' Rosie said suddenly. 'I could name them after the famous dogs descended from Gleeson's Kelpie! The ones I've been reading about.'

She ran into the quarters and came back with a piece of paper, tracing her fingers along the lineage.

'The two females could be Sally and Jess. And for the three males, what about Clyde, and Coil and –'

'Chester!' added Jim.

'Perfect!' said Rosie.

And so the pups were named.

Twenty-six

Driving into the courtyard after a morning spent checking the newly-marked lambs, Rosie heard the loud bell of the phone echoing around the walls. Her mother appeared from the direction of the vegetable garden with a large armful of spinach.

'I'll get it,' Rosie called as she kicked off her boots and ran inside the house.

She picked up the phone. 'Hello?'

'Rosie?' came her brother's voice on the other end of the line.

'Julian, hi! How are you?'

'I'm so sorry I haven't got back to you sooner to find out how things are going there. I've been trying to work things out this end.'

'That's okay. Jim and I are doing fine.'

'Good. I'm planning a visit, so I can help you out with anything that's going,' he said.

'Great! What's the trip for?'

'I guess I want to see if the place feels different now Dad's not there.'

'Oh, it does. Believe me, it does. When are you coming?'

'Tomorrow okay?'

'You just missed out on lamb marking.'

'Damn!'

'Knew you'd be disappointed.'

'Can you tell Mum I'm on my way? And I'm bringing a friend.'

'Aha!' sang Rosie. 'A *friend*, eh?'

'See you tomorrow,' Julian said with a smile in his voice.

When Rosie delivered the news, Margaret tossed down the spinach and clapped her hands together.

'And a *friend* too!' she said in delight. 'I'll have to get cooking!'

'Don't go overboard,' Rosie cautioned, thinking of her mother's overspending and the long wait until the next lot of farm income was due. She'd made a point of getting her mother involved in the book-keeping and it seemed to be working so far.

'Don't worry,' Margaret said. 'No trips to town. It'll be all home-grown.'

'Thanks, Mum,' Rosie said gratefully before turning away.

'How about a nice meal tonight?' Margaret said almost urgently. 'Will Jim join us for dinner?'

Rosie sighed. How long would this pretence go on? Her mother knew she spent her nights in the quarters with Jim. Yet she wouldn't speak about it openly. And she still wouldn't be drawn on the subject of Rosie's father. Rosie conceded that her mother had been a lot better since almost losing her daughter in the flood, but she still clung to the hope that Gerald would come home and life would return to her form of normal. And Margaret's form of normal did not include a relationship between her daughter and a stockman. Still, she said little, aside from the odd, pointed question such as 'Is he really your type?' or 'Does he plan to stay long in the job?'. Rosie was torn between her mother's loneliness and her own burning need to be with Jim.

'Sorry, Mum. Jim and I are really tired. We've had a big few days. We'll just have some toasted sandwiches in the quarters and we'll see you in the morning.'

'Oh,' was all Margaret said.

* * *

Late the next day, Margaret and Rosie were installing a cash-book program on the computer when they heard a truck lumbering up the hillside. Jim heard it too and came out of the workshop to see a vehicle roll through the garden gates and pull up with a hiss of airbrakes. On the side of the truck, in large letters, were the words 'Trees to Please . . . reclaiming land for our native environment'.

Rosie and Margaret stepped down from the verandah onto the drive. Tumbling out of the cab came Julian, tanned and slim, wearing baggy khaki clothes and thin strips of black leather about his neck and wrist. His hair was streaked blond. He wore lace-up bushwalking boots and a broad grin. His collie leapt down from the cab before he slammed the door shut. A short, black-haired man sprang down from the driver's side. He was wearing the same khaki uniform as Julian.

'Crikey!' said Rosie to Julian. 'You look like the Croc Hunter!' Then she flung her arms about him. 'Welcome home!'

Margaret also hugged him warmly. Julian indicated the man standing beside him.

'This is my partner, Evan. Evan, my sister, Rosie, and my mum, Margaret.'

'Great to meet you both,' Evan said, shaking their hands, the skin around his brown eyes creased in a smile.

'And this must be Jim,' said Julian as he stepped forward and shook Jim's hand. 'Heard a fair bit about you.'

'Indeed you would've,' Jim said.

'Ha!' exclaimed Evan. 'You sound just like Dougall off that *Father Ted* show!'

'Only hopefully not as thick,' replied Jim.

'I don't know about that,' said Rosie teasingly and Jim gave her a shove. 'What's with the truck?' she asked.

'It's Evan's business. I've been working with him on regeneration projects.'

'It's a government and private cooperative,' Evan explained. 'We protect inner-city wildlife and re-establish natural habitat for them.'

'And we control feral animals.'

'Can you do anything about Jim? He's not native . . . so that would make him feral. Eh, Mum?'

But Margaret wasn't paying attention to their conversation. She was still stuck on Julian's introduction of Evan.

'So you said you're in partnership with Evan?' she asked, trying to sound chirpy.

'Um, well, we're not business partners,' Evan explained.

'But we are *partners*,' Julian added, moving closer to Evan.

'Oh. I see,' said Margaret, turning pale.

There was an awkward silence until Jim said, too loudly, 'Right then,' and clapped his hand on Julian's back. 'How about a drink at the pub? Rosie's keen, I'm sure. Are we all in?'

'Crikey!' Rosie said again, taking in her brother's news. She felt a warm sensation rush over her. She'd always known there was something different about Julian, ever since they were children. It finally all fell into place. And after everything that had happened in her family, this turn of events seemed minor. In fact, it was something to celebrate.

'Mum, we'll take your car,' she said. 'Come on, Evan. I'll look after you.' Then she lowered her voice as she steered him away. 'Beware. She can bite.'

As they stepped into the hotel's warmth, James Dean came out from behind the bar and took a swirling, theatrical bow.

'Welcome, welcome, *welcome*, friends and family of long-lost Rosie!'

'What *are* you on?' Rosie asked.

'Just practising for the Oscars,' he said. Then he flamboyantly extended his arm towards the bar.

'More like practising for a job on *Sale of the Century*,' Rosie grinned.

'James Dean at your service, madam,' he said elegantly to Margaret. 'You are beautiful enough to be Rosie's mother.' He helped Margaret up onto the bar stool. Then, leaping over the bar, he poured a scotch on the rocks and presented it to her with a flourish, and reached over to shake hands enthusiastically with Julian and Evan.

'Any friends of Rosie and Jim are friends of mine,' he said warmly. 'And now, trusty boozers, you must meet the lovely, large-bosomed Princess Amanda.' He flung open the swinging door to the kitchen and the smell of sizzling steak drifted into the bar.

'Mands! Come and meet Rosie's rellies,' he yelled in his own ocker voice. Amanda emerged, grinning, with a book tucked under her arm.

'Oh hi, guys! God, Rosie, we haven't seen you for ages. Must be busy on the farm.' Then she remembered what she was carrying and held up the book, *Puppetry of the Penis*.

'Look what I found in the outside dunny!'

A few drinkers looked over and whooped in delight. James Dean held up his hands as if surrendering.

'If I'm to crack the big time in entertainment, I need to be multiskilled. It's good to have a wide repertoire.'

Amanda put the book down in front of Rosie.

'Check out the "KFC", Rosie. You'll never eat chicken again!'

Listening, Margaret tipped her scotch back with conviction.

'That'll tickle your bits,' James Dean said, setting her up with another scotch straight away, then darting up and down the bar pulling beers for the boys and sloshing together a rum and Coke for Rosie. As she smudged the condensation from the chilled glass, Rosie sensed most of the girls were staring at them, stunned to see Sam's ex and Mrs Highgrove-Jones at the bar. No one approached them. The girls stared at Evan and Julian too, but it was Jim and Rosie their eyes settled upon. Rosie felt her cheeks burn red. She wondered what they were thinking. Did they think it was too soon after Sam for her to be out with someone else? She tipped back her rum. Stuff them, she thought ruefully.

Because it was a long weekend, the pub was unusually full

and a raucous crowd was already primed by an afternoon of drinking. Lee Kernaghan tunes were belting out from the jukebox and a group of shearers were clustered about the pool table, swilling beer and taking haphazard shots at the black. Rosie recognised a few of them as former Highgrove station regulars. They watched Margaret with amazement as she perched at the bar with her handbag in the crook of her arm and a scotch in her hand. Her eyes darted to them warily and she shifted her weight so she had her back to them. She began to ask Evan the questions that had been burning inside her during their drive to town.

'So,' she asked, 'how did you meet my son?'

Rosie and Jim leant forward to hear Evan's answer.

He pulled up a stool and sat beside Margaret.

'With all due respect, Margaret, before you sentence me, I'll have you know you're not a patch on my Italian grandparents! Wait till you meet my nonna,' he said warmly. He put on the voice of an old lady and began gesticulating wildly.

'Evan! Why you not married? There is good Italian girls about here, no? You beautiful boy. You need wife!' He grabbed his own cheeks and pinched them.

Rosie laughed. Cute *and* funny, she thought.

'Jules and I were in the same class at school. We were friends. Good friends. But nothing . . . you know. I took care of him, country bumpkin that he is, shielded him a bit. You probably know he found boarding school hard at times. Then when I met up with him again in Melbourne recently, I finally figured out that . . . that we're meant to be together.' Evan's deep brown eyes smiled into Margaret's. 'And we got together. And he became involved in my family business. And your son, well, he's perfect.'

Margaret nodded and smiled.

'I know he's perfect. He's my boy.' She looked at Julian, reached out and squeezed his hand. 'And I've never seen him look happier.' She turned back to the bar and held up her glass. 'Now where's that barman? Goodness me, he's slack.'

Rosie and Julian looked at one another and pulled 'Can you believe it?' faces. After all that had happened, maybe her mother was finally letting go, thought Rosie. She looked up into Jim's eyes and smiled. Then she stood on her tiptoes and kissed him on the cheek.

'Your shout,' she said.

Just then, Dubbo burst through the door of the pub with a group of Sam's old mates. His eyes scanned the crowd and fell on Rosie.

'Hi!' he said enthusiastically, walking up to her. 'Great to see you out and about. You look well!' He gave her a warm kiss on her cheek and squeezed her arm. 'Bottom pub's just closed, so we thought we'd rock up here.'

Dubbo looked at Jim with a quick nod of acknowledgement. He'd been drinking, Rosie thought. His eyes were shining yet he seemed lost without Sam by his side, egging him on to be the larrikin. He had lost a lot of weight in the months since the accident.

'Have you still got a pup for me?' Dubbo asked.

'What are you after?' Rosie asked.

'An all-rounder.'

'They all say that,' said Jim to Rosie. Dubbo glanced at him.

'All right. One that's more paddocky.'

'I've got one for you,' said Rosie. 'But for the right price.'

'What happened to giving me one? They're Sam's pups, after all.'

Rosie felt the sting of his comment, but before she could retaliate her mother was cutting in, drunk already.

'David, darling!' She kissed him on both cheeks.

'Mrs Highgrove-Jones?' Dubbo was stunned to see her there. 'Having a night on the town with Rosie and your stockman, are you?'

'Yes! And Julian's home again. Have you met Jim Mahony? He's our manager, alongside Rosie, that is. And have you met Evan, my son's . . . Evan, my . . . Evan,' she finished unsteadily.

Evan nodded at Dubbo.

'I've not met Jim, but I've heard all about him,' Dubbo said.

Dubbo and Jim were the same height, but Jim was fitter and stronger. As they shook hands, an image of two male dogs growling with their hackles spiked flashed into Rosie's mind.

'Jim's absolutely rescued our Rosie,' Margaret continued. 'We're so grateful. He's kept the farm going these past few months, haven't you, Jim?'

'Is that so?' said Dubbo suspiciously.

'Well, Rosie's put in the hard yards too. She's a tough lass,' Jim said.

A red-faced, red-haired shearer suddenly came lurching over and put his arm round Margaret's shoulders.

'Hallo, Mrs H-J,' he said with boozy breath. 'Remember me?'

Margaret looked at him through narrowed eyes, her face showing no recognition at all.

'Carrots,' he said. 'Was a shearer on your place in the late seventies . . . up to 1980. Was with Billy O'Rourke's team before we all got the sack. Remember?' he asked again.

Margaret flinched and flushed red. 'Yes,' she said quietly. 'I remember.'

'That the daughter all grown up?' Carrots went on, nodding towards Rosie. 'She's a looker. She's a chip off the old block.' Then he began to laugh and dug a finger in her rib. 'Eh? Don't you think so, Margie darlin'?'

'Nice to see you again, Carrots,' said Margaret firmly, turning her back on him and sipping on her scotch, her cheeks still flame-red.

Jim put a hand on the shearer's broad back.

'Carrots!' he said warmly. 'How would you be? Looks like Damo's waiting for you to play your shot.' He nodded towards the pool table where the blokes were leaning on their cues and watching the exchange.

'Yeah, you're right,' said Carrots, ambling away.

My god, Rosie thought in horror, could that man be my

father? She downed her drink. When she turned around Jim and Dubbo both jumped in to offer her another. She held up her hands. Then she sighed, as if giving in. 'Yes, please. I'll have two drinks.'

It was nearly closing time. Dubbo, Margaret, Evan and Julian, Jim and Rosie had their arms slung about each other's necks as they sang Tania Kernaghan's 'Lasso You' at the top of their voices. They were all on the pub's tiny dance floor, hips swaying, pretending to swing their imaginary lassoes high above their heads.

'How's it feel to get wrangled?' Rosie sang, moving slinkily to the music. *'Heart's in a tangle.'*

Dubbo sidled up to her and put his hands on her slim hips, trying to look deep into her eyes. He was singing, *'I'm not going to hurt you, we'd be too good together.'*

Rosie politely tried to extricate herself from his grip, but Dubbo pulled her closer. She wrestled free from him and danced in front of Jim. *'This was bound to happen . . . you're too cute under your stetson.'* And Jim cast a smile at her that made her melt.

Singing 'Bup, bup' in deep baritones, Evan and Julian bounced up and down pretending to be backing singers as Margaret spun around in a drunken world of her own.

As Rosie sang the last line of the song loudly, *'My heart's made up its mind . . . lasso you'*, Dubbo again grabbed her and whirled her away from Jim.

'Let me go!' Rosie flashed Dubbo an angry look and tried to shake off his strong grip.

'You heard her,' yelled Jim.

The next thing Rosie knew, Jim had swung a punch. Dubbo's head snapped back as Jim's fist hit his cheek. Then Jim grabbed at Dubbo, pushing him into the tables and chairs, scattering people. The song ended and was replaced by a chant of 'Fight, fight, fight' from the crowd. Dubbo flew back at Jim and they grappled with each other, landing solidly on the floor.

'Stop it!' yelled Rosie.

Diving into the ruckus, James Dean, Evan and Julian prised the two men apart and told them to settle. Rosie cast Jim a hurt, angry glance, then turned and pushed her way through the crowd.

In the Ladies', Rosie leant her forehead against the mirror and shut her eyes for a moment. She felt so drunk. She opened her eyes again and saw her reflection. There she was in her Wrangler jeans, her tight, checked shirt that was highlighting her blue eyes, and her blonde hair no longer bobbed and neat but growing to her shoulders. She started to wonder about the girl in the mirror. Was that really her? Then she heard people coming in so she dashed into a cubicle and locked the door.

'Snobby cow actually turns out to be a slut,' said a girl's voice. 'Getting it on with the workman! Who'd have thought she'd be up for that?'

'Yeah. Maybe her mother's shagging the staff too? Gang bang with the gardener!' another slurred. Both girls giggled. Rosie heard the slam of a cubicle door as one of the girls went into the toilet next to her.

'Don't you miss him?' she said.

'Who?'

'Bloody Sam, you idiot. You could always count on getting one off him after a big night like this.'

'Huh? Oh, yeah. I wouldn't mind getting one off that stockman Miss Highclass-hyphen is on with. He's a looker, and have you heard his *voice*? Dee-licious! I'd do him.'

'He must do anyone if he's doing *her*.'

The toilet flushed, the taps ran for a moment, the door slammed and the girls' voices trailed away.

By the time Rosie went back out to the bar Amanda was pulling down the blinds and clearing away the glasses.

'Alas, dear patrons,' said James Dean as he stood on a chair, 'last drinks.'

He ducked for cover as the drinkers flung coasters at him.

'Princess Amanda needs her beauty sleep!' he called to them. 'And if you don't leave in the next ten minutes, I'll give you my own penis puppetry creation . . . new and innovative . . . yes, it's my interpretation of the half-shot possum!'

He began to mime undoing his fly, causing most of his patrons to run screaming from the pub in mock horror. Rosie walked out into the cold night air, holding back tears.

Twenty-seven

Too tense to sleep, Duncan Pellmet was watching the shopping channel and worrying about his burgeoning waistline. His wife had taken the all-in-one gym equipment, along with their fitball and Red, the Irish setter. At least she'd left Derek, Duncan mused, running his fingers over the Jack Russell's soft ears. Derek bared his teeth in response, annoyed at being disturbed. Duncan sighed. He couldn't decide which he missed more – his wife or the setter. He had recently seen both on the Gold Coast, at their daughter's graduation in Brisbane. His wife had looked bronzed, lean and lizard-like in a hibiscus print suit, her new man on her arm. The dog had looked fat.

When the phone rang, Duncan answered it full of hope. It might be his wife. Perhaps she wanted to come back? Instead, it was Rosie.

'Duncs . . . can you *please* rev up your phallic symbol and come down to the pub? We need a lift home. It's an emergency.'

'Rosie Jones,' said Duncan tiredly. 'Why would I want to do that?'

'Because my mum's here with me and she needs a gentleman like you to take her home.'

'Margaret Highgrove-Jones at the pub? Don't give me that, Rosie . . .'

Suddenly Margaret's voice was on the line.

'Duncan, darling,' she purred. 'Won't you please help a lady in distress?'

Duncan stood tall and sucked in his belly. 'I'll be right there, Margaret . . . you can count on me.'

Duncan's sports car idled nosily outside the pub, setting all the town dogs barking.

'It's a two-seater, you dork,' Julian said to Rosie. 'We can't all fit in there! I thought you said Duncan's car was long and huge.'

As they all peered into the car Carrots staggered up, put his big hand on the bonnet and proceeded to vomit into the gutter in the gleam of the headlights.

'Ah. I see why they call him Carrots,' said Julian.

'I assumed it was because of his red hair,' said Evan.

'Carrots all round,' Margaret said.

God. Please don't let him be my father, Rosie prayed. The night had started out so well, and now it was all falling to pieces. Jim stood nearby, his hands shoved deep in his pockets, a stern expression on his face. Rosie just wanted to get away from the crowd.

'Can't we all pile in?' she begged.

'I know,' Julian said. 'Duncan can drive the Pajero. We'll all fit in that.'

But before they knew it, Duncan had helped Margaret into the passenger seat of his car. Then, like a suave man from *Miami Vice*, he flicked his collar up and slid into the squelchy leather of the driver's seat. With a throb and a rev, they were gone into the night.

'Mum?' Rosie said, flabbergasted. She shivered in the cold night air. Part of her wished that Jim would put his arms around her, but she was still angry at him too. Dubbo was in the crowd outside the pub, glancing over at them every now and then, nursing his swelling eye.

'So now what?' Evan asked. 'Can't we get a taxi?'

'A taxi? In Casterton?' said Julian. 'There's only one cabbie in town and it's past his bedtime.'

'I don't know about you, but I'm going to bunk down at Ronnie Seymour's place,' said Jim. 'He's probably still up watching Austar. It's not luxury accommodation, by any stretch, but it'll do me. Not sure if it'll be up to standard for some.' Jim cast Rosie a look as if to imply it wouldn't suit her.

Rosie thought of the dingy old cottage she had visited with her mother that day, and the senile old man who lived there. She shivered in the cold. This was her only option, aside from following Dubbo to a party somewhere, and she didn't want to do that.

'Can we come with you?' Julian asked.

'Sure,' said Jim. 'It's up that way.'

Rosie began to walk. She was desperate to get away from the rowdy crowd hanging around outside the pub. She felt as if all the girls were talking about her, and she could sense Dubbo was psyching himself up to confront Jim again.

With Evan and Julian a little way behind them, Jim reached out for her hand.

'Are you still mad at me?' he asked.

'What was *with* you in there?'

'Come on, Rosie. It's a cultural thing. Get pissed and punch your mate, drink with him later. All my Irish mates do it!'

'You're far from Dubbo's mate, and you know it. He was being harmless. And I don't need you to defend me, anyway.'

'But he's a prize dickhead, the way he gets about.'

'There's no need to act like a bloody thug in public though!' Rosie said angrily.

'Ah, that's just the problem, isn't it?'

'What's the problem?'

'That we're in public. You're ashamed of me.'

Rosie stopped in her tracks, shocked. 'That's just not true!'

Jim shrugged, pulled his coat over his shoulders and strode off up the street, leaving Rosie to trail reluctantly behind.

* * *

'Hello?' Jim sang out in Ronnie Seymour's hallway. The sound of the greyhound racing replays greeted them and the television's cool blue light flickered on the walls.

In the chair in the corner of the room, Mr Seymour dozed. His cat sat on top of an old piano, looking at them with untrusting eyes. Julian, Evan and Rosie stood looking at the old man.

'Ronnie?' said Jim.

Mr Seymour's eyes shot open. He sat up in his chair and frowned at them. His wispy grey eyebrows were pulled down over his hazy reddened eyes. Then, in an instant, his posture changed.

'Ah, it's *you*, Jim,' he said, leaping up from his chair, his face no longer sagging. 'Had a big one at the pub and now you're too pissed to drive back to Highgrove, eh?'

Jim introduced Julian, Rosie and Evan.

'Nice to meet you all. But I believe I've met the pretty lass. A while back now.'

Rosie frowned at the old man, amazed to see him standing, let alone making sense. He smiled at her.

'Yes! I know. You were thinkin' I was a daft, senile, rude old man. I'm not actually daft and senile, but I'll agree, I am rude, and as for old . . . well I'm certainly that.' He looked at Rosie's questioning eyes.

'The senile act started out as a bit of a lark . . . it certainly sucked in the likes of your mother. Then I just kept it up. I wouldn't get my Meals on Wheels from 'em if I didn't act up a bit. Plus the more of the "old fool" act I give them, the more I get to hear what they really think of me. Silly old chooks. They think I'm as deaf as a post and nutty as a Picnic Bar.' He tapped at his head and gave a high-pitched, gleeful laugh. He strode over to the sideboard and pulled out a bottle of Tullamore Dew whisky.

'Sit yourselves down and we'll have a nip. But first I'll clean out the blessed kitty litter, it's giving me the shites. I was hoping one of the old chooks would be by to do it for me, but they've been thin on the ground this week,' he said with a wink.

Rosie sat on a sagging armchair and watched as Mr Seymour carried the kitty litter outside.

'Wow!' whispered Evan as he picked up a snow dome of Phar Lap and shook it. 'This place is so retro! Some of this stuff would sell for a mint in Melbourne!'

Mr Seymour returned and poured them all large glasses of whisky before settling back into his armchair. On the piano, the cat continued to crouch, watching them through narrowed eyes.

Mr Seymour raised his glass. He looked directly at Rosie. 'Jim tells me you're digging up the ghosts of history . . . tracking down the past of "Kelpie Jack".'

Rosie wondered what else Jim had told him about her.

'That's right,' she said politely. She looked around at the old photos and sketches of long-dead racehorses on the walls, and the stacks of yellowing newspapers on the floor. 'Maybe I should ask if *you* have any books or clippings on him?'

'Don't get him started,' Jim said.

Rosie didn't feel like talking about kelpies with Mr Seymour. She wanted to climb into bed with Jim and reassure him that she didn't care what the rest of the town thought.

'A bit of oral history would be good,' Rosie said dreamily, casting Jim a flirty look, which he ignored.

'Well,' Mr Seymour said, 'I can tell you all about the bloodlines, and which dogs were crossed with Jack's Kelpie to start the breed off.'

'Oh,' said Rosie, resigning herself, 'that's . . . great.'

Banks of the Murrumbidgee River, circa 1871

Jack urged Bailey on to a trot when he heard the lowing of cattle ahead on the track. Since leaving Ballarook, he had spent the days drifting north on his way to Mary at Wallandool. But when he heard that Mark Tully was looking for him, Jack turned his horse to the east. He knew Tully was in charge of a mob of drought cows and was grazing them alongside the Murrumbidgee.

Jack's skin prickled with excitement when he saw through the trees the black gelding with the white snip on its nose, and the mottled red hides of the cattle.

On the other side of the mob, Mark Tully was hitching rails up around the yards. He looked out from under his hat when his dogs barked in greeting and ran towards Jack.

'They said at the hotel that you were about here with the herd,' said Jack as he slid from the horse and shook Mark's hand vigorously.

'I'd heard word you'd left Ballarook too . . . chasing a lady, I believe.'

'Yes, well,' said Jack, kicking at the dust. 'That's yet to be seen.'

Mark put a hand on his mate's shoulder. 'Come with me. I've got something that will take your mind off Miss Ryan.' He walked with Jack over towards the camp site.

There, tied to a tree, was a handsome black dog with a short, smooth coat. He had prick-ears and bright brown eyes and his tail beat up clouds of dust when the men walked towards him.

'I've been holding on to him for weeks, trying to track you down. His name's Moss. I thought a dog as classy as this would be perfect for Kelpie. He's the same lines as my dogs. Rutherford-bred, from northern Scotland. When I saw him working, I knew his style would suit your Kelpie.'

Jack stooped to pat the young dog's shiny coat.

'He's a beauty.'

'It's time both of us put our skills to the test and went trialling. With dogs like these I reckon we'd be hard to beat.'

'But how did you come to have him?'

'Ah, Jack . . . let's just say the odds were with me that day.'

Jack unclipped Moss's chain and he danced about Jack's legs wagging his tail. Kelpie came to bounce in front of him as an invitation to play, her solid little forepaws thumping on the ground. Moss pulled back his ears in response and grinned as he leapt from side to side.

'He's a character,' said Jack.

'That he is. Like you said that first night we met again, on our way to Ballarook . . . this is the start of something bigger than just you and me and these few dogs. We're going to make a difference, Jack. I just know it.'

As the birds began to stir before dawn outside the window, Rosie woke up on Mr Seymour's couch. In the chair across from Rosie, Mr Seymour sat with his mouth open, snoring.

Jim, Julian and Evan had disappeared hours before to the musty-smelling spare rooms, while Mr Seymour droned on about dogs.

'Velour bedspreads with tassels! We had these when we were little,' was the last Rosie heard from Evan, before he and Julian both fell into a deep sleep.

Feeling seedy from too much rum, Rosie tiptoed along the hall and peered into one of the bedrooms. There, in each other's arms, lay Evan and Julian, sleeping peacefully. Rosie couldn't help but smile. It was the happiest she'd ever seen her brother. She closed the door gently. In the next room, Jim slept on an old camp bed. Rosie crept in and sat on the edge of the bed. Jim stirred and opened his eyes to look at her.

'I think we've had our first fight,' she whispered. 'But the best part is making up, you know.' She pulled back the old quilt and snuggled in next to his warmth.

'You're not wrong. This making up feels very nice indeed.'

'Can I ask you something?'

'Mmm?' he said sleepily.

'Do you really think I'm ashamed of being with you?' Rosie asked, resting her chin on his chest and looking up at him. Jim shut his eyes again.

'I don't know.'

'If you hadn't noticed, Jim, you're in Australia now, not Great Britain. We're a classless society down here.'

'Oh, are you now? I don't believe that for a second.' Then

he added more gently, 'We're from such different backgrounds, Rosie. Maybe it's just not going to work?'

'Don't you dare say that!' Rosie said. 'Of course it can work!' She snuggled back into his chest.

Jim held her tight for a moment, then gently pushed her off him and sat up.

'Come on,' he said. 'We've work to do today. I'm sober enough to drive now, so let's get cracking.'

'So have we stopped fighting?' she asked.

'All is forgiven,' he said as he stooped to pull on his jeans.

Twenty-eight

It was now late afternoon and the sleepless night at Mr Seymour's was catching up with Rosie. She and Jim had spent the morning out at Cattleyard Swamp mustering up the cows and calves for marking the next morning. As they trailed the cattle, bringing them back to the homestead yards, Rosie squinted at Jim.

'Are you sure we're not still fighting?'

'Of course we're not,' he said, reaching over to pull Oakwood's rein so that the gelding came to stand next to his mare. Then he kissed her. 'I'm just tired. That's why I'm not chatty.'

Back at the homestead, Rosie couldn't wait to climb into bed with Jim. All they had to do now was feed the dogs, mix up the chaff for Sassy and Morrison, and prepare the vaccine, ear tags and knives for tomorrow's work. Then eat and slip into bed. Her thoughts were interrupted when her mother rang the dinner gong.

'Surprised she's up for cooking,' said Jim, looking up from his knife sharpening. Rosie smirked. According to Julian, Margaret had only arrived back at the homestead that morning, long after Jim and Rosie had headed out to muster the cows and calves. Apparently she had alighted from Duncan's sports car, kissed him fondly on the lips, and run inside giggling like a schoolgirl.

When Rosie and Jim walked into the homestead they were met by the delicious aroma of Indian curries. They found Margaret, Julian and Evan sitting at the kitchen table, laughing and drinking beer. They greeted Rosie and Jim with cheers and raised stubbies.

'That'd be right,' said Rosie, her hands on her hips and a smile on her face. 'Jim and I slave our guts out all day while the bloody squatters party on!'

She accepted the bottle of beer that Julian was pressing into her hands and hungrily scoffed some naan bread.

'Come on, everybody,' said Margaret. 'Dinner is served!'

In the dark, wood-panelled dining room they passed delicious steaming dishes around the table, everyone talking at once. Jim held Rosie's hand beneath the table. In the glow cast by the silver candelabra, Rosie sat back in her chair, watching her family. Her mother looked different. Younger, somehow. Her clothes didn't look like they had been ironed on to her, for one thing. And her hair, normally lacquered into place with masses of hairspray, fell in soft, natural waves. She acted differently too. When had Margaret stopped hassling her about her appearance? Rosie wondered. She no longer complained about Rosie's torn work shirts, threadbare jeans and long, untrimmed hair. Rosie couldn't quite put her finger on it but her mother had changed . . . or at least, something had shifted within her. Rosie stifled a smirk. Something had definitely shifted within her last night, she thought wickedly. Something like Duncan Pellmet. Rosie spluttered and began to laugh.

They all turned to look at her. Her hand covered her mouth and her eyes scrunched up as she shook with laughter.

'What?' they chorused. It made her laugh harder. Here she was, she thought, sitting at her great-great-grandfather's dining table that had been imported from England. She was holding hands with the stockman and playing footsies with him under the table. What's more, the stockman was sitting at the head of the table, where Highgrove-Jones men had sat for generations. Meanwhile, on the other side of the table, her gay brother was talking to his boyfriend. Then there was Mrs Highgrove-Jones, who had just spent the night with her new toy boy (given that Duncan must be a good seven years younger than Margaret). The Highgrove-Jones ancestor who had imported the table wouldn't just be rolling in his grave. He'd be spinning like an Afro-American rapper. But then, Rosie realised, Mr long-dead Highgrove-Jones was no longer her great-great-grandfather anyway! Her real great-great-grandfather could've actually been some swagman who had once called in here to beg for food.

'What's so funny?' asked Julian.

She brushed tears of laughter away and struggled to speak.

'This!' she said, sweeping her hand around the room. 'Us!'

'What do you mean?' asked Margaret.

'Well, there's Julian . . . a horse's hoof. No offence, Evan. And you, Mum . . . shagging the editor of *The Chronicle*, while your husband's run off with your sister. It's such a crack-up! And then there's me . . . a bastard, so to speak. With a father so awful Mum can't admit who he is. And now *I've* taken up with the workman.' She held up Jim's hand from under the table. 'Can you imagine what Prudence Beaton would say? Or the Chillcott-Clarks?'

The room fell silent as all eyes came to rest on her. The smile on Rosie's face slid away as she looked around her. Jim stared at her poker-faced, her mother pursed her lips and Evan put his hand on Julian's shoulder. Then, as if a switch was flicked on, Margaret, Evan and Julian began to splutter too and soon they were laughing loudly enough to rouse the ghosts of the servants in the attics. But even as her family laughed around her, Rosie felt uncertainty settle in the pit of her stomach. Jim had quietly slipped his hand out of hers.

By the time Rosie made it out to the quarters after clearing up the kitchen, Jim was asleep. Instead of spooning against his warm body, Rosie lay with her back to him. What was upsetting him so much? And how could she sleep when she longed to find out who her true family was? Sighing, she reached out for the tattered Working Kelpie Council newsletter beside the bed and began to read.

Bolero station, NSW, circa 1874

A hot, windy day was coming to life beneath a sunrise splashed with colour. Jack looked up at the crazy clouds that hung over the red-soil plains of the Riverina. Bright pinks, blues and reds were streaked across the sky like the brushstrokes of a madman's painting. Jack pulled his hat down low over his brow and made his way to the kennels. Kelpie wasn't in her normal place waiting for him, ears pricked and tail flogging the ground. Instead she was inside the dark hole of her kennel. He stooped and looked inside.

'Well, bless me!' he said, grinning broadly. 'You might have waited for me, girl! You weren't due for another two days!'

Kelpie was curled around a litter of fat, glossy pups, five in all. Jack scooped up each tiny pup in his hands, surprised at the range of colours Moss and Kelpie had thrown. One pup was jet black, one black and tan like Kelpie, two were of rusty red colour and yet another came with a slate-grey coat.

He couldn't wait to tell Mary that the pups had arrived safe and well. Normally he'd write to her. But he would be seeing her the next week, as he had time off from Bolero to journey to the Ryan's local church for Easter Mass. It was there the Ryan family clustered in the front pews each Sunday after a dusty journey from their home on Wallandool. Launcelot Ryan would glare as Jack and Mary stole gleeful glances. Afterwards he would lurk near the couple like a shadow, making sure they exchanged only pleasantries, and nothing more. Jack shrugged away the thought of Mary's father and the difficulties he created between them. He had five beautiful pups! He went to find his fellow workman, Tom Keogh, who would be excited to hear the pups had arrived. Jack had promised Tom a pup from Kelpie's first litter.

* * *

As the winter moved into spring on Bolero, the pups began to grow into classy types. Rain had failed to fall in the Mirool district, so Jack spent many of his days carting water to thirsty stock. Because of the dry he couldn't have leave to visit Mary on Wallandool. Instead he wrote her stilted letters, always with the vision of her father breaking the wax seal and reading his private words. When he did have a day off from work, to forget Mary he absorbed himself in training the pups. Soon other workers and young graziers from neighbouring stations were drifting over to Bolero on Sundays. The men would share training methods with one another, standing about the yards with their dogs on the ends of long ropes like fallen kites. Some coaxed pups with pieces of dried kangaroo meat and others used kindly words and sounds.

John Cox of Mangoplah station came by regularly to play at the dog trialling. He kept his smile hidden behind a long moustache and raised his voice to the heavens if the dogs took a wrong turn. When John Cox first saw Jack working a dog without cursing or raising his voice, his caterpillar-like eyebrows rose high on his forehead.

'Your skills are too good for that of a mere overseer, Jack. If I could have you as my manager on Yalgogrin, I could tend to Mangoplah without a worry in the world. What do you say?'

'It sounds tempting, John. But I haven't long set my boots down here on Bolero. Give me a bit of time to think on it.'

Jack loved it when graziers such as John Cox chose to spend their spare time working their dogs alongside station hands. In the yards, Jack thought, the dogs made all men equal. They gathered outside Jack's tiny wattle-and-daub hut to talk dogs until sundown, admiring Jack's pups as they ran about on the crackling dry house paddocks. The lightly timbered mountain of Yalgogrin rose up from the Riverina plains as if seeking out the sky. Jack's hut nestled at the base of the mountain amidst a cluster of lazy-looking pepper trees and sturdy, upright kurrajongs. Galahs screeched in the drooping branches and danced in front of the hut. The men were gathered here in the shade beneath the split shingle roof on a particularly hot Sunday, waiting for the afternoon to cool before riding home with their dogs. When the sun sank lower and the flies began to give up their chase, Jack's boss, Mr Quinn, stood up.

'S'pose we ought to bid you lads farewell and get on with our work. Jack here must muster that mountain, and I must ready myself for a journey home.'

The men stood to leave, but Jack poured himself a cup of tea, took another hunk of damper and pulled up a chair on the verandah.

'I think I'll use this chair for the muster instead of me horse, if you don't mind,' he said.

'Stop playing silly buggers with me,' Mr Quinn said. He was already familiar with Jack's humour and liked to play along with him. Jack had fitted in comfortably on Bolero.

'Oh, I'm not being silly at all,' Jack said with a glint in his eye. 'Bets are on, gentlemen, that I can muster that there Yalgogrin Mount with this chair here . . . instead of my horse.'

'Right then! You're on!' said Quinn, taking off his hat and throwing a coin into it. The other men tossed their own coins into Quinn's hat.

'Now, how do you propose to do it?' asked Jack's boss.

Jack strode over to a flat clear area in front of the hut.

'Just you watch.'

Jack called Moss and Kelpie to him and told them to sit. With his back to the hill. Jack looked at both dogs. They quivered with anticipation, ears pricked, eyes locked on Jack, waiting for his word.

'Moss, get away over,' Jack said, inclining his head to the right, and Moss took off, casting out clockwise towards the mountain. Jack followed his command with a piercing whistle that seemed to propel the dog up the steep slope. At Jack's feet, Kelpie whined softly with impatience, waiting her turn.

'Kelpie, get away back,' said Jack, inclining his head the other way. Like a rabbit on the run, she shot out in an anticlockwise direction towards the mountain. Then Jack strolled back to the hut and sat on the rickety old chair, resting his feet up on the verandah post and folding his hands across his flat belly. Both dogs ran further and further away. Soon they were just tiny black blobs darting between the trees on the crest of the mountain.

The sheep grazing on the steep slopes threw their heads up in the air and pulled their ears back. They began to trot, congregating in a whirling mass. Jack cupped his hand on one side of his mouth and whistled a 'steady' command so that both dogs slowed to a walk. Then the dogs guided the mob steadily down the mountainside, like a flowing river. Jack barely said a word, only occasionally directing Moss to work the wing harder or whistling Kelpie to stop to take a bit of pressure off the mob. He sipped at his tea.

'This chair is wonderful for mustering, gentlemen, I can tell you. Why take a horse on the Sabbath when you can obey God's law and take a chair?'

Within a few minutes the sheep had flowed down the side of the mountain and across the paddock. Now they were milling about in front of the verandah. Moss and Kelpie, tongues lolling and feet dancing, moved their eyes over the stock, intent on keeping the mob in order. Even the pups, who had been playing at the men's feet, had cast out on their little legs and, ears pricked, were setting the sheep and padding around them, showing natural hold and cover. The men shook their heads in disbelief, and smiled.

'But can they shut the gate behind them?' teased Quinn, knocking Jack's legs away from the verandah post so that tea splashed over his britches.

'Well, if your yard gates swung properly they could!'

'You're a bloody show-off, Jack Gleeson,' said Tom Keogh. 'You'll be mustering sheep in your sleep next, and the boss'll have me out working to re-swing all the gates!'

The men burst out laughing.

'Well, to prove I'm not a skite, I'd like each of you gentlemen here today to pick yourself one of those little pups,' Jack said. 'Go on! Take your choice!'

The men stood still, not believing what Jack proposed.

'Are you certain?' said Steve Apps. 'Surely you'll want payment for pups as sound as these?'

'Oh, no!' said Jack. 'I've vowed never to sell a pup for money. They're to go to men like yourselves, men who have an understanding of what it is to train the likes of a *proper* dog *properly*!'

'But, Jack,' said Tom, taking him aside for a moment and whispering, 'you could make a small fortune selling dogs as good as these. It'd be enough to buy you land . . . and then, young Mary Ryan would be yours for the taking!'

Jack shook his head and replied so that all the graziers could hear. 'Lance Ryan can take me as I am. Land or no land. I'll not sell a dog to buy a wife!'

John Cox shook his head. 'You're a daft bugger, Gleeson. Old Ryan was hell-bent on not letting my young brother Pat court his daughter Grace. But since Pat bought a run of his own on Yalgogrin, Ryan's approved of the match! A property's a secure home for a girl.'

'I disagree,' said Jack, a flash of hurt bringing colour to his cheeks. 'A *good man* is a secure home for a girl . . . and for a pup. That's why you, John Cox, can have one of these.' His face brightened as he strode out to scoop up a pup and carry it over to the men.

Word of Jack's Sunday afternoon muster-by-chair spread quickly around the district, along with the news that he had handed out Kelpie and Moss's fine pups for just a smile and a handshake. The story of Jack's generosity reached the ears of Launcelot Ryan as he sat in the London Hotel. Ryan's cheeks turned an angry pink when he heard that the Irish stockman had refused money for the pups. If the man wanted his daughter, why didn't he aim for a handsome profit on such a litter and put it towards some land?

On the ride back to Wallandool, Launcelot Ryan mulled over the fact that Gleeson had followed the Ryans to the Mirool area. It was clear Jack was well liked in the district, but what did he have to offer his daughter? Already his older two girls, Kate and Grace, had been matched with fine, hard-working graziers. He had given Kate away to Harry King, who owned the impressive Wollongough station, and Grace was certain to have a good life with Pat Cox on their patch of red-soil country on the Yalgogrin run. But Mary! His thoughts became tangled when they turned to his fairest daughter. He wanted the very best for her, but she just would not give up when it came to Jack Gleeson. Ryan turned to his son who sat astride Mary's old black pony.

'No word of Mr Gleeson's exploits to your sister Mary now,' he said sternly.

Then Launcelot Ryan spurred his horse into a canter and banished all thoughts of Jack Gleeson from his head.

Twenty-nine

Rosie felt the calf's sharp hoof meet her shin.

'Ouch! You little bugger!' she exclaimed, hopping on one leg, before she reached up between his legs for the sac of his scrotum. She got the knife in position, the way Jim had shown her.

'Can't say I blame him,' said Jim as he loaded another electronic tag into the applicator. It was his first attempt at a joke all day and Rosie looked up at him and smiled with relief. She'd been worried by his silence.

Today they were drafting the early calves off the cows and running them up the race. At first Rosie assumed Jim was tired and just didn't feel like talking. But as the day wore on, it was obvious there was something wrong. With cows bellowing in the next yard and calves crying out from the shock of the knife as they were earmarked, Rosie didn't even attempt to ask what it was. It would have to wait until tonight.

She reached for the vaccine and jabbed the needle through the calf's tough hide. Then she moved to get the next calf up.

'That's the one I've been looking for,' she said at last, as she let the final calf out of the crush.

As she sat on the tailgate of the ute and began to tidy up the eartags, Rosie looked up at the distant ridge where the hut was hidden in the bush. She thought back to the nights she had spent there with Jim. Even though it had only been a few months, it felt like a lifetime ago now. So much had happened with her family and the farm since then. Rosie sighed. In those early days she had felt that they were meant to be together but lately Jim was often distant and withdrawn. She wondered what she could say to convince him how much he meant to her. That she didn't just want him around to work on the farm. That she didn't give a damn what people might think.

He came to sit beside her now. She put her hand on his thigh and, with relief, felt the warmth of Jim's hand as he laid it over hers. She turned to him, ready to tell him how much she loved him, but Margaret called from the homestead.

'Visitor for you, Rosie!'

Dubbo stepped out from behind Margaret. He walked over to the cattleyards, neat and tidy in moleskins and a red-striped shirt. His boots gleamed and his fine blond hair was freshly trimmed.

'Blimey!' he said, taking in Rosie's battered hat, grimy face, and the dried blood on her hands and clothes. 'Never seen you in your work clobber!'

Rosie looked down and shrugged. Jim hauled the half drench drum filled with the marking gear noisily out of the tray of the ute. He nodded briefly at Dubbo.

'I'll get this gear washed up,' he said to Rosie and disappeared inside the quarters.

'I've come to see Sam's pups,' Dubbo said. 'If you've got time.'

Sam's pups, Rosie thought with a jolt. Of course. But she now thought of them as hers. Hearing Sam's name gave her a strange, guilty feeling. She realised she hadn't thought of him in weeks, and now here was Dubbo reminding her. She turned on her heel.

'Come on then. I'll show you *Sam*'s pups,' she said, but Dubbo missed the sarcasm in her voice.

She ushered him through the stable, pointing out Sassy's

colt, Morrison. Dubbo, not keen on horses, glanced quickly at him.

'Very nice,' he said absently.

At the dog pens, the pups jumped and clawed at the wire. Rosie made them all wait and settle before she let each one out.

'They've all had obedience training so they sit, stay and come when they're called,' she said. 'Jim says the next thing will be to start them on stock. Do any catch your eye? Do you want a bitch or a dog?'

'What's going on with him anyway?' Dubbo asked suddenly, turning to face Rosie.

'With who? Jim? What do you mean, *going on*?'

Dubbo shook his head.

'I hate to have to say this, but you can't be too trusting of workmen, you know.'

Rosie frowned.

'How well do you know this Jim bloke anyway?' Dubbo asked.

'Well enough,' Rosie said, anger prickling her cheeks.

'Well, I've been doing some checking up on him. Asking about his background. Just as a precaution, you know.'

'No. I don't know.'

'Look,' Dubbo stepped forward and put a hand on her arm, 'I'm just watching out for you. I kind of feel I owe it to Sam.'

'I don't need your protection!'

'I care about you, Rose. That's why I'm here. I know you don't want to hear this, but I need to tell you what I've found out about Jim.'

'What?' Rosie said. She felt sick in the stomach.

Dubbo lowered his voice. 'From what I've heard, our friend Jim has used his Irish charm like this before.'

'What do you mean?'

'Let's just say the man is after property. Apparently, he's been engaged twice before – at the same time. You know, hedging his bets. Both girls were the daughters of big grazing players up in the Territory. One had an arse the size of a fitball and the other was part-way dippy. Apparently both weddings fell through when the fathers sussed out his scam.'

'It's not true,' Rosie said, backing away.

'Just think about it, Rosie. How fast has he wheedled his way into your life? He turns up just after you've lost your fiancé. Bang. Right on time to save the day. Look, I've spoken to a former employer. He confirmed it all.'

Rosie felt confusion swamp her. Jim had seemed like a dream come true. But the same sick feeling crept into her that she'd felt when she'd found out about Sam and Jillian. Jim always seemed to be there to support her, but was he really just like Sam? Doubt crept through Rosie's whole system like a virus. She felt as if she couldn't breathe.

The next thing she knew Dubbo was holding her in his arms. She had her face pressed to his chest and tears were pricking at her eyes. Just then, Jim walked out from the stables and stood stock still. Rosie pushed Dubbo away.

'I'd better go,' Dubbo said. 'I'll pick out a pup another day, eh?'

He walked straight past Jim, ignoring him, and was gone. Jim stood in front of Rosie, silent. She could see his jaw muscle twitching in anger.

'Please tell me it's not true,' she said, tears rising up to her eyes.

'What's not true?'

'That you're just after me for the property. Like you were with those girls in the Territory.'

'Is that what he told you?' Jim said.

Rosie nodded.

'And you believed him?' he said, flinging down the bridle he was carrying.

'I don't know what to believe! Maybe all men are arseholes after all!'

'It shows how much you think of me then.'

Jim turned and stormed into the quarters, slamming the

door so hard that the windowpanes shook and the pups scuttled nervously to sit at Rosie's boots. Rosie, sobbing, called the pups back into their pens. She sat for a time, clinging on to Chester as he licked at her tears. She knew as soon as she'd said the words to Jim that they couldn't be true. Dubbo was lying. He was jealous, and still grieving for Sam. Rosie hugged Chester once more and stood up. She had to apologise to Jim.

She found him in the stables, leading his horses from the stalls.

The door of his float was open in the courtyard beyond. His grim face was flushed red.

'What are you doing?' Rosie said, trying to cover the quaver of fear in her voice.

'What does it look like?'

He loaded the mare and his colt and hauled up the heavy float door with a bang. Then he brushed past Rosie and went into the men's quarters. Rosie followed him, panic bubbling up inside her as Jim began to fling clothes into his grubby old canvas bag.

'I've had it with this family, and being treated like scum by your snobby mates,' he said tightly.

Rosie opened her mouth to argue, but no words came as she watched Jim ram his clothes into the bag.

'It's not going to work between us, Rosie. We're from different worlds.' He tugged at the zip.

'But you can't leave me!' Rosie said, grabbing his arm.

Through narrow eyes Jim glared at her.

'Why? Because you need your hired hand?'

'That's *not* what you are to me! Will you just drop it? You know it's so much more than that. Don't you feel it too?'

'After what you said before, I don't know what to think.'

Jim strode to the ute, slammed the bag on to the tray and whistled his dogs on. He opened the passenger door for Bones and scooped the old dog in.

'Jim. Don't. Please.' Rosie was sobbing. Jim slammed the

ute door. He wound down the window and looked at her. There were tears in his eyes.

'You know I love you, Rosie.' His voice seemed to choke for a moment, but he soon gained control. 'But you'll be better off with someone else.'

'Jim, don't go. Please. Let's talk this through.'

But he turned the ignition over and he drove away.

Wallandool station, 1878

As the fiddler dragged his bow across the strings, Jack swung Mary high in the air, his large hands clasping her tiny waist. Her white gown was trimmed prettily with tiny roses made from silk. Her cheeks were flushed from dancing. Friends from the district clapped and danced around the bride and groom, while the younger Ryan children and their gang made mischief on the side verandah where the grog was kept.

When Jack held Mary close he could smell lemon blossom in her hair. He shut his eyes and swung her around again on the dance floor. Mary Ryan was now Mary Gleeson. At that moment, dancing in the dusky evening in front of Wallandool homestead, Jack felt he was the happiest man alive.

'Surely it's time to go soon?' Jack said, kissing Mary on her neck and breathing in her scent. She laughed and kissed him on the cheek.

'I'll find Ma to organise my things. Da can get the buggy.'

Jack pushed through the rabble of dancers and went to find Launcelot Ryan. He was sitting by a bonfire that was sending sparks shooting into the dark July sky. He nodded at Jack.

'Mary's set to leave. Are the horses all tacked up to go?' Jack asked.

Ryan stood.

'You've got persistence, Jack Gleeson, I'll grant you that.' He put his hand on Jack's shoulder and looked directly at him. 'But you hurt her in any way and I'll be after you.'

Jack shook off his touch.

'You're the one who's been hurting her these past few years, by keeping us apart! Her life begins now, tonight, with me.'

'You might be the hero about these parts with your fine stockmanship, but you're well beneath my Mary. You always will be.'

'No man would be good enough for her in your eyes,' Jack said.

Ryan sighed. Jack had a point. Mary was his golden girl, his favourite child out of eleven.

'I'll go fetch the buggy,' he said wearily, then walked into the darkness surrounding the garden.

Jack watched the rising sparks darken and die as they shot heavenward. He closed his eyes and thought back over the years that had led to this wedding night.

He recalled his time in the Mirool district on Bolero, Kelpie had whelped with a second litter in the eighteen months that he had worked there. The pups were another bright-eyed batch sired by Moss.

At twelve weeks of age they were bursting with herding instinct in their style of play. Again Jack sent them into the world to the trustiest of flockmasters, whether they were shearers or squatters.

It had also taken eighteen months for John Cox to persuade Jack into resigning from Bolero as overseer to become manager on the Cox family place, Yalgogrin. With Jack climbing the ladder, and word of his stock skill spreading far and wide, Launcelot Ryan could no longer ignore him. Through his gentlemanly ways and his generosity with stock dogs, Jack had earned enough standing to ask for the hand of Ryan's daughter. And so a deal had been struck.

'You can only have my Mary if you promise to take up land for selection and build her a decent home.'

Jack had at last agreed.

Mary's sister Grace was married to Pat Cox, and it was Pat who had shown Jack a portion of land on Bolero where a house could be built.

'Take it, Jack,' he urged. 'There's forty acres of open plains country for you. And because it's next to Yalgogrin, Mary can see her sister whenever she needs. Ryan is bound to like that idea.'

'Ah. Forty acres, Pat,' said Jack doubtfully. 'You'd barely be able to swing a cat.'

'What do you want with cats? It would run a few milking cows, some killers for mutton and think of the vegetable garden that can be grown in that red soil around the homestead. Mary will love it.'

'And water? What of water, Pat?'

'There's bores can be dug.'

Jack thought of Mary and the years they had spent, longing to be together. It was time he settled.

'I guess it will do.'

'That's the spirit, Jack,' said Pat.

In his hut Jack folded the application for the forty-acre title and wrote the address of the Department of Lands in his best hand. As hot wax dripped onto the parchment Jack felt as if his fate was sealed.

Now here he was on his wedding night, with his bride making herself ready for him inside the house and his friends outside, leaning all topsy-turvy about the bonfire, singing loudly to the stars.

Tomorrow, he'd set about building Mary a house on land he would soon own.

'Promise me, Jack,' he heard Mary's light-hearted voice in his head, 'you won't build me a kennel to live in.'

Thirty

Fresh spring winds bit into Rosie's skin as she turned Oakwood into the icy blast. In the two months since Jim had been gone, Rosie hadn't left the station. Instead, she had thrown herself into work, trying to keep the numbness at bay.

She had begged Julian to come home and help her and, reluctantly, he'd packed his bags and returned.

'It's only short-term, mind you,' he'd warned her after he'd dumped his bags at the foot of the stairs.

Margaret had been genuinely sympathetic, but Rosie knew her mother was secretly relieved Jim was out of her life, though she now knew better than to point out that Jim wasn't right for Rosie in the first place, as she would once have done. The power had shifted and it was Rosie who seemed to be in charge.

Rosie stayed on in the men's quarters and worked on her Jack Gleeson articles, trying to shut out the memory of Jim. She was determined to bury all the traumas of the past eight months and start afresh as the spring landscape came to life. She urged Oakwood into a trot towards home.

As she neared the house, Rosie could hear the rev of Duncan's sports car rising up through the bare limbs of the winter elms. She pulled Oakwood up at the front gate and saw Duncan in the passenger seat, his eyes creased with laughter as Margaret jerked and revved his car around the circular driveway. She was laughing too, and carving deep wheel-ruts in the lawn each time she turned the steering wheel too sharply and let the clutch out too quickly. Rosie stepped Oakwood onto the drive to flag them down. The car careened to a halt.

'What on earth are you doing?' Rosie said.

'You sound just like I used to,' said Margaret, almost falling out of the car.

'I was going to teach your mother to drive the car,' said a breathless Duncan, getting out of the passenger seat. 'I thought a quick trip to the front grid would fix her . . . but we still haven't got past first gear!' Duncan put his arm around Margaret. 'Still, I'll make a Peter Brock of her yet!'

Rosie rolled her eyes and smiled. Her mother and Duncan had been seeing each other since the night at the pub and she had never seen Margaret happier, or Duncan healthier – or better dressed. At first he had used the pretence of coming out to help edit the Jack Gleeson articles, but soon he was staying over most nights of the week.

Now Duncan was there so often, Rosie hadn't found the right time to confront her mother again on the subject of her real father. And with Jim gone, she felt she just couldn't take any more shocks. For now, she had buried the questions deep inside herself, though sometimes, in the dark at night, she allowed herself to wonder. Did her father know about her? Was he thinking of her? What did he look like? Did she have sisters or brothers? Rosie glanced at her mother, looking so happy with Duncan. It couldn't have been *him*, he was 'new' to the district and had only lived here fourteen years.

'Come on, you two,' Rosie said, jumping down from Oakwood. 'There's work to be done. You need to come and talk dogs with me.'

Half an hour later, Rosie sat at the kitchen table with her papers spread out in front of her and her feet warm in a pair of ug boots. She looked up at Duncan.

'It seems Kelpie had two main men in her life.'

'Oh?'

'Gleeson joined Kelpie to Moss twice and then he fraternised some more with the landed gentry and got on to a sire which was by an imported pair of dogs. He was a dog called Caesar and he was Kelpie's second boyfriend.'

Narriah Station, Circa 1878

Jack was uncomfortable in the starched collar that buttoned tightly at his neck. But he and Mary were dining with property owner John Rich this night.

While Mary chatted with Mr Rich, Jack copied her moves, picking up the silver cutlery between his rough hands. It had been a long time since he had needed such manners. He unfolded the starched napkin and laid it on his lap. He lifted the silver utensils to dish out steaming food onto fine china plates. But the friendly conversation, the warm red wine, and the crackling fire in the blackened grate soothed him. By the end of the night Jack was clasping a tiny crystal glass confidently between his large fingers as he and John Rich retired for port and cigars.

In the wood-panelled smoking room, John Rich told how a black and tan dog called Brutus and a bitch called Jenny had recently come to the district.

'It was Gilbert Elliot and Allen of Geraldra station, near Stockinbingal, who imported the two collies from Scotland,' John announced, as if it was the latest news though Jack already knew of the dogs, as did all the stockmen in the district.

'They joined on the ship . . . knotted tighter than the ship's rigging. Even the highest of seas couldn't untie the two. And not long after Jenny came to Geraldra she whelped a bonny litter. And the sire, Brutus . . . surely you've heard of his wins at the trials?'

'Indeed I have,' said Jack, nodding and feeling his cheeks burn red from the warmth of the port and the fire. The pups from that union were the very reason why Jack had pressed for a meeting with John Rich, and Mary, in her charming way, had orchestrated it. Rich strode over to pull a leather-bound scrapbook from the bookshelf and placed the book open on Jack's lap. Then he pushed the lamp closer. Jack then read the account of Brutus' win:

The performance of this dog was something wonderful. Three sheep were let loose and taken outside in the ground and the dog upon word being given brought them into the ground and across through a crowd of people running here, there and everywhere in a manner which would confuse a human being, to the pen, without so much as a bark. So uncommonly well did this shepherd's friend behave himself that the other competitors resigned all claim to the prize, and would not put their dogs upon trial.

'Three pups!' John declared, stumbling slightly from too much port as he returned the book to the shelf. 'Three pups she had in the first litter: Nero, Laddie and Caesar.'

Jack of course knew all this.

'I want to put to you, my dear man,' John continued, 'that you join my Caesar to your Kelpie. It's a cross that can't fail. I have searched high and low in this district for a bitch of her class.'

'Oh, she's the one, all right!' declared Jack. 'If you'd said so earlier, Mr Rich, you could've saved yourself a meal and all that fancy port. If you'd requested this out in the paddock with just a stale biscuit and a pannikin of weak old tea, I would've agreed. In fact, you could say, you've read my mind!'

John Rich laughed and came over to slap Jack on the back. The two men shook hands, and the mating deal between Kelpie and Caesar was done.

Rosie shut the book. Regret welled up in her. She and Jim had been talking about which bloodlines to put over Dixie next time she came on heat. She would have to make the decision on her own now.

Duncan, seeing Rosie's face grow sad, urged her on with the story.

'Well,' Rosie continued, 'one of the pups out of the Kelpie–Caesar litter looked so much like her mum, Jack called her "Young Kelpie".'

'Really? So that's how the name was passed down,' said Duncan. 'And what's Young Kelpie's claim to fame?'

Wollongough station, circa 1879

'Oh, you're the image of your mother,' Jack said as he held up the solid little black and tan bitch. For a moment, squatting on the red Riverina ground, Jack was transported back to that misty, eerie night on the banks of the Glenelg River, when he had first tucked Kelpie into his coat.

'You'd have to be *Young* Kelpie,' he said, gently scratching the pup's pink belly. Jack was sorely tempted to keep the little slut, but here he was, set to deliver her to Wollongough station on Humbug Creek. Jack's brother-in-law, Charles King, was walking towards him now with a welcoming smile on his face.

'You won't regret giving her to me, Jack,' he said.

Jack felt a sadness clutch him as he passed the pup over. It was like handing Cooley's lead rope to George Robertson-Patterson all over again, though he knew it was for the best. Charles King was a man of standing and had the funds to trial Young Kelpie all over the countryside at the biggest events.

Jack recalled how Launcelot Ryan had cracked open his best whisky when it was settled that his daughter Kate would marry into the King family. Now she lived in style and comfort – unlike her sister Mary. Jack looked at the scuffed toes of his boots with a frown. Sometimes, when he rode home after dark and found Mary asleep in the chair, he would search her pretty, sleeping face for signs that her passion for him was dying down, like the embers in the fire. She was a strong, patient, cheerful girl, but the constant work about the house, and the long hours of waiting for his return from the runs wore her down. On little money she had to keep food up to them, and all the clothes mended and clean. She was too proud to take the help her mother and sisters offered her.

Jack looked at the well-dressed man before him. Handing Young Kelpie to Charles King would further the name of Jack's line of kelpies. Unlike King, who toured the dog trial circuit, Jack preferred to work his dogs in a real environment, casting them out on the vast Yellow Box plains to bring in toey stragglers and strays. He gave Young Kelpie one last scratch behind the ear.

'Make sure you train her well. And let's hope she has some handy work for you at Forbes,' Jack said.

Margaret pushed two more steaming cups of tea towards Rosie and Duncan. Duncan looked up and Margaret gave him a grateful smile and patted him on the shoulder. Rosie put on the plummy voice of an old newsreel reader and began to read out an article.

'*"Forbes pastoral and Agricultural Show,"*' she said importantly. '*"At the trial of sheep-dogs to-day, there were seven entries including some of the best dogs in the colonies. After some severe tests the judges divided between Mr Charles King's Kelpie and Mr C F Gibson's Tweed. The latter dog was sent for specially from Tasmania to compete. Both dogs worked magnificently, and it is likely that the amount of first prize of 20 Guineas will be doubled, so that both owners will get equal money. Flockmasters came from distances of 150 miles to see the trial, and avowed it was the grandest contest they ever saw. The dogs worked one and three sheep respectively, and notwithstanding the continuous rain, some hundreds of people watched the trials for six hours with unflagging interest."*'

'Oh, jolly good,' mimicked Duncan.

Rosie looked up from the article.

'That was the trial that essentially advertised how fantastic Jack's lines were. Demand for the pups of Kelpie and Young Kelpie skyrocketed. King's Kelpie was mated to old Moss several more times after that. Some of the famous pups out of that cross were Gibson's Chester and Grand Flaneur.'

Margaret seemed to have stopped listening, but Rosie didn't notice. She continued as excitedly as Mr Seymour did when talking dogs.

'Then there was King's Red Jessie and MacPherson's Robin. They were the best show and paddock dogs about and won trials all over.'

Duncan nodded encouragingly.

'From what I can work out,' Rosie said, 'in the late 1890s there came two pups descended from Young Kelpie's blood-lines, Barb and Coil. It says here: *"Barb was a close working black dog that was good in the yard and Coil was owned by the Quinns."* He won at Sydney with a full 100 point score in each of his runs. And in the final he won with a broken leg set in splints. Mr Seymour goes all gushy when he talks about him. Calls him the "Immortal Coil". So there you have it . . . the descendants of these dogs became the kelpies we know today.'

'Speaking of Mr Seymour – you should go in and see him,' Duncan said.

'Yes,' Margaret said. 'Last time I dropped a meal in to him, he mentioned that he wanted to see you.'

Rosie shuddered at the thought of going back to Mr Seymour's house, and the memories of Jim that awaited her there.

'Why would he want to see me?'

'I think he has something for you,' was all Duncan said.

Rosie turned back to the history books and pretended to read. Since Jim had left, she'd had just two phone calls from him. She remembered her mother calling from the house late at night. The floor beneath her feet felt cold as she picked up the receiver.

'Hello?'

She could hear music and people laughing and yelling in the background. Then a voice came on the line. It was Jim. He was singing 'Uptown Girl' in a slurred, drunken voice.

'Where are you?' she yelled.

'I love you, Rosie Jones without-the-fecking-hyphen.'

And then the line went dead.

The next time he'd called, it was to apologise for the first call. There'd been awkward, painful gaps in their conversation.

He wouldn't say where he was. Only that he was working somewhere 'up north'.

'Come back,' Rosie had pleaded.

'No, Rosie. It just wouldn't work.'

When she hung up, she began to think that perhaps he was right, perhaps it wouldn't work. History, she told herself. She had to stop thinking about him.

Rosie sipped her tea and refocused on the books in front of her. Suddenly Julian burst through the door clutching an old file.

'Look, look, look!' he said. He swiped Rosie's books and papers aside and set the file down.

'What?' chorused Margaret and Rosie.

'Dad phoned and told me about it,' he said. 'Look!'

Rosie stared at the official-looking documents. They said something about a water right.

'So?' said Rosie.

'It means our family has a right to irrigate from the river. It's not a big quota, not enough for crops, which is why it wasn't ever used by Dad or Grandad, but it is enough water for a tree nursery!'

'Really?' said Rosie, suddenly realising what Julian was proposing.

'Yes! I've been on the phone to Evan. He and his sister are doing some costings. It could mean we relocate his business out here and expand it!'

'But I thought you were longing to go back to the city,' Margaret said.

'I was longing to go back to Evan, not the city. I'm loving being back on the farm. But I know Evan would love it here too. His business can't grow any more where it is because of real-estate prices and a whole load of reasons. He says he's prepared to move and go into a partnership with Highgrove in tree production. That's if you're prepared to have us. I mean once we've had a formal meeting and done the sums.'

'Yes!' chorused Rosie and Margaret loudly at once.

'Of course we want you here,' Margaret said, tears coming to her eyes.

Rosie picked up the dusty file and sifted through the old documents as an image of greenhouses filled with healthy native plants sprang up in her mind. Suddenly, a new future on Highgrove station was starting to unfold. A future that included Julian and Evan. Her mum and Duncan. And herself and the animals.

No Sam. No Jim. Just horses, dogs, sheep and cows, and now, trees.

Thirty-one

The phone and fax ran hot for a week as Margaret, Rosie, Evan and Julian worked furiously on getting plans in place for the proposed tree nursery. There was government red tape to gnaw through, banks to negotiate with, scientists' brains to pick, and irrigation systems to cost.

By Saturday morning, Rosie thought it was high time she had a break and left Julian and Evan to it. She decided to head into town to the ute muster and dog trial. And it was a good chance to face her demons by visiting Mr Seymour.

Neville the ute backfired loudly as Rosie pulled up outside Mr Seymour's house. She slammed the ute door and ran her hands over her new Wrangler jeans and tight-fitting Beccy Cole T-shirt which had 'Storm in a D-Cup' printed on it in pink. Her hair, still damp from the shower, hung in pretty blonde strands to her shoulderblades. She walked down the weedy path and steeled herself to go back inside the house where she had first seen Jim. Dixie, Gibbo and Diesel sat watching her from the back of the ute, their ears pricked.

As she walked into the dim hallway a startled bark made Rosie jump and set her own dogs barking with excitement. A large black shape lumbered towards her, and as her eyes adjusted to the gloom she saw it was Bones, greeting her with a thrashing tail. Her heart skipped a beat. Was Jim here? She crouched beside Bones and scratched the back of his dome-like head while his back foot moved as if scratching the air. Emotion welled up in her as she ran her hands over his lumpy old body.

'Hello?' she called out in the empty sitting room. There was a clatter in the next room.

'Ah, lass,' said Mr Seymour as he shuffled in from the kitchen. There was no sign of Jim, and Rosie's heart sank. 'You've been a long time coming.'

He strode over to the sideboard, pulled out a bottle of Tullamore Dew and picked up two glasses.

Rosie perched on the edge of the sagging couch. Lazy Bones lay on a brown gritty rug in front of a hissing fire, licking at his splayed paws. He looked up at Rosie and slapped his tail slowly on the rug, raising small clouds of dust that danced in the light. On the piano, the cat watched her through narrow eyes.

Mr Seymour raised his glass to Rosie.

'Good health to you.' He took a sip and gasped as the whisky warmed his throat. 'I expected you weeks back. He left Bones here for you to collect . . . to remind you.'

'*Remind* me?' Rosie said. As if she needed reminding.

'Yes. So you remember to keep good genes flowing through the blood of your dogs. Don't just join your females to any old dog. He's got to be special.'

'Special,' Rosie echoed as tears welled up in her eyes. Mr Seymour saw the colour drain from Rosie's face.

'He's mad about you, you know. But he reckons you're better off with your own kind,' he said sympathetically.

Rosie shook her head. If only Mr Seymour knew that she didn't even belong with her 'own kind'.

'Where is he?'

Mr Seymour shrugged. He offered to refill Rosie's glass but she shook her head.

'No more, thanks. I'm driving.'

'Where are you off to?'

'A dog trial and ute show. Jim had talked me into entering

Gibbo in the novice section of the trial, and Neville in the Old Clunker section of the utes.'

'Old clunker? Sounds like I'd be eligible for that section!' Mr Seymour laughed. 'And Bones too, for that matter!'

'Well,' said Rosie, 'why don't you come?'

Mr Seymour looked at her with a wry smile.

'I like your style, girl.'

Rosie helped Mr Seymour into Neville's passenger seat. Beneath an old coat Mr Seymour wore his best shirt of beige geometric patterns, and his brown nylon pants were pulled up nearly to his armpits. He smoothed his hands over his grey hair, which he had slicked over his bald spot. In the back of Neville, Lazy Bones settled his fat body next to the other dogs and turned his nose to the rushing wind. His pale tongue blew back and flapped beneath his grey muzzle.

'Rides well,' Mr Seymour remarked as the ute bumped over the show-ground grid and pulled to a halt with another deafening backfire.

Rosie handed the man on the gate their entry money and drove towards the line of utes that ringed the oval. There were brand-new utes with gleaming paintwork, and a motley mob of ancient paddock-bashers. Old Neville limped past the shiny modern utes lined up like young soldiers, their massive bull-bars jutting out importantly. Some had truckie mudflaps that hung beneath their tailgates, others had aerials shooting up like spears. All of them were covered in stickers that said things like 'I'm totally UTED' and 'Wrangler Butts Drive Me Nuts'. Most had big round spotlights mounted on their bull-bars and all of them had Bundy Rum stickers or artwork of the Bundy Bear painted on their gleaming surfaces. The young crowd leant around the utes, shirtsleeves rolled up, big hats jammed on and beer cans encased in various stubby holders grasped in their hands.

Someone banged suddenly on the roof of the ute. James Dean stepped forward, raising his beer. He leant in through the window.

'Hey, baby . . . fast mover! I like your new boyfriend!'

He reached across Rosie to shake hands with old Mr Seymour.

'James Dean,' he said.

'Clark Gable,' Mr Seymour said.

'I reckon this here jezebel would keep you on your toes?' said James Dean, inclining his head towards Rosie.

'I haven't got her in the sack yet, boy, but I'm working on it,' Mr Seymour said, rasping with laughter.

'Gentlemen, please!' said Rosie, pulling a face. Then she ground the gearstick into place and floored the accelerator so that damp soil spun up from the tyres.

'I'll speak to you later,' she yelled to James Dean as he waved goodbye.

'Really,' she huffed to Mr Seymour. 'And I thought our relationship was purely platonic.'

'Sometimes you gotta skite in front of the boys,' he replied. Then he turned his attention to the line-up of ancient utes featuring dinted panels, rust spots and trays cluttered with old junk.

'Oh, this takes me back,' he said.

Rosie parked Neville in the line-up and, as if announcing he'd arrived, the ute gave off one of the loudest backfires yet.

'I'd better go enter Neville, then I'm due at the dog trials. What do you want to do?'

'Me and Bones can poke about here for a bit and look at these old boys.'

'Okay,' Rosie said as she unclipped Gibbo. 'Just make sure you and Bones are in the ute when the judge comes past. Remember, you're part of the old-clunker image!'

She smiled at him and walked off towards the show secretary's caravan.

'Hey, lass,' Mr Seymour called after her. She turned and squinted into the sun. 'Jim was mad to leave you behind. You're a good type.'

'I'll take that as a compliment,' Rosie said brightly, but she felt sadness settle inside her.

In the secretary's caravan, her mother's ex-rent-a-crowd batch of graziers' wives fussed over their celebrity guest, Allan Nixon, the ute judge.

'Do we call you Uteman or Allan?' twittered Susannah Moorecroft.

'I answer to anything,' he said lightly. He looked up from beneath his Ford peaked cap to see Rosie standing in front of him.

'G'day,' she said. 'I'm here to enter in the Old Clunker section.'

'And which is your mongrel ute?' Allan asked.

He leant out of the caravan to see where Rosie pointed. Uteman was greeted with the image of Bones shakily lifting his arthritic back leg on the front tyre as old Mr Seymour leant against the ute, rolling a smoke and hacking up a phlegmy gob onto the ground.

'I'm afraid the two old fellas go with the ute,' Rosie said, wrinkling her nose.

'Was that part of the trade-in deal?' Uteman asked.

'Um, well kind of.' Rosie looked over to the glossy yellow Ford ute that was parked by the caravan and had a Uteman number plate. It looked like it had just driven off the showroom floor. 'That your ute?'

'Yeah. Paintwork's a little bit flasher than yours but I don't have such unusual accessories,' Allan said, glancing back to Mr Seymour and Lazy Bones. 'Right then, we'd better get you entered.' He turned towards the secretaries. 'Ladies?'

Mrs Moorecroft pushed a form forward and began to write Rosemary Highgrove-Jones in the space that said entrant.

'Ah. Actually, it's Rosie Jones,' Rosie said.

Mrs Moorecroft's face gave nothing away, but Rosie could tell she was bursting to ask a million nosy questions about the goings on at Highgrove station, what with Gerald having left the property – with Margaret's sister! Then the carry-on between Margaret and the newspaper man. *And* the rumours that her son was homosexual. Now here was Rosemary, who'd apparently taken up with a stockman and had turned up today in that terrible old ute with that disgusting old man . . . and she'd dropped her hyphen!

'I need to enter the dog trial too,' Rosie said, smiling up at her.

'Over at the porta-yards there's a blue tent,' Mrs Moorecroft said crisply, waving her pen in the general direction. 'You can enter there with the Yard Dog Association.'

'Thank you,' Rosie said, 'and yes, you can tell Mum's friends – it's all true.'

Rosie didn't hang around to see Susannah Moorecroft's cheeks flame red.

Rosie and Gibbo's names were announced over the loud-speaker and a murmur went through the small crowd. Rosie knew they were talking about Gibbo being Sam Chillcott-Clark's young dog, bought as a pup from the Pandara Kelpie Stud and shipped over from Tasmania. But while some in the crowd were harsh and judgemental, the people who trialled dogs were kinder. Especially the dog-trialling girls, who knew the truth about Sam. They welcomed Rosie and encouraged her to take her first nervous round in the competition yard.

'You'll be right,' one said.

'Gotta be a first time for everything,' said another. 'Once you've done one, the rest will follow.'

They smiled at her warmly.

'Make sure you familiarise yourself with the gate latches. In my first trial I couldn't even unclip the chain,' laughed the first.

Rosie swallowed down nerves.

In the yard, Gibbo cast out naturally enough but was too forceful on his sheep as Rosie hadn't yet worked out how to steady him down. He was hit-and-miss on his stops so it took her some time to get the sheep flowing into the first pen because Gibbo always overshot the shoulder of the small mob and turned the leaders in on themselves. When they got to the race, instead of jumping up on the sheep's backs, Gibbo disappeared underneath them and was buried completely under wool and hocks. Rosie, red-faced, had to peer underneath and coax him out again. The judge helped her out when the sheep blocked in the drafting gate, and again he put down his clipboard to help her with the put-away latch. Despite her pitiful score, whittled down from her original starting points of 100, the crowd gave Rosie an encouraging round of applause when she at last put the sheep away.

She was heading back to the ute when she felt a hand on her shoulder.

'He shows fine promise, that young dog. Well done.'

Rosie spun round. It was Billy O'Rourke.

'Shame about the handler,' she said quietly.

'You won't learn if you don't have a go.'

Rosie looked up into Billy's laughter-lined eyes. He clapped a strong hand on her shoulder.

'Good to see you again,' he said.

'How are the plans for the kelpie auction going?' Rosie asked.

'Oh, we're getting the town organised. It's scheduled for winter. The long weekend in June.'

'Great!'

'How are you coming along with the Gleeson research?'

'Slowly,' she said ruefully.

'We want to start running the articles in the new year,' Billy said. 'We need to get the word out so that people have time to select dogs to offer for sale.'

'I know, but I've been so busy with the station that I've barely had time to train the pups, let alone finish Jack's story.'

'I heard you lost your stockman,' Billy said gently. 'I'm sorry about that. Must have rocks in his head.'

Rosie looked down at her boots, but didn't answer. Sensing her hurt, Billy steered away from the subject of Jim. 'What stage are you up to with the pups?'

'We'd got as far as putting them round a few sheep in a

yard . . . you know, teaching them the left, right and stop commands. But I don't know how to finish them off. Get them backing and barking, and casting.'

'I can teach you that in a flash. How about you bring them over to my place and I give you a lesson?'

'That's really kind of you, but are you sure you've got time for me?'

In truth, Rosie felt as though things were spiralling out of control on the farm. It was great to have Julian home, but the new tree business had absorbed all his time and energy. She needed someone else to help her. The pups *had* been neglected, and Sassy's foal, Morrison, was downright wild from lack of handling.

'Really, Billy. I wouldn't want to put you out,' she said again.

'I've heard how good the pups of yours are. I'm doing this for the sake of the auction, too. We need really good-quality types for the first sale so that Casterton gets a good name for kelpies. And if I can train you at the same time, you'll be able to demonstrate them so you'll get a good price.'

'It sounds fantastic,' Rosie said, almost sighing with relief.

'How about we start tomorrow? Do you want me to come to Highgrove to save you time?'

'That would be great. Thank you so, so much.'

Feeling buoyed by Billy's kindness, Rosie walked through the crowd with Gibbo at her heels. As she weaved past the people clustered round the utes she heard a shrill voice call out, 'Rosemary! Rosemary!' There, tottering in her heels, a camera slung about her neck, was Prudence Beaton. She grasped Rosie's upper arms and kissed the air on either side of Rosie's cheeks.

'My God! I haven't seen you in *ay-ges*! How *are* you?' Without waiting for an answer Prudence prattled on, 'But look at your *hair*! It's so long. And you're so thin! Too thin. But enough of that . . . how about a shot of you and the dog for *The Chronicle*?'

She held up her camera but Rosie could feel Prudence looking her up and down and noting the dirt under her short fingernails and the calluses and cuts on her hands.

'Fine, but can we take one with my friend in it and the Uteman?' Rosie gestured towards Mr Seymour, who was talking excitedly with Uteman. Prue frowned. Mr Seymour was the last person needed for the social pages. But before she could argue, Rosie felt two hands over her eyes.

'Guess who?' came a voice.

For an instant her heart leapt with joy. But when she turned she saw it was Dubbo standing before her.

'Sorry I missed your run with the dog,' he said. He gave Rosie a kiss on the cheek before she could step away.

'Perfect!' said Prue. 'Can you do that again for the social pages?' She held up her camera. Click.

'Lovely,' she said. 'Well, time to gather more news. Toodle-loo. We'll catch you for that drinkie later, David. And you owe me a kiss too.' And she was gone, scribbling their names into her notebook.

'How have you been?' Dubbo said.

'You lied to me,' Rosie said coldly.

'What?'

She began to walk away but Dubbo caught her up.

'Look, Rose, if this is about the stockman, I was just relaying what I'd heard. I was trying to help.'

Rosie looked at him incredulously.

'That's bullshit, Dubbo, and you know it.'

'Come on, it was with good intentions. Whether it was the truth or not, the fact is he wasn't right for you.' He touched her arm.

Rosie pulled away. She couldn't believe Dubbo's arrogance. How would *he* know what or who was right for her? But she didn't want to fight with him. It just wasn't worth it.

'Why don't you just go and find Prue for that drink?' she said eventually. 'Now there's someone who's perfect for you. And if you still want to come and buy one of my pups, you'll be paying full price!' She turned her back on him and walked away.

That was it, Rosie decided. She'd had enough of men. From now on she'd just throw herself into running Highgrove and training her kelpies up for next year's auction.

'Come on, Mr Seymour,' she said, 'we're outta here.'

Mr Seymour shook his head. 'Can't go yet! The judge is about to announce his decision. Just you wait. I told him my special joke, the one about the Pope, the Virgin and the gerbil. He loved it. It's in the bag . . . just you wait . . . that Adam brand CB will be ours!' He rubbed his hands together.

Rosie frowned. 'CB?'

'Yes! You can win a CB radio!' Mr Seymour said.

Rosie sighed and shook her head, then laughed. The encounter with Dubbo had upset her, but now, back with Mr Seymour, she started to relax again.

'Not a CB, a *CD* – they mean a compact disc . . . you know, like a record.'

'Well, what's this Adam brand? Is it like Black and Gold brand?'

'You mean *who*'s this Adam Brand? He's a spunk in tight jeans who sings good songs. Oh, never mind, if we win, you'll find out.'

As Allan Nixon switched on the microphone the group of boys who stood beneath their big hats with hatbands made from black bale twine and yellow Bundy Rum lids raised their stubbies and whistled.

'Ladies and gents . . .' Uteman began to woo his devoted crowd of fans by telling the joke Mr Seymour had told him. Some of the ladies in the caravan pursed their lips in disapproval, but the young guns howled with laughter. Then he began to summarise the winners in each category, which included Most Mongrel Ute, Best Bull-bar, Fattest Ute, Best Chick's Ute and, at last, the Old Clunker section.

Uteman leant towards the microphone.

'Runner-up in the Old Clunker section is The Brown Stain,

owned by Craig Gardener – congratulations! But the overall winner is . . .' Uteman paused for dramatic effect, 'Neville! Exhibited by Rosie Jones, Old Mr Seymour and Lazy Bones the dawg!'

Rosie stepped forward and Allan presented her with a signed copy of his latest *Beaut Utes* book and the Adam Brand CD which she promptly handed to a confused-looking Mr Seymour.

'Come on, gorgeous,' she said, helping Mr Seymour into the ute. 'We'll get you home before too many of the old biddies from Meals on Wheels get wise to how sprightly you are. They might cut off your meals if we party on too hard here.'

'You're a good girl,' he said as he reached for his rollies.

At Mr Seymour's house, just as Rosie was settling him into his chair, he reached over to his side table and grabbed a heavy old scrapbook of clippings. God, she thought guiltily, she didn't want to talk kelpie history right now! She needed to get back to Highgrove to feed all the dogs and horses. Sensing her reluctance to stay, Mr Seymour nodded towards the door.

'Off you go, then. We'll talk about what's in this later. Take it with you. Just bring it back when you can.'

'Thanks.' Rosie gave Mr Seymour a grateful kiss on the cheek.

'Don't forget to take Bones with you,' he reminded her gently. 'Some of the old chooks are threatening to have him put down with the green dream.'

'God!' shuddered Rosie as she pulled Bones towards her. 'Come here, boy. We'll get you home and you can sleep in my room.'

Thirty-two

Tucked beneath her doona, with Bones snoring gently on a mat beside her bed, Rosie opened Mr Seymour's scrapbook. There in the pages were pictures of him as a boy in Ireland.

'Cor, you weren't a bad looker back then,' she said as she studied Mr Seymour's handsome features. Glued on the next page were photos of a family standing in front of a stone cottage. Beneath was scribbled 'The Mahonys'. Rosie looked at the two little boys standing in front of their mother. She recognised the smaller one as Jim. She ran her finger gently over his image.

'Cute,' she said.

Further on in the book were clippings, held fast with yellowing sticky tape. In one Mr Seymour had underlined the words: *It is remarkable how, at that time in Australia, many of the best known breeders and workers of sheep dogs were located in the one small, remote district: Gleeson, the Kings, Quinns, Willis, Beveridge and McLeods of Bygalorie.*

Rosie wondered if Jim had headed up to New South Wales, to the very same district of the Riverina, near Ardlethan, in search of work and the old kelpie bloodlines. She sighed and turned the page. It was all very well to trace the bloodlines of the dogs, but Rosie really wanted to know what had happened to Jack and Mary all those years ago. Did they make it work, despite the differences between them? Rosie laid her head on the pillow and tried to conjure up the feeling of Jim's touch. Soon she slept.

Water trickled into her dreams and began to rush in torrents. Silver rivulets spread like veins over green winter pastures. Water glistened in wide grey sheets across paddock flats and surged towards deep gullies and creek beds. The creeks, in response to the roaring rain, rushed through ever-deepening clay beds so that giant rocks tumbled loose and fell into dark caverns that churned with angry water. A hut had come loose from its foundations and was swept along in the torrent.

Terrified, Rosie lay on a camp bed, a scratchy blanket covering her naked body. The hut swirled through the flood, bashing against trees and nudging the upturned bloated bodies of cows and horses. Rosie was wet all over, and shivering. But even as she panicked that she would be washed away, she could feel the warmth of a hand moving over her body. A man was above her, sliding his fingers into her own dampness. She was heavy with tiredness and drunk with desire. She breathed deeply, panting almost like a dog. In the darkness of the flooding hut, with rain sliding down inside the rough-cut walls, Rosie looked up to see Sam's face hovering above her. She tried to cry out, but she couldn't speak. Sam was smiling at her but his smile was savage, and the pleasure of his touch turned to jolts of pain as he began to jab his fingers into her. She tried to struggle, but her arms were so heavy she could barely lift them from the bed. She couldn't move. There was nothing she could do but cry silently as Sam invaded her whole soul.

When she gave up struggling, she opened her eyes and saw Jim moving above her. He was kissing her, riding her in waves as rain thrashed on the roof. Again, desire flooded her soul. She pulled Jim close and sunk her face into the warmth of his neck. But when she looked up she saw another man's face. The light brown stubble on his face was rough, his blond hair soft, his eyes the same blue as Jim's. He was calling out as he pushed himself into her rhythmically.

'Mary,' he said over and over. 'Mary.'

Lake Cowal West, circa 1880

Jack woke with a start and moved away from Mary. His body was slick with sweat. His head pounded. The rough sheets on which he lay were sodden. Sitting up, he felt a wave of nausea take hold of him. He clasped his hand over his pounding heart and tried to control the panic rising within him. He looked at Mary, sleeping beside him. Moonlight slipped through the cracks in the hut walls and shone on her hair, which spread softly over the pillow. She stirred a little but didn't wake.

Jack swung his legs over the side of the bed and shakily stood up. He quietly lifted the latch of the hut door and stepped outside. Shuffling over to the trough in the horse yard, he splashed water on his sweating face. The coldness made him start, but it seemed to relieve the fever momentarily. Then he began to shake again with cold. He looked up at the moon that had risen high in the sky above the Lake Cowal West homestead. The lamps had been extinguished and every soul in the homestead was asleep.

'Oh, Lord. Am I being punished for what I have done?' he said.

He ran his fingers through his sodden hair. He thought back to the long nights of pleading with Mary. He had barely got started with building a tank and a hut on his forty-acre run before the restlessness began to stir in him again. His irritability grew. By the time he began to build a chock-and-log boundary fence around his land, he would wake at night in panic. As the fence grew longer, and turned at the corners, and then was sealed with a gate, Jack thought he would asphyxiate. For a while Mary's touch soothed him, calmed him, sheltered him. But she knew it wouldn't last. And, finally, it was Mary who had said, 'Let's move on.' Sad though she was to leave her family, Mary was a young wife in a new marriage and she loved Jack. She would do all that she could to support him and his dreams. She would walk away from her homestead that was never built. She would walk with Jack Gleeson to the ends of the earth.

When Jack told the Ryans that he had accepted a position at Lake Cowal station, further north beyond West Wyalong, Launcelot Ryan had slammed down his plate of food and walked out of the house. The door banged angrily behind him. But Jack had followed his father-in-law with a grim look of determination on his face. Standing in the dust the two men squared up to each other.

'I knew you wouldn't do right by our Mary,' spat Ryan.

'We'll have a better life than if we stay and rot on forty acres of good-for-nothing scrub.'

Ryan looked at Jack with furious eyes and shook his head at the tall young man who stood before him.

'Our Mary will be back to us before a few years have passed . . . of that I'm sure.'

Jack stood proud, but he tucked the words into his heart and carried them about for months afterwards. In the nights they came back to him, like a black omen. But their first year of marriage was a happy time. They had some new pups coming on that showed excellent promise, and Mary helped him with their training. The strong bloodlines of Kelpie, Moss and Caesar were definitely carrying through. The glory days of Kelpie and Moss were slipping by though. Kelpie, worn out from long years of work and whelping, was showing her age. Her muzzle was now grey, her eyes cloudy, and she got about the place like old Idle who had died years before. She was even refusing to leave Mary's side when Jack called her . . . even if Jack wanted her for her company alone. Kelpie was arthritic now, stiff in her hips, and her front legs bowed out, while her back dipped down. She panted heavily in the summer heat and shivered in the cold of winter.

The day they loaded up the dray to leave for Lake Cowal, Kelpie sulked in the shadows.

'It's as if she's saying she's had enough of my moving about,' said Jack sadly. He whistled her again but Kelpie looked away from him, guilty for not obeying. She continued to lie in the shade of her kennel, even though she wasn't chained.

'Come on, Kelpie, old girl,' Jack pleaded.

The end of her tail flickered to life, but instead of trotting to him, she crawled deeper into her kennel and sighed.

'Oh, Jack,' said Mary. 'She's not long for this world.'

Tears came to Jack's eyes as he thought of the journey he and Kelpie had shared. She had been the start of all he had created. She was his best mate. Mary put her arms around Jack.

'Get her from the kennel, Jack. She can ride up on the dray with me. Look, I've even stitched an old horse blanket for her.'

Crouching down, Jack coaxed Kelpie from her darkened den. He scooped her up in his arms and set her down on the blanket. Her tail was jammed between her legs and several times she tried to leap off the seat of the dray and make her way back to the kennel.

'Stay, Kelpie,' Jack said firmly.

'Perhaps she should,' said Mary gently.

'Stay?'

'Tim Garry offered to have her. You know that, Jack.'

'I know.' Jack sighed, thinking of his good friend at Ungarie who had been shocked to see how quickly Kelpie had aged.

'We could drop her off on the way,' Mary said, tears coming to her eyes.

Jack swallowed. He knew Mary was right. The poor old bitch would find the journey hard. Tim had offered a kennel lined with wool and promised to give her good tucker from his very own table. She would have peace and quiet and comfort in her final days. As Jack flicked the reins on the rump of the horse and the dray jerked forward with a start, he held back tears. Last year he had lost his old mare, Bailey. He had found her lying dead by the dam. He had stroked her cold chestnut muzzle and cut a lock of her flaxen mane. Now he knew Kelpie would be next.

'Ungarie it is, then,' he said, then fell silent.

As the dray rocked over the rutted road Jack thought back to the painful goodbye he'd said to Moss, just a week before. Charles King, the man who had worked Young Kelpie so skilfully in the trials, was now at Gainbill near Lake Cargelligo. He had offered to keep Moss and stand him as a stud dog. Such was the reputation of Moss and Young Kelpie pups, the demand had spread across the countryside for their bloodlines. Rather than drag Moss about and spread his genes haphazardly with other station dogs, Jack knew it was best to keep him in one place, so that his bloodlines could be traced and recorded on paper as King's Kelpies. It was something King was fastidious about.

Charles had seen the pain in Jack's eyes when he stroked the black dog's ears for the last time. He had put a hand on his brother-in-law's shoulder.

'I'll write to tell you what good pups he throws, Jack. He'll be in the best care.'

Jack knew both Charles King and Tim Garry were men of their word. He knew it was best that both his precious old dogs be given an easier life. But the pain of the era ending shot through him. His hand came to rest on Kelpie's lean back as she lay between Mary and him on the seat of the dray. Kelpie rested her head on Jack's lap and looked up into his eyes with her soulful brown ones. It was as if she knew. Mary, in turn, placed her hand on Jack's in an offer of comfort.

Jack swiped away a tear as he looked up at the night sky over Lake Cowal West. He missed both Kelpie and Moss so much. The work on Lake Cowal hadn't been as rewarding as he'd hoped. And now, with this fever sending cold shudders through his body, he longed for a place that was familiar and comfortable, and to have his old friends and family about him. Sitting by the trough, his temperature running from hot to cold, he now craved Mary's warmth.

As he climbed back into bed, heavy-hearted, he knew that he wouldn't be working tomorrow, such were the aches of his joints.

'Dear God, make me well again,' he murmured as he pulled his young wife to him and curled his body around hers.

Thirty-three

In the morning, waking from her strange dream, Rosie longed for Jim's comfort. She sat up in the bed in the men's quarters and tried to shake the feeling of doom from her.

A little later, in the homestead, Rosie settled down to the computer with her notes spread about her as her fingers flew over the keys, reconstructing the story of Jack Gleeson and how it had all begun, the kelpie line, on the banks of the Glenelg River. A swap of a horse for a pup one misty night at midnight. One man's passion that grew as rivers of bloodlines intermingled and a flood of good stock dogs began to flow from the Western District of Victoria up into the Riverina country of New South Wales and beyond.

The sound of the phone ringing broke Rosie's train of thought.

A while later, Margaret popped her head around the door. 'I didn't want to disturb you before, but there's a message for you. From Billy O'Rourke. He's coming to see you this morning.'

For the first time in months, Margaret's voice sounded tight. She glanced at her watch. 'He'll be here soon. Meet him in the yards if you don't mind.'

* * *

In the yards Rosie showed Billy the style of each dog, casting them out individually around a small mob of weaners. Never did she shout or lose her cool. The dogs, waiting their turn, sat quietly on their short chains, straining and quivering.

'Jim's trained you well,' Billy said.

'Don't you mean trained *the dogs* well?'

'No. He's trained *you* well. Most of it's in the handling. These dogs have got the natural herding ability in their genes already. And you must have natural stockmanship in your genes too, that's why, with Jim's training, you've got so far so fast. Some people take years to learn and others, they just never get it.'

Rosie felt the warmth of Billy's praise as she raised her hand. 'Sit,' she said to the blue and tan female, Jess.

'That's your pup for Dubbo,' Billy said, nodding at Jess. 'She's showing good natural paddock style. Tie her up, and we'll work on the other four. I'll show you what they need for the auction.'

'Should I start with the easy-natured ones?' Rosie pointed to the big blue and tan male. 'Chester's as arrogant as anything and can be a real pain.'

'You've gotta have one like him to learn from,' Billy said. 'Start with him while you've got the energy. After him, the other pups will seem easy.'

As she picked up a piece of poly pipe and cast Chester around the mob, Rosie vowed she would stand up to him, but soon he cut into the sheep and forced them far too hard.

'Settle him,' Billy coached.

Rosie steeled herself. She heard Jim's voice saying 'Get some grunt about you girl!'. Within seconds she was towering over Chester, blocking him with her body. She rolled him over so he lay beneath her in the dust.

'I'm not taking any of your crap, Chester,' she growled at him through gritted teeth as she grabbed his jowls with her fingers like teeth. 'You listen to me.'

He wagged his tail meekly at her and looked away, as if

ashamed of himself. When she let him back up for work, he shook himself as if shaking respect for her back into place. Then he herded the sheep steadily and dropped to his belly when she whistled a stop.

'That's better!' coached Billy from the yard's edge. 'Now open the race gate and I'll show you how to get him backing and barking on command.'

Later, when she worked Clyde, the stocky red and tan dog, he threw himself onto the backs of the sheep. Billy had shown her with Chester how to use the lead to call the dog back to her.

'Push, push, push,' she said again and Clyde flew up the race again, his big paws splaying over the sheep's wool as he let out deep throaty barks.

Next, Rosie worked Clyde's brother, Coil, who was a little more steady and shy.

'Let him get up on the first sheep, then let him straight back down so he feels he's got an escape route. Make sure he feels safe every time,' said Billy.

Soon Coil was padding up and down the sheep's backs and barking on command.

Lastly, Rosie took the runt pup, Sally, into the yard. She was a lively little black and tan with eyes like buttons. She slunk low at Rosie's heels and waited for the command. Rosie whistled and cast her round to the left. She zoned in quite close and bustled the sheep forward into the race. Within minutes, Billy and Rosie had Sally backing the race.

'We'll have to work on her bark. She's not natural at it. But I think she's had enough for now. Short sharp lessons are all they can handle.'

Billy scooped up Sally and scratched her behind her ears, then plonked her into Rosie's arms.

'You should be really proud of yourself,' Billy said. 'You've done a great job on them. They're a little rough in places, but we'll work on it. We've got plenty of time. And remember, I'm here to help. You can call me any time.'

Letting Billy's praise sink in, Rosie put Sally's paw to her nose and inhaled. She had discovered dogs' paws smelt like fresh-cut lawn on a summer's day. She sighed with relief.

'Thank God you think they're okay. I thought I'd been neglecting them.'

'You've done well,' Billy said. 'But they'll need constant work. Now I'd better get out of your way. Margaret said you were working on the articles before I interrupted you.'

'Oh, it's okay. I've got all the information. It's just a matter of writing it up. The only trouble is, I don't know how to finish the series. I haven't found a book yet that tells me where Jack and Mary ended up.'

'Keep digging and you'll find out,' Billy said.

As the sun began to dry off the green flush of spring and the days grew warmer, Rosie spent most of her nights writing the Jack Gleeson articles, and her days out in the paddocks of Highgrove. Evan had moved in and the greenhouses were up. It was now a matter of laying the irrigation pipes. When Rosie wasn't working on the farm, she was working her kelpies. Billy had set up a small trial course and from it she had learned the importance of clear commands and the use of her voice and her body language. These were all techniques Jim had begun teaching her before he left. Billy would often call over in the evening, and together they handled Sassy's foal. He showed Rosie that training horses was similar to training dogs. It was all about pressure and then reward. Steady, quiet, gentle stockmen skills, that she practised and practised.

When Julian worked alongside her in the yards and paddocks, even he began to ask how he could get more out of his own dog.

'Come on, sis,' he said, 'share your trade secrets.'

'It's no secret. Buy a decent dog to start with,' she teased, as his floppy-eared, shaggy collie lay panting in the shade.

She was so glad Julian was home to stay. He and Evan had helped her draw up a business plan to convert the ram sheds into a business growing housed superfine wool. If the old silos could be filled with grain in a good season, the gross margin for the labour-intensive wool-growing enterprise far outweighed the traditional grazing methods on Highgrove.

Despite the energy that sustained her by day, Rosie collapsed exhausted into bed in the quarters each night. Some nights she dreamed of Jim, but his features became blurred with the ghostly face of Jack Gleeson, and Rosie woke feeling empty and confused, as if Jim had never been there at all. For company and comfort, Bones slept on the mat beside her bed. She came to enjoy the sound of his gentle snoring, and when she felt alone she reached down to stroke his silky ears. Sometimes it seemed to Rosie that the old dog was her only evidence that Jim had once been real.

One hot December night, Rosie had just finished another good draft on Jack and was about to switch off the light, when there was a knock on the door.

'You awake, sis?'

Julian sauntered into the room. Rosie knew he'd come to offer her some comfort. Tomorrow was the anniversary of Sam's death.

'You okay?' he said.

'Yep. Really I am,' she said, putting her papers down. 'It seems like it all happened in a different life.'

Julian stood at the foot of the bed.

'Do you miss him?'

'I hardly think about him any more. Though I'm ashamed to say it.'

'It's okay. Sam was never right for you. You probably would've been divorced within a year.'

'Or shagging his shearers,' she joked.

Julian smirked for a moment.

'And do you miss Jim?' he asked.

'Jim?' Rosie bit her lip and nodded. 'Every minute.'

'What about Dad? Do you miss him?'

Rosie frowned and looked at Julian. Then they both burst out laughing.

'Sometimes,' she said fondly. 'Sometimes I do miss the old bugger.'

'After Christmas, let's go down and see him then,' Julian said.

Rosie nodded.

'Yeah. That'd be nice. Let's.'

'Well, see you tomorrow, sis.'

Just before he shut the door, Julian pulled a letter from his back pocket and lobbed it onto her bed. 'Forgot you had some mail.'

'Thanks,' said Rosie, snatching up the envelope. Her heart leapt at the sight of the strange, spidery handwriting scrawled across it. Was it from Jim? Had he finally written? She could barely stop herself from ripping it open.

'Night then,' she said to her brother.

'Night,' and he closed the door. Rosie was tearing the envelope open when Julian ducked his head back round the door. 'Is that smell you or the dog? It's a shocker!'

'Dog,' said Rosie. 'One thing Bones is not lazy about is farting.'

'Foul,' Julian said, wrinkling his nose before closing the door again.

Rosie's heart sank as she pulled out a letter which was folded around a pamphlet with a kelpie on the cover.

The letter wasn't from Jim at all, but came from a local homestyle historian – an ancient historian at that, judging from the shaky writing, thought Rosie. He was offering information for the kelpie articles. She felt a wave of disappointment sweep over her. Then her disappointment turned to sadness as she began to read the pamphlet and discovered the tragic conclusion to Jack Gleeson's life.

Thirty-four

LAKE COWAL WEST, CIRCA 1880

The doctor pulled down Jack's lower eyelids and peered at the whites of his eyes. A yellow tinge had crept into their corners, making his normally brilliant blue eyes seem dull. The doctor stepped back from the bed, folded his arms across his belly and looked at Jack with a frown.

'Nausea?'

'Yes,' said Jack.

'Vomiting?'

Jack nodded.

'I see,' said the doctor as he gathered up his things. 'I recommend continued bed rest. There's not a lot I can do at this point. It's a matter of waiting to see how recovery goes.'

He turned on his heel and pulled the curtain shut behind him, leaving Jack alone.

A million questions flooded through Jack's mind and fear gripped him. He thought of old Albert lying in his bed, dying, with his yellow old-man's fingers curled up on the grimy sheets. Jack held up his hands and peered at his skin, which was also yellowing. The pain in his abdomen gripped him again and he shut his eyes against it and tried to think of something else.

From behind the curtain he could hear the doctor and Mary talking in hushed tones and he strained to hear. He couldn't make out any words. Anger simmered in him. What were they saying? Why weren't they talking in front of him?

In the kitchen, Mary's face was pale and drawn as she listened to the doctor. Her hand instinctively came to rest on her unborn baby. She held back tears as the doctor's whispering voice washed over her.

'Hepatitis,' he said. 'That's my diagnosis.'

'And what does that mean?'

'It's an infectious disease of the liver . . . hence the yellowing of his skin and eyes.'

'How did he come by it?'

The doctor shrugged.

'Any of a number of ways,' he said. 'The condition is spread through food and water. I'd say there may have been an outbreak here on the station . . . the children here may have had it, but the symptoms are usually mild in children. Their parents could have just thought they had a flu.'

Mary thought back over the weeks. She tutored the Lake Cowal station children here in her kitchen. There was a time, about a month ago, when the numbers had dwindled to just two because the others were at home in the main house, sick with flu.

'And our child? Will it harm the baby?'

'No, Mary. It's not likely.'

She looked at the doctor's earnest face, a face that reminded her of an owl. He blinked at her from behind his round spectacles.

'And Jack? When will he be better?'

The doctor fell silent and looked down at his shoes, as if the answer could be found somewhere at his feet.

'I'm afraid I can't say. It's . . . it's a more serious condition for adults. He may not recover.'

Mary's hand flew up to her mouth and tears began to fall. Panic raged in her brain.

'You mean he could die?' she whispered.

'Well . . . over time . . . perhaps . . . yes. I suggest you make provisions for you and your child. I'm sorry.'

When Mary pulled back the curtain and came to sit by Jack's bed, the expression on her face told Jack most of what he needed to know. She lay down next to him and stroked his strong, handsome face with her cool fingertips. She pushed back the strands of fair hair that now lay in damp slivers on his forehead. She kissed him with love on her lips. Jack moved his hand to her belly and let his hand rest on the place where his child slept within her womb.

Jack was too ashamed of his illness to farewell his in-laws at Wallandool. Instead, he left Mary at her parents' house and travelled on alone to the Cobb & Co coach change-over hotel in West Wyalong. Mary had wanted one afternoon to say goodbye to her mother and father before they headed south to Jack's family at Koroit. But for Jack, goodbyes seemed senseless – especially goodbyes to Launcelot Ryan. Ryan's bitter words at their last parting now cut even deeper into Jack's heart, for he knew they were true. Mary *would* come back to this place to be with her family . . . and it would certainly be without him.

Jack sat hunched on a bench outside the hotel in a patch of weak evening sunlight, waiting for Mary and the Cobb & Co coach to arrive. Some of the locals who passed him on the street were afraid to talk to him. This great strapping Irish lad, this legendary stockman, was a mere shadow of his former self. His skin was yellow, his face gaunt, the muscles of his arms were wasting away and his spine seemed to curve as though the gravity of earth was too much to bear. The strangest thing, though, was that there wasn't a kelpie dog leaning by his leg, or sitting with its paws crossed by his boots. Jack Gleeson was horseless and dogless. A walking dead man.

On a bleak morning in August 1880, cold winds sped over the paddocks at Crossley in southern Victoria. As if tormented by the wind screaming in the cottage roof, the baby woke and cried in his cane basket by the fire. Mary stooped to pick him up, a furrow in her brow. She held the warmth of the little boy to her breast and breathed in the sweet smell of his soft skin. She kissed him on the crown of his head.

'Don't worry, little man. Spring is on its way. It won't be cold for long now. We're through the worst of the winter. This wind and this winter is just Mother Nature having her say.'

She bent to stoke the fire and then sat in the rocking chair. She clutched her baby and rocked back and forth, back and forth, as the wind threatened to lift the roof from the cottage.

She was waiting for Jack's Aunt Margaret and his cousins to arrive. She had sent word and they were surely making the four-mile trip from their home in Koroit to the cottage in Crossley now. She pressed her lips to her son's head as she hummed. Tears spilled from her eyes and landed on the baby's soft cheeks.

'Oh dear God,' she said, beginning to wail along with the wind.

In the bedroom behind her lay the body of her husband of two short years. She had placed heavy pennies on his eyelids and washed him all over with warm soapy water. She had kissed him and whispered her love into his unhearing ears. She had picked up his hands and kissed each finger. She had seen those hands so often, pressing down gently on the soft skin of a working dog. Patting it with strength, command and love. She had felt that same power in Jack Gleeson's touch. Now his hands were still and cold and curling. Mary held them to her cheeks but the magic of his touch was gone.

The spirit of Jack had been blasted away by the cold Crossley wind. It was blowing north, blowing his soul back to the vast open country where all his dogs were. Back to where he belonged. His soul, embedded forever in the brown eyes of a thousand prick-eared dogs. Mary kissed her husband for the last time and waited for his family to collect his body.

On that very same day in August, Charles King walked down to the kennels to let his dogs off for a run. While the other dogs danced in delight in the morning sunshine, he noticed Moss, on the end of his chain, lying on his side. The black dog was still. Charles crouched to place his hand on the old dog's side. Moss was cold and stiff. And then Charles King *knew*. He *knew* his friend Jack had gone. He was suddenly crying. Unclipping the chain, he carried Moss over to a log and sat stroking him for a long time.

As Charles King stared through tears at the red soil beneath his boots, he realised Moss had gone to find his master. He had joined Jack and Kelpie on a road that was not of this earth. They were all together, Jack, Kelpie, Bailey and Moss, riding high on a road that had neither past nor present, nor future. He gently laid the dead dog on the cold winter earth and turned away to search for a shovel.

When Rosie woke it was morning and the anniversary of Sam's death. She ran her hands over her wet cheeks with the sudden realisation that she had been crying in her sleep. She stretched her hands out of the covers and her fingertips came to rest on the pamphlet the historian had sent her. She looked again at the black and white photo of Jack Gleeson's gravestone at Tower Hill cemetery. She couldn't make out the inscription, but in type below the author of the book had written: *'Erected by Mary in memory of her beloved husband John Denis Gleeson who departed this life 29th of August 1880 aged 38 years.'*

It sent a shiver through her. Jack had died so young. He was supposed to die a happy old man, with his children all around him. Training his dogs until he could no longer walk. He wasn't supposed to die young, Rosie thought again. Poor Mary. To bury her young husband and to look ahead to a lifetime of raising her son without his father. Rosie felt the old panic rising within her as Jack Gleeson's death stirred up emotions she'd tried so hard to control: her feelings over Sam's death; Jim's departure; her parents' mess of a marriage. She couldn't see a future for herself with anyone. What was the point? Tears began to well up in her eyes. Angrily, she swung her legs out of bed and accidentally stood on Bones's tail.

'Get out of the way!' she said crossly. But he didn't move. In the shaft of morning light she noticed his staring soulless eyes.

'Oh God,' Rosie said. 'Lazy Bones?'

She reached out to stroke his side. He was stiff beneath her touch. She wasn't aware that she let out a strangled cry.

'Oh no. Please, no!' She knelt next to the old dog and said his name over and over. Then she began to fear the worst. She looked up at the pine-lined ceiling and closed her eyes.

'Jim?' she called out. 'Jim?'

But in her heart Rosie Jones knew Jim Mahony had left her world.

Rosie stooped and rolled up the stiffening body of old Lazy Bones in the mat on which he had died. As she lifted him, fetid air escaped from his bowels. The familiar stench made her turn her head away.

'That'd be right, Bones,' she said. 'Leave me with something special to remember you by!'

She carried him to the wheelbarrow in the stables and laid him down inside it.

'There you go, Lazy Bones – a perfect spot for you. You just lie there and I'll push. No need for you to expend any more energy in life.'

She swiped away tears as she laid a shovel next to him and began to wheel him through the side gate into the orchard.

Beneath a lemon tree, Rosie began to dig. She felt the muscles in her arms flex and smelt the fecundity of the soil that squirmed with tiny living things. She winced as she sliced through the bodies of fat worms and they continued to wriggle, despite being severed in two. Here in the orchard, there was life all around – from the birds skittering noisily in the branches above her to the spider that was weaving her web on the back of a rich green leaf. Using her muscles to drive the shovel into the soil, feeling her breath quicken with effort, Rosie felt so young and alive. Yet lying there next to her was a stark reminder of death. Bones's glassy eye stared up at the clouds that slid silently along in the blue sky above. His pink tongue was now pale and dry. His black lips looked plastic and his nose no longer shone with the moisture from his breath. She stroked his shaggy back before she lowered him into the grave on his mat. She began to shovel earth over his body and watched him slowly being covered by the dark soil. He would lie there like that for months in his death-sleep, slowly rotting away, though his body was still connected to life through the bellies of worms and tiny creatures that fed on him. Eventually, old Bones would become just that . . . bones.

Rosie closed her eyes. She felt like she should say a prayer, but what good were prayers? She knelt down on the grass and patted the soil into an even hump. There beneath her was a grave. A grave that she now felt contained her past. She let out a breath and felt like she would cry . . . but no tears came. Her tears were now in the soil beneath her. She had just buried them along with Bones. She felt as if she was at last burying Sam and the memory of him. She was burying her hopes for a future with Jim. He was gone with his dogs. Along with Jim she was burying the tragedy of Jack Gleeson's sad widow and his fatherless child. And, at long last, she was burying Rosemary Highgrove-Jones, and the past that had held her back for so long. Such a tiny grave, she thought, to fit so much.

Rosie stood and began to stamp down the soil. It was as if she wanted the soil packed down so tightly, none of these things could ever come back into her life. She began to jump up and down, leaping high and then landing with a thump on the freshly turned soil. Stomping. Stamping. Burying the old. Trampling death. She gritted her teeth, laughing hysterically. What was the alternative to life? Rosie knew it was death. So there she was in the orchard, jumping up and down like a mad woman. She was living, leaping, breathing, all for now. For now, and for the precious life she had.

Thirty-five

Rosie pushed off from the rock and floated, trailing her fingertips through the water. She looked up at the blue summer sky and exhaled, letting the current slowly take her back downstream. She heard a splash. Then another. Rosie spun over to float on her stomach and see what had made the noise.

On the river bank, Julian, wearing a Santa hat, and Evan, in reindeer antlers, skipped stones into the water. Around them danced the dogs, all eight of them: Dixie, Gibbo and Diesel, and the auction pups, Chester, Clyde, Coil and Sally. Duncan's little terrier, Derek, was there too, looking offended at having to share his company with working dogs. A Jack Russell, thought Rosie, is a big dog trapped in a little dog's body. She whistled and the ears of all the dogs pricked up.

'Come, kelpies!' she called. Some leapt into the water, others tiptoed over the stones and lowered themselves in gingerly. Soon they were all swimming around her, while Derek barked at them indignantly from the shore.

'Lunch!' called Margaret from her deckchair beneath a giant river red gum. Derek instantly fell silent and trotted over to beg beneath the table where the drinks and picnic hampers had been arranged.

Rosie felt the warmth of the day wrap around her as she

waded out of the river and hobbled over the hot river stones to her boots and sarong. The dogs splashed out behind her.

'Go and sit down,' she commanded, and the dogs ran up the river bank to lie under the shady trees.

Evan and Julian, wet from the river, plonked down in the deckchairs and reached for their drinks.

'Charge your glasses for a toast,' commanded Duncan, the sweat on his brow shining.

They all raised their glasses.

'Merry Christmas!' they chorused.

In the silence while everyone sipped, Rosie realised she had never felt this happy.

'This is great,' Rosie said. '*The* most relaxing Christmas *ever*!'

'So you haven't told her then?' said Evan, glancing at Julian. Julian put his finger to his lips and frowned.

'Told me what?' Rosie sat forward.

Julian sighed. 'Nothing really. I'll tell you later.'

'*What?*'

'It's just Evan spotted a fly-struck sheep on the way here.'

'As my papa would say, Donworryaboudid,' said Evan. 'Eat now, slice off maggoty wool later.'

'Ah!' said Margaret. 'Speaking of maggoty wool, my present for Rosie!' She rummaged around in the back of the Pajero and pulled out a box, wrapped in Christmas paper.

'For you,' she said, handing it to Rosie.

'Mum, I thought we agreed. It's a no-present Christmas until we make a profit on the farm,' Rosie cautioned.

'I know,' said Margaret. 'But you won't be cross with me once you open it.'

Rosie tore at the paper.

'Oh, wow!' she said, genuinely ecstatic as she pulled out a pair of metal fly shears. 'Brand new. And my very *own*. Thank you *so* much, Mum.'

'Look, I even had them inscribed.'

Rosie ran her finger over the lettering. *Rosie Jones*. She stood and gave her mother a damp, river-watery hug.

'The man at the merchandise store said he'd show you how to sharpen them properly next time you're in town,' Margaret said, waving a fly from her face. 'Thought I'd give them to you now so you can use them on that sheep on the way home.'

Rosie set the shears down at her feet and sipped her drink. She looked at the dogs lying in the shade. Some were licking their wet coats, others dozing, or snapping at flies. She looked at Julian and Evan, who were munching on sandwiches, then Duncan and Margaret, who were feeding each other long skinny pretzels. She wished Gerald were here to see his family so happy. But then, if he hadn't been brave enough to leave Highgrove in the first place, none of this would be happening.

Rosie realised she was genuinely glad that Gerald was happy at last. He had phoned that morning from Giddy's with Christmas wishes for them all. Although he and Margaret weren't officially speaking to each other, she had heard her mother wish him Happy Christmas when she answered the phone.

'I'll get one of the children for you then,' she said promptly afterwards and put the phone down to call out.

'Julian? Rosie? It's Gerald wanting to speak to you.'

Rosie had noticed real changes in Gerald over the past months. He now treated her in the same way as Julian, giving her lots of information and advice about the running of the farm. He didn't seem to miss the place at all, but he said he missed Julian and her. Today on the phone he'd even said he was proud of Rosie and the job she was doing for the whole family.

Rosie sighed as she looked at the sleepy summer river that quietly slid past their Christmas picnic. Despite the heat, Rosie shivered as she remembered the fury of the icy winter river, tugging at her clothes, dragging her down. Crushing the breath from her. Jim's terrified face flashed into her mind, and the fearful roll of Oakwood's eye, her panicking dogs being swept out of sight. Her memory longed to wander to the hut and relive the tenderness of Jim's touch. She could almost hear his comforting, gentle voice, and feel the warmth of his body against hers. But Rosie determinedly pushed these memories aside. She'd resigned herself to never seeing Jim Mahony again. Suddenly the dogs leapt up and barked, looking towards the rise. A ute was approaching.

'Time for a swim,' said Julian, getting up. Evan followed him.

'Aren't you going to see who it is?' Rosie asked.

But Evan and Julian had skidded down the river bank and slipped into the cool water.

'Beers are getting too hot here,' said Duncan. 'I'll just stick them in a shady pool,' and he left too.

'Mum? What's going on?' Rosie said, as Margaret remained sitting while the ute came nearer.

'Maybe it's another surprise for you?'

'What are you all up to?' Rosie asked. Through the haze of heat Rosie recognised the vehicle and smiled.

Dressed in his best work clothes, his hair combed and trimmed beneath his hat, Billy O'Rourke walked over to Rosie and Margaret as the dogs danced about him in greeting. He was carrying a large square parcel. What on earth was Billy doing here on Christmas day?

'Hello,' he said. 'Merry Christmas to you both!'

'Hi,' said Rosie, puzzled. 'Merry Christmas to you too.' And she gave him a quick kiss.

'I've come to give you this,' he said, handing her the parcel. 'Margaret, Duncan and I organised it.'

Rosie tore away the paper. Framed in dark timber was the first article in the Gleeson kelpie series.

'It's a proof page that Duncan did for you. It'll be run in *The Chronicle* in the New Year,' Billy said.

'Wow!' said Rosie. 'It's fantastic.'

A photo of a proud prick-eared kelpie was at its centre and beneath the title, *Casterton, Birthplace of the Kelpie*, was written in bold type: *The first in a series by Rosie Jones*.

'It's to thank you for all your hard work,' Billy said.

'And to let you know how proud we are of you,' Margaret said.

Rosie looked down at the framed article. She could hardly believe she had done it. After all she'd been through, she'd completed her job.

'It's come up all right, hasn't it?' Billy polished a corner of the glass with his sleeve.

Rosie looked down to the river bank, where Duncan waved a beer in the air at her. Then she looked at her mother.

'There's something else, Rosie,' Margaret said nervously. 'Billy and I have been talking. And we agree that it's time to tell you.'

'Tell me what?'

'Here,' Billy said, 'let me take that.' He took the frame and leant it against the picnic table.

Margaret took a breath. 'It's Billy,' she said at last. 'He's your father.'

Rosie felt emotion surge through her as she looked at Billy's kind, smiling face, as if for the first time. Their days together training the dogs and horses flashed back in her mind. That time by the river at the races, when his dog had come to sit beside her. Billy had always been there, hovering, nearby. He had been her safety net, and she hadn't even seen it. She pointed at him.

'Oh my God!' she said, laughing and crying at the same time. 'You!'

Billy stepped forward, tears in his eyes, and scooped her up in the biggest hug. Rosie held him at arm's length and looked from Margaret to Billy.

'But why didn't you tell me sooner?'

Billy shook his head. 'At first I didn't know. Not for sure.'

'And I kept it from him,' Margaret said quietly, shame-faced.

'When I saw you all grown up, getting about town and in at the newspaper, I twigged. I just *knew* you'd have to have O'Rourke in you. It was when I saw you work a dog – then

I *really knew*. But I kept it to myself. No sense in stirring up trouble. I just thought I'd keep an eye on you from a distance. I know you've been through a lot.'

Rosie looked at Margaret accusingly. She should have told Billy the truth years ago.

'I know I've been stupid and selfish,' Margaret said reading her daughter's look. 'When the truth finally came out and Gerald left, I thought it was high time I cleaned up my messes and let Billy know.'

'You need to forgive your mother, Rosie,' Billy said. 'We were both young and silly.'

'Now some of us are old and silly,' Margaret added.

Rosie shook her head and smiled. She looked at Billy as if for the first time, taking in his short stature, like hers. His naturally tanned skin, like hers. And his blue, blue eyes. Like hers.

'And all this time I thought it was Carrots,' Rosie said at last.

'*What?*' said Margaret. 'Give me some credit!'

And they all began to laugh.

Thirty-six

When Rosie drove into the main street of Casterton, it was as if the sun and the clouds were having a tussle over who would dominate the day. It was the Saturday morning of the Queen's Birthday weekend in June. Clouds blew across the sun and sent a fine spray of rain onto the street. Then the sun would emerge again, seemingly victorious, making the road glisten.

Before she reached the cordoned-off area where the parade would take place, Rosie pulled up outside Mr Seymour's house. When she walked into the living room she found him still in his flannel pyjamas.

'You're coming to the kelpie parade like that?'

He seemed as nervous as his cat, which sat staring at her with big eyes from beneath the coffee table. Perhaps he was embarrassed that his pyjamas had polar bears with beanies patterned all over them.

'Oh, lass, I overdid the Tullamore Dew last night. I'm not in the right state of mind for it. Plus the Meals on Wheels ducks are bound to catch me. They'll be down the street selling their raffle tickets and checking out who's pregnant or who's got fat, or who didn't dress too well. If you don't mind, I'll give it a miss today.'

As if to confirm his state, Mr Seymour gave a loud rasping cough and clutched his chest.

'Ooh! Doesn't sound good,' said Rosie. 'But then, I never know if you're acting or not . . . you've got that number down pat. Reckon you'll get an Oscar for it!' She wrinkled her nose at him. 'So I guess that means you're not my hot date for the kelpie black-tie ball tonight?'

'Looks like you'll have to find some other fella,' he said.

'Oh well. I think I'll go it alone. I'm too wound up about the auction tomorrow to party hard tonight. Going to get an early one.'

'Good on you, lass. Good luck with your dogs. You'll be grand. Jack Gleeson would be proud of you.'

Rosie flinched. Didn't he mean Jim Mahony would be proud? Perhaps he did.

'I'll come out the front in my slippers, just to get a peek at your fine dogs.'

Outside his ramshackle house, Rosie pointed to each dog as the kelpies bashed their tails against the ute, wagging them furiously.

'The blue and tan dog is Chester – he's the alpha dog of the litter. Challenges me to my core. Then there's Sally, the black and tan runt. Then the two red and tans are Clyde and Coil. Clyde is the larger of the two, with the bit of white on his chest.'

'Oh, they're a grand collection. If you work them well, you'll make some money on them this weekend.'

'Money's not why I'm doing it.'

'Oh? What then?'

'Not sure really,' said Rosie. 'Just because I love it, I suppose.'

'How will you be when it comes to saying goodbye to them all?'

'Mmm? I haven't got to that bit. I figure there'll be more litters. And I know they're born to work so I can't keep all of them. My other dogs have already been missing out . . . so, on the bright side, it'll be great to finally have fewer kelpies. But in truth, I'm sure I'll bawl like a baby.'

'Well, when you're done, bring us a bottle of Tully and we'll farewell them in style.'

'Deal,' she said, rising on to her toes and kissing Mr Seymour lightly on his grey stubbly face.

'Crikey! What are you thinking, girl? The neighbours will see!' he said, winking at her. 'Now get going, you brassy young thing!'

Smiling, Rosie turned and ran down the path towards the ute. She could hear the band warming up as the sound of tubas tumbled up the street towards her. The parade would start soon and she wanted to be part of it.

Evan and Julian, decked out in Driza-Bones, held onto Sally and Chester, while Coil and Clyde stood at Rosie's heels. The young dogs were excited by the sight of the other kelpies that danced around them. Some dogs ignored the others, standing quietly beside their owners. Others play-bounced and pulled on their leads. Most of the handlers wore Driza-Bone coats and hats to celebrate the classic image of the stockman. At the start of the parade, the rain came down in a light shower, then suddenly the sun was back again and as the parade rolled down the street people came out from under the shop eaves to clap and cheer. There were kelpies herding Indian runner ducks along the way, and floats that the schoolchildren had decorated with banners, posters and larger-than-life cut-outs of sheep and dogs. On the Scouts' float, a little boy in his khaki uniform sat on an outdoor dunny, toilet paper in one hand, waving with the other. There were old bikes, vintage cars and fat utes. And men and women riding Australian Stockhorses and Walers that kept their cool even though the bagpipes blared behind them and the bass drum boomed and echoed off the high walls of the middle pub.

As the stockmen cracked their whips, Rosie felt goosebumps

rise on her skin. She pictured Jack Gleeson riding down the unsealed street of Casterton with Kelpie at his heels. She looked at the stockmen ahead of her and at the kelpies all around. It felt like Jack was here today.

The sun burst through the clouds with even more vigour just as the parade finished and the participants congregated near the bridge. The Glenelg River swept silently by and the river gums glistened with the morning's rain. Julian was introducing Evan about and people were shaking their hands and asking about the new tree business. Rosie looked around and saw many of the skilled men and women she had watched competing at the dog trials over the past few months. Though Rosie had worked Gibbo in a few of the novice events, she hadn't managed to win any, but each time she felt she was closer to a trophy. Not that winning was important. For Rosie, the main thrill was in meeting the other dog handlers who knew so much about the sport and the breed. The reports she had back from the old men who watched her were good. They were sparing with their praise, but it was heartfelt.

She felt an arm being slung about her neck and a finger prodding her ribs. She turned to see James Dean, with Amanda by his side.

'Who let you out of the pub?'

'Christine's got it all under control,' said Amanda. 'We just nicked out to see the street parade.'

'Would've been more interesting if the theme was Kelpies and Kinis . . .'

'Kinis?' asked Rosie.

'Yeah. Reckon you should've worn your bikini in the parade. Shown us all a bit of nip,' said James Dean, waggling his head and smiling.

'Oh, Andrew,' said Amanda flatly, rolling her eyes.

Rosie was just punching him on the shoulder when a lady with neat blonde hair and a brand new Akubra approached them. She smiled a polished, professional smile.

'Hello,' she said smoothly but not insincerely, 'my name's Annie Morgan-Smith. I'm from the Nine Network.'

Rosie, Amanda and James Dean looked at her blankly. Clyde sniffed at her neat white moleskins and brand-new R M Williams boots as the lady stooped to scratch his ears. She looked up to them.

'Are you local?'

'Yes,' Amanda said.

'Oh, good. I'm scouting for extras for the next series of *McLeod's Daughters*. We film it not far from here, you know. In South Australia. Do you know the show?'

'Watch it every Wednesday,' said James Dean, stepping forward.

'You all look pretty fair dinkum,' she said in her city-chic voice.

'Well thanks, I think,' said Rosie cheekily. 'We do try.'

'We're interested in casting some real-life young country guys for a couple of the episodes. You've got the sort of look we're after,' she said, eyeing Andrew.

'Really?' he said, his eyes opening wide.

'*Really*,' purred Annie Morgan-Smith.

'Oh, come on,' said James Dean, rolling his eyes as the penny dropped. 'Billy's set you up for this, hasn't he? Well, tell him he's a funny bastard and there's a talent scout after him for a part in *Catherine Comes on Casterton*.'

'Sorry?' she looked at him blankly. Then she pulled out a business card and handed it to James Dean. 'Why don't you give me a call?'

James Dean looked at the card and suddenly realised Annie Morgan-Smith was deadly serious.

'Yeah. Um. Sure,' he said, blinking with disbelief.

'Or better still,' butted in Amanda with her friendly, pretty smile, 'come up to our pub for lunch. You can have one on the house and we'll fill you in on his acting talents.'

'Acting talents? So you've got experience? It just gets better!' said Annie, smiling.

Amanda pointed up the street. 'You'll find us there in the middle pub, on the left.'

'I'll see you around lunchtime then,' said Annie, before disappearing into the crowd.

Rosie looked up at James Dean's handsome profile and shook her head.

'Acting experience,' she scoffed. 'Are you going to show her your *Puppetry of the Penis* repertoire? That'll definitely get you a gig!'

'I'm going to show her everything, baby . . .' James Dean said, shimmying his hips and shoulders like Peter Allen. 'This is it, the launch of my new career – the bright lights and the big time! Me and Mands are on our way to the stars! I'll be co-hosting a show with Steve Irwin and Troy Dann before you know it, and Mands will be my right-hand sexy pin-up girl. We'll take Australian telly by storm –'

'More like *The Dorks and Dimwits Show*,' said Amanda dryly.

'Come on, lovely titties,' he said to Amanda. 'Let's go and tell my mum. She'll wet herself when I tell her I've been scalped. See you later, Rose-by-name, horny-by-nature,' he said, grinning at her. And with that James Dean turned and strode off up the street, strutting like a puffed-up pigeon.

Amanda pulled a 'Can you believe him?' face for Rosie and followed him up the street, pinching his backside and stirring him as they walked along. Rosie looked at the laughing couple as they disappeared into the crowd. They seemed so comfortable together, and so in love. The loneliness started to creep in, but then Rosie felt the warmth of Clyde leaning on her leg. Who needed men when you had dogs and horses? she thought. She began looking around for Evan and Julian. The festivities would soon be under way and she wanted to enter the dogs in some of the events. The dog high jump was on next. Then the kelpie hill climb, on the big hill overlooking the main street, and, later, the Indian runner duck herding trials, where competitors had to steer five unruly ducks through obstacles with their dogs. Later that night, at the kelpie black-tie ball, the band belted out a rock-and-roll tune in the high-ceilinged town hall. Rosie sculled another test-tube full of vile-looking green cocktail, and thought to herself that she should head home soon. The auction was early the next day and her gut was twisted with nerves at the thought of demonstrating four dogs in front of a massive crowd. The duck trialling today had been scary enough. Dixie had come third and Rosie had sighed with relief after it was all over. She had never worked a dog in front of such a large crowd and the number anticipated for tomorrow's auction was even greater.

The hall was filled with locals and with men and women from across Australia. Everyone was relaxing before tomorrow's big event. Evan and Julian swung Rosie about and danced with her until she was breathless. Billy took her for a waltz. James Dean and Amanda made her dance the chicken dance and Duncan and Margaret were in each other's arms most of the night. From across the room, Dubbo and Prue waved to Rosie. Prue's hair was curled and pinned up at the sides with diamante hairclips and she was swathed in pink silk. Dubbo was looking chubby again, red-faced and shy in his dinner suit with a matching pink cummerbund. Rosie roamed over to them.

'I must say you both look very dapper tonight!' she said.

'And you look nice too,' said Prue, looking over Rosie's simple black dress. Dubbo looked down at his suit.

'The pink bits were Prue's idea. The dogs didn't recognise me when I walked past them tonight. Barked at me like I'd come to rob my own sheds!'

'How's Jess going with her training?' Rosie asked, but the band was too loud and drowned out Dubbo's reply. In the end he just gave her the thumbs-up about the pup before Prue whisked him away again, pulling his head down into the chasm of her cleavage. Rosie smiled after them. Now *they* were made for each other, she thought.

Beneath a large papier-mâché kelpie suspended from the

ceiling, the whole town danced. As the band drummed out 'Should auld acquaintance be forgot . . .' the crowd joined arms, forming a rough circle, kicking their legs and singing. Some footy club boys pushed to the centre of the circle and, now stripped naked from the waist down, began to waltz around together. Margaret stepped into the circle and started smacking the boys on their bare white bums. The Western District women, who had once shared Melbourne Cup Day champagne and small talk with Margaret, watched with nervous smiles on their faces while their husbands cheered and clapped.

'Definitely time to go home,' laughed Rosie as she scooped up her mother and steered her to the door. Outside in the winter's night she tugged open Neville's door and slid her mother on to the bench seat. She was about to go back inside to find Duncan when Carrots stumbled out of the hall.

'Bleaurrrk,' was all he said as he bent double and vomited into the gutter.

Rosie watched him with an amused expression.

'Thank God for small mercies,' she said to Billy, who stood inside the doorway. She kissed her father goodnight and disappeared back inside the hall.

Thirty-seven

The next morning Rosie made her way to the sportsgrounds beside the river. She stood in front of the stock and station agent's truck with a hangover settling in her head and stomach. Like the rest of the vendors, she wore her kelpie auction cap and a large auction number pinned to her Driza-Bone coat. As the auctioneer read out the conditions and proceedings for the day, Rosie swallowed down nerves and the stale taste of alcohol.

Billy put an encouraging hand on her shoulder and winked at her as he walked past, while from afar, sitting on top of big square bales, Evan and Julian waved their catalogues at her and gave her the thumbs-up. She waved back.

'Make sure you're here well before your demonstrations so we're not having to chase you up,' said the auctioneer to the vendors. 'If you miss your time slot, you'll have to demonstrate last. I think that's all we need to cover. So enjoy yourselves and good luck with the sale.'

The crowd of vendors dispersed and Rosie went over to Neville to unclip her sale dogs from the back of the ute. She led them into a big white marquee that was lined with golden straw bales and short, evenly spaced dog chains. Rosie searched for her lot numbers, walking with all four dogs behind her on their leads.

''Scuse me, 'scuse me,' she said as she pushed past both vendors and buyers. Men turned to look at the pretty girl with the four handsome dogs. The local women looked at her too, trying to connect her to the same sheltered girl who had been set to marry Sam Chillcott-Clark.

At last Rosie saw the spot for her dogs on the far side of the tent and made a beeline for the empty chains. Pinned above the chains were signs that read Clyde, Coil, Chester and Sally, with Rosie Jones printed in bold type beneath each dog and the individual lot number. Despite all the noise and excitement generated by eighty dogs, her dogs seemed comparatively settled and spent most of their time looking up at her face for eye contact and reassurance.

After she had clipped them to the chains, she patted each one and watched buyers wander down the rows, looking up at the lot numbers and comparing the dog with the catalogue notes. Most of the kelpies on offer were black and tan or red and tan, so Chester really stood out with his blue-coloured coat.

From where she sat on the straw bales, Rosie looked up at the potential buyers. It would be a long day. She had four dogs to demonstrate, spread out over the whole program. Then the auction would begin in the late afternoon. She looked along the rows of kelpies and thought of Moss and Kelpie and Caesar. Imagine if Jack Gleeson could see this, she thought. He would be smiling, that's for sure.

Rosie was third on the list to demonstrate Sally in the arena. She stood looking at the crowd that sat perched on large square hay bales and on grandstands and semitrailers. She'd heard at least three thousand had come through the gate so far. The wind blew strongly from the west and chilled her as she tried to quell her nerves. Billy climbed onto the truck and clicked on the microphone.

'Ladies and gents. Welcome to the demonstrations at the first Casterton working kelpie auction. Today's event is the culmination of years of work from our community and we hope it will become a long-running national and international fixture. Numbers here today reflect the need for an event that showcases the highest-quality dogs in this country. But before we move on to seeing what the kelpie dog can do, I'd like to thank a few people . . .'

Rosie was so nervous she barely heard Billy mention her name.

'I should add,' Billy said, 'that this whole event was inspired by one man . . . an exceptional stockman by the name of Jack Gleeson. It's a celebration of his life and his achievements, and of the bonds he forged with other skilled stockmen and dog breeders from here to New South Wales. The vision and generosity of this young Irishman made this event possible today. So, in closing, may the work of Jack Gleeson, and men and women like him, be celebrated when you are bidding for the high-quality kelpies on sale here today. To those of you who buy dogs: treat them well, treat them kindly, because their blood is more valuable than gold. Thank you. Now over to our agent to tell you about each dog in your catalogues.'

Applause swelled up in the crowd and was carried away on the wind.

Out in the large yards, Rosie licked her lips. She didn't have a hope of whistling when her mouth was this dry with nerves. Using body language instead of a whistle, she cast Sally out around the mob of sheep. Sally's wide cast steadied the mob in the strong winds that seemed to have put the sheep on high alert. Rosie shut out the noise of the commentator, the flapping sponsorship banners and the colour and movement of the crowd. She had to support Sal in her every move from now on. It wasn't like a trial; here she could move about and encourage the dog and sheep as much as she liked.

'Just work her like you'd work her at home . . . none of this plant-your-feet-and-whistle trial stuff,' Billy had said. 'Show her off, praise her up. Be a showman.'

Rosie thought of Jim and his focus on using energy when working a dog. She thought of Jack casting his dogs up the hillside at Yalgogrin station . . . showing off and having fun.

As Sally brought the skittish sheep steadily towards her, Rosie began to relax. She called out, 'Yes, good dog!' Sally flicked her tail in recognition of the praise but kept low to the ground as she anticipated covering any breakaway sheep that dared run from the mob. In the race and the draft, Sally worked like clockwork and the crowd laughed when Rosie said 'Thank you, Sally' in a polite voice when the bitch had done what was asked of her. At the end of her demonstration, a smile beaming from her face, Rosie scooped up Sally and patted her as she climbed out of the yards. The crowd clapped loudly, impressed by the pretty blonde girl and the biddable little kelpie bitch.

Later in the program, Clyde and Coil put in solid demonstrations too, although Clyde did get buried in the race and Rosie had to coax him out. He was a tough dog, so he was back among the action without a whimper, despite being trampled by the sharp hooves of the wethers. After she had worked three of the four dogs, Rosie's nerves had settled, but now she was confronted with Chester – Mr Arrogant. He could potentially do anything. She thought he might single out a sheep and chase it down just to spite her, or challenge her leadership by not sitting when she asked. But instead, when she cast him out in the large yard he dropped to his belly on balance and waited for the sheep to steady. From then on he worked smoothly and worked for her. He seemed to sense her needs. He was a little reluctant on his stops in the yard when she asked him, but Rosie played along with his games, talking to him as if he was a naughty child.

'Excuse me, Chester!' she said to him. 'I said stop! Now STOP . . . please! Thank you!' She held up her hand to enforce her command so that soon Chester reluctantly laid his belly on the ground and gave her a sideways glance.

Rosie feared people would think he was disobedient, but,

in fact, the crowd collectively decided he was a character and laughter rippled through them as they appreciated his antics and the strong relationship he clearly had with Rosie. Potential buyers marked asterisks next to Chester's name in their catalogues. He was a dog that stood out . . . and not just because of his colouring.

The day raced by. Rosie barely had time to eat. When she wasn't demonstrating she sat in the big tent on the hay bales by her dogs, talking to the people interested in bidding on them in the auction. She stroked each dog as she talked and told the buyers about their strengths and weaknesses in work and temperament. She asked each person what they wanted the dogs for. Some wanted a dog for cattle work, others for sheep; some for work on Kangaroo Island, others for the vast plains of the Riverina, or the bush run country of Tasmania. People seemed to have come from all over. As the auction time neared, Rosie's nerves again began to rattle.

An agent called out for vendors to bring their dogs in lot order and asked them to assemble at the back of the big semitrailer. Stairs led up to the makeshift stage where the broad-shouldered auctioneer with a booming voice stood at a microphone. Rosie looked up at the football stand in front of the truck and it seemed to be overflowing with people.

Sally was seventh in the draw. When she took to the stage the little kelpie looked out and gave a gruff woof at the sea of people. The crowd laughed.

'Now here's a good-looking bitch, ladies and gents. And I know you know I'm talking about the little kelpie that's here on display, even though her handler's easy on the eye too,' he said cheekily.

Rosie laughed and crouched down to pat Sally as the auctioneer opened the bidding. She felt colour rise to her cheeks when the bids reached $2000 and kept moving up. The hammer came down at $2500 and the crowd clapped loudly. The best price so far. But Rosie knew there were another seventy dogs or more to come.

It was like a blur. Clyde sold for $3000. Up on the stage with Coil, Rosie, a little calmer now, tried to spot where the bids were coming from, but she couldn't place them. The auctioneer rattled on at such a pace she had a good job to hear the final price. The crowd clapped loudly when Coil sold for $3700. The bids were really hotting up. The kelpie before Coil had sold for $4000 . . . a record so far.

Back in the tent Rosie felt a wave of sadness wash over her as she clipped Coil to the chain and put Chester on the lead to take him to the stage. In a few moments all these dogs would be gone from her life. She prayed they would go to good homes. She was giving a twelve-month guarantee on each dog, in case of personality clashes with their new owners.

She made her way up onto the stage for the final time and sat Chester down by her feet. The auctioneer gave the description of him that was printed in his notes.

'This blue and tan male of sixteen months has Beloka, Pandara, Capree and Moora bloodlines on his side. He's good in the paddock, very good in the yard, shed and truck. With a strong personality, he has all-round toughness that carries through in the yards; a forceful dog that backs and barks freely. He will work cattle and could, with an experienced handler, be used for trialling once mature. Ladies and gents, Rosie Jones has done a fabulous job of training this dog. Who will start me on Chester . . . what am I bid?'

Rosie couldn't believe the response. The bids flew up from $2000 and kept climbing. She tried to spot the bidders, but all she saw was a lady in a red jacket nudging her partner's elbow. She must've wanted the dog badly. Perhaps it was his colouring that appealed, or his strength in the demonstration. Whatever it was, several people were keen to buy him. When the bids reached $4500 the auctioneer paused for breath. As far as Rosie could tell, it was between three parties and one had just pulled out. When the auctioneer started again, he offered to go up in halves, and the hammer finally fell on

$5000. The crowd applauded loudly and Chester barked as if thanking them. Rosie leapt down from the truck and people came to slap her on the back.

'Well done,' one man said.

'You'll be getting top price with him,' said another.

Rosie walked back to the tent feeling a mix of joy and sadness. She had made good money on the dogs . . . at least three times the amount she'd expected. But the money left her hollow. She loved these dogs and would miss each one. She'd have to get tougher if she was going to keep on breeding dogs for sale, she thought to herself.

The buyers trickled in to show their receipts to the agents and collect their dogs, and the tent began to fill again with barking, chatter and laughter. People came and left with their dogs. Rosie shook hands with Sally's buyer and was pleased to see the man's wife stooping to pat and talk to Sally. The small woman with grey hair glowed with happiness at meeting both Sally and Rosie. Rosie remembered talking to them earlier in the day and had hoped they would buy a dog from her.

'She'll be fine, love,' the woman said in a broad accent. 'She'll have three thousand sheep to play with when she gets home. I've got a kennel all set up on the back verandah. We'll ring and let you know how she's getting on.'

Coil and Clyde had been bought by a father and son who ran cattle in Gippsland. Both had liked the way the dogs had worked with the same style, yet one was softer and had more distance from the stock, while the other had more force.

'They'll make a great team,' said Rosie. 'And I'm so glad they're going to the same home. Any problems, let me know.'

It was almost dusk when Rosie sat down again on the bale and called Chester to her. He rested his head on her lap. He was tired from the excitement of the day and seemed sick of all the action. The tent was nearly empty and lights shone out enticingly from the footy clubrooms where people were drinking, but Rosie had to wait for the last buyer to come. Sadly she stroked Chester's head, fighting back tears. When the buyer approached, Rosie's head was bowed over the dog. She was talking to Chester, telling him it would all be okay, when she sensed someone standing above her. She saw his boots first, and as her eyes roamed upwards to his broad shoulders she was struck by the height and size of the man who stood before her. Then her eyes came to rest on the face that was shadowed by his hat.

'This would be lot 73 then?' came the voice as rich as honey. He held out his receipt in a broad, tanned hand.

Rosie felt tears well up in her eyes.

'Jim?' she said, barely believing it.

She stood up and threw her arms about him. Jim returned her embrace with passion and strength. She hugged him closely and breathed him in. He smelt of horses and of the dust of the road. He smelt of faraway places. He smelt so good. He looked down at her with questioning eyes, searching for her reaction. At first she thought she was going to punch him. He had left her. He had been away so long. He'd barely called her. She had thought he was dead. But instead she found herself clambering up onto the straw bale so that she could kiss him. Drinking in the taste of his warm mouth on hers. The electricity of his touch running through her.

'Rosie, I'm sorry, I'm so sorry,' he said, stroking her back. 'I should never have left you. I was an eejit.'

'Yes, you bounding bastard!' Rosie pulled away and looked him in the eye. 'Tell me you've realised that *you* were the one being the bloody snob!'

'Yes, I know,' he said. 'I was wrong. *So* wrong.' He looked at her with tears in his eyes. 'I can't live without you, Rosie Jones.'

Rosie kissed him hard and held him tight, running her hands over his neck.

From behind them, the voice of the auctioneer cut in. 'If

I'd paid top price for a kelpie would I get that kind of bonus? It sure looks like it'd be worth it!'

Rosie pulled away and laughed, but Jim's face was serious. He looked into her eyes.

'Rosie, I *am* sorry. You know I love you, and I'll never leave you again. I promise you that.'

'I love you too,' Rosie said, hugging him close.

Chester, sensing their excitement, barked and put a paw up on Rosie's leg. They both looked down at him.

'What do you want?' Rosie said to him. He looked at her and made clicking noises with his teeth and wagged his tail.

'I think he's trying to tell you that he's glad to be going back to Highgrove station to live,' Jim said.

'Now he's a five-thousand-dollar dog, he'll be wanting to live in the homestead,' Rosie said.

'Actually,' Jim said, 'he'll be wanting to live with us.'

'With us? Where? In the quarters?'

'No,' Jim said. 'In our hut up on the ridge.'

'Are you serious, Jim Mahony?'

'Why not?' he said. 'Old Ronnie Seymour said if you'll have me back he'll make it worth your while.'

'What's he talking about?' asked Rosie, laughing.

'Believe it or not, Ronnie's one of the richest men in Casterton. Everything he's won on the dish-lickers and horses has been invested for years. We're the closest he's got to family, and he thinks we should stick together. He says he wants to help us out in some way.'

'With the hut?'

'With whatever you like. But if you did want to live up there, like you said, it'd mean we could afford solar power. And build some sheds and yards. Doze a proper track. Do the hut up a bit . . . well, *a lot* actually. Don't you agree? It's possible?'

Her skin tingled with excitement as she began to see a future with Jim up in the bush. A log cabin with no fences and a garden of gum trees, with a track down to the river and the farm beyond. Just her and Jim and the horses and the dogs . . .

'So?' Jim asked, waiting anxiously for her response.

And Rosie grinned.

'With you, anything's possible.'

Epilogue

SIX MONTHS LATER

The flag fell and Rosie felt Oakwood's muscles bunch beneath him as he sprang forward. The rest of the horses jumped with him, their hooves ripping up the turf in a galloping frenzy. And there was Rosie, dust in her face, the roar of the crowd in her ears, and half a tonne of horseflesh thundering along beneath her. Jim belted up beside her and gave her a cheeky grin, before hissing his horse on faster.

Rosie laughed as adrenaline coursed through her. She clutched the reins, damp with sweat, and leant over Oakwood's neck so that his long mane flew in her face.

'Come on, Oaky,' she whispered in his ears and she felt him surge forward. The rush and bustle of the galloping horses around her fell away. Soon Oakwood was on his own out in front, his ears flattened back, his muscles straining, trying his hardest to catch Jim's mare. Sweat trickled into Rosie's eyes. Wind rushed past her. She savoured the thrill of being as one with the magnificent creature beneath her. Oakwood increased his stride and soon they were level with Jim. Then they were past him. As Rosie galloped into the straight, the crowd rushed to the rail, cheering her on. Derek dived onto the track, his little tail held high, yapping at Oakwood. She could hear

Duncan's excited commentary echoing around the track. He was shouting her name.

'It's Rosie Jones! Rosie Jones! Rosie Jones on Oakwood! She's just won the Stockmen's Challenge!'

Oakwood crossed the line in front by a good three lengths and Rosie felt joy flooding through her.

'Good boy! Amazing, wonderful boy!' She stroked Oakwood's sweating neck and shifted her weight back in the saddle so he began to slow his stride. The sound of the crowd and Duncan's commentary faded away as Oakwood, breathing hard, cantered on to the far side of the track. Exhilarated, Rosie knew she was, at last, exactly where she belonged. Happiness spread through her whole being.

She rode on at a steady pace, talking to Oakwood gently and cooling him down. As she turned to ride back in search of Jim, she caught sight of the Glenelg River, sliding lazily beneath the shade of the majestic river red gums. And then, through the trees, she saw a young man and his horse standing in the long green grass of the river bank. A black and tan dog sat leaning against the man's leg. The man followed the dog's gaze, looked at Rosie, and tipped his hat. Then he stepped up lightly into the saddle and turned his horse towards the shining river, his dog following close behind.

Rosie watched them go, and kept on watching, until Jack Gleeson and Kelpie had disappeared from sight.

Notes for Timeless Land

While *Timeless Land* is based on the actual life of Jack Gleeson, I'm a fiction writer, not an historian. I have hung my imaginings on the factual hooks provided by wonderful historians such as Barbara Cooper, Robert Webster and A.D. (Tony) Parsons – my gratitude to these clever people runs deep – but my imagination also took me to places beyond those that can be found in the historical record.

I've tried to remain true to the events that led to the birth of the kelpie breed, and to do justice to the memory of John Denis Gleeson, better known as Jack. I hope his family will see this book as a celebration of Jack's contribution to Australian culture and legend, and as a recognition of Jack's part in giving us that magic creature, the Australian working kelpie dog.

Age (Melbourne), 17 October, 1854

Australian Wool Corporation, *National Merino Review*, Ross Dunkley & Barry Millett Publishers, 1989

Barbara M. Cooper, *Founders of the Working Kelpie Sheepdog*, Working Kelpie Council website, 1998

Raimond Gaita, *The Philosopher's Dog*, The Text Publishing Company, 2002

Jack Gorman, *Tales of Casterton – The Waines Murder and other Stories*, Osborn Mannett Printers

Katrina Hedditch, *Land and Power – A Settlement History of the Glenelg Shire to 1890*, National Library of Australia Cataloguing in Publication Data, 1996

Frank Jackson, *The Mammoth Book of Dogs – A Collection of Stories, Verse and Prose*, Carroll & Graf Publishers Inc, 1997

Frank H. Johnston, *Cattle Country*, FH Johnston Publishing Co. Pty. Ltd, 1960

Graeme Lawrence, *Souvenir History of the Casterton Racing Club*, Casterton Racing Club, 1982

H.A. McCorkell & Peter Yule, *A Green and Pleasant Land – A History of Koroit*, Collett, Bain & Gaspars, 1999

Allan M. Nixon, *More Beaut Utes*, Penguin Books Australia Ltd, 2000

Allan M. Nixon, *Beaut Utes 3*, Penguin Books Australia Ltd, 2001

Allan M. Nixon, *Beaut Utes 4*, Penguin Books Australia Ltd, 2002

Noonbarra Kelpie Stud web site

A.D. (Tony) Parsons, *Training the Working Kelpie*, Penguin Books Australia Ltd, 1990

Tony Parsons, *The Australian Kelpie – The Essential Guide to the Australian Working Kelpie*, Penguin Books Australia Ltd, 1986, 1992

Shire of Glenelg Bi-Centennial Committee, *Echoes of the Past*, 1968

Shire of Glenelg Centenary, 1863–1963

Jean Uhl, *Still Stands the Schoolhouse by the Road*, FRP Printing, 1987

Rob Webster, *Bygoo and Beyond*, Canberra Times Print, 1985

Rob Webster, *The Dog That Nearly Never Was – Ardlethan, Home of the Kelpie*, JA Bradley & Sons, Temora, NSW

Acknowledgements

This book wouldn't be here without Ian O'Connell's enthusiasm and love for Casterton and the kelpie. It was Ian who convinced John and me to sell a kelpie at the Casterton auction in 2002. It was Ian who plied us with red wine and put Peter Dowsley's hauntingly beautiful poem, *Kelpie*, in front of me and said, 'Wouldn't this yarn about Jack Gleeson make a great movie or book?' So thank you to Ian . . . persistent, larger-than-life, infectious, wonderful Ian! Heartfelt thanks also to Ian's family, especially Kay who now experiences annual Tasmanian invasions during the Kelpie Muster weekend.

Accolades to the incredible Deb Howcroft, who originally dug out the history of Gleeson and inspired a whole township to build a monument and celebrate the story. My thanks to the people of Casterton, including the Glenelg Shire Council, the Casterton Library and the Tourist Information Centre, and especially to Jim Kent of the Casterton Historical Society. Thanks to Joey Smith for riding past on that green-broke thoroughbred when you did, triggering a creative rush for me. To David Levy and the organisers of the Kelpie Muster and Auction, you are an amazing bunch of volunteers who move mountains every year to put on a dazzling festival, and I hope this book entices visitors to your magical town on the Queen's

Birthday long weekend in June. (The Meals on Wheels ladies are lovely, not like the ones portrayed in this book!) Thank you to the station owners who welcomed me as I retraced Gleeson's path, including the Larkins family on Warrock, the Murphy family on Dunrobin, the Walker family on Bolero and Peter Darmody near Beckom. Thanks to my friends Marg and Barry Price of Moora Kelpies for taking me to Jack Gleeson's grave. Thanks to the descendants of Jack Gleeson, Geoff, Pat and Peter Gleeson and Anne English, for giving this fictional account of his life your blessing. I hope it's done him proud.

My lifelong gratitude goes to the modern-day stockman who inspired me, Paul Macphail of Working Dog Education. You gave me such a precious gift when you taught me to train and work dogs nearly a decade ago. Thank you, Paul, for your continued generosity and friendship. And to my classic kelpie friend and superb stockman, Mathew Johnson, you and Margie are a big part of why John and I love being involved in the kelpie breed so much.

To Barbara Cooper of the Working Kelpie Council, thanks for your years of dedication in recording details of the breed. And to the fount of knowledge on kelpies, Tony Parsons. Your books began my journey both in writing fiction and in training dogs.

Gratitude to the very busy Tania Kernaghan who read an early draft and allowed me to use her song lyrics, and got my toes tapping as I typed when playing her brilliant CD, *Big Sky Country*.

At Penguin, as ever, your support, sincerity and integrity have been unfailing. Love and thanks to Clare Forster who helped me on this very difficult journey of juggling a new baby with a new book. Accolades to the gifted John Canty and his design skills, and a massive thanks to the whole big Penguin team. Special, special thanks to my gorgeous editor Belinda Byrne who nurtured this book from its very shaky beginnings and nurtured me along with it. For my agent Margaret Connolly, you have been my safety net and my friend. I thank you for always being there for me.

Thanks to the people who froze in Tassie in the sleet on the 'blustery cover shoot'. Thanks to Bill Bachman, Amy McKenzie, Alasdair Crooke, Joe Holmes and my John and our gorgeous animals, including Greg Cowen's pups. Thanks also to Rachel Parsons, our cover rider.

On the home front, without my Levendale legend Maureen Williams, who cared for my baby while I wrote, *Timeless Land* would never have been finished. Maureen, you were sent by an angel! Thank you! To my dear dotty dog woman, Kathy Mace, thanks for the river swimming hole and six pack therapy when it all got too much, and thanks for being as kelpie-crazy as me. Thanks to my darling Heidi and James for their love, kindness and fish. Thanks to Mum for feeding us when I was too tired to cook and to Dad for getting wood for me. To my brother Miles and Kristy, thanks for always being there for me and for Dr Kristy's insight into Jack Gleeson's illness. Thanks to my almost-lost girlfriend Pip for nearly drowning in a river after trying to rescue sheep. Your scary adventures inspired me to throw my characters in the river too. Thanks to Steph Brouder, my real-life, inspiring chicky-babe stockman; my Levendale Lighthorse comrades, Luella and Prue; and my dear two buddies, Mev and Sarah. To the Malahide crew, John and Sandy Hawkins and Cat and Ian, thanks for minding our little miss and for all your love and support. To Doug and Mary, Rob and Sharon and the whole Victorian gang – thanks for flying down to cheer me up when it all got too much.

Many many thanks to Andrew, Amanda and Christine Dean for being my pub characters . . . now Andrew has to read his first book ever – that was the deal!

Most importantly, all my thanks to John, the love of my life, my stockman and my soul mate, who supported me through the roughest of it all . . . and to my baby, Rosie Erin, who had to share her birth with a book and her name with my heroine. Thanks for being a funny, lovely baby who sleeps lots, laughs lots and hardly cries! And finally, to my dogs,

Gippy, Blunnie, Sam, Manfred, Gemma, Diamond and Ralph, and horses, Tristan, Jess, Maxine, Marigold, Edith and Morison, for being outside my window, ready to inspire me as I write.

The poem that inspired *Timeless Land*, by Casterton poet Peter Dowsley, is reprinted here with Peter's kind permission.

Kelpie

A tear rolled down Jack Gleeson's cheek
For the son he'd never see,
For the dogs he'd never work again,
And what he knew they could be.

He'd ridden all the eastern states,
And bred a strain of dogs, in time;
Now he was about to die,
A stockman cut down in his prime.

He left his wife an unborn child
And his dogs already famed,
His black and tan sheep dog bitch
After which a breed was named.

* * *

It all started on the Warrock run
Where Jack saw dogs that could work sheep,
Collies brought from Scotland
And a pup he wished to keep.

George Robertson wouldn't sell her,
Not to Jack or anyone.
'When you've got dogs like this,' he said,
'They pass them father on to son.'

But he gave one to a nephew
Who didn't follow in that course,
He knew Jack Gleeson pretty well
And had a liking for his horse.

He said he'd swap the dog
For Gleeson's stockhorse tall and stout,
By the old Glenelg at midnight
To save his uncle finding out.

And so down by the river
On an eerie moonlit night,
Where the Red Gums touch the water
And the yellow-belly bite,

Jack Gleeson sat there waiting
With the stockhorse on a lead,
Listening to the rippling waters
And the roos and emus feed.

Then a rustling from the bushes
Sent a shiver down his spine,
He looked up to see a horseman pause,
Then wave a knowing sign.

So Jack rode on towards the ford,
Where Warrock met Dunrobin run,
They exchanged the pup and stockhorse
And the midnight deal was done.

Both horsemen rode off quietly
Through the fast descending fog,
Until Jack stopped above the river
To take a good look at his dog.

The sky was clear as crystal
And cold air made him shiver
As the full moon cast his shadow
Down across the fogbound river.

His thoughts turned back to Ireland,
Of haunted fords and streams,
By the spectre they called Kelpie
And how it filled his early dreams.

He could hear a horse at canter
As he fixed a thoughtful gaze
On the tops of lifeless Red Gums
Jutting out above the haze.

He glanced down at the pup
Who pricked her ears up at his sight,
Then smiled, called her 'Kelpie',
And rode off into the night.

Perhaps he knew Jack Gleeson's Kelpie
Would be known throughout the land,
Her descendants strong-willed working dogs
Just as the stockman planned.

Jack headed north with Kelpie
And broke her in along the way,
A station north of Cootamundra
Was where he'd find the work to stay.

As he crossed the Murrumbidgee
He met Coonambil Station's boss.
It was here Jack mated Kelpie
With a Collie dog called Moss.

From Forbes to Yarrawonga,
Kelpie's pups would show their guile,
In the woolshed, on the paddocks
With mobs of thousands, or at trial.

They became, simply, Kelpies,
Sought for their desire to work,
For their pride, for their intelligence,
With so little that they shirk.

Now if you're heading into Casterton
And the sky is crystal clear,
Make a stop down by the river
And if you're quiet you will hear

A whistle through the Red Gums,
A mob of sheep take flight,
Then horses' hooves and barking
Will echo through the night.

But there is no horseman out there,
No real dogs or running sheep,
Just Jack Gleeson working Kelpie,
A spectre Casterton will keep.

Now read the first chapter of Rachael Treasure's next novel

The Cattleman's Daughter

Coming soon from Preface

One

When Emily Flanaghan hit the tree and her heart slammed out of rhythm, she didn't hear the rush of hooves as the other bush-race riders belted past her. Nor did she hear how her silver-grey mare, Snowgum, roared in agony, screaming out a hideous guttural sound like some prehistoric creature. She didn't see the mare's river-stone hooves flailing in the air on the dusty bank, nor did she smell the blood. Instead, Emily felt herself drift up through the filter of gum leaves, the panic from the accident subsiding in her, as she wondered at the imperviousness of gum tree trunks and how ridiculous it was that she should ride full pelt into one. She marvelled at how solid they were, in all their gentle silvery beauty. Gone was the rush of fear she had felt when she and Snowgum had taken the full force of the big chestnut hitting them broadside. Silver stirrups irons had clanked, the horses grunted punch-drunk, as Snowgum was shunted off course. As she saw the tree in front of her, she had for an instant wished she'd never fought with bloody Clancy. She wished she'd never gone in the race just to claim some ground back from him out of pride.

Images of her two little girls, Meg and Matilda, flashed in her mind. They would be down at the marquee; lean country kids, with messy sun-kissed pony tails and grubby painted faces, one as a cat and one as clown, both waiting nervously to see Mummy race her horse across the line. She recalled how her youngest, Meg, had clung to her whispering, 'Mummy, don't go in that horsey race. Please.' And how she'd felt Meg's tears on her neck, prompting the sting of her own. Then, in the second before she hit the tree, she thought of her dad, Rod, and the pain it would cause him to know she had wiped her life out at just twenty-six. She felt the weight of guilt that she would leave him alone at such a time. A time when a stroke of a pen in a far away Parliament would soon take their family mountain cattle runs from him. Then there was a flash of her brother, Sam, somewhere on the other side of the world in a Nashville recording studio. Or more likely, in a bar with a bourbon in his hand, wearing irresponsibility on his face along with his too-cute grin. Then came an image of Clancy. In the last split second of the life Emily had known, she felt the horror of Clancy's rage. There was an overwhelming sense of regret that she'd mucked her life up so badly. The stinging realisation that she'd sold out to being ordinary and subservient. She had let herself be buried alive and allowed herself to be stolen away – from herself, from her family and from her mountains.

Then the pain came in an instant as she met with the tree. As Snowgum gave way beneath her, all there was, was a kind of drifting – a kind of peaceful nothingness. She heard the sound of the water rushing by, and wondered why the water was slowing to a trickle. She didn't realise that it was the sound of the blood in her veins moving slower and slower. She listened to an axe falling somewhere in the distance, at first fast, then slowing to a few lazy haphazard strikes. She didn't know it was her heart, beating slower. Then slower. Then almost still. Just . . . one . . . lazy . . . hack . . . at . . . a . . . time.

As her body lay crumpled on a dry rocky creek bank, a frenzy erupted around her. Race officials in fluoro-orange vests clambered over tussocks. They scrambled through shallow rocky waters. One of them punched words into a two-way radio as he ran.

'We got a rider down! We need an ambulance! It looks bad. Real bad.'

On the golden river flat where the makeshift tent city of the the Mountain Cattlemen's Get Together had sprawled itself out for the two-day celebrations, people were still watching the race. The commentator, oblivious to the fall on the other side of the rise, continued to call The Mountain Cattlemen's Cup as the field of horses half-slid down the jagged slope towards the finishing straight. Horses sides were sheened with sweat, riders gripped tight with denim-clad thighs and gritted teeth, hissing their horses home. The veins of both horse and rider awash with adrenaline. The two leaders hugged tight the curve of the track. One rider's boot toes hit at the fluttering triangular blue and yellow flags strung between star-pickets as his horse was bunted and shunted home. They flew past in a blur, belting for the finish line. Only three people in the the crowd were ignoring the neck-and-neck finish. Rod and his grandchildren, Meg and Matilda, were searching the rough mountainside track, looking desperately for Emily on her grey mare.

At the time of the running of the Cattlemen's Cup a pretty bush nurse was doing up the silver press stud buttons of her blue overalls in the back of the ambulance. She smoothed down her long chestnut hair from the tussling he had caused and pulled it back into a ponytail. Penny ran her hands over the sheets of the stretcher bed, trying to regain the crisp whiteness that they once held. Her rosy lips were still raw from his stubbly kiss. She smiled at the thought of his handsome, wicked looks under his hat and the firmness of his tanned arms in his blue bushman's singlet. She could still taste the beer, cigarettes and dust on his lips. She'd felt dizzy and giggly all at once as she recalled the full force of his lust. The encounter fast and furious. She knew he had been watching her, all day, like a tiger laying wait in the grass. She'd felt a thrill when he'd run to her, curved his hand around her waist and dragged her into the ambulance, the very moment Kev, her ambo crew partner, had walked away to get a drink and to watch the race.

Clancy had kissed her rough and hard on the lips and began, straight away to reef open the studs on her overalls to clutch beneath her clothing and cup her breast in his hand. He'd lifted her onto the trolley as she swiped aside the drip stands and oxygen equipment. He had wrenched down her overalls, her ambo trousers, then tugged at his own leather belt and unzipped his jeans.

She pictured his hips, as snake-thin as a bull rider, thrusting into her. He'd set at her at a flat-out gallop, the rhythm of his thrusts rising in crescendo as the commentator called the mountain race outside the ambulance. As she thrust her hips equally as hard against his, she threw her head back and gripped tight his perfect backside. She felt like a galloping, sweating, blowing horse, and he, her rider. The ambulance rocked and she had wanted to scream, but she had felt her hand on her own mouth as she bit hard into the flesh of her palm. When it was done, he lay on her for a time and kissed her all along her neck. She had shut her eyes and almost sadly, began to long for the next encounter. They could only ever steal moments like that. She had hoped no one had seen – he was not so subtle when he was drunk. But, she smiled coyly, as she'd smuggled him out from the ambulance, everyone's eyes had been on the race. She knew she had evicted Clancy from the back of the ambulance just in the nick of time as Kev had wandered back, ready for a doze in the driver's seat in the heat.

Kev now held a coffee held loosely in his hand and set his feet up on the dash. In the lead up to the Mountain Cattleman's Cup, he'd been watching Penny in the side mirror flirt mercilessly with that selfish bugger for the past half hour. He'd eventually turned the mirror away in disgust and then taken himself a little distance away. He couldn't bear to watch.

Suddenly now, the radio was alive with urgency and Kev

knew that it was bad. He tossed the paper coffee cup down on the dry grass, it's syrupy contents disturbing the ants.

'Penny!' he yelled, 'Get your arse in the front!'

In the creek bed, one of the men had unclipped the buckle of Emily's helmet and was gingerly loosening the velcro of her protective vest. He listened desperately at her pale lips for breath. The translucent white glow of her normally tanned skin, the blood trickling from the corner of her mouth and the lifelessness of her limbs injected fear through him. This girl simply could not die. Not Rod Flanaghan's daughter. When she was younger, before she moved away, she had been the life and soul of the mountain community. God, not Emily, he thought. Not with those two little kids and that mongrel of a husband. He lay his hand on her cheek.

'Emily? Can you hear me?'

The other official was now desperately trying to move Snowgum away from Emily's body. Hauling on her reins, pleading with the mare to try and stand. The man who crouched beside Emily found the sounds of the horse in agony so excruciatingly disturbing that he wished it would just lie down and die. He couldn't bare to look at the way the white flanks of the mare were coursing with blood and how it twisted and contorted in pain. He wished he had a gun. He would shoot the mare there and then. It would be much safer for all of them. He looked up from where he knelt beside Emily towards the direction of the Cattlemen's, his face contorted with anguish hoping the ambulance would arrive, knowing it was up to him to begin the task of CPR in the blind hope that he could save her. He looked down to Emily's pretty heart shaped face. He was shocked to see that her normally long dark hair was just tufted remains, the scissor hacks still angry and angular against the softness of her face.

'Emily?' he said desperately. 'Emily. Stay with us. Emily!'